SPIDER
MOUNTAIN

SPIDER MOUNTAIN

P.T. DEUTERMANN

St. Martin's Press
New York

Deu

This is a work of fiction. All of the characters, organizations, and events portrayed in this novel are either products of the author's imagination or are used fictitiously.

www.stmartins.com

Library of Congress Cataloging-in-Publication Data

Deutermann, Peter T., 1941–
    Spider Mountain : a novel / P. T. Deutermann. — 1st U.S. ed.
        p. cm.
    ISBN-13: 978-0-312-33379-9
    ISBN-10: 0-312-33379-X
    1. Ex-police officers—Fiction. 2. North Carolina—Fiction. I. Title.

    PS3554.E887S65 2007
    813'.54—dc22

                                                            2006051190

First Edition: January 2007

10   9   8   7   6   5   4   3   2   1

This book is dedicated to all the seemingly anonymous folks, government, faith-based, or just plain charitable, who work out in the hills and hollers of Appalachia, tending to the people and their children who only think they can take care of themselves.

ACKNOWLEDGMENTS

I want to thank the real Vivian Creigh, a lovely carriage-driving lady who "won" the auction at a fund-raiser to use her name as a character in this book. She specifically told me to make her character an evil person. Be careful of what you wish for, Vivian . . .

SPIDER MOUNTAIN

Prologue

They were going to hang him, Janey realized. She could just barely see an old man lying in the back of a battered pickup truck, his arms and chest wrapped in at least fifty pounds of chain coiled from his neck down to his hips. His eyes were wide with terror. A heavily bearded fat man was trying to toss one end of a rope up over the limb of an oak tree, while a second, older man, tall and thin with a ferret-like face, was fashioning an elaborate hangman's noose on the other end of the rope.

She'd been taking water samples on Crown Lake when she'd heard the truck laboring in the woods and climbed up to the ridge to investigate. Her Park Service Jeep was nearly two miles away around the shoreline, along with her radio. Only now she remembered the senior ranger telling them to keep their radio with them at all times. Too late now, she thought. She squinted into the late afternoon sunlight, trying to decide. There were two of them, and she was alone. Being a probationer, she had no weapon other than a pepper-spray cylinder on her work belt. But she couldn't just squat down behind these bushes and watch them hang the old man.

The fat man succeeded with the rope and began to pull the slack over the branch. They had parked the pickup so that the bed was just about under the tree. The thin man dropped the tailgate with a bang and hopped up into the bed. The chained man tried to roll away from him, but the thin man casually kicked him in the crotch, doubling him over as much as the chains would allow. The old man's hands groped to reach his pain, but the chains completely pinned his arms, and all he could do was groan. The thin man slipped the noose over his prisoner's head and tightened it around his scrawny neck. Then he heaved the old man up onto his feet while the fat man pulled all the slack out of the rope. The prisoner could barely stand, but every time he swayed the rope reminded him that standing was the only option.

"Hey," she shouted, stepping out from behind the bushes and walking toward them. She had the pepper-spray canister in one hand, while she kept the other hand planted in the small of her back, hoping they'd see her ranger uniform and think she had a gun back there. "What's going on here? You all stop that."

The would-be executioners whirled to stare at her.

"You let that man go," she ordered in what she hoped was her best ranger voice. "This has gone far enough."

The big man casually dropped the end of the rope. He was wearing blue overall bottoms and a stained green wife-beater T-shirt, which barely covered his enormous belly. His black beard came down to the top of his stomach. His face was round and red, with small, belligerent eyes. He had a greasy-looking black pigtail hanging down the back of his neck.

"I said, let him go," she ordered. She'd stopped a dozen paces from the pickup truck. The chained man was looking at her as if he'd seen the Second Coming. The thin man stood motionless in the bed of the pickup truck, glaring at her, still holding his prisoner upright.

"Well, hell, little lady," the fat man said, in an unexpectedly amiable voice. "We just funnin', ain't we, Will? Ain't we just funnin' here." He kicked at something in the dirt, bent forward slightly, then put his hands on his massive thighs, a lazy smile spreading across his fat face.

She relaxed her guard for just a second, which is when the fat man reached down, scooped up the rock, and threw it at her. It was a baseball-sized rock, and it hit her right in the solar plexus. She doubled over with a painful whoof and he was on her in a flash, grabbing the hand with the pepper spray and whipping it around behind her back while he twisted her arm. She yelled with the pain and tried to escape, but he had her pinned hard. She could feel the mat of his beard against her neck and smell the sweat on him. He grabbed her other arm, pulling it behind her, and then kicked her feet out from under her, dropping her to the ground on her knees. He pushed her right down onto her face. While she was spitting out pine needles, he pulled both her wrists together behind her and tied them with something, and then he reached under her, undid her belt, and yanked her uniform pants down around her ankles. He stood up and planted one heavy boot on her back.

She tried to move her face, but he put his considerable weight on that one foot and she got the message. She lay still, her left cheek plastered to the ground.

"Looky here, Will," the fat man said softly. "Ain't that a pretty sight, though. Drawers like that, wonder why she bothers, hunh?"

The thin man spoke for the first time. "Leave her be and git on that rope," he said.

The fat man took his foot away and knelt down on one knee beside her. While one meaty hand fondled the back of her panties, the other grasped her hair. "You stay right there, kitten," he said softly. "'Cause if'n you so much as twitch, I'll come back over here and kick your teeth right down your throat. You hearin' me?"

She didn't say anything. He jerked her hair. "You *hear*?"

She grunted a yes and he stood up. He kicked the black pepper-spray canister away from her and went to get his end of the rope. She watched him pull tension back into it. She heard a commotion in the truck and turned her head just in time to see the thin man push his prisoner off the tailgate and into the air. They'd left no slack in the rope, so she knew that the victim was not going to die of a mercifully broken neck. She closed her eyes but could not shut out the sounds of the old man grunting and gargling frantically while he kicked the air. The coils of chain clinked in time to his frantic struggles.

After what seemed like forever it stopped and she opened her eyes. The prisoner was dangling under the tree, his legs splayed and motionless a few tantalizing inches above the ground, his bulging eyes and black tongue protruding from a plum red face. The fat man, who had been standing on the end of the rope while their prisoner strangled, stepped back and dropped the body onto the dirt. The thin man jumped down from the bed of the pickup and removed the noose.

"What about this one?" the fat man asked, walking over to where the probationer lay in the dirt. "This is damn prime."

"Business before pleasure," weasel-face said. "He'p me get his ass in the lake."

But the big man had other ideas. She could almost feel him staring hungrily at her exposed limbs. "Shit, Will, I ain't a'goin' nowheres," he said. "Right now, I'm gonna tear me off a piece'a this right here."

"Goddammit, Lee, Grinny'll kick your ass, you mess with—"

"Don't hafta know, now, does she," Lee said, his voice thickening. He straddled her lower legs and knelt down. When she felt his weight, she tried to lunge forward like a fish in the grass. He smacked her solidly on the back of her head, momentarily stunning her. When she felt him tugging at his overalls she tried again to wiggle out from under him. She felt that big paw coming down again and this time she saw stars and then nothing.

1

The uniformed park ranger looked up from his newspaper. "You're Lieutenant Richter," he said with a frown.

"That's right," I said. "Except for the lieutenant part. I'm not with the sheriff's office anymore."

The ranger gave me a stony look, as if this news somehow made my appearance there worse. "I'll tell her you're here," he said curtly. He got up from behind the visitors' information counter and walked over to an office door. He paused before opening it. "You're not exactly welcome up here, you know," he said.

I just waited. The ranger gave me another hard look. I debated quailing in the presence of such ferocity, but yawned instead. He then went into the office, shutting the door behind him. Truth be told, I hadn't exactly expected a marching band and festive bunting upon my first visit to the Thirty Mile ranger station since the cat dancers case. But that had been two years ago, and I'd almost managed to bury those events in my moving-on box. Almost.

The station hadn't changed a bit. The unfriendly park ranger was a new face, so whatever he knew about it he'd been told by others. They'd been furious then because I'd put Mary Ellen Goode in grave danger. Apparently they weren't over it. Nothing I could do about that. She had called me, not the other way around.

Then she was standing there. Still remarkably pretty, although there were some dark circles under those blue eyes and a tinge of gray in her hair. Her smile seemed a bit forced.

"Thanks for coming," she said. "Let's go back to my office."

I followed her down a short hall. *She's thinner*, I thought. The sign on her door read M.E. GOODE, PH.D., PARK ECOLOGIST.

"How's the arm?" she asked as we went into her office.

"Better," I said. "I can hold it on the steering wheel for almost an hour now. How're things in the Great Smoky Mountains National Park these days?"

She sat down behind a cluttered desk. "Comparatively quiet," she said with a rueful smile. "Until six weeks ago."

I eased myself into a wooden chair and massaged my upper arm. What was left of it. "I've missed seeing you," I said, and meant it.

She looked down at her desk for a moment before answering. "I'm sorry about going radio-silent," she said finally. "I—it's been—very difficult." She took a deep breath. "I've not been well."

I leaned forward. "Hey? That wasn't an accusation. Just an observation. I *have* missed seeing you. Now, tell me: Am I going to get out of this station alive?"

She smiled. "Don't mind them," she said. "You made them look bad. They'll get over it."

"And how about you—are you getting over it?"

"Are you really a private investigator now?" she asked, sidestepping my question.

"After a fashion. I left the Manceford County Sheriff's Office after—well, after that incident at White Eye's cabin." I saw her flinch when I mentioned White Eye. I guess I had my answer. "I couldn't very well stay on in law enforcement once I refused to testify. So now I do investigative work for the district court system in Triboro. When I want to."

She gave me an appraising look. "Sheriff Baggett explained that to me," she said. "Why you wouldn't testify. I don't believe I've ever thanked you for that."

I shrugged and immediately regretted it. There were some things my left arm could do, but lifting suddenly wasn't one of them. "Well, it was my butt, too," I said. "Until we know we have them all, both of us would have been dreaming about crosshairs for the rest of our lives."

"Dreaming of crosshairs," she said softly. "That's very well put. And are they working it?"

"I think so," I said, rubbing my arm again. "But of course I'm on the outside now, so I don't really know."

"And how about you—are you working it?"

It was my turn to smile. "Oh, yes," I said. I'd formed a one-man-band consulting company when I left the sheriff's office, offering myself to handle investigative projects for various court offices. The Major Criminal Apprehension Team, or MCAT, leaderless after I left, had been disbanded, and the team members reassigned within the major crimes division. I'd offered moonlighting

jobs to three of my ex-teammates, who all knew the real reasons behind my re-
fusal to testify in the cat dancers case. Together we were quietly assembling a
database of candidates for the as yet unapprehended cat dancers.

She nodded, not quite looking at me. She seemed distracted, I thought. Remembering the cave and those big cats hunting them in the dark? My mother
had been on antidepressant meds after my father died. She'd been like this.
Wistful. Quick to drift. "You called?" I prompted.

She pulled herself together. "Yes, I did. Did you read about the Park Service
probationer who was beaten and raped up here in the park? About six weeks
ago?"

"Sorry, no," I said.

"One of ours. New rangers are assigned to an experienced ranger as a mentor when they start their probationary year. Janey Howard was assigned to me.
She'd been here almost three months. The chief sent her to one of the backcountry lakes to take water samples. She didn't come back that afternoon.
Once it got dark and we couldn't raise her on the radio, we launched a search."

"The local cops join in?"

"Absolutely. Park Service. Carrigan County deputies. Volunteer firefighters
from Marionburg. But we concentrated on where she was supposed to have
gone. Found her vehicle there, so that's where we looked. Some hikers found
her two days later, wandering down one of the trails, about ten miles from the
lake. Wearing nothing but an old blanket. Barefoot. Dehydrated. Beat up.
Among other things."

"Did she get herself loose or did they dump her?"

"No one knows. She doesn't know. She remembers nothing, which is probably a good thing. She's home, over in Cherokee County, in Murphy. Her parents are being—very protective."

"They mad at the Park Service?"

" 'We trusted you to take care of her,' " she recited. " 'She was supposed
to be a park ranger, not a rape victim. Walking tours, nature hikes with the
tourists, butterfly lectures, sweet bunny rabbits, bird watching. See Bambi run.
That kind of thing. Instead you people sent her off into the deep woods and
some twisted bastard got her. What was she doing out there all alone?' "

"Her job, perhaps?" I said.

Mary Ellen sighed. "It is a beautiful park. And we do all of those nice
things. But you and I know that evil can get loose in the backcountry from time
to time."

"Do we ever," I murmured.

She shot me a sideways look. "And," she continued, "Janey was working very close to Injun country."

I raised my eyebrows at her. "Meaning?"

"Meaning that she was working up on the edge of Robbins County."

"Ah." I'd heard of Robbins County back when I'd been with the Manceford County Sheriff's Office. The Great Smokies Park extended into both Tennessee and North Carolina. Robbins County enveloped the southeastern boundary of the park on the Carolina side. It was a place where the hill people lived remote and were determined to keep themselves that way. It was also rumored to be the mother lode for methamphetamine in western North Carolina. The Robbins County Sheriff's Office was also reputed to be a really interesting organization. Their official motto was "Taking care of business." I'd heard they'd painted that right on the patrol cars.

"Yes," she said. "Our local sheriff, Bill Hayes, apparently has to ask permission to operate in Robbins County. They were not exactly forthcoming."

"The Park Service is federal—you don't have to ask permission."

"Yes we do, outside of the park. Anyway, we got her back, but that's all we got. Which is why I called you."

I leaned back in my chair. "The Park Service has sworn officers. And I would have guessed they'd get the Bureau into it, especially if you guys suspected criminal collusion from local law."

She hesitated. "It's complicated," she said. "It seems our regional director is scared of starting some kind of feud with local mountain people. Send the FBI in and stir up a hornet's nest of hillbilly outlaws who would then come into the park for recreation involving the tourists. We're not staffed to cope with that kind of mess. The visitor count is down already because of what happened to Janey Howard."

"And the visitor count is important?" I asked.

"It determines the budget, among other things. Especially if it goes down because of bad publicity."

"Does it have a bearing on other things—such as promotions, seniority, performance evaluations?"

She nodded. "What can I say: We're a federal bureaucracy. Anyway, I thought perhaps you might have some ideas on how we can find out who did this."

"What's Sheriff Hayes doing?"

"The Carrigan County people got nowhere in Robbins County, whose sheriff maintains it didn't happen on his patch. And, of course, if it didn't happen in Robbins County, then it probably happened in the park."

"Either way, technically not Hayes's problem, either."

"Not his jurisdiction," she corrected. "He's mad as hell about it, and they did more than they had to. It's just—"

"Right," I said. "Some cases are just no-win for anybody. So you guys want to hire me? Is that it?"

She put a hand to her mouth in surprise. "Us? The Park Service? Oh, no, we can't do that. I mean—"

I grinned at her. "I know that. I was just teasing. Besides, my name isn't exactly enshrined in a place of honor here. I thought I was going to have to call for the dogs, the way that ranger was looking at me."

"You've brought them along?"

"Don't go anywhere without them," I said. I saw the alarm flicker in her eyes again and mentally kicked myself. "Why don't we have dinner," I said. "We can talk about it some more. I may have some ideas for you."

She appeared to think about it. "I don't know if that would be such a good idea," she said finally. "Marionburg is a very small town. And, well—" She stopped.

And my being here has resurfaced some very bad memories, I thought. Which she was not, apparently, able to expunge. No wonder the rangers were still mad at me. Before the cat dancers case she had been the brightest object at the station.

"Well," I said, getting up. "I'm assuming there's still only the one decent place to eat in Marionburg. I'll be there around eight if you change your mind. Otherwise, I'll check around a little and then give you a call. Okay?"

She nodded quickly. Too quickly, I thought. I sensed that she wanted me out of there, and that now would be nice. Plus, she was probably embarrassed. I'd driven almost four hours from Triboro, and now she was probably thinking that her call had been a mistake. "Thank you," she said in a small voice, again not quite looking at me. "And I'm sorry for being such a drag."

"Don't beat yourself up, Mary Ellen," I said gently. "It takes some time. You getting help?"

She nodded. "And you?" she asked. This time she did look at me. The fear was still visible in her eyes. If anything, brighter.

"Scotch at night, the gym during the day, and lots of quality time on the firing range. I'll be in touch. You stop worrying."

*   *   *

As I headed out to my Suburban I heard a voice behind me calling my name.

"Lieutenant Richter? A word, please?"

I thought it was the hostile ranger I'd run into when I first arrived, so I turned around very quickly, ready to quash any more bullshit from the hired help. But this ranger was older, and the title on his nameplate read CHIEF RANGER. He stopped abruptly when I spun around.

"Yes?" I said in as official a voice as I could muster. For the record, I'm six-one and I hadn't been kidding about spending much of the last two years in the gym. The older man had to look up to speak to me.

"I'm Bob Parsons, chief of the station here. My people told me you'd come to see Mary Ellen Goode."

"That's right," I said. I could see two sets of German shepherd ears outlined against the back window of my Suburban. The vehicle's windows were open and they'd heard my tone of voice. I was about to add that she had called me, but then decided against it.

"My predecessor told me the story," Parsons said. "About what happened up here and what happened to Mary Ellen." He paused. "Look, Lieutenant—"

"I'm not a lieutenant anymore," I said. "I took early retirement from the Manceford County Sheriff's Office. And I suspect you didn't get the whole story about what happened."

Parsons nodded. "Right," he said quickly. "She said you were a private investigator now." He hesitated again. "Look," he said again. "I'm sure there's stuff I don't know, and probably don't need to know. But what I do know is that Mary Ellen is pretty fragile these days. Is it absolutely necessary for you to be here? Can maybe one of us help you instead?"

I considered the question. The chief ranger sounded sincere. "That'll be up to her, Mr. Parsons," I said. "For the record, I'm intimately familiar with what she went through. I was there for part of it. And the last thing I want to do is to upset her."

"Up to her?" Parsons asked, and then he understood. "Ah—she called you?"

"That's right," I said.

"Then this is about Janey Howard, isn't it."

"Why don't you ask her, Mr. Parsons. Or you can wait for her to tell you. That actually might be the kinder course of action."

Parsons shook his head. "The Howard case is complicated, Lieutenant. Very complicated. It involves more than just the Park Service."

I pretended to be surprised.

Parsons sighed. "We're not sure where the attack took place. Whether it was in the park or in Robbins County."

"You are sure about the attack, though?"

"Oh, yes. God, yes. That girl's lucky to be alive."

"So. You jailed any bad guys for it?"

Parsons frowned. I suspected he probably did that a lot. "Um, no," he said. "But that doesn't mean people have stopped trying."

"People?"

Parsons avoided the question. "Like I said, it's complicated. Politically sensitive within the Park Service. I guess what I'm trying to say is you'd be doing everyone a favor if you just went back east. Really, you would."

"Nice to meet you, Chief Ranger Parsons," I said. I turned away from the ranger and walked to my vehicle. Parsons stood there for a moment, shook his head, frowned some more, and then walked back into the ranger station.

I took my shepherds for a quick nature walk and then left to find my motel. I wondered how long it would take Parsons to get on the telephone to talk to those mysterious "people," and how long before they would get in touch with me.

I went into Marionburg and stopped at a grocery store to pick up some supplies for the cabin. Then I drove around the area for half an hour, refreshing my bearings and making sure I remembered where the restaurant was. There was actually quite a bit of traffic. Marionburg was the county seat of Carrigan County and had maybe eight thousand permanent residents. There was one main drag with mostly tourism-oriented shops and restaurants, a center square with the county offices, and rustic-looking residential neighborhoods.

It being early fall, rooms on short notice had been very scarce anywhere near the Smoky Mountains National Park, so I'd ended up acquiring the so-called bridal suite at the Blue Mountains Lodge on the south side of town. It was available because it cost a small fortune to rent it, but since money wasn't something I had to worry about anymore, I said yes. When I'd told the reservations clerk that I might want the cabin for an entire month, there had been no objections. Weekly rate times four, bride not included.

The lodge featured a standard, two-story motel building next to the road and several outlying cabins in the back for guests who wanted extended stays. The complex was situated on a low bluff overlooking a wide, tree-lined mountain stream. I checked in at the front office at five thirty and then drove around the motel building into the lower parking lot. The cabins were stair-stepped along the creek, and according to the diagram, the bridal suite was at the very end of the left-hand row of cabins. The lower parking lot was almost empty. I surmised that the rest of the guests were still out whitewater rafting, hiking, trail riding, fishing, or even gambling over on the Cherokee Reservation.

I nosed the Suburban into the curb and was about to shut down when another vehicle slid close in alongside mine, so close that I could not have opened my door more than about four inches. It was another Suburban, as big as mine, and there were three men inside. The dogs were alarmed and I gave them a down command. The two windows on the other vehicle's right side slid down. I lowered my driver's-side window and looked over at the man in the right front seat. He was middle-aged and extremely hairy—beard, mustache, and a wild mop of grayish black hair on top folded into a ponytail behind. He wore a multicolored hippie headband and dark glasses on a neck rope. He was fox-faced and reminded me of some of the lawyers I'd encountered out riding their weekend Harleys when I'd been a cop. This guy's coolly superior expression told me they were probably federal drug agents.

"You're blocking my door," I said. One of the men in back, dressed more conventionally in a khaki windbreaker and ball cap, snorted out a laugh.

"We need to talk to you," fox-face said. "You're Lieutenant Richter, am I right?"

"You're blocking my door," I said again. "Back up, please."

"We'll back up when we're good and fucking ready to, Lieutenant. Oh, I guess I forgot, you're not a lieutenant anymore, are you."

"Once more, with feeling," I said. "Back up."

Fox-face grinned and raised a set of credentials for me to admire. "DEA," he announced. "And we're here to invite you to stay away from the Janey Howard case. We think you're not qualified, not authorized, and not wanted here."

"You've got me confused," I said calmly.

"*What?*"

"With someone who gives a shit about what you think about anything. Back up, please."

"In case you've forgotten, *Mister* Richter," fox-face snapped, "you're not a cop anymore. In fact, some people think you were a bent cop. If you'd like, we can reinforce that notion locally. So why don't you leave? You know, easy way or hard way?"

"Let's try my way," I said, and then I punched down the left rear window button and gave a sharp command. The two German shepherds launched serially through the window directly into the other car, where they proceeded to cry havoc. They barked, roared, growled, snapped, slobbered, and pounced between the front and back seats until all three occupants had submerged from sight. I recalled them with a whistle and they happily jumped back into my Suburban, looking very pleased with themselves. The whole thing had taken maybe twenty seconds. Longer for some than others, I thought.

I backed my Suburban away from the DEA-mobile, where no heads had yet reappeared, and parked it about twenty feet away. I let the dogs out and told them to watch the agents' vehicle. They sat down ten feet away from it. The first head to pop up was the driver's, whose white-faced visage was greeted with angry barking and raised hackles. The man quickly raised his window and then backed the car all the way out to the ramp leading to the upper parking lot. I watched them go. I wondered if I should wave, but decided not to. Once they'd changed underwear and showered, they'd discover that no one had actually been bitten. That would probably make them really unhappy. Crying shame.

The bridal suite cabin was appropriately designed. It was perched on a large rock that overhung the creek and was separated from the nearest cabin by a thick stand of Leyland cypress. It had all the important bases covered: an enormous bed in the single bedroom; three refrigerators, one each in the bedroom, living room, and kitchen; a large screened porch extending over a small waterfall with yet another bed. There was a pine-paneled living room, complete with a heavily padded bearskin rug and a huge stone fireplace. The bathroom had a large hot tub, which had a built-in cooler within easy reach. Each of the refrigerators was a fully stocked minibar, including the one in the kitchen. The bedroom had a large-screen TV and a stereo system that had been wired throughout the cabin. There did not appear to be any telephones. There was an interesting DVD collection stacked inside some kind of vending cabinet.

The shepherds looked at me as if to ask, *And where do we go?* I was tempted to put them back in my Suburban. On the other hand, they had done a first-class monster mash on the uppity DEA guys. I went back out to the Suburban and got their dog beds. The shepherds were called Frick and Frack. My dog-aficionado friends had been appalled at the names, but they had the advantage of sounding different, dog commands being mostly an audio business. Frick was a sable spayed female, about eighty pounds and fairly intense. Frack was an all-black East German border guard number, an easy hundred pounds plus, whose specialty was sitting down and staring with those big amber eyes of his, which seemed to scare the shit out of most people. I set them up on the screened front porch and told them to watch for bad guys. Frick immediately assumed the alert; Frack, not one to sweat the load, yawned and lay down for a nap.

I'd been wrong about the phone. I hunted down the chirping noises and found it stashed inside a tiny pantry closet in the kitchen. I picked it up. Fox-face was back.

"I suppose you think that was funny," he said. "I could have you arrested for assaulting federal officers."

"I didn't assault anybody," I said. "My dogs may have gone to investigate some impolite assholes who didn't know how to park their car."

There was silence on the line. I made a quick decision: I couldn't operate up here if the feds went to the local sheriff and made trouble.

"You have a name in addition to 'special agent'?" I asked.

"Greenberg."

"Okay, Special Agent Greenberg. You want to sit down and have a conversation like an adult, I'm willing to meet with you. But enough of this *Miami Vice* bullshit."

I heard Greenberg take a deep breath. "Okay," he said. "Where and when?"

"You've got this number, so you know where I am. I'll meet with you here. Lose the other clowns. Whenever you're ready." I hung up.

Greenberg knocked on the front screen door about ten minutes later. Both shepherds watched him but did not otherwise react. Greenberg watched them very carefully. I gave the dogs a command and then let Greenberg in. The DEA agent was actually kind of short, maybe five-six in his stocking feet, made two inches taller with the aid of expensive-looking cowboy boots. He wore jeans and a truly repulsive untucked Hawaiian shirt. He was broad-shouldered, though, and I thought he'd probably be dangerous in a street fight. Little guys built like this often were. He seemed full of nervous energy, eyes flitting this way and that as he checked his perimeters.

"Scotch okay?" I asked as we sat down on the screened porch over the creek.

Greenberg relaxed fractionally and nodded. I poured. The agent asked if he could smoke, and I said sure. "What *is* this place?" Greenberg asked. "You've got beds everywhere."

"Honeymoon suite," I said. "Only thing available on short notice."

Greenberg grunted. I tipped my glass at him. "Shall we start over?"

The agent sipped some scotch and nodded. "I apologize for that bullshit in the parking lot," he said. "That was unprofessional."

"I apologize for setting my dogs on you."

Greenberg nodded solemnly and then, surprising me, grinned. "That was fucking amazing," he said. "All three of us are armed to the teeth — belt guns, ankle guns, knives — and nobody even *thought* about going for a weapon. And then they were just — gone."

"It takes some training," I said. "I take it Chief Ranger Parsons called you?"

Greenberg nodded. "He's apparently a bit of a politician. Your being here has his wires humming. Puppets hate that."

"Okay," I said. "Let me tell you why I'm here."

I explained the background of my relationship with Ranger Dr. Mary Ellen Goode. How she had been drawn into the cat dancers case while I was still with the Manceford County Sheriff's Office. How she had been taken hostage and held for several days in a cave in the mountains strapped into a homemade electric chair, and how she and I had fought our way out of the cave while being pursued by two starving captive mountain lions.

"Not exactly a great first date," I said. "She had the living shit scared out of her, and she's just now getting over it."

Greenberg sipped some more scotch. "What's with this dirty-cop rap, then?" he asked. "We checked you out with the Bureau guys in Charlotte after Parsons called. They said you refused to testify in that mountain lion thing."

"True. And the reason for that is that some of the bad guys involved are still at large. We're talking local Carolina law and maybe even some feds. Their wire-woman offered us a deal: We both go radio-silent, and there'd be no long guns in the night for Ranger Goode. Otherwise . . ."

Greenberg nodded. "That reads. I heard some weird shit about that whole business. Heard you became a millionaire when that judge got clipped in Triboro?"

"That judge was my ex-wife. We'd gotten back together when that happened. Frankly, I'd rather have her back."

"Oh," he said. "That why people think you took a fall?"

"My boss in Manceford County had some good advice. He said my enemies would think the worst, and my friends would know better. What strangers thought didn't make a shit either way."

Greenberg considered that for a moment. "So why'd she call you?" he asked. His left foot was doing this tapping routine, and I wondered if maybe this guy had gotten a little too close to his trade. He was positively wired.

"Like you said, she called me. Said that the Howard case has gone cold and that the Park Service head-shed is afraid of stirring up the ten-gauge, black-hat crowd in Robbins County. Local law here isn't on speaking terms with the sheriff next door. She basically asked me to look around."

"You licensed?"

I nodded.

"Okay," Greenberg said. "My turn. We got called into the Howard case because the Park Service thought she'd maybe stumbled onto a meth pit. There's never been a case of a park ranger being assaulted up here, not like that, anyway."

"You think that's what happened?"

"Who the fuck knows—we've got zip-point-shit. That girl was so traumatized she can barely remember her name, so we don't even know where the hell it happened, in the park or in Robbins County. Which is definitely a place of interest."

"Meth?" I asked, knowing the answer.

"Meth, indeed," Greenberg said. "It's becoming a fucking epidemic. No, not becoming—we're there. And most of the crank in this region is coming out of these here hills; apparently it beats the shit out of picking ginseng roots when you're looking for cash money."

"How in the world can the DEA infiltrate the coves and the hollers in these mountains?"

Greenberg finished his scotch. I pointed at the bottle, but he shook his head. "Short answer—we can't, of course. Oh, we can do the usual techie shit: night flights looking for infrared plumes, analysis of geo-science satellite imagery, the occasional roadblock collar. But going among the great unwashed, undercover? Fuh-geddabout it. All my guys have most of their teeth and can speak using the occasional two-syllable word."

"So how do you work it?"

"We look for an angle, anything that can justify us going into Robbins County."

"Like the Howard assault?"

"That would be nice. If we can't get a search warrant based on a rumored drug deal, we get one in connection with an ongoing investigation of this assault on a federal officer. Or we can sample creeks and lakes where they throw their used chemicals and then file environmental charges. Anything we can hang our hats on. Which, admittedly, ain't much."

"And the last thing you need is for some Lone Ranger to come in and stir the pot."

"Right again."

"Unless maybe I stir it your way?"

Greenberg sat up and gave me a thoughtful look. "You made your manners with Sheriff Bill Hayes yet?" he asked.

"First thing tomorrow morning," I said. "We've met before."

"Why don't you do that," Greenberg said, fishing out one of his cards. "See how much he'll reveal about the local two-legged wildlife. Especially next door in wild and wonderful Robbins County. If he gives you the okay to work his patch, then maybe you and I can do some business. How's that sound?"

"Like the makings of a deal, Special Agent. By the way, my name's Cam."

Greenberg nodded and got up. "Name's Ruthe," he said, looking me right in the eye.

"Ruth."

"That's right. But with an *e* on the end."

"And if I say anything at all, I'm going to get hurt."

"Yup."

"Lemme guess—you go in low and fast."

"Drop to one knee, left hook into their nuts, and then I stand up as their face comes forward and down. Trick is to remember to keep your teeth together."

"Ruth."

"Yup."

"Nickname?"

"Can't you guess?"

I thought for a second. "Baby?"

"There you go."

I nodded, trying not to grin. I thought we were going to get along. "So, Special Agent Ruthe Greenberg, glad to meet you."

"Look," Greenberg said. "One thing I've learned up here is that the outlaws are networked better than fucking IBM. Dollars to doughnuts somebody who cares already knows you're on their web."

"We hear you," I said.

Greenberg glanced toward the front room and rubbed his beard. "I hear *you*," he said. "But one of my guys stopped on the road to nosh a greaseburger two weeks ago? Little roadside pull-off, you know, park benches, trees, burbling fucking brook? He's sitting there, scarfing fries, and this .65-caliber Civil War minié ball comes down the mountain and blows up his Happy Meal bag."

"One of those 'we could have if we'd wanted to' love notes?"

"Right. Bullet first, then the boom. Three-, four-hundred-yard shot."

"Long guns are the scariest," I said.

"Okay, then, just so you know," Greenberg said. "They like to reach out and touch someone once in a while. Call me."

"Call you what, exactly?" I asked.

Greenberg grinned, cocked and fired a finger gun at me, and left. After he'd gone, I wondered if that had been too easy. Most of the information flow had come from me, not Greenberg. On the other hand, the meth problem nationwide was big and getting bigger, so it made sense for the DEA to be out here along the Georgia–North Carolina–Tennessee wilderness nexus. I made a mental note to see if any of my friends in the North Carolina SBI knew "Baby" Greenberg. Either way, the chances were good that the DEA guys would try to use me to their best advantage. Fair enough, I thought. I was perfectly capable of using them right back.

The setting sun had made the porch uncomfortably warm, so I decided to go down to the creek bank, find a rock, and put my feet in the water. As I was sitting on my rock, enjoying the sunset and my scotch, I saw a figure coming down the creek who appeared to be walking on the water. I checked to see how much scotch I'd had and then realized he was wading *in* the water. I couldn't make out his features because he was up-sun and there was one hell of a glare in that pristine mountain air. He was wearing hip waders and carrying what looked like a mesh laundry bag and a stick. I realized he was fishing for trash in the creek and, based on the lump of debris in the bag, succeeding.

When he got about ten feet away, I finally said howdy. He turned to see where I was, and I just had to stare. He had the face that you see on the back of a buffalo nickel, and I mean identical—the stereotypical American Indian face, complete with sculpted nose, thick lips, pointed cheekbones, and pretty much the same expression. It was such a resemblance that he was probably not surprised by my reaction.

"Scary, isn't it?" he said with a small smile, resting on his pickup stick for a moment. I had to laugh. He was heavy in the chest and shoulders and had to be at least six-foot-something in height. He had jet black hair pulled back in a short ponytail and was wearing a buckskin shirt above the rubber waders. I had half-expected a grunt or even a Hollywood "How," but his accent was not even remotely western Carolina. The shepherds appeared just then from the underbrush and looked him over.

"Nice dogs," he said. "You staying here at the lodge?"

I said yes and asked him what he was doing out there in the creek.

"My contribution to the environment," he said, shifting his weight from foot to foot. That water had to be very cold. "All this natural beauty, people come out here, gawk at it, ooh and aah, then throw their shit in the creek." He glanced at the drink in my hand.

"Scotch," I said. "Join me?"

"Absolutely," he said, wading over to my side of the creek. He sat down on a rock and began to undo the elaborate wader rig. I went up to the cabin and got another glass and the bottle. The shepherds stayed with me up and back. He was sitting on a dry rock when I got back down to the bank. He was wearing what looked like two sets of red woolen long johns and extra-thick socks, and the boots and waders were piled in a sodden heap beside him. He accepted the drink gratefully and knocked half of it back, following up with a satisfied sigh. Up close, I could see that he was probably in his late fifties, if not sixty. His face was permanently tanned, telling me he spent all of his time outdoors.

"Perfect," he announced. "I needed that."

"You live up here?"

"Retired," he said. "Came from these parts about a hundred years ago. Robbins County, actually, right next door."

"You don't sound like western Carolina," I said. The shepherds sat behind us; from their posture, it was plain they hadn't made up their minds yet about this guy. It was hard not to stare at that face; it was just such a perfect resemblance to the Fraser sculpture.

"Got the hell out, like most folks who had the chance and half a brain," he said. "How about you?"

I told him I was retired from the Manceford County sheriff's office back in Triboro.

"Don't look old enough," he said, eyeing me as he finished the scotch. I offered him a refill, but he shook his head. "Thanks, gotta drive my Harley."

"I thought a snoot-full was a prerequisite for righteous hog wrangling."

"A snoot-full and a Harley is a summons for the undertaker," he said.

"They come after you for reenactments up at that Cherokee Village?" I asked.

"All the time," he said, chuckling. "I don't, but I do go downtown sometimes and do my wise old Indian act when I'm looking to pick up women." He grinned and suddenly looked ten years younger. Retirement was agreeing with him.

"What brings *you* up here?" he asked. "Vacation?"

"I do a little consulting work on the side for the courts back east," I said. "A friend needed some help with something, asked me to come up."

He nodded, but didn't pursue it. "I do private guide work in the backcountry of the Smokies," he said. "Name's Mose, by the way. Mose Walsh."

"Cam Richter," I said. "Those guys behind us are Frick and Frack."

He laughed out loud. "They must hate you for that."

"No, it's a sound thing. Easy name differentiation for commands."

He looked over his shoulder at the shepherds, who looked back. "Keep 'em with you all the time?"

I nodded.

"Good deal," he said. "Especially for a cop. I had a shepherd once. He got eaten by something in the woods. Bear, feral pig, I don't know what, maybe even a big cat."

I felt a tingle on the back of my neck. "Big cat? You mean like mountain lion?"

He shook his head. "Folks say they're out there, but I've never seen any real sign of 'em. Too bad, in a way. Some'a these tourists would be more respectful of the park if there was something out there could eat 'em."

"People keep saying they've seen big cats," I said.

"The park rangers are hard-over on that subject," he said. "The big ones are long gone. No, if it was a cat got Kraut, it was probably a bobcat. Damned dog liked to corner woods critters. Something cornered him back, that's all."

I thought about telling him about my own experiences with some all too real mountain lions out there, but decided not to. It was history best left alone. Then I remembered what Greenberg had said about Robbins County, and I asked Mose about that.

"Robbins County is a place unto itself," he said. "Me, I keep to the park."

"I ran into some DEA guys this afternoon," I said. "They make Robbins County sound like, um—"

"Injun country?" he said with a mock suspicious look on his face. Then we both laughed. That was exactly what I'd been about to say.

"Most of that county is classified as state game lands," he said. "Hunters go up there more than tourists; you just have to be circumspect about what you see sometimes."

"How long you been guiding?"

"Going on ten years now. Made a nice change. You found your chapter two yet?"

"Not really," I said. "Still figuring it out."

"Well," he said, getting up from his rock. "Thanks much for the firewater. You ever need some guide services, give me a holler. Moses Walsh, Esquire. I'm in the book."

"Esquire—you a lawyer?"

"Na-ah," he said. "The 'esquire' keeps those pesky telemarketers away." He grinned again, and I said good-bye. He gathered up his wet gear, the bag, and the stick and headed up the gravel walk toward the parking lot, looking faintly ridiculous in those baggy red long johns. A couple of teenaged girls were on the pathway. They stared at him as he lumbered by them. He raised his right hand and gave them a very convincing Big Chief grunt as he passed them, and they broke into fits of giggles. A minute later I heard the unmistakable rumble of a Harley firing up in the parking lot. Sitting Bull on a Harley; that must make quite a sight.

At nine, I was finishing dinner in town when Mary Ellen Goode came into the bar and looked into the dining room. I waved her over. Despite those shadows under her eyes, she was still pretty enough to cause most of the men in the dining room to fumble what they were doing. She was wearing jeans and a short-sleeved blouse, and she was definitely thinner than the last time I'd seen her. Her face exuded that slightly haunted, lingering, longing look. But not for me, I suddenly realized. I started to get up, but she waved me down and slid into a chair.

"You're bigger than I remembered," she said. "Weights?"

I nodded. "After I left the sheriff's office I was really feeling sorry for myself. Left under a professional cloud, my best buddy dead up in the mountains somewhere, and an unknown number of the bad guys still out there. The sheriff came by one evening and was unsympathetic. Next day one of the SWAT team supervisors showed up and hauled my sorry ass down to his gym. Introduced me to the notion of applied pain as therapy."

"Did it help the arm?"

"Actually, it did. I was mostly doing the Napoleon bit after the incident, but now I can hold a glass when I pour my scotch. But you're right—two years of free weights and you tend to bulk up. Had to buy all new clothes. How about you?"

She smiled. It did wonders for her face, but it wasn't the dazzling, sunny smile I remembered from when I'd first met her. "I came back to work after a month's leave. Told my boss everything. Big mistake. They wanted to transfer me out west, or to Washington headquarters. I couldn't stand the thought of leaving the Smokies."

"So then they, what—put you in a cocoon?"

"Exactly. I was having trouble sleeping, so they sent me to a counselor. He fell in love, or at least lust, and I had to disentangle myself from that mess. If I wanted to go out to the backcountry they always sent someone along. That screwed up the duty rotation, had people standing extra duty. I thought about quitting, but what else would I do? I had no idea."

"I know the feeling," I said. "I was a cop. That's a job that defines you in to-day's society. Now I'm supposed to be some kind of private eye and I feel a lit-tle ridiculous most of the time. Plus, everyone knows I don't have to work anymore."

"So the big bucks came to pass, then?"

"Boy, did they ever. Even after taxes and grasping lawyers, it was a hell of a lot of money. You eaten?"

She shook her head. "I typically have a late lunch and leave it at that."

I talked her into dessert and coffee, and we talked about the past two years. She had written me a letter after the dust settled that seemed to invite a rela-tionship, but it hadn't panned out. I'd been too busy reestablishing my identity to get away from Triboro, and she had become increasingly reclusive. I asked her why she really wanted me to look into the Janey Howard incident.

"It's become a political football," she said. "The incident involved two counties and the national park, and no one wants to own it. Meanwhile Janey is a whimpering wreck over in Murphy, and, of course, she's provided zero use-ful information. Her parents finally got disgusted and told everyone to go away. She was my newbie, and I feel responsible."

"What'd the investigation reveal?"

"Not much. We found her Jeep and tracked around the lake with dogs, but it had rained and they got nowhere."

"What kind of dogs?"

"Labs, as I remember."

I snorted; I despised Labs. Blockheaded, passive-aggressive lumps, every one.

"Anyway, she was found some miles away from the lake, so she may have been abducted, taken somewhere, and then assaulted."

"And she's said nothing?"

"One of the EMTs reported she said two words on the way to the hospital—'hangman' and 'grinning.'"

I sighed. "Not much. Almost sounds like that tarot stuff."

She touched my hand. "You can forget the whole thing if you'd like to," she said. "At least three authorities did look and came up with zero. I've no right to impose on you this way."

At that moment she looked over my shoulder and withdrew her hand. I turned to see the young ranger who had been so unfriendly earlier come in and give Mary Ellen a disapproving look as he went into the bar. "Oh-oh," I said. "You've been spotted consorting with the devil."

"They're just being protective, Cam," she said.

"Well, let's face it, Mary Ellen—last time I came out to these parts two people died and you were taken hostage. I guess I can see their point."

"That case was very different," she said. "This was just a straightforward assault."

Ain't no such thing, I thought. *Especially up here in the western Carolina mountains.*

2

The next morning I called on the sheriff of Carrigan County, William Hayes, whom I'd met before. He'd been sheriff for a while and looked it. Sixty-something, gray hair, politician-cop face with paternalistic eyes. I explained over coffee why I'd come up to his neck of the woods, trying to cast my mission more in terms of doing Mary Ellen Goode a favor than of actually hoping to solve a case that, presumably, the sheriff and his people had already taken a good swing at. The sheriff was not fooled for a moment.

"Last time you came around, you cut quite a swath," Hayes said. "Mountain lions, dead guys. You still got those two shepherds?"

"Out in the car as we speak," I said. "Bobby Lee Baggett ever give you the whole story about all that?"

"Enough to know I didn't want any of that Triboro shit up here," the sheriff said.

"It was a lot bigger than Triboro," I said. "Tell me: What do I need to know about Robbins County?"

"Two words—stay the hell out of there."

"Two words?" I asked.

"'Stay' and 'out' are the operative ones. Sheriff M. C. Mingo is the law over there. He takes the notion of territory serious-like. You know their motto?"

"I've heard it," I said.

"Well, in Robbins County, everything is M. C.'s business, if he says so."

"Mary Ellen said they weren't cooperative in the Howard investigation."

The sheriff snorted. "Master of understatement, that woman," he said. "M. C. flat declared that it didn't go down in Robbins County, 'cause if it had, he'd have known about it and he would have shot the bastards responsible, most likely for resisting arrest."

"Resistance is good," I said. "But, bottom line, if it did happen in Robbins County, that answer cuts both ways."

Hayes nodded. "Not much I can do about what goes on over there. Our cooperation is limited to notifying M. C.'s office that there might be a mutual problem. We get an official acknowledgment, and then, *if* M. C. sees fit, what usually happens is that some battered hillbilly appears out on the county line road just dying to jump into the back of one my cruisers and confess to any damn thing at all. You know about the Creighs?"

"The Indian tribe? Cree?"

"Nope, the Creighs." He spelled the name. "They just pronounce it that way. They're *the* clan in Robbins County. Run by an old woman lives up on the side of a mountain. It's got one name on the maps, but everyone in Robbins County calls it Spider Mountain. Guess why?"

"Lovely," I said.

The sheriff grunted. "I've never seen her. Not many folks have, apparently. There's not too many ways you can make a living in Robbins County other than tourism, and the Creighs tend to scare off the flatlanders. So lots of the folks up there subsist on welfare and supplement their existence by running 'shine, weed, meth, mushrooms, and any other damned thing they can grow, dig up, boil down, or sell in the dead of night. And this Grinny Creigh is supposedly at the center of that web."

"Grinny?"

"As in the way a hungry witch grins at a fat little child who blunders into her cauldron room asking about lunch. Her real name's Vivian."

"So why don't the state guys or the feds take her out?"

He sighed. I realized he looked a good deal older than the last time I'd seen him. Older and a bit preoccupied.

"It would take an army to root those people out," he said. "The bad ones, I mean. Robbins County is all up and down, and mostly empty wilderness designated as state game lands. The Creighs and their like have been at this kind of stuff for over two hundred years. Block the roads, they run the rivers.

Block the rivers, they'll hump it out on mules. Some Bureau types went in there back when they were hunting Eric Rudolph. Had to be rescued from an abandoned gold mine shaft. Said they had no idea how they got down there."

"And this Sheriff Mingo protects them?"

The sheriff leaned back and hitched up his trousers. "Well, that's a little blunt, maybe. The way I see it, he's riding herd on a wolf pack. He offers up a sacrificial lamb just often enough to keep the SBI from coming in force. It ain't like he's a regular at the annual Carolina sheriffs' convention, so not many people outside Robbins County know him."

"But he keeps getting elected?"

The sheriff guffawed. I realized that had been a dumb question. "He's a Creigh," the Sheriff said. "That's what the C stands for."

"Mary Ellen suggested the Park Service is scared to really pursue what happened to their probationer."

"That got just a bit murky," the sheriff said. "They had a feds-only meeting—some Bureau types, Park Service, the local DEA guy—and decided to back off for the time being."

"The time being?"

"We had no leads—nobody did. The girl is a semi-gorp. The DEA said they had some irons in the fire that ought to take precedence."

"DEA: That would be Special Agent Greenberg?"

The sheriff grinned. "Met him, have you? That was quick. That old boy's a pistol. Fuzzy looking, but don't let that fool you."

"He and his goon squad irritated my shepherds," I said. "Frick and Frack convened a short meeting with them in the back of their Suburban."

"Now that I'd like to have seen," the sheriff said, laughing.

"Greenberg and I worked it out over some scotch last night."

He finished his coffee. "Well, lemme tell you: Don't try any of that shit with M. C. Mingo and his boys."

"If I were to go over there, should I go see him?"

"What part of 'stay' and 'out' didn't you understand?"

"But if I did?"

"You go over there pokin' around into the Howard case? He'll find *you*. Believe it."

"But you have no objections to my looking into what happened to her?"

He rubbed his face with his hands. "Long as I find out what you find out, okay?" he said. "I do have to get elected, if you get my meaning."

I told him that I absolutely would do that, and then asked him about Moses Walsh.

"Mose? Where'd you run into him?" Hayes asked.

I told him.

"He's a retired city homicide detective," Hayes said, surprising me. Mose hadn't shared that tidbit with me on the creek bank. "Funny old duck," Hayes said. "He's been here a while, keeps to himself, hires out as a guide. People see that face, think he's the original Indian scout. Then they see the Harley. He's okay, best I can tell. Really likes to chase skirt during tourist season."

I thanked him for seeing me again and left to find Special Agent Greenberg.

In the event, Greenberg wasn't available until that night. He and his squad had been called to Gatlinburg over on the Tennessee side of the national park for a meeting. I spent the rest of the afternoon orienting myself in Carrigan County. I also visited the local newspaper and read accounts of the search for Janey Howard. I dropped by the Carrigan County social services office and was able to glean a little information about the socio-economic state of affairs in neighboring Robbins County. The census-verified population was quite small, just over seven thousand, although it was thought that the real population would be a third larger than that if the hill people had bothered to cooperate. The head count had been complicated by some ambiguities on the number of children in the county outside of the town of Rocky Falls itself. The Robbins County welfare office supposedly had some postulated numbers, but they had not been verified in quite some time.

My questions about the Creighs produced deliberately blank looks. One lady in the welfare office told me flat out that running one's mouth about the Creighs was a good way to become toothless, and it didn't much matter which county you lived in. I asked her if her counterparts in Robbins County just sent out welfare checks to the Creighs based on what the recipients told them, and she said, yes, that was exactly how it worked. The sheriff's office over there did periodic verifications, no one was complaining, and it wasn't likely that anyone would, if I got her drift.

I went back to my newlywed paradise, changed into running gear, and took the dogs for a run down the creek road. When I got back, Greenberg was sitting on the bank of the stream behind the cabin. I flopped down beside him, kicked off my shoes and socks, and let the icy water revive my feet while I told him what the sheriff had told me. He seemed a little less bouncy today.

"He's not kidding about M. C. Mingo," Greenberg said. "That guy's a piece of work. He's all smiles and snake oil whenever we show up, but we can't go anywhere without one deputy we can see and a few we can't within visual range. Answers every one of our questions, and none of the info's worth two shits."

"How about the Creigh clan?"

Greenberg skipped a stone across the creek. "Lot of myth and legend over there about the Creighs. That said, getting your hands on one is apparently really hard, and if you do, they bite."

"It seems to me," I said, "that if the local law is in bed with a meth gang, then there ought to be the mother of all sting operations running. Especially on the federal side."

Greenberg smiled. "Don't get ahead of yourself, there, sport," he said.

I put up my hands in mock surrender. "I know. My brief is Janey Howard. I'm going to get Mary Ellen to take me to see the victim. Maybe together we can prod something loose."

"Good luck with that," Greenberg said. "But if you do go up to that lake, please let me know. That girl may have been taking water samples for a reason, okay?"

"Would she have known what that reason was?"

He smiled. "Not necessarily," he said.

I said I'd keep him in the loop. I asked him about Moses Walsh, still mildly curious about the guy. I told him about our conversation of the evening before. It turned out that Greenberg did know him.

"You see him in the bars sometimes; can't miss that face. Big hit with the women."

"Hayes called him a funny duck," I said.

"Well, he was homicide police—some of those guys come out a little bit gonzo when they're done. He's never come up on our radar since I've been working up here."

"He said he was from this Robbins County originally," I said.

Greenberg shrugged. "He might be," he said. "I don't know. Why—you gonna hire him to be your guide over there?"

"Thought crossed my mind. First I'm just going to go over there and snoop around a little."

"You tell Bill Hayes you were going to do that?"

I nodded.

"And he said what, exactly?"

"I got the 'two words' lecture."

"You might want to listen to the man," he said. "That would show great intelligence on your part."

"Why start now?" I asked.

He grinned and shook his head. "Where are your furry friends?" he asked.

I spoke Frick's name and both shepherds appeared behind us in about two seconds, ears up, ready for action.

"Man, I love that shit," he said.

"So do they," I said.

He watched the shepherds for a moment and then asked me if I was married. I said no, how about him?

"I make it a point to keep women out of my life," he said. "I plan to retire a semi-wealthy man, and women have a way of screwing that up for guys in my line of work."

"Not the good ones," I said, thinking of the millions my ex had left me.

"Both of 'em?" he said with an ironic grin.

After Greenberg left, I showered and called Mary Ellen Goode. It took some sweet-talking, but she finally agreed to pick me up at my hotel and take me over to beautiful downtown Murphy, North Carolina, where the Howard family lived. Janey Howard's mother met us at the door of their two-story house, which was on a tree-lined street straight out of Mayberry. She was a tiny woman, and while she seemed genuinely glad to see Mary Ellen, she gave me a decisively wary look. Mary Ellen had called ahead. I didn't know what she'd told the woman about me, but I could see that Mrs. Howard wasn't exactly thrilled with my being there.

Janey Howard was waiting for us in the living room. She was sitting in a rocking chair and did not look up when we came in. I winced when I saw her face. Her body language was that of a small child who knows she's going to be hit again and is resigned to the first blow. Mary Ellen and I took seats on the couch opposite the rocking chair, while Mrs. Howard stood next to her daughter. I had told Mary Ellen what I wanted to ask, but agreed to let her do the actual talking.

"Janey, you're looking a little better than the last time I saw you," she said gently.

Janey blinked but did not respond. Her mother patted her shoulder and the girl twitched. I saw that Janey was not as small as her mother, but she didn't look old enough to have been a park ranger, or even a probationer. Her face was still badly bruised, one eye bandaged shut. Her knees were locked rigidly together and there was a noticeable tremor in her right hand.

Mary Ellen told Janey that I had come all the way from Triboro to find out who had done this thing to her. Janey shot me a quick, furtive look, but then resumed her thousand-meter stare. The tremor increased. The medical report had said that she had been raped, sodomized, and beaten. Four cracked ribs. Multiple hematomas. Broken nose. Four teeth permanently gone. Jaw dislocated. Retinal tear in one eye. Hearing damage in one ear due to a ruptured eardrum. Sunburn, insect bites, and a bacterial infection from contaminated water during the time she had wandered the woods.

"Janey, the ambulance driver told us you said two words when they took you to the hospital. Do you remember going to the hospital?"

Janey licked her puffy lips and nodded once, although she still didn't look directly at either of us.

"He said the words were 'grinning' and 'hangman.' Do you remember saying that?'

Janey shook her head emphatically.

"She doesn't remember anything," Mrs. Howard said. Her expression said that that was probably for the best.

"Did they hang you?" I asked.

Janey looked at me for the first time. There was a tremor in both her hands now.

"She doesn't remember *anything*," Mrs. Howard said again. "Isn't that right, dear?"

Janey took several breaths and then nodded. Mary Ellen had been right, I thought. This was a total waste of time. The poor thing had simply cleared core on all her memories of the incident. This was pointless. I nudged Mary Ellen and indicated with my head that it was time to go.

Mary Ellen looked relieved. She got up and went over to Janey. She took the girl's hand and told her everything was going to be all right and not to worry. Nobody was going to hurt her anymore. Nobody was mad at her. As far as I could tell, very little of it was penetrating. The one question that was really bothering me was why she was still alive. Had the bad guy just let her go, or had she escaped? With all that damage, they may have just dumped her. So maybe this total amnesia was related to some final warning, such as *You say one word and I'll come back and do it all again.*

Mrs. Howard escorted us to the front vestibule. "I told you this wasn't going to be of any use," she said to Mary Ellen. "It's only because it's you and not that other ranger that I agreed to this." She spoke as if I weren't standing right there.

"I think she was warned off," I said to no one in particular, but loud enough for Janey in the other room to hear me. "As in, she saw something and she was told to keep quiet or more bad things would happen." I paused for a long moment. "And I completely understand," I added. "I'd do the same thing. I'd just clam up."

Mrs. Howard gave me an angry look. But as she started to reply, Janey said something from the living room.

"What's that, dear?" Mrs. Howard asked, visibly surprised.

"Look in the lake," Janey said, her voice breaking. "By the red rocks."

Mary Ellen looked blank. I immediately wanted to go back in there to see what else I could elicit, but Mary Ellen shut me down. "We'll just be leaving now, Mrs. Howard," Mary Ellen said. "Thank you for letting us talk to her. A little bit at a time—that's the way to take it, right? We'll just be on our way."

Mary Ellen had my arm now and was tugging me firmly toward the front door. I watched Mrs. Howard try to hide her confusion and then quickly agree. She'd made a big deal out of the fact that her daughter remembered nothing, and now the girl had told us something.

Back out in the car, I said nothing until Mary Ellen had had time to drive off and gather her thoughts.

"Okay, why'd we eject just when she started to talk?" I asked.

"I recognized that look in her eyes, Cam," she said. "I've seen it in my own mirror. Telling us anything at all cost her. I don't know what any of that means, but you wanted something more and you got it. I just thought one more question would be too much."

I considered that and then accepted it. "You're probably right. So: What lake, and where are those red rocks?"

3

The following morning, I decided to drive over to Robbins County and make a formal call on the notorious Sheriff M. C. Mingo. Mary Ellen had been undecided about following up on Janey's cryptic information, as the Park Service had officially closed the investigation and her boss most definitely wanted the whole incident to stay in its box. She said she'd talk it over with some of the other rangers and call me later that day.

M. C. Mingo was in a meeting, so the desk officer asked me to come back in an hour. I went to a local diner for breakfast and then took a windshield tour of Rocky Falls. That didn't take long. The town had sprung up along a two-lane road that paralleled the Roaring River as it cut its way down toward the Chance Reservoir. The river was about fifty feet wide as it ran noisily through Rocky Falls, dropping nearly five hundred feet in elevation along the two-mile notch occupied by the town. On one side of the road were most of the businesses and gas stations, with a single street of homes above and behind that. On the river side of the road were larger homes, interspersed with whitewater rafting outfitters, restaurants, B and Bs, and two motels. Across the river, the shoulders of Blue Home Mountain rose dramatically above the town, where they faced the slopes of Scotch Blood Mountain on the other side. There was a single rusted steel-trussed bridge crossing the river, and where it intersected the main street of town stood city hall and the sheriff's office. I parked in the visitors' area, opened the windows for the shepherds, and went back in.

The desk sergeant asked me to take a seat and then made a phone call. A few minutes later a young woman came out of the sheriff's private office. She was very pretty in a disco-trashy fashion, tall, black-haired, lots of lipstick, sloe-eyed, and amply endowed in all the right places. She was wearing painted-on jeans, a straining halter top, and bright red cowboy boots. She smiled at the sergeant, who was unabashedly locked on to that lush body, gave me the once-over, and then sashayed out the front door with a very deliberate, traffic-stopping walk. An invisible stratum of flowery perfume lingered in the air behind her.

"That there's Rue Creigh," the desk sergeant announced, proudly. "Ain't she somethin', though." The phone on his desk rang, and the sergeant, after clearing his throat, told me I could go in now.

Sheriff M. C. Mingo was in his early fifties and was about as plain a man as I had ever seen in a sheriff's uniform. He was five-eight or -nine, wore large bifocal eyeglasses, and had the soft, round, mealy-mouthed face and superior churchwarden expression I usually associated with Carolina politicians, all smiling eyes and teeth with just a hint of B'rer Fox glinting behind the glasses. His hair was dyed an unnatural dark brown. He had tiny hands, but his grip when he shook hands with me was surprisingly hard. He wore a perfectly pressed khaki uniform, which could not disguise a tiny potbelly. He had a .357 Magnum chrome-plated revolver on his hip, and his badge positively gleamed.

I gave him points for not wearing one of those ridiculous four-star-general collar devices beloved of so many police chiefs these days. He indicated a chair for me and sat down behind his desk, which was piled high with neat stacks of paperwork.

"You're that cat dancer fella, aren't you," he said in a mild, high-pitched voice. "Up from Manceford County, right?"

"I'm retired from the sheriff's office there," I said. "Doing some private work these days."

"A *private* eye," the sheriff said dramatically. "My gracious. Right here in Robbins County. Who'da thunk it. What can we do for you there, Lieutenant?"

The mention of my old rank spoke volumes. Someone had made a call during my hour-long wait to see the sheriff. I thought I could detect that big-haired bombshell's perfume lingering in the air.

"A friend has asked me to look into what happened to a probationer ranger assigned to the Thirty Mile ranger station over in Carrigan County," I replied.

"A friend," the sheriff repeated encouragingly. His expression was pleasant, but those crinkly eyes had not lost their hard edge.

I smiled. "One of the rangers at Thirty Mile. She was Janey Howard's mentor. Apparently, the Park Service has put the case into a let's-move-on box."

The Sheriff nodded. "Didn't happen in Robbins County, that much I know," he said.

"Yes, sir," I said. "I understand that nobody knows very much about what happened."

"Now, now," the sheriff said. "You weren't listening. I said: It didn't happen in Robbins County. See, if it had, I'd have known all about it, and we'd have some guilty bastards sweating bullets out in the back cells. Whatever did happen, it must have happened in the national park. That would be on *federal* land."

"Bastards, as in plural?" I asked.

M. C. Mingo sat back in his chair and showed some teeth. "Lord love a duck," he said. "Aren't you the quick one. Bastards. Plural indeed. Figure of speech, that's all. Bastards tend to come in small herds in this part of the state."

"Of course," I said. "So: Would you have any objections to my asking some questions around here in the county?"

"Why don't you ask me your questions, Lieutenant? Or should I say mister?"

"Definitely mister," I said. "I'm not a lieutenant anymore."

"That's right, you're not," Mingo said. "So: What are all these questions?"

I hadn't prepared for this. I'd assumed that I would just start asking around to see who knew what, if anything, about the case. This was supposed to have been a simple courtesy call. A little voice in my head was saying maybe I should have listened to Sheriff Hayes. "Oh, I just want to see what folks have heard about the case," I said. "Maybe spark up a name or two. I mean, a park ranger raped and beaten? That must have been news."

"Even up here in backward old Robbins County, that what you're saying?" the sheriff said. "As in, that kinda thing doesn't happen here more'n, what, once a week? Is that it?"

I leaned forward. "Sheriff, I didn't come in here to sass anybody. I just thought it basic professional courtesy to let you know I'd be walking around town asking questions. I have a Section 74 PI license, so I think I could do all that without seeing you."

"Well, now, you're both right and wrong there, *Mister* Richter," the sheriff said. All the pleasantness, whether faked or real, had drained out of the conversation. "You were absolutely right to come see me. But you're no longer a law enforcement officer, so you can forget all that *professional* courtesy business. And you are absolutely wrong to think you can come into *my* county and do one goddamned thing without *my* permission. And you know what? I do *not* give my permission. In fact, I invite you to get back in your vehicle and get out of my county before I throw your licensed ass in jail and pitch said vehicle into a mine shaft." He leaned back in his chair and pasted his smiley face back on. "Anything else, there, *Mister* Richter?"

"Oh, c'mon, Sheriff—what grounds would you have for putting me in jail?"

"Trying my patience? Disturbing my office routine? Interrupting me when I was in a meeting?"

"Oh, yeah," I said. "I saw the meeting. I guess that would be a crime, interrupt that kind of meeting."

I'd made a mistake. The sheriff stiffened, picked up a ballpoint pen, and began tapping it on the table in a slow four-beat rhythm. His face settled back into a cold mask. "I suppose I'll just let that pass, *Mister* Richter," he said finally. "I'll lay it down to your being ignorant of how things work up here in the western mountains, you being of the *urban* persuasion. But we can cure that ignorance lickety-split, and we will, if you're anywhere in my county in the next thirty minutes. Good day, sir."

I didn't linger. I drove back down the two-lane toward Carrigan County, my rearview mirror filled with the image of a Robbins County cruiser practically riding my Suburban's bumper. Wasn't like I hadn't been warned, I thought. The shepherds, sensing my mood, kept looking back at the cop car behind them.

The deputy turned around about three miles out of Rocky Falls, and I relaxed a little. The sheriff could not legally arrest me for simply asking questions, but I knew damn well that I was in the very western, and very remote, end of the state, where one annoyed a county sheriff at his peril. I recalled Sheriff Hayes mentioning FBI agents going into a mine shaft. Come to think of it, Mingo had also mentioned a mine shaft. I wondered who the black-haired bombshell really was.

Ten minutes later, as I slowed down to negotiate a hairpin curve to the left, I suddenly hit the brakes. At the bend of the curve a mountain stream went under the road through an old redbrick arched bridge and dropped into a deep ravine. At the bottom of the ravine, I'd spotted a man running wildly down the creek bank, flailing through the underbrush, falling as often as he covered ground. He was a fat man with a full black beard, and he was being pursued by a pack of baying dogs. I pulled over and got out of the Suburban. The shepherds had heard the other dogs and started barking. I shouted at them to shut up. By now the man was a hundred yards down the bank.

I ran over to the guardrail in time to see the first and biggest dog catch up with the fleeing man and grab an ankle in his teeth. The fat man yelled in pain and went down heavily, landing with his head and shoulders in the creek and the rest of him still on the bank. The remainder of the pack arrived and, to my horror, swarmed all over the man until he was no longer visible from the road. Even from my distant vantage point, I could hear the snarling, see the bloody jaws tearing from side to side. When I saw the whitewater in the creek turn red I backed away from the guardrail.

I thought about getting my .45 and seeing what I could do, but the scene below was out of effective range, and, judging from the blood in the water, it was already too late. I looked back down and saw that the dog pack was still going to town and the creek was still running red. Then movement caught my eye high up on the slope above the bridge, right at the tree line. A very tall, thin man was standing up there, dressed all in black, with what looked like a very long, antique rifle crooked over his arm. The man was watching the carnage below through a set of binoculars. I saw a glint of light on lenses as the binoculars swung around to train on me. I backed away from the guardrail toward my Suburban. The watching man put the glasses back on the dog pack, as if to say he didn't much care if there had been a witness. Then I saw a small group of men, maybe five or six, standing above the lone watcher on a nearby ridge. None of them seemed to have binoculars, but they did have rifles. I decided it was definitely time to get the hell out of there as fast as I could safely drive.

Back at the lodge, I placed a call to my old boss, Bobby Lee Baggett, high sheriff of Manceford County. He called me back in fifteen minutes.

"What in the world are you doing up there in black-hat country?" he asked.

I told him, and then described my conversation with M. C. Mingo and what I'd witnessed out on the mountain road. "Normally," I concluded, "I'd have called that mess in to the sheriff's office. However . . ."

"Yeah," Bobby Lee said. "I see your problem. You think those dogs killed that guy?"

"Several times over, based on the runoff. Then I think they ate him."

"Wow. Maybe you should do just what M. C. told you to do—get out and stay out of Robbins County. Sounds like they have their own rules up there."

"What can you tell me about M. C. Mingo?" I asked.

"Not much, Lieutenant. As I recall, he's not a member of the North Carolina Sheriffs' Association, and, of course, here in Triboro, we hardly ever have any contact with Robbins County. Heard some stories, but you know how that goes."

"Well, now you've heard a new one."

"But that wasn't the sheriff up there on that tree line, was it?" Bobby Lee asked.

I had to admit that he was right. Bobby Lee was often right. I asked if I should make a call to the North Carolina SBI and report what I'd seen. Bobby Lee said he'd make the call and get someone from the SBI to contact me up there in Marionburg, which was exactly what I had hoped for. I gave the sheriff my number at the lodge and thanked him. He suggested I also make a report to Bill Hayes.

When I got back from lunch, there was a message from Mary Ellen Goode. I got her on the phone at the ranger station.

"I have to make a trip up to Crown Lake this afternoon," she said. "Park Service business, of course. Want to come along?"

"What's Crown Lake all about?"

"Red rocks?"

It took me a moment, but then I remembered. "Of course it does," I said. "Where do you want to meet?"

*   *   *

Ninety minutes later we drove into a scenic overlook pullout and parked. I had followed Mary Ellen's Park Service SUV so that I could bring the shepherds along. She had thought that was a wonderful idea. The view was spectacular indeed, which is typical of the Smokies. Most people came up there to do stuff but spent a lot of time just looking at it. The air was clear and cool, and Crown Lake spread out in front of us in a silvery expanse of lightly rippled water, reflecting the lower end of the Smokies in the distance. The opposite shore was easily a half mile away.

"Are we in the park or in Robbins County right now?" I asked, joining her at the low stone wall. The shepherds were running around the parking lot with their noses down. She was in uniform and wearing a sidearm, I noticed.

"This is the park," she said. "Robbins County is over on the other side, down that shore maybe two miles. This is where we found Janey's Jeep. We have no idea of which way she went after parking here, or where she was taking the water samples."

"Why was she taking water samples?" I asked.

"We keep track of lake acidity to see how much damage the western power plants are donating, season by season. Mainly looking for sulfuric acid, mercury, and other heavy metals."

"Nothing of interest to the DEA, then?"

"The DEA? Not to my knowledge."

I saw a trail leading off to the right that roughly paralleled the margins of the lake. "Would she have taken the samples here or walked around?"

"The lake is twenty-seven miles in perimeter, so she would have walked around part of it but not all of it. She was supposed to concentrate on the outflow of streams into the lake, and they're predominantly coming from that long ridge on the north side. Feel like a walk in the woods?"

"Absolutely," I said, calling up the shepherds. "Do I need one of those?" I asked, pointing at her sidearm.

"Technically that would be illegal. Practically speaking . . ."

"Right," I said, walking over to my Suburban. "Avert thine eyes, madam ranger."

We set out on the lakeside trail, walking initially north and then curving around to the west once we turned the end of the lake. I carried my trusty SIG-Sauer .45-caliber model P-220 in a belt holster, partially concealed by a light windbreaker. Within minutes we'd each acquired a walking stick from the debris along the shore. The dogs were loving it, ranging far ahead and then loping back to make sure the humans hadn't quit on them. For the most part the trail stayed within fifty feet of the shore, and came right down to the water where spines of the big ridge plunged into the lake. Mary Ellen, like every ranger who goes into the woods, carried a plastic trash bag along for the inevitable litter.

I told her about my reception at the Robbins County Sheriff's Office. I did not tell her about what I'd witnessed out on the road. She said that she had talked to some of the rangers in the office, but not to her boss, about what Janey had said. They'd all been in favor of her going to take a look. As she said, they were all behind her. *Way* behind her.

"And what if we turn something up?" I asked. "How are you going to explain that to Ranger Bob?"

"Um, well . . ."

"You could always tell him that going to see Janey Howard and then coming up here was all my idea. You only came along to keep the Park Service out of trouble."

She laughed. "I may take you up on that, except I think he already knows I called you in."

"You're not afraid you'll get in trouble?"

She turned to look at me. "You know what? Janey Howard was a nice young woman. She's a college graduate. She wanted to be a park ranger for the best reasons. Maybe a little idealistic, but, hey, she's young. And some knuckle-dragging, slope-faced, slack-jawed, drooling brute who can't even speak English grabbed her, beat her, raped her, sodomized her, and then threw her down a ravine to fend for herself with the coyotes and the bears. I want him dead. I don't want him arrested. I don't want him to have a lawyer. I don't want him to plead insanity. I want him dead. I want him gutted, and I want to film the scavengers eating his guts. And, no, I'm not afraid I'll get in trouble."

I stared at her. "Hello, Mary Ellen Goode," I said.

She looked down at the ground and sighed. "Okay, that's just me, venting. At some point, reality will intrude. And, sure, we may both get into trouble. You want to turn back?"

"Hell, no. It's not like you or the Park Service has retained me to do anything. And if I want to ask questions, I can." I grinned at her. She was embarrassed, but she gave me a defiant smile. The one I remembered. The one that lit up the ranger station. "How much farther to the red rocks?" I asked.

"I have no idea," she said, surprising me. "I actually don't remember any red rocks on Crown Lake. But we've got at least four hours of daylight left, so I say we walk for another ninety minutes or so. If we come up empty, we turn around."

"Sounds like a plan," I said, and called in the shepherds to make sure they didn't roam too far or scare up a mama bear with cubs. "Did you ever find Janey's water samples?"

"No, we didn't. They're white plastic one-liter bottles. And her uniform and pepper spray are missing, too. Her radio was in the Jeep, along with the usual gear."

We picked our way through the wreckage of a large tree that had blown down over the trail. "So she left her gear in the Jeep, walked probably on this trail, taking her water samples. So where are they?" I asked.

"What do you mean?"

"If she took, say, six empty sample bottles, and began sampling at that last creek we just crossed, she wouldn't then continue to carry the full bottles—she'd leave the full ones at each sample point and then pick them all up on the way back, right?"

Mary Ellen stopped and nodded. "Right—so we should be looking for sample bottles to confirm that she even came this way."

I pointed up the shoreline to where a wide creek flowed into the lake from the ridge above. "Let's take a look up there."

It took us fifteen minutes to find the bottle, which had been wedged between two rocks in the lake itself. "Okay," I said. "So now we know she did come this way. When we run out of bottles or find a pile of empties, we'll know where she started her not-so-excellent adventure."

The next creek gave us nothing, but it was also quite small. The one after that yielded a full bottle. By now we were almost two miles around the shoreline, and the western slope of the big ridge was flattening out. I thought I could make out a firebreak road above us running through the trees. The trail was getting increasingly wilder and difficult to negotiate. Even the shepherds were having to pick their way through the underbrush. Mary Ellen said that budget cuts had resulted in many of the park's walking trails being neglected. Frick took off after a squirrel and ran up a game trail, with Frack right behind her. When they came back a few minutes later, each was carrying an empty white plastic bottle.

"Bingo," I said softly, relieving the dogs of their prizes. "I'd say she went thataway."

"But why?" Mary Ellen asked.

"Saw something? Heard something? Went to investigate and found trouble. Let's give it a try. We still officially in the park?"

"Not when we leave this trail. Actually, the lake belongs to the power company; there's a fifty-foot margin around the shoreline that belongs to the park. Up there is your favorite county."

"Terrific," I said, and sent the dogs out ahead of us along the game trail. If there were black hats up there in the trees, the shepherds would find them first. I hoped.

We climbed up the rocky slope and into a stand of pines, where the game trail disappeared. The ground was covered in a thick carpet of pine needles. The shepherds ran silent zigzag patterns with their noses down, exploring all the woodland scents. The ground leveled off about a hundred yards into the trees, and then we broke out onto the fire lane that cut across the face of the larger ridge beyond. I inspected the ground but saw no ruts or tracks that looked at all recent. There were hoofprints and the multiridged striations of a tracked vehicle of some kind underneath the weeds. Rainstorms had cut some deep runoff grooves down the lane where deer tracks were visible.

"Maybe she heard something up here on the fire lane," I said, "but there's no sign of what it was."

We continued uphill for fifteen minutes and then retraced our steps, passing where we'd come out of the pines and going down the fire lane an equal distance. We came to a switchback in the lane that widened out into a small plateau. A huge old oak stuck thick limbs out over the bend, but again, there were no recent vehicle signs. The sun was slanting down toward the western mountains, whose ridgelines were backlit by an increasingly orange sky. The trees were starting to throw long shadows, and the shepherds flopped down along the side of the fire lane, panting.

"This happened a month and a half ago?" I asked.

She nodded, knowing what I was thinking. Looking for tracks was pointless.

We went back up to the point in the pine woods where we'd first come out and started back down toward the lake. I kept looking for any signs that the probationer had come this way, but there were none. The woods were thick enough to be getting dark, and I wondered what might be watching us. Halfway down through the woods, Mary Ellen stepped into a stump hole hidden by the pine needles and turned an ankle, so we had to stop and let her rub the soreness out for a few minutes. I held her hand while she hobbled the rest of the way to the edge of the trees, but when we stepped out onto the hillside, she pointed excitedly down at the lake.

"Look," she said. "Red rocks."

I saw what she was talking about. Where a spine of the big ridge came down into the lake, there were three large boulders about twenty feet offshore. The setting sun was painting them dark orange, if not red.

"Okay," I said. "But what are we looking for?"

"Beats me, but let's go down there," she said. "I'm ready for some flat ground."

The two shepherds started down with us but then stopped and looked back up into the woods. I noticed and turned around. Both dogs were looking intently into the tree line, but the advancing shadows made it impossible for me to see anything. I called them to come on, and they turned around and rejoined us, albeit reluctantly.

When we finally reached the rocks, they weren't really red anymore, even though the western sky was. They were just three twenty-foot-high boulders that had rolled down the slope ten thousand years ago and stopped here, probably many years before the lake had been created by the TVA dam at the other end. A dead tree created a bridge of sorts from the shore out to the first rock, and I, using my stick for balance, went out on the trunk to look into the water.

Where something glinted on the bottom. I bent down to see what it was and then swore softly.

"What?" Mary Ellen called from the shore.

"This lake belongs to the power company, right?" I asked. "Not Robbins County?"

"Right," she said. "What do you see?"

"I think it's a body," I called back to her. "All wrapped up in chains."

I got back to the lodge just after ten o'clock that evening. I let the dogs run around for a few minutes while I fixed myself a scotch and then called them back in. Carrigan County deputies had been the first responders to our report of a body in the lake, followed by the Park Service. Mary Ellen and I had managed to extract ourselves from the fun and games around eight. We'd had a quick dinner in town, and then she'd gone home. I had the sense that discovering the body had upset her, and that I'd resumed my role as harbinger of death and destruction. She hadn't said anything, but I'd felt it.

Sheriff Hayes had given me a head-shaking look when he arrived on scene. Typhoid Mary's older brother was back in town. No one had recognized the body, because the fish had been at it for a while, so identification was going to take some time and applied organic chemistry. The sheriff hadn't been happy when he found out why we'd gone up there looking. Mary Ellen hadn't quite

understood that, until I pointed out that our getting the girl to talk and then reveal a solid lead might just possibly make the Carrigan County Sheriff's Office
look bad. I had called Bobby Lee Baggett back in Triboro to tell him what we'd
found. Bobby Lee pointed out that if the girl had witnessed a murder, then dis-
covery of the body put her in danger. I hadn't thought of that, but I got Mary
Ellen to say something to Sheriff Hayes. It turned out that he *had* thought of that,
so now Mary Ellen was on his shit list as well. I called Baby Greenberg's number
and told the voice mail what we'd found and where. I decided not to add to my
reputation by telling Sheriff Hayes what I'd witnessed on the road to Rocky Falls.

The single malt was a welcome relief, and, as best I could tell, the shepherds
weren't mad at me. I walked out to the screened porch that stuck out over the
creek bank. The night was cool and clear. A million tree frogs were chirring in
the darkness, and the creek splashed pleasantly under the cabin. I was about to
sit down when the shepherds woofed from the front porch. Then someone
knocked on the screen door.

I hadn't left any lights on, but there were some solar sidewalk lights out
front and I could see that a slender, dark-haired woman was standing out there.
The shepherds were sitting up, but they'd been trained not to execute a canine
feeding frenzy display just because a stranger showed up at the front door. They
made their presence known, and that usually took care of the Bible salesmen
and prospective intruders.

"Yes?" I said from behind the screen door.

"Lieutenant Richter?" she said in a husky, low-pitched voice. I couldn't see
her features. "I'm Carrie Harper Santángelo, SBI. Sheriff Baggett made a call?
If you can turn on a light I can show you my ID."

I laughed and opened the screen door for her. "I would but I don't know
where the switch is. Come on in. Don't mind them—they've been fed."

"That's good," she said, eyeing the two big shepherds as she came in. "I'm
told that it's the ones who don't go nuts when the doorbell rings that bear
watching."

"All dogs bite," I recited. "I'm having a scotch on the back porch—care to
join me?"

"Sure," she said. She was five-seven or -eight, jet black hair, with a classical,
aquiline nose. She was of either Italian or American Indian descent. She was
wearing jeans, a white blouse, and a loose-fitting, lightweight blue blazer.
Once in the kitchen she presented her creds, which I dutifully examined. I got
her a drink, and we went out onto the back porch. I brought the bottle. I saw
her eyeing all the wedding suite accoutrements.

"Which office?" I asked.

"Raleigh. I'm an inspector in the professional standards division at head-quarters. I drove out today. If this is the bridal suite, I hope I'm not interrupting anything."

"All I could get on short notice. Plus, if I drink too much, a bed's never far-ther than about five feet away."

"You don't look like a man with a drinking problem," she said. Her com-plexion was very smooth in the light spilling out of the kitchen. She had dark, almost black eyes, and she looked right at me when she spoke. Professional standards work, known as internal affairs in some jurisdictions, encouraged the direct approach.

"No, I guess not," I said. She kept her blazer buttoned even though she was sitting down. I could make out the lump of a shoulder rig just under her left shoulder.

"So," she said. "M. C. Mingo. I understand you've met?"

"Today," I said. I then explained what I was doing up here in Carrigan County, my prior relationship with the Park Service and Mary Ellen Goode, and why I'd touched base with Bobby Lee. She listened without interrupting. I had the impression that some part of that dark-eyed brain was record-ing my every word. Or the other lump in her pocket was a voice-activated recorder.

"Tell me something, if you don't mind," she said, when I'd finished. "What was the deal with your not testifying in that mountain lion case?"

I sighed. Inquiring minds always wanted to know, especially if they were cops. "How much time you got?" I asked warily.

"How much scotch you got?" she replied.

"*That* much time," I said. "Okay, let's do the abridged version."

When I'd finished, she nodded and sipped some scotch. "And now you're private and working for the district court. What's that like?"

"It's not like being boss of the MCAT in Manceford County."

"What's the Park Service think about your being here?"

"Less and less," I said. "Apparently their headquarters wanted this mess with the probationer all to go away. Bad for park business. After today, it's probably going to reflash. So: M. C. Mingo?"

"Right," she said. "M. C. Mingo. Sheriff of Robbins County for the past twenty-odd years. No opposition at election time. Ever. Related to the evil hag who runs most if not all of the drug trade in Robbins County."

"That would be Vivian Creigh."

"The one and only Grinny. Our intel is that she runs it like a Mafia don—stays up on Spider Mountain and controls every pound of meth, grass, hallucinogenic mushrooms, and even the damn ginseng. She has soldiers, and they work for a capo, her son, Nathan. Her father ran it before her and reportedly invited his three grown sons to settle who'd be in charge when he checked out. One brother died exploring an old gold mine, which caved in following a mysterious explosion. A second brother accused Grinny of having a hand in the matter, and then he died after being set upon by a pack of wild dogs."

I nodded. "I've seen those bad boys."

"Probably not," she said. "This all happened when Grinny was eighteen. She's fifty now, or thereabouts."

"Then their descendants, maybe." I told her about watching the dog pack take down the fat man. She whistled quietly.

"What happened to the third brother?" I asked.

"He became the sheriff of Robbins County."

"Ah-ha!"

"Yes, indeed."

"So—then there's Nathan. Grinny was married?"

"Probably not. There's Nathan and a daughter, Rowena, who are reportedly by different fathers, who have themselves long since gone into the cold, cold ground. A Creigh family tradition, apparently."

"*Spider* Mountain. As in black widow."

"That's what some of the locals call it. Interestingly, nobody in law enforcement has ever seen her. We know where her place is, but that's about it."

"Why is that?" I asked. "I mean, you and the DEA guys seem to know a lot about the Creigh clan. Why hasn't some state or federal task force gone in there and hauled the whole bunch in for questioning?"

She tinkled the ice in her empty glass, and I poured her a refill. "You know how it is," she said. "The SBI comes in only when we're invited in. M. C. Mingo declines to invite. The DEA prefers to work alone. The Bureau comes in only if it's big enough and there's positive PR potential. Right now they don't consider western North Carolina as having positive PR potential, especially after the Eric Rudolph fiasco. Homeland Security is obsessing with grubbing out crazed Muslims. The state attorney general has his hands full with urban crime. The sheriff is related to the kingpin. That's why not."

"Amazing."

She shrugged. "Personally, I don't think anyone cared all that much until the meth epidemic began. Hillbillies running 'shine, maybe some grass, whacking each other out with nineteenth-century rifles over some hundred-year-distant insult—big deal, as long as they kept it in the hollers."

"But meth is changing all that?"

"Yes. There's a river of the stuff coming out of these hills, all under the control of Grinny Creigh. We think. We just can't prove it."

"Big money?"

"At the retail end, yes. But we don't believe it's all about the money for her. I mean, hell, you've been to Rocky Falls. What would big bucks get you there—a double helping of grits? She lives on the side of a mountain in a log cabin with a privy, for crying out loud. No, it's about control. The Creigh clan has run the dark side of things in Robbins County for decades. Grinny Creigh *is* a spider: Step out onto her web and here she comes, fangs and all."

"So it's the sheer quantity, not just the basic crime?"

"Yes. That's supposedly why Greenberg and his crew are working up here."

"Why do you say supposedly?"

"Because they don't seem to do much. On the other hand, that's a secretive bunch, so nobody really knows."

"I met him the other day."

"We heard," she said. I thought I saw the ghost of a smile cross her severe face.

I grinned back. "They got uppity around my shepherds. What can I say?"

"Baby's a city boy," she said. "A little jumpy and aggressive. But as far as we know, he's a good cop."

"He's a frustrated cop right now," I said. "Says he can't figure a way into Robbins County, either. He was interested in the fact that I might be able to go up there and shake some bushes."

"Well, there you are," she said. "Work a deal. It wouldn't be a bad idea to have some feds behind you."

"Only thing is, I think they'd be *way* behind me," I said, recalling Mary Ellen's comment. "Besides, I didn't come up here to solve the meth problem. I came to help Dr. Goode find out what happened to her probationer. And I think we got closer today."

"Interesting that you're helping her but not the Park Service."

I nodded. "True, but they're apparently scared shitless of getting into a blood feud with the Creigh clan, who probably know the park better than any ten rangers. I guess I can see their point."

"I can't," she said. "You let a bunch of crooks, even colorful ones, know you're scared of them, they get bolder and bolder. What we need up here is a SEAL team. Send them into Robbins County and let them start cutting some prominent throats in the night until all this meth crap stops. Unfortunately, they're all otherwise engaged these days."

I laughed. "Don't remember ever meeting a bloodthirsty SBI agent before," I said. "Usually you guys are all about the paper chase."

She didn't smile back at me. "There's another thing," she said. "One we don't understand at all. The state police collared a guy for vehicular homicide in Robbins County. Basically, a case of serious road rage. Nudged a tourist minivan off a cliff with his pickup because they were going too slow. At one point he implied that they better not mess with him because he worked for Grinny Creigh."

"The state guys just love to be intimidated."

"It's almost as good as resisting arrest. Anyway, long story short, their detective bureau tried to turn him, without success. In the process of questioning him, though, he dangled a tidbit, saying that Grinny was a 'florist.' The cops were baffled, and when this guy realized they didn't understand the code, he stopped talking."

"A florist? As in, say, hallucinogenic botanicals?"

She shrugged. "Who the hell knows? Street slang morphs daily. Nobody's ever heard the term. But if you do get involved in Robbins County and hear that word, we'd love to know what kind of new and original evil shit that is."

She fished in her pocket and produced a business card. "Keep this handy," she said. "You find a hole in Robbins County that regular law enforcement can drive through, please call me. If I can't talk my bosses into exploiting it, I'll take some leave, come up here, and go after it myself."

"That sounds like there's a personal angle," I said.

She looked right back at me. "Anything's possible, Lieutenant. By the way, I haven't informed the local law that I'm here. I'd appreciate your keeping that confidence. In the meantime, be careful. The hills really are alive and all that good stuff."

After she'd left, I slipped on a jacket and took the dogs out for a last call among the defenseless trees. The cabins were mostly dark and the shepherds had ranged ahead down a creekside path. This was getting interesting, I thought. First a DEA agent, and now an SBI agent, both complaining about not being able to penetrate Robbins County, and both offering to partner up if I should succeed. And why should I succeed where law enforcement had failed? All I'd done was to prize some useful information out of the injured probationer. We'd found a body, but there was still no direct evidentiary tie to

Janey Howard. I wondered if that "grinning hangman" business meant the guy in the lake, assuming it was a man, had been hanged. It certainly hadn't been your usual park excursion.

And what in the world was this "florist" stuff? The druggy world came up with more interesting code names for their addictions than even the government. But I'd come up to find out what happened to Janey Howard, not to chase druggies. I think that chasing druggies has become a form of white-collar welfare for law enforcement. As far as I'm concerned, drugs ought to be decriminalized and sold at government outlets for tax revenue. Let the addicts shoot up and die if they want to—meth, heroin, 'ludes, coke, tranks, ups, downs, you name it, they are all just manifestations of Mr. Darwin's theory of natural selection. I just wanted to quit finding the miserable bastards climbing through my basement windows.

The dogs had gone out of sight down the creek banks. My boots were crunching through pea gravel, so I knew I must still be on the lodge grounds. I noticed a side path that branched away from the main path to my right. I wondered what personal connection the handsome SBI agent had with Robbins County and the Creighs, and I made a mental note to check that out before I called her, *if* I ever called her. Her not checking in with the local sheriff's office was not only unusual but outside of standard procedure. The SBI was usually called in by local law, but occasionally they were investigating said local law.

Then I saw the two men standing on the path, pointing shotguns at me.

I stopped in my tracks, just barely restraining myself from saying something stupid like *What do you want?* Both of them wore dark pants and shirts, and they were sporting full beards. No black hats, but definitely a pair of faces born to decorate a wanted poster. One of them stepped forward and motioned with his shotgun for me to come with them. I hesitated, hoping the dogs would reappear, but when the second man reversed the shotgun in his hands to form a club, I said all right and went with them. Both of them looked perfectly capable of clubbing me senseless and then dragging me to wherever it was we were going.

We walked quickly down the narrow path toward a pickup truck, with one of them in front and one behind me. Their clothes smelled of wood smoke and pine needles. I thought of a dozen different escape moves, but none of them stacked up well against shotguns at three feet. If they'd meant to kill me, they could have already done that and then thrown my body into the fast-moving creek.

Once we got out to the parking lot, one of them got in on the driver's side while the other motioned for me to get into the bed of the truck. The man jumped up behind me, told me to lie down on my belly, and then clipped my wrists and legs to chain manacles welded to the corners of the bed of the truck. He prodded me in the back with the shotgun.

"Lookin' to go see the Baby Jesus?" he whispered. His accent was mountain, but not tree-stump ignorant. The pine scent from the man's clothes was really strong up close. Which was why the dogs had missed them, I realized. It was an old deer hunter's trick. They'd double back eventually and then go nuts when they couldn't find me.

"Not especially," I said.

"Then keep still," he growled.

Thirty minutes and a gear-grinding climb later up a very dark mountain road, the truck slowed, turned so hard I thought we were going to tip over, bounced over some serious ruts and then choked to a stop. I felt tenderized after all that time on the steel bed of the truck, and I had no idea of where we were, except that it was up. They got me out of the bed and marched me along a crooked path leading still farther up, one of them again leading, one behind. I stumbled a few times as I worked the kinks out, but they didn't restrain me. After a ten-minute walk through the trees and out across a mountain meadow, I saw dim lights above, where a long log cabin was perched on the hillside.

They marched me up the slope to the cabin, where I could see two people sitting in rockers on the front porch, flanked by lanterns hanging on the front wall. One of them had to be Grinny Creigh. She was a heavy woman, with short, graying red hair cut in a surfer bowl, a broad forehead, a round, florid, double-chinned face, narrow-set eyes, a down-turned, thin-lipped mouth, and a pug nose. She wore a shapeless black dress to cover her ponderous body. There were massive fat rolls on her upper arms, but plenty of muscle, too. Her ankles had cuffs of fat above them and were indistinguishable from her calves, but she had small feet. In her left hand she held an old-fashioned paddle fan with which she was keeping her face cool. Her right hand held a sweating glass of what looked like tea.

Sitting next to her on the porch had to be Nathan, Grinny's son. Even sitting, he was very tall, well over six feet, with elongated arms and legs, massive hands, and an oversized, bony head. He had a pale, square forehead and a long-bearded lantern jaw that made him look like a caricature of Frankenstein's monster. His beard was long enough to rest on his chest. He wore loose-fitting blue denim overalls over a long-sleeved white cotton shirt and canvas-topped, size really-large Army surplus tropical combat boots. There was a deerskin bag at his feet from which the handles of several knives projected. He watched me with calm eyes while whittling on a piece of wood.

Standing just inside the front screen door was another woman, whom I recognized as the buxom hottie I'd seen at M. C. Mingo's office. The two lanterns cast enough light to shadow the interior of the cabin, so I could barely see her expression, but I thought she recognized me. *Now here's an unholy trinity*, I thought. For a moment I thought I saw some other faces, smaller, pale ovals bobbing around in the interior shadows behind the young woman, but I couldn't be sure. I heard some noises off to either side of me and realized that there were other people out there in the shadows. Good deal. I heard some dogs stirring behind a fence made out of solid sheets of galvanized tin roofing nailed vertically to posts and boards.

"This him?" the fat woman asked.

"He's the one," said the girl from behind the screen door. She pressed her front up against it, creating two white circles against the screen in the shadow of the doorway. I'm sure I was supposed to get all hot and bothered.

Grinny Creigh leaned forward in her chair, making it and the porch floorboards creak. "Where you from, mister?" she asked.

"Manceford County," I said. I'd decided not to waste energy protesting my abduction, hoping that, if I acted calmly, none of them would get violent.

"You been nosin' around, askin' questions down'ere in Rocky Falls?"

"Not yet," I said. "I did talk to the sheriff."

"You the one found that deader in the lake yonder?"

"That's right."

"How'd you know where to go lookin'?"

"I'm an investigator. I investigated."

Grinny leaned back in her rocker and gave me an annoyed look. My sarcasm was apparently not much appreciated.

"Got a smart mouth on him," Nathan said softly. His voice was high-pitched and nasal, like M. C. Mingo's.

Grinny tilted her head fractionally, and I sensed the man behind me raise his fist to smack me on the head. I bent forward and whirled to his left, blocking the blow with an upraised left forearm and clubbing him in the groin with my stiffened right forearm. The man gasped as he doubled over, but instead of quitting, he bared his teeth and tried to bite my arm. I drove my right elbow into his temple, dropping him like a stone. My second captor, much older than the first, hadn't moved yet, so I kicked him in the shin as hard as I could.

He yelled, dropped his shotgun, and collapsed over his splintered shin. I extended my knee as he went down, catching him right under the chin in a tooth-clicking crack that knocked him cold. It all took less than fifteen seconds. I turned around to face the people on the porch and found myself looking into the bores of a double-barreled ten-gauge held by Nathan. The girl behind the screen was staring openmouthed at me. My left arm ached.

Grinny was looking down at me with a furious expression on her face. "You got some nerve, boy," she growled, "comin' up here and doin' that."

"I didn't *come* up here," I said angrily. "They brought me. That's called kidnapping back in the World. You have a reason for doing that?"

"You ain't kidnapped. You was brought here so's I could ask ye straight: What're you here for? Why you pokin' around in Robbins County, askin' folks 'bout Creighs?"

"I want to know what happened to that park ranger, the one who was beaten and raped at Crown Lake."

"What's 'at got to do with us?"

"Don't know," I said. "But we want to find out who did that and bring him in."

"Who's we?" Grinny said. Nathan and his shotgun had not moved one inch. The old man groaned on the ground, but the other one exhibited the stillness of the grave. I wondered if I'd hit him too hard in the temple. I hadn't meant to hit him there, but those snaggly yellow teeth had looked both serious and toxic.

"The National Park Service," I replied. "The Carrigan County Sheriff's Office. The rangers at Thirty Mile station. And probably the decent, law-abiding people in this county, both of them."

She snorted at this insult. "They hire you up?"

"That's right," I said. The truth would have been too complicated. Grinny leaned forward, and the heavily stressed rocking chair complained again.

"Well, you hear me, mister," she said. "What goes on in Robbins County ain't none of your bizness nor anyone else's. If we got menfolk out in them woods doin' that kinda shit, we take care of it, our way, not your way. Our lawyers come in two sizes: ten-gauge and twelve-gauge. You follow?"

"Well, that *sounds* good," I said. "But a body or two delivered to the Thirty Mile station might be more convincing."

Grinny raised her eyebrows, as if she hadn't thought of that.

"You remember 'em dogs?" Nathan asked. "On the Rocky Falls road?"

I looked at him blankly for a second, then remembered the tall man up on the ridge with the binoculars. Had that been Nathan? I nodded.

"That convincing enough for ye?"

"That was the man who assaulted the ranger?"

"It was. You want meat for your lawyers'n such, you go on down there, pick up what's left. Ain't much, I reckon, but you's the one needs convincin'."

"Like I was sayin'," Grinny said. "We take care'a things *our* way. You get on outta here now, and don't you come back to Robbins County."

I assessed my situation. The men in the shadows had gathered closer, but they weren't doing anything except watching. Yet. The old man on the ground was crabbing his fingers toward his dropped shotgun. When he saw me watching, he withdrew his hand. The other one still hadn't moved, although he did appear to be breathing now. Nathan's shotgun still hadn't wavered. I concluded that this was not the time for speeches. All this complex calculation took me a good three seconds.

"All right," I said. I turned around and started walking down the meadow toward the tree line by the road. My back prickled in fearful anticipation, but I forced myself to simply walk away without a backward glance at all those shotguns. When I got down to the actual road, the cabin was out of sight. I turned across the hill to the road and picked up the pace. The road was a glorified dirt track, and the woods on either side were entirely dark. It was going to be a long night, I thought, as I rubbed the aching muscles, what was left of them, in my left arm. Then I heard a large dog start baying somewhere behind me, joined quickly by several others. An image of the pack tearing up the fat man crossed my mind and I cranked on a few more knots, although I could stumble only so fast down a rutted road in the dark. The dog noise kept up, but it didn't sound like it was getting any closer. Grinny Creigh sending me one last message: *Keep going, stranger, or worse things can happen than getting shot at.* I pulled out my cell phone, but, as I'd expected, there was no service. Cell phone service seemed to be available in inverse proportion to how badly you needed it.

I had walked for almost forty-five minutes, still not reaching level ground or a paved road, when I heard a vehicle approaching from behind me. I stepped off the road into the trees and watched a pickup truck with too much engine come around the corner above me, showing only parking lights. When it drew abreast, the offside window came down and Rowena Creigh's face appeared.

"Need a ride?" she asked.

I hesitated.

"C'mon, it's fifteen miles back to Marionburg. I don't bite, less'n I get really excited."

I said okay and climbed in. The truck was not new, but there was obviously a huge mill under the hood. The interior smelled of perfume and cigarette smoke. She was wearing a white sleeveless blouse knotted under her breasts, cutoff blue-jean shorts, and sandals. Her long legs gleamed in the light from the dashboard. She put the truck in second gear and let it roll itself down the road, the engine rumbling in protest.

"Better'n the way you came, don't you think?" she asked.

"I didn't have a lot of choice in the matter," I said. "But I do appreciate the lift."

She laughed. "Grinny wants to see you, she's gonna see you. One way or another. That's how it is around these hills. You'd best believe that."

"I saw a fat man get run down and torn to pieces by a dog pack the other day," I said. "Those the same dogs I just heard back there?"

"Wouldn't know anything about that," she said, fishing a cigarette out of her blouse pocket and punching in the truck's lighter. "That there's menfolk business." She looked across at me, a teasing look in her eyes. "I just live there."

"Sure you do," I said.

She lit the cigarette and returned the lighter. She took a deep drag and blew out a big cloud of smoke. "Uncle M. C. wasn't too happy with you bein' in Robbins County. You some kinda lawman, ain't you?"

"He really your uncle?" I asked, avoiding the question.

"Hell if I know," she said, rolling down the driver's-side window to let a little of the smoke out. "Uncles, brothers, cousins, husbands—what's it matter when the county phone book has only eleven different names listed?"

I laughed despite myself. The dirt track ended at a two-lane blacktop, and she turned right. She flipped on her headlights and put the hammer down. The truck jumped forward and I found my seat belt. She wasn't wearing one. "Rocky Falls looks a little bigger than all that," I said.

She grunted derisively. "Rocky Falls ain't what I'm talkin' about. I meant the county. You really a lawman?"

"Nope," I said. "Used to be, but I'm retired. Now I do investigative work for hire. How about you? What do you do?"

"Me?" she laughed. "I'm Rue Creigh and I cause trouble. I drive around makin' all the menfolk crazy and their women huffy. I smoke and I drink and, lemme see, there's a third thing, but damned if it hasn't slipped my mind just now. But it'll come to me."

I could just imagine, which was probably the object of the lesson. "Nice truck," I said.

"Meanin' what—how do I come to have it, seein' as I'm just a layabout?"

"Interesting choice of words, but let me guess. Grinny Creigh got it for you."

"Good guess, lawman. And *I'm* guessin' you know how she manages that. But you need to be real careful if that's what you're really doin' up here, 'cause Grinny don't abide strangers pokin' into her business. Got her a regular hate-on for that."

"I told her why I was here, to find out—"

"That's finished business," she interrupted. "You want some sign of the old boy done that, you'll need to get you a pooper-scooper."

Suspicions confirmed, I thought. I saw a sign indicating we were crossing into Carrigan County and relaxed fractionally. The road paralleled a rushing mountain stream, with towering green hills on either side. There was no moon, but the air was incredibly clear. "That's awfully convenient," I said. "But we have only your word for that."

"We?" she said. "Got a mouse in your pocket there, lawman? But, what the hell, if it's proof you want, reach under your seat."

Surprised, I felt around under the front of my seat and discovered a small, cold, heavy cylinder among the empty beer cans. I pulled it out. It was a law-enforcement-model pepper-spray canister. There was a decal on it saying that it was property of the U.S. Park Service and, if found, should be returned to the nearest ranger station immediately.

"This hers?" I asked.

"Ain't no one knows, lawman. But the fat boy you saw doin' the Alpo marathon? He had that thing in *his* truck. Y'all can make of that what you will. Convinced me. Good enough for them dogs, too."

"Nobody from Robbins County has done anything like this to a park ranger before," I said. "The cops are speculating she witnessed something, maybe even tried to interfere."

Rowena shrugged and then readjusted her blouse before she fell out of it. "Where you stayin' at?"

I told her, and she drove through the town going at least twenty miles over the speed limit. At this hour there was almost no traffic, but I did see a sheriff's cruiser parked on a side street. They had to have heard that engine, but didn't seem to be interested. When we pulled into the parking lot at the lodge, however, there were two police cars and a Park Service Jeep out in the middle of the lower lot. Rowena drove right into the middle of the cluster, put the truck in park, and leaned an elbow out her window.

"Well, here you are, lawman," she announced, as several cops began to get out of their vehicles. Mary Ellen Goode climbed out of the Jeep, and my two shepherds came bounding out behind her.

"Well, thanks again for the ride," I said. "I guess I probably won't be seeing you again."

She pushed both hands through her luxuriant hair, which did interesting things to her superstructure. "Not in Robbins County," she said with a seductive smile. "But now that I know where you're stayin', who knows?"

Mary Ellen was close enough to the truck to hear that last bit, and I saw a pained expression cross her anxious face. I got out of the truck and closed the door. Rowena waved at me, smiled at all the staring cops, and thundered out of the parking lot. The two shepherds were all over me, but over their fuzzy shoulders I could see that the cops wanted some answers.

"Where did you get that?" Mary Ellen asked, pointing at the pepper-spray canister in my hand.

"It's a long story. Let's all go to my cabin."

Once in the cabin, the senior Carrigan County sheriff's deputy told me that a guest on the second floor had seen a pickup truck leave the parking lot with what looked like a body in the bed. He'd called 911, and the responding deputies found my two German shepherds racing around the parking lot looking for me and displaying just a bit of aggression, meaning no one in the lodge could get to a vehicle. It also kept all the cops in their patrol cars until their sergeant, who'd shown me into Sheriff Hayes's office the other day, had called Mary Ellen Goode, a known associate of the possibly missing ex-lieutenant Richter, to corral the agitated shepherds. A ninety-minute search through the surrounding area had produced nothing but the facts that I appeared to be missing, my cabin was unlocked, and my car keys and wallet were in the kitchen. They also had a second witness statement about a woman seen leaving my cabin earlier in the evening. Mary Ellen had called her supervisor at Thirty Mile station, the redoubtable Ranger Bob, who'd brought along the senior law enforcement ranger from the station.

I got everyone situated out on the creekside porch and held an impromptu debrief, leaving out only my visitation from the lady SBI agent. Then Sheriff Hayes himself arrived, and we had to go through it all again, while the other cops verified and added to their notes. When I had finished, the sheriff gave me a long look and then commented on my continuing propensity to instigate trouble.

"You are a regular shit magnet, Lieutenant," he said.

I grinned. "Guilty," I said. "But you have to admit, you know more about what happened to that girl than when I first came here."

"And now that we do, will you be leaving soon?" the sheriff asked, sounding hopeful.

"That depends," Mary Ellen said, provoking an annoyed look from Ranger Bob, who'd been about to speak.

"On . . . ?" prompted the sheriff.

"Mrs. Howard called me earlier this evening," she said. "After she heard about our finding that body, she sat down with Janey and had a heart-to-heart. She said Janey was ready to tell me what happened, although she did not want to talk to the police. So I went back to Murphy. I took along a tape recorder."

She fished the recorder out of her bag and set it on the table. We all listened to Janey Howard tell her tale of witnessing the execution and being taken down, assaulted, and then driven away out into the woods dressed in only a blanket.

"So now we know what the word 'hangman' was all about," Mary Ellen said.

"And that there were two men involved in it, not just the fat boy I saw getting eaten by a dog pack," I said. "Grinny Creigh did not tell the entire truth."

The sheriff just stared at me, until I remembered that I hadn't told him about the dog-pack incident. I did now.

"Ain't that something, now," the sheriff mused, shaking his head. He turned to Mary Ellen. "We can't use that tape as evidence, you understand. If there's gonna be a prosecution, she's gonna have to make a statement, ID a bad guy, and testify in court."

"I understand," Mary Ellen said. "I just thought you would appreciate finally hearing from the victim. At least you know where to look."

"Yeah," the sheriff said unhappily. "That's not necessarily progress. Means I now have to call M. C. Mingo." He turned to me. "You want to press charges?"

"I'll think about it—it was more of a summons before the throne than a kidnapping. Will you need a formal statement as to what I witnessed out there on the road with those dogs?"

"Can you describe the victim?"

"Ragout?" I said, prompting suppressed grins among the other cops.

"Let's see what M. C. has to say tomorrow morning," the sheriff said. "In the meantime, give some thought to going back to Manceford County. Actually, give it a lot of thought; I can't stand all this goddamned excitement."

I promised I would, and the meeting broke up. Mary Ellen stayed behind, after having exchanged what I sensed to be a few tense words with Ranger Bob as he left the cabin.

"Your boss seems unhappy tonight," I said.

"Let's say he isn't thrilled with developments," she said. "I have been suitably cautioned about bringing outsiders into Park Service business."

I thought about a scotch and then decided to make some coffee instead. Mary Ellen and I went back out to the porch.

"Given all the hostile vibes up here, maybe the sheriff is right," I said. "I should back out and let you folks get on with your interesting lives."

She gave me a wan look and nodded. "I really appreciate your coming," she said. "I'm just sorry . . ."

"That it turned up yet another dead body and more violence?"

"That wasn't your fault," she said with a sigh. "But . . ."

"Yeah, but. It does seem to happen a lot. Like every time you and I get together. Maybe the sheriff was also right about my being a shit magnet. I wish things were different."

"This is such a beautiful place," she said, looking out at the creek rushing through the night below our feet. "The Smokies. The park. This whole end of the state. It's sad to think there are people who come out here to hurt other people, make narcotics, hunt people down with packs of dogs. That's the stuff that happens in big cities, not out here in God's country."

"Violence in these mountains was here long before Mr. Vanderbilt bought the Smokies and gave them to the government for a park," I said. "I imagine it takes a hard individual to live off the land out here."

"Who was the girl in the truck?" she asked, a little too casually.

"Rowena Creigh," I replied. "Grinny's daughter. She seems to think very highly of herself. She showed up in her truck after I'd been dismissed. It beat walking back."

"Was she the one the man said he saw leaving your cabin earlier this evening?"

I was surprised, but then remembered that second witness. "No," I said. I didn't elaborate. I sensed that somehow all these unknown women had become important to Mary Ellen, although, superficially at least, she had no claims on my loyalty. And vice versa.

"There going to be formal repercussions from Ranger Bob?" I asked.

She smiled. "I don't think so. I think he's more upset about you than me." She hesitated. "Bob's carrying a bit of a torch, I think. I keep fending off, but someone must have told him persistence pays. One day I'll have to get firm, I suppose. Mostly it's harmless."

I remembered the hostile looks Bob had been shooting my way during my little debrief. I wondered how harmless the guy really was. Mary Ellen was a striking woman who took her beauty in stride; she might be a whole lot more important to Ranger Bob than she knew.

"All the more reason for me to get out of Dodge," I said, finishing my coffee. "I'm glad I could be of some help. I think."

She smiled. "We'll have a ton of paperwork to do after today. I'll let you know what they find out about the victim and the second hangman."

Once she'd left I thought about taking the dogs out for a final night walk. I decided against it. One unscheduled truck ride was enough for one evening. I decided on a nightcap after all. As I sat out on the porch in the dark, I wondered if my association with the lovely Mary Ellen Goode wasn't drawing to a close on more fronts than just the Howard case.

We'd met by chance during the cat dancers investigation, and I'd been smitten, probably like every other normal man who saw her for the first time. But the fact was, the entire context of our time together had been violent and especially frightening for a park ranger with a Ph.D. A man and a woman may draw very close under those circumstances, but in the cold light of day, it was common ground you both wanted to go away.

Frack came out to the porch and flopped down on the rug. We both decided to sit there and listen to the creek go by.

4

The muttskis roused me early the next morning with some tentative woofing on the front porch. I grabbed my bathrobe and went to the door, where a deputy stood waiting patiently, flat hat in hand and mirrored sunglasses firmly in place. He looked to be at least thirteen. Or perhaps I was getting old.

"Morning, Deputy. What's up?"

"Sheriff needs to see you," the deputy replied, looking nervously at the shepherds now that I had the screen door open. They were sitting behind me, waiting for breakfast. "Problem in Robbins County."

"What kind of problem?" I asked, wondering why the early-morning summons.

"Um," the deputy said, knotting his hands. "Sheriff Mingo says you killed a man over there last night?"

I blinked in the bright morning sunlight. "News to me," I said, "but you tell the sheriff I'll be right over."

"Do I need to wait for you, Lieutenant?" the deputy asked, pointedly.

"Nope. I need a shower and some coffee, and then I'll be right along. Want to come in and meet my shepherds?"

"No, sir, reckon I don't. Big dogs make me nervous."

"Okay, then. Tell him thirty minutes."

The sheriff was waiting for me at his office a half hour later.

"Shit magnet, reporting as ordered," I said. The sheriff smiled grimly and offered coffee. He then explained that M. C. Mingo had called over from Rocky Falls and asked him to round up one *Mister* C. Richter and deliver him to the Robbins County Sheriff's Office, forthwith, as they say in the big city.

"Says he has a complaint report of a fight at Grinny Creigh's place on Spider Mountain wherein you assaulted two men, one of whom was sixty-three years old. The Creigh people say one's got a broken leg and the old guy's dead from a fist to the head."

"It was an elbow," I said. "It still hurts. He have a warrant out?"

"Now that you ask, he didn't actually mention any warrant. You said last night two guys tried to administer a little discipline and you put 'em down. Care to amplify?"

I went through the fracas in detail, reminding the sheriff that I had been abducted by these two men, chained into the back of a pickup truck, and taken against my will to the hills for my "conversation" with Grinny Creigh. "The older guy was out cold but definitely breathing when I left; the other guy did seem to have a broken leg. But I'll claim self-defense in the context of a kidnapping. And I *will* get a warrant for the whole damn clan."

The sheriff drummed his fingers on his desk for a moment. "Lemme call him back. Why don't you wait out in the bullpen."

"Ask him if he can produce a body," I said from the doorway. "You know, habeas corpus?"

"Don't tell me my business, young man," Hayes snapped, and waved me out of his office. He summoned me back in ten minutes. I had taken the time to make a call of my own to my estate attorney in Triboro, J. Oliver Strong, Esq. Lawyer Strong was a wills-and-probate guy, but his firm had a stable of criminal defense lawyers. Strong told me to sit tight and that one of them would call me back within the hour.

"Seems M. C. does *not* have a warrant," the sheriff reported. "Although he says he can scare one up one pretty quick. FYI, the magistrate over there is married to a Creigh. The habeas question got a little bit murky, though. He hasn't personally seen a body, nor have any of his deputies. Whole thing's 'verbal' at the moment, pending lots and lots of further investigation."

"They're really all over it, aren't they."

"I told him what you said about getting a warrant out for Grinny and her whole crew. He started in with nobody having proof of any abduction until I told him we had witnesses at the lodge, plus the fact of Rue Creigh delivering your tired ass back to the lodge around midnight. That definitely slowed him up some. I asked how likely it was that she'd be offering you a ride in her pick-'em-up truck if you'd just killed one of their people with your bare hands right there in her front yard."

"What'd he say to that?"

"That it would probably have turned her on. Rue's got kinda of an exotic reputation in these parts."

"Yikes. So where are we? I have lawyers in motion."

The sheriff shrugged. "Ball's in his court right now. If the Creighs can produce a body, and he can get his warrant, he may or may not follow through with it. He has to know that the feds have been looking for a way into Robbins County for months now."

"And?"

"Kidnapping is a federal crime. A perfect handle for them to get right into the middle of all this. You know how they do—come in riding one charge and then suddenly growing arms like an octopus. My guess, even if that guy did kick? Mingo's gonna think on it and then fail to produce a corpus. One less Creigh isn't worth a federal invasion. In the meantime, however, I need you to stick around."

"Damn, I was just about to declare victory and leave town."

"Be still, my heart," he said wistfully. "Right now I need to see what the jungle drums are saying up in the coves and hollers. Maybe find out who this supposedly dead guy was. And, more importantly, whether or not he has kin of his own."

"As in, if M. C. isn't going to handle it, some irate relatives might?"

"As in, you bet your flatlander ass. You better stay out of open windows and keep those dogs with you."

"They're out in the car right now. But wouldn't I be safer waiting this out in Triboro?"

The sheriff scratched an ear. "That might pose me a political problem," he said. "Folks will be watching to see what happens with this. You and I are sitting here drinking coffee because you're an ex-cop. If I let you leave the county, I'll hear about it. So stick around. This won't take long. And in the meantime, can we get your formal statement about how y'all came to stumble on that body up at Crown Lake?"

I dictated a statement to the sheriff's secretary, signed it, and drove back to the lodge. I lectured the dogs on the way back about wandering off when there were bad guys hiding in the bushes. They paid close attention for a good thirty seconds before yawning in unison and going to sleep. The defense lawyer called on my way back to the love cabin. I briefed him on the situation. He told me to say nothing to anyone until I knew what the real situation was, and that his retainer for a felony criminal charge was fifteen thousand. I noted the advice and the price and said I'd be in touch if there were any further developments.

Back at the cabin I called Mary Ellen Goode and told her what was going on. She said she'd already heard. Her voice was strained and she was speaking formally.

"Lemme guess, Ranger Bob standing right there?" I asked.

"Yes, sir, that's correct," she replied. "Let me look into the matter and call you back."

I said okay and hung up. I then called Tony back in Triboro and brought him up to date on developments in the provinces. Tony had already heard. The lawyers' courthouse gossip circuit had been humming ever since my first call to Lawyer Strong. Women had nothing on lawyers when it came to gossiping, unless they were lady lawyers.

"Bare hands?" Tony exclaimed. "That's what you get for turning into a gym rat. Think you're the Terminator now or what?"

"It felt a little bit like Sicily," I said. "All those guys standing around in the dark with their *luparas*. I guess I'd had enough of being pushed around by toothless cretins. Listen, I need some stuff sent up here."

After about three months of relative idleness, a friend in the Marshals Service had offered me a job doing routine investigatory work as an independent contractor for the federal court in Triboro. Once Annie Bellamy's estate cleared, I no longer needed to do anything but read my financial statements, but the walls had begun to close in. Anything was better than just sitting around. It wasn't exactly demanding stuff—background checks, witness management, short-notice paper scrambles during a court session—but it got me out of the house and interacting with other people again, and it was also a great excuse for Sheriff Bobby Lee Baggett to stop hounding me about getting back out in the world and doing something besides pump iron and brood about getting some revenge down the line.

Sergeant Horace Stackpole, one of my guys who'd been on the original MCAT, took retirement a few months after that and looked me up for a drink. We were joined by another cop and got to talking about what cops can do after leaving the Job. I bitched about the boring nature of the work I was doing, and the third guy suggested that I form my own company and hire only ex-cops, like Horace, and we could all work as much or as little as we wanted to. The courts had an unending need for people who could retrieve information and documents, witnesses who might not know they were witnesses, and other odds and ends quickly. Cops knew how to do all of that, and had the networks to get to certain people and information quickly. I suggested that Horace found the company, but, as he pointed out, I was the one who both had money and didn't need to work.

So I did, and Hide and Seek Investigations, LLC stood up a month later, with a condition of employment being that you were an ex-cop who had retired in good standing with your department. Coming from me, that was something of a dark joke among the guys, but what the hell: I knew I hadn't done anything wrong. I justified the ex-cop criterion because of some semimysterious security requirements of the courts. That of course was BS, but it kept the professional job-discrimination Nazis off our backs. I made it a rule that everyone working there had to approve any new hires. Any cop who makes it to retirement has both an established professional reputation and people who know him and will vouch for him—or not, as the case might be.

There were now six of us, with the other five doing most of the work while I dealt with the larger management issues, such as making the office coffee and handling the mail. We had an office on the second floor of a bail bondsman company in downtown Triboro. It was pretty Spartan, but it had the advantage of being near Washington Street so the guys could still hit the sheriff's office and city cops' watering holes for lunch and afterward. Two of the "guys" were women, both of whom had been street cops with the sheriff's office. Both of them had gone through the trauma of having husbands go astray. They now did a flourishing business of predivorce reconnaissance work for suspicious wives, and they *loved* their work. We loved their after-action reports.

Like Horace, Tony Martinelli had joined us from the MCAT when it was broken up after the cat dancers case. None of us worked full-time, and the money from the contracts went proportionally to the people who put in the most hours. Most of them were filling up 401(k)s, and I took a dollar a year and the biggest office, a massive corner suite twelve feet square and overlooking a culturally intriguing back alley. With more cops finding out about our little operation, I knew we'd soon need more office space, something I'd have to attend to when I got back from helping Mary Ellen Goode. But all in all, none of us took our second "career" very seriously, and I the least of all.

I gave Tony a list of the things I needed and asked him to overnight it all to the lodge. I also asked him to see if he could find out what the street term "florist" meant in contemporary druggie circles. Then I retrieved Carrie Santángelo's card, called her, and asked her for the GPS coordinates of Grinny Creigh's cabin.

"I can get you those," she said. "Should I ask why you want them?"

"Probably not," I said. "I'm about to exercise one of the privileges of not being a cop anymore. Think deniability."

"Deniability's good," she said. "Hang on and I'll get you the coordinates. And if you're going to go do some recon, make sure you file a flight plan."

"With whom—Carrigan County?"

"If it were me, I'd tell Baby Greenberg. You really ice some guy with your bare hands?"

For God's sakes, I thought, *did anyone not know about it?*

I put a call in to Baby Greenberg. The agents had motel rooms down the road in Murphy, and he called me back in thirty minutes. I explained what I wanted to do.

"Been nice knowing you," the agent said.

"Can't be that bad," I said. "And it seems I'm stuck here for the weekend anyway."

"Yeah, I heard."

I sighed. "The guy was alive when I left. I think it's all bullshit. He just wants me in custody in Robbins County."

"So you're gonna what? Waltz over there and solve the man's problem for him?"

"He's gotta catch me first, and I'm not going anywhere near Rocky Falls."

"The closest we've been able to get to Grinny Creigh's place is twenty-four thousand miles—that's where the satellite cameras live."

"Anybody ever try just driving up there? I mean, if you think they're going to give you guys some shit, go get a few dozen marshals to go with you."

"The problem is that we have no grounds for one of our usual home invasions. And no supervisor is willing to put his agents at risk of an anonymous bullet through the windshield just for a face-to-face meeting with this woman."

"But if they shot at you, then you can bring a crowd."

"If *who* shot at us? And from what crag? That's the problem. I can't feature Grinny Creigh taking a muzzle loader down from the mantel and opening fire on a car full of feds. But there are some guys up there who would make a wager out of it. None of us wants to die on the off chance that we can score a bust. Your theory's good up the point of who volunteers to be the *casus belli*. It's that simple."

"Where the hell are Elliot Ness and the Untouchables when you need them?"

"We've been modernized," he said. "Director's a lawyer."

"Then maybe my way is the best way, Special Agent. Somebody shoots at me, I'm going to shoot back. Or I may even shoot first. Give the black hats a taste of their own tactics."

"I officially didn't hear that," Greenberg said. "Call me *if* you get back."

"Why don't you come along?" I asked, not entirely in jest.

"Because I'm chicken, that's why," Baby said.

5

On Saturday morning, I found myself working harder than I'd expected, paddling a large aluminum canoe across Crown Lake. The shepherds were onboard, curled up one in front and one behind me among all the gear. I'd left a note back in the cabin in case Sheriff Hayes came looking for me. It said simply that I was going camping for the weekend and would be back Monday midday. I'd toyed with the idea of telling Mary Ellen Goode, but then decided against it. However reluctantly, I knew it was time to begin separating myself from her life, which was a pity, because I really did like her. But if she did not have the internal fortitude to cope with the kinds of things that seemed to erupt in my wake from time to time, Ranger Bob might yet prove his theory about persistence.

The lake was gorgeous, and I now understood its name. It was an impoundment for the TVA, as were some of the other big lakes in western North Carolina, which meant it wandered around the hills and mountains for many miles following the course of a long-drowned river. There were even some islands, the tops of submerged hills, still covered with trees. The Park Service map showed where the long-lost roads and villages had been submerged back in the thirties and forties when the dams were built to send electricity to the power-ravenous atomic bomb project at Oak Ridge.

I'd arranged for Moses Walsh to drive me, the boat, and my gear to one of the overlooks on the national park side of Crown Lake, and to retrieve me again Monday at noon. I'd told him to wait an additional two hours if I was late, but not to worry about declaring me missing if I didn't show up. I did ask Tony back in Triboro to alert Sheriff Hayes's office if I hadn't called in by Monday at 8:00 P.M.

Mose had offered to guide until I'd told him I was going into Robbins County. "You're retired," he said. "You don't do death-wish stuff once you've closed out of the Job."

"I'm just going for a little look-see," I told him. "The real cops are all wrapped around the axle with probable cause, warrants, etc. You were in homicide—you know how it is."

He'd grinned at me as he realized I'd checked him out. "There's a reason we have all that constitutional stuff in place," he'd said.

"Right, of course there is."

"No, I'm talking the selfish reason: By jumping through all the hoops, you make sure the excitement is going to be worth the risk. I don't believe you appreciate the danger, my friend."

I'd thanked him for his concern and admitted that he was probably right, but the truth was, I often didn't appreciate the danger, if only because danger seemed to grow in the telling of it.

I had a rifle, a telescope, a handheld GPS unit, head-mounted night vision gear, and minimal camping equipment. If the local fire service maps were correct, there was a straight eight-mile shot across the face of Rockslide Mountain via fire lanes to the eastern front of Book Mountain, below which the GPS coordinates of Grinny's cabin were centered. My plan was to set up a small camp on one of the offshore islands, rest this afternoon, go in by night, set up my hide, watch all day Sunday to see what went on around the cabin and the other buildings, and then go back out Sunday night.

* * *

I awoke at just after sundown and stretched on the air mattress. My left arm was still sore from the fight the other night. The shepherds were curled up in the pine needles but opened their eyes when I moved. It was getting cooler, and there was already a pale full moon rising over the lake. I got up, washed my face, and fed the dogs. The moon was painting a wide path of light on the still waters of the lake. I lit the Primus stove and heated up one of the MREs provided by Mose. I made sure that neither my camp nor the tiny flame was visible from the shore in the direction of Book Mountain. I doubted that Grinny kept permanent sentinels out on the hills and ridges, but I didn't want to attract attention in case I was wrong about that. The hills above the lake were getting darker by the minute, and it was easy to believe I was all alone out there.

I cleaned up, buried my trash, and then made a cup of instant coffee. Despite the execrable coffee, it was a real pleasure to watch night fall on the lake. The wind that had been cascading off the nearby ridges died down. An occasional night bird called across the lake. A distant pack of coyotes made their obeisance to the rising moon as the forest noises subsided. I'd just decided to get going when the dogs sat up and stared out at the lake in the direction of the park. I had put in below the scenic overlook and then paddled more than four miles, rounding a point that now obscured my starting spot.

The dogs were staring hard into the gloom of the lake in that direction. I made sure the little stove was off and watched their ears twitching. I realized there had to be something or someone out there. I was reaching for my NVG headgear when I heard the thump of a paddle against aluminum, a splash, and then some unpleasant language. A moment later a canoe materialized out of the darkness and grounded at an odd angle on the gravel shoreline. Baby Greenberg climbed stiffly out of the canoe and massaged his knees.

"I saw that movie?" he said. *"The Last of the Mo-what-the-fucks?* They made this canoe shit look so easy. Damn! My knees hurt. My shoulders hurt. My hands hurt. And I cannot steer this thing worth a shit." He staggered over some wet rocks. *"Damn!"*

"It gets easier if you have ten war canoes full of serious hostiles chasing your paleface ass down said river," I said with a grin. "It's all about motivation. How'd you find me?"

"Brother Mose told me where you started off from, and then I looked for light." He held up the smallest night vision telescope I had ever seen.

I looked around my Spartan campsite. "What light was that?" I asked.

Greenberg pointed at the Primus stove, which was still warm from heating water for coffee. *Those must be really sensitive glasses*, I thought. The dogs came over to get reacquainted, while I made up another cup of coffee.

"What changed your mind?" I asked.

"Carrie Santángelo?" Greenberg said. "She called me. Said you really were going Creigh hunting. Wanted to make sure that someone besides her knew what you were doing. Asked me why I wasn't going along. Told her I was chicken, but if she'd spend the night with me I might reconsider. She said she might go as far as phone sex, so I said okay. Then she asked me how I'd enjoyed it, and there I was. She is the *best*-looking slinky-toy in the whole SBI."

I handed him the coffee. "She have any personal connection to this part of the world that you know of?" I asked.

Greenberg didn't know. "She can surprise you, though," he said. "Shows up at interagency meetings in one of those DKNY outfits? All the coffee-and-doughnut cops trying not to drool. But then she, like, sits at the back of the room, taking notes like somebody's executive whatever, while some other suit sits at the table as the SBI principal. Only later you find out she's the senior internal affairs inspector in the outfit, and the suit at the table works for her. They call her Santa Claws; that's with a *w*, by the way, not a *u*. What's our plan?"

"You sure you're up for this?" I asked. "I mean, see that mountain? I'm going up to the topline of that one via the forestry fire lanes, then over to a second, higher one. Eight, nine miles by the map, and probably more with all the wrinkles. I have to go fast enough so that I can be in my hide by daylight. That's daylight tomorrow."

Greenberg smiled. He was starting to bounce around again. "I run ten miles every day," he said quietly. "I won't slow you down. You are gonna leave most of this shit here, right?"

I nodded. "I've got a small backpack, a camo shelter half, canteen, knife, the spotting scope, two MREs. Going up tonight, gonna watch all day tomorrow, come out tomorrow night, late."

Greenberg pointed at the black rifle with his chin. "Whatcha got there, sport?"

"Remington 700P TWS model, .308 Win rounds."

"We going to war?"

"We might," I said. "Although, from what I hear, the black hats see a couple of strangers, they usually fire a warning shot to shoo them away."

"Usually? Is that like 'assume'?"

"Well, life's a risky business, Special Agent. I get a warning shot, I propose to scope the hillside and blow an arm off. You have official top cover to come along on this little hike?"

Greenberg sniffed and shook his head. "Officially, I was concerned that a crusading civilian might get himself hurt going up into Grinny Creigh's cave and irritating the demons. I can follow you at fifty yards if you like."

I laughed. "That might not be a bad idea, you know, in case that 'usually' shit doesn't work out. But mostly I want to watch for an entire day. I've been there once, at night, and besides Grinny, what I remember most is Rue Creigh making headlights against the screen door."

"Tell me your impression of Grinny Creigh—you're probably the first LE guy to lay eyes on her for a long time."

"Carrie said that her whole deal was about power and control: She radiates that. Big woman, fat, but probably strong as an ox. Cunning, pig eyes. Accustomed to command and obedience. Didn't move out of her chair or raise her voice particularly, but when I pissed her off, the guys hanging back in the trees started sliding toward cover, like she might have been about to pull a gun and start blasting away. Her son, Nathan, looks like he ought to have bolts in his neck. Tall, skinny, one of those ball-bearing-eyes types. I think he gives the detailed orders to the black hats once Grinny sets the general objective."

"Modern weapons?"

"None that I saw. Lots of shotguns, but all double-barreled, nontactical. A pack of dogs that's pretty scary. Outbuildings, but I don't know if there's electricity. Really primitive look and feel to the place, but bigger than most of the cabins in these parts."

"Primitive makes for pretty good electronic security," Greenberg said. "Nothing for us to listen to when they're whispering messages down the mountain trails in some eighteenth-century dialect, as we have found out. How many soldiers were there the night you went up there?"

"A dozen? It was dark. And that's not counting the two who took me there."

Greenberg nodded. "The population outside of Rocky Falls is estimated to be something between one and two thousand people," he said. "That's all in. But the state demographers really don't know shit, and the federal census bureau has zero credible data. The Creigh clan isn't that big, but they all tend to react negatively to strangers. The decent folk just try to keep out of their way."

"So anyone who spots us is likely to at least raise the alarm."

"And the usual warning shots. Don't forget them."

I looked at my watch and roused the dogs. "Why don't we go find out?"

"How about these canoes—hate to have them stolen while we're up that hill there."

"We'll sink them, pile some rocks in them. They're aluminum. Easy."

"How do we get the water out, we come back?" he asked.

"Now that's hard."

It took most of the night to get across the aptly named Rockslide Mountain to a position about a thousand feet above the cabin on the east flank of Book Mountain. The firebreaks, which had looked smooth and open from a distance, had turned out to be overgrown and very difficult to walk through without a machete. A bulldozer would have been a great help. We'd ended up traversing the slopes by staying just inside the tree line and using the firebreaks more as a navigation aid. We'd seen some cabins down in the hollows, but few lights. There'd also been some barking dogs, but no reaction from inside the houses.

I had put my dogs' bark collars on and then deployed them fifty yards ahead of us, where they scouted, making regular returns to touch base with their struggling humans. Greenberg had been true to his word, though, keeping up with me all the way. Our biggest problems had been night insects and not enough water. Fortunately, our perch on the side of Book Mountain included a substantial weep of spring water flowing practically under our feet, so the dogs had water and we could fill our canteens, albeit with a hefty dose of Halzone purifier to kill off the ubiquitous giardia bugs.

We set up our hide between two massive boulders, which looked like they were ready to unlimber from the hillside any minute now and roll directly down on the cabin complex below. I had put the dogs on a long down above the boulders to give warning of anyone approaching from behind our position. Our own view into the cabin's yard was partially obscured by a spotty line of pines, which also screened us, but the scope gave us a pretty good look. We counted twenty-five dogs of uncertain but uniformly large breeding in the dog lot, three even larger pigs in a pen next door, and a pair of goats wandering around eating invisible delicacies throughout the dirt yard.

Three men had come up the front meadow just after sunrise, leading a mule with bulging saddlebags. Nathan had come out of the building to the right of the main cabin. They'd talked for a few minutes, and then the men departed, leaving the loaded mule behind. Nathan took it into the barn, then came back outside. He slopped the pigs and threw chunks of something red to the dogs, causing an immediate dogfight, clearly audible from our hide. Greenberg wondered aloud if the red things were local babies while I sketched details of the cabin layout on a notepad.

The spotting telescope was a sixty-power Swarovski number shielded against making a lens flash. Greenberg pointed out that there were firing ports cut in the logs of the cabin, and that the ground behind the cabin was higher than the visible grade on either side.

"That's been built up," he said. "They've either got a basement that goes back into the hill, or maybe even a cave."

I shivered mentally. The last cave I'd been into had been occupied by two starving mountain lions.

Greenberg said he saw a pipe running down from the springhouse to the cabin. "We ever do any kind of siege down there, we'd need to cut that pipe."

"They have electricity that you can see?"

He said no, nor had I seen any power poles.

Grinny herself appeared midmorning on the back porch of the cabin, sweeping some dust and debris out into the yard. She was wearing a tent-sized housecoat, and from our hilltop vantage point her head looked too small for her body. I was watching her through the telescope and was startled when she stopped sweeping for a moment, cocked her head to one side, and then looked up the hillside and appeared to stare right back into the lens. I didn't move, and neither did she, for almost ten seconds. Then she went back into the house.

"Shit!" Greenberg exclaimed. "She see you?" He'd been watching through his own small binocs.

"There's no way," I said. "But she might have sensed us. Some of these mountain women have what the locals call 'the sight.' Wouldn't surprise me if she's detected someone or something watching the cabin."

"She looked right up here, and that's, what, a thousand feet of elevation difference? We should move."

"No," I said. "Movement is a dead giveaway. She couldn't have seen the lens; it's recessed at least three inches into the tube."

I watched the back windows for signs of curtains moving, but no further movement disturbed the morning calm. "I don't think it's anything," I said, with more confidence than I felt.

*   *   *

Fifteen minutes later we saw a big dog burst out of the barn and go sprinting across the front yard. Nathan stepped into view for a moment, but the dog disappeared into the woods and kept on going.

"Looks like a dog got out," Greenberg said, watching the show through the telescope. "The tall guy looks pissed off."

I was using Greenberg's binoculars now, which had a much bigger field of view than the telescope. It was getting close to noon, and it was hot in the little hollow between the two big rocks. I wondered if my dogs needed water. I was about to slide my way out to them when I saw a flash of metal through the trees below the cabin.

"Vehicle," I announced.

Greenberg looked up to see where I was pointing the binocs and then swung the telescope in that direction. "Well, looky here," he said. "The high sha-reef himself."

"Mingo?"

"Yup. I can see him through the windshield. Apparently he's allowed to drive on the grass, because he's coming right up to the cabin."

We watched as the sheriff's patrol car drove up the meadow to the front of the cabin. Nathan came out of the barn to meet him. We couldn't see whether Grinny was on the front porch because the cabin blocked our view. Nathan and M. C. Mingo talked for a minute, and then Nathan opened the left rear door of the cruiser and removed a young child, none too gently.

"Boy or girl?" I asked.

"Girl, I think, although with all that hair in her face . . . she's done something wrong, the way Nathan's manhandling her." He kept his eye glued to the scope. "This thing have a camera port?" he asked.

"Yes, but no camera," I said. "Sorry."

"Lemme see if this fits," he said, fishing in his vest pocket while keeping his eye on the scene below. He produced a small digital camera. "Screw this onto the top and shoot some pictures of Mingo talking to these bad-asses."

I took the camera and tried it. The threads were wrong. "No go," I said.

"Shit," he replied. "Whoa—here comes the Big Mamu."

I watched M. C. Mingo, Nathan, and the child, all standing next to the cop car in front of Grinny's cabin. Then something large took over the image. It was Grinny Creigh's ponderous backside, coming down off the front porch, one haunch at a time. Her head still looked too small for that enormous body as she shuffled painfully down the grass to the police car. She put her tiny little hands on her massive hips and bent down to address the child, who appeared to be terrified. At one point the child tried to run and Nathan restrained her by her hair. He pushed the kid back in front of the angry woman.

The tongue-lashing went on for almost a minute, and then Grinny did a strange thing. She stepped forward and, hooking her forearms under the child's armpits, pulled her up into an ample embrace.

"I guess they made up," Greenberg said.

But I wasn't so sure. "Can that kid breathe?" I asked quietly.

Greenberg watched and then swore. It became obvious to both of us that Grinny's embrace was anything but motherly love. We could barely see the girl now as Grinny hugged her to that huge, soft belly, but we could see her hands and feet struggling to escape those meaty arms. Grinny bent further forward and then really gripped the little girl's body. Nathan and M. C. Mingo watched from a few feet away, Nathan with what appeared to be clinical interest, while M. C. seemed to be studying the ground until it was over. Grinny finally straightened up and threw out her arms in a dramatic gesture, and the girl's limp body dropped in a heap of skinny arms and legs at her feet. Grinny nudged the body a couple of times with her foot, causing the girl's head to loll like that of a broken doll. Then she turned to go back into the cabin. I thought I saw her glance up at the rocks, but the binocs were not strong enough to really see where she was looking.

Nathan helped the sheriff roll the child over, and then Mingo cuffed her hands behind her back. Together they loaded her into the patrol car's backseat. They talked for a minute, and then the sheriff got in the car and drove back down the hill. Now he seemed to be in a hurry.

"Mother*fuck!*" Greenberg whispered. "She just kill that kid?"

"I thought so until Mingo cuffed her," I said, swallowing hard. "Now I think she just smothered her until she passed out."

"Damn. I wish I had a picture of that."

"The kid would have been invisible," I said. "But, man! What are these people doing?"

"Well, now we know all we need to know about M. C. Mingo," Greenberg said.

"We have to report this."

"Wanna go now?"

"We should wait till dark," I said. I couldn't get Grinny's final glance upward out of my mind. Something wasn't quite right here. Then it came to me.

"You know, maybe we should get out now," I said.

Greenberg looked over at me and raised his eyebrows.

"She damn near smothered that kid," I said. "Right out there in the open. Where anybody could see her do it, including any watchers up here on the ridge. Why would she do that in full view?"

"Because she never did see us?"

"Or because she's already sent for reinforcements."

"How?"

"Who knows?" I said. "Cell phone? Landline telephone that we don't know about? Ham radio? Homing pigeon?"

Greenberg took another look through the telescope. "Homing *dog*, maybe?" he said softly. "You're the dog man—is that possible?"

"Hell, yes," I said, and we started breaking down our gear. Five minutes later we crawled on our bellies out from between the big rocks and up to where my dogs had been stationed. I was hoping that the pines in front of us would conceal our movements, aided by the fact that the eastern slopes of Book Mountain would be moving into sun shadow as the afternoon progressed. We made no sound as we moved through a deep bed of pine needles until I gave a low whistle to summon the shepherds from their hides above the big boulders. They came at a run, and I gave them some water. Then we headed back across the eastern face of Book Mountain, trying to keep trees and other vegetation between us and anyone watching from down at the cabin.

It took us a half hour to reach the first firebreak lane, where we stopped to catch our breath. I drank some water and gave the rest to the shepherds, who were panting pretty hard. We were going to have to cross the open firebreak to keep going down and across the mountain, and even though it was overgrown with chest-high weeds, we would be clearly visible from the heights above. The woods on the other side were denser than what we'd been toiling through, and those shadows were inviting.

"Any better way across this?" Greenberg asked, as I gauged the hundred-foot-wide clearing and felt the forested ridges towering above us.

I shook my head. "We can stay in the woods, but that's the way we need to go to get back down to the lake. Cross this and then move parallel to it. We can wait for dark, but they might use dogs to find us. I'd rather be out on the lake after dark than still up here."

Greenberg sighed. "So," he said. "We just run for it?"

"I'll send the dogs across first to make sure no one's over there in the woods," I said. I summoned the shepherds, deactivated their bark collars, and sent them across the open space of the firebreak. Once into the woods they looked back at me and I gave them the hand signal for a down. They dropped obediently into the tall grass.

"Love that shit," Greenberg muttered.

"I'm going to move right fifty yards and then do a little broken-field running. If there are shooters up behind us, I'll try to make it hard. Once I'm out in the middle, you break out here and go straight across."

"Divide the targets," Greenberg said. "Good move."

"Unless there's a dozen of them," I said. I grabbed my bag, my rifle, and the now-collapsed telescope and headed down the hill. When I got to what I judged to be fifty yards down the slope from where the shepherds had crossed, I slung the rifle, slipped into the pack, took a deep breath, and bolted out into the fire lane, jinking right and then left but really pumping it, trying to accelerate as I ran to make it as hard as possible for a long rifle to set up on me. I blasted through some scrub pines and into the welcome gloom of the pine forest on the other side and stopped. I bent over to catch my breath and listened for any gunfire. Moments later, Greenberg came pushing through the undergrowth, followed by the shepherds. I gave them a stern look; technically they should have remained in place.

"My fault," Greenberg said. "Once I got across, I told them to come on, and they were only too willing."

The shepherds sat down in front of me and tried not to look too guilty. "What do you think?" Greenberg asked. "We clear?"

"There aren't any more open firebreaks to cross," I said, scanning the slopes above and the tree line on the other side. The sun was farther down in the sky, so the shadows along the eastern slopes of Book Mountain were lengthening. "We've got four, maybe five more miles to go, across that next big slope. Then down five, six hundred feet in elevation to the lake. *Then* we're in the clear."

"I remember the up phase of that," Greenberg said. "Down sounds better."

I gathered my gear. "Actually," I said, "down is harder. Be on the lookout for some good walking sticks."

We headed southwest through the pines, keeping close enough to see the firebreak from time to time to make sure we remained on course. The dogs ranged ahead, crisscrossing our line of advance, ears up and noses down. We went as fast as we could without making too much noise, and I began to feel slightly more confident about our chances of getting back to the lake without a confrontation with the black hats. After that, things would get interesting, I thought. Especially when we reported what we'd seen that woman do to the child.

Then the shepherds froze in their tracks and stared into the woods ahead.

I made a sound and dropped to the ground immediately. Greenberg, fifteen feet to my left, followed my lead. We were on a downslope section of the hillside, still within the dense pine stands, and we had been approaching a narrow brook that had carved a rocky **V** down the face of the hill. On the other side were more trees, but these were a mixture of pines and thin hardwoods, which provided even denser cover. I hissed through my teeth, and the dogs turned around and came back to me. I snapped them into a long down and then carefully, slowly, unslung the rifle. Out of the corner of my eye I saw Greenberg inching over toward a large pine to get some cover between himself and whatever was on the other side of that creek. I had dropped next to a flat, moss-covered rock, which gave me about a foot and a half of protection. For now, I thought, we were in decent defensive position, although when we crossed that brook, any shooters at the top of the **V** would be in even better position.

The slope facing us went back uphill at a fairly steep angle. I chambered a round, slipped the safety off, and then began to scan the forest on the other side through the Leupold VX-III scope, looking for anything out of place. Greenberg was doing the same thing with his binoculars, and he had his SIG .45 out on a rock beside him. I realized that there could be someone approaching from behind us, but trusted the dogs to detect that problem. They'd hear footfalls and twigs breaking long before we humans would.

So what was over there? A deer? A bear? Or some of Grinny's crew with an armful of shotguns? I lay on my side and began to methodically traverse the barrel of the rifle degree by degree, studying the scope picture for anything that didn't look like a tree trunk or a boulder. The scope wasn't as powerful as the telescope, but if I suddenly saw a man aiming a gun in our direction, I wanted to be able to shoot first.

The first puffs of the late afternoon breeze were stirring leaves across the way, and the pines were making that sweet whistling sound above us as their tops bent to welcome the cooler air coming down from the higher slopes. While my left eye studied the scope picture, my right eye saw that both shepherds were still interested in something across the way. Their ears were erect and not moving. I kept looking, tree by tree, across one line of elevation, and then back, slightly higher. There were no bird sounds other than what sounded like a large woodpecker working on something across the way. I kept searching the tree line, studying the shadows and the bushes, the reticles of the scope seeming to drill into the greenery. I was looking for a face, a hat, the glint of steel, eyes.

Eyes?

I steadied the scope and centered on a gleaming reddish eye looking back at me. My finger came off the trigger guard and settled on the trigger. I cleared my throat quietly, and Greenberg looked over at me. Seeing the rifle steadied, Greenberg swung his binoculars around, trying to locate the target. For an instant I lost it, and then the bushes moved slightly and I saw it again—a single red eye, surrounded by what looked like a black Brillo pad. The woods were silent except for the clatter of the woodpecker. I pulled the butt of the rifle in tight.

"Animal," I whispered.

"What kind?" Greenberg asked. The shepherds were still down, but they sensed our excitement and were leaning forward.

"Can't—" I began, and then I fired, almost involuntarily, as a four-hundred-pound black boar exploded out of the bushes in front of us and charged down the hillside in our general direction, grunting and growling and coming down like a four-legged avalanche, knocking down bushes and small trees and coming faster than I had ever seen any pig move. The shepherds launched forward, barking furiously.

"Tree!" I yelled to Greenberg, as I slung my rifle and leaped into the lower branches of the nearest pine tree. Greenberg did the same, and we both scrambled as high as we could get, dislodging a hail of dead branches, pine needles, and a few thousand startled insects as we pushed our heads up through the dense foliage. The furious pig blasted right past the shepherds and headlong into the tree Greenberg had climbed, shaking it from roots to tip and almost dislodging the scrambling DEA agent.

I swung around my own sticky trunk, unlimbered the rifle, and tried to get a shot, but by now the shepherds were circling the beast, barking and snapping, while the pig got down on its haunches and circled with them, tearing up great gouts of dirt and pine needles with its hooves while making a continuous roaring sound. I finally got a shot and fired down into the pig's back, but the monster merely grunted once and kept circling. It lunged at Frick, who barely escaped being disemboweled by a whipping tusk, but the move allowed Frack to get a jaw-full of the pig's right hind leg. The dog backed hard, pulling the squealing pig right off its feet. As it tried to bend around to get at the shepherd, Frick closed her jaws over the pig's snout and began to pull back in the other direction. The pig thrashed hard enough to flail the two shepherds like furry rags, but the moment gave me a second shot. This time

I aimed for the back of its head and the pig collapsed instantly. The two shepherds continued to pull and snarl until they finally heard me calling them off. The pig's stubby legs twitched uncontrollably for about a minute and then it expired with a long, wet gasp that sprayed a flat cone of bright red blood onto the pine needles.

I swallowed hard and looked over at Greenberg, who was staring down at the black, hairy body below. His face was white as we watched the two shepherds sniffing around the body.

"What the *fuck* is that thing?" he asked.

"Wild pig," I said. "I should have recognized the warning she was giving—remember the woodpecker sounds?"

Greenberg nodded, not taking his eyes off the pig, as if to make very sure that the thing was really dead.

"She was snapping her jaws at us, warning us to go away. There's probably a litter up there."

"Litter same as smaller?"

I laughed, but it was a nervous laugh. The yellow tusks sticking out of the pig's mouth were at least twelve inches long. Okay, two. But the dogs had been lucky.

Dogs?

We both heard it at the same time—a long, melodious baying sound from the ridge behind and above us. Then another dog joined in. The pack was coming to the sound of our gunfire.

"Rock and roll," I said, and slid down the pine tree in a shower of sticky bark and outraged pine beetles.

Forsaking any semblance of caution, we grabbed our gear and took off down the slope to the brook. Greenberg slapped his side and turned around to go back and retrieve the gun he'd left in the grass. I waited anxiously on the other side, trying to wipe pine pitch off my hands. I reloaded the rifle, and then we were off again, trotting right along the edge of the firebreak to make better time. From the sounds of it, there were even more dogs behind us now and they were onto a solid scent. The shepherds were ranging out ahead again, occasionally looking behind to see where that dog pack was.

"That dead pig will slow them up for a few minutes," I said, trying not to puff. We were climbing again, and the branch-littered ground made for rough going.

"Can we make it to the lake before they catch up?" Greenberg asked. He seemed to be doing just fine physically, without any signs of being out of breath. Of course, he wasn't carrying as much gear as I was. That had to be it.

"If the men keep the dogs with them, on tracking leads, then we can beat them. If they turn them loose, I don't know. We get over this spine, it's all downhill from there."

"That's good," Greenberg said.

Actually it wasn't. The slope was much steeper going down, and my thighs were burning within a few minutes of starting down that hillside. The footing on Rockslide Mountain was loose shale, rocks, and tufted grass, and I felt as if I were falling forward more than running down the hill. Greenberg started to slow down, as I had thought he might. It was always much harder to go down than up. The dogs weren't doing too much better. Frack lost his balance and tumbled for ten yards before getting back up, and then he did it again. Behind us the noise of the dog pack seemed louder, but I kept telling myself it was just the acoustics caused by the rock walls above us. The bad news was that it didn't sound like the dead pig had slowed anyone down.

We finally reached the bottom, which was a jumble of large boulders in front of a tangled pile of winter-killed pine trees. The line of debris stretched hundreds of feet in both directions along the base of the mountain. Greenberg collapsed in front of a big rock.

"Fuck it," he gasped. "You were right—my legs are done. We've got a pretty good field of fire here. Those dogs show up, let's waste 'em."

I glanced down at Greenberg's .45; lovely weapon though it was, the pursuing dogs would have to be at our throats for pistols to do any good, especially shooting uphill. I dropped my gear and picked a suitable rock for rifle work. The shepherds flopped down in the woods beyond the debris field, panting heavily. The sounds of baying hounds echoed clearly now from within the trees up above our position. I shook my canteen, but it was empty. Somehow the top had come off in the big scramble down the slope. I yelled a command at the shepherds to put them into a long down.

The afternoon shadows were deepening fast down here, but there was plenty of light for the Leupold scope. I attached the rifle's arm sling, contracted my body into a sitting position behind the rock, and pointed the rifle up in the direction of all the noise. I began to scan the edge of the trees from which we had escaped. I had enough ammo to thin out the pack leaders and hopefully convince the followers to stop and talk things over.

"There they are," Greenberg said. "Swing right."

I traversed the rifle and saw the first three dogs clearing the edge of the forest and coming down the hill in our direction. I lined up on the biggest one and squeezed off a single shot at about two hundred yards. At first I thought I'd missed, but then the dog tumbled down the hillside in a hail of dust and gravel and lay still. The rest kept coming, and there were more appearing at the edge of the woods. I set up on one running in another pod of three and dropped that one, too. The dog nearest to that one looked over its shoulder but never broke stride. Greenberg was crouching over his rock, watching.

"Get under cover," I said to Greenberg while stuffing more rounds into the magazine. "The handlers will have rifles."

Greenberg dropped and then crawled on his stomach to the rock behind which I was hiding. He began sweeping the ridge with his binoculars, looking for the men behind the dogs. I fired again and swore when I saw dirt fly. I dropped a third one, a through-and-through lengthwise, and this one died hard, screaming as it rolled down the hill. That stopped the ones behind it, and I took the opportunity to shoot one more before the pack finally scattered. But the lead wave, now down to three truly ugly dogs, was inside of a hundred yards away and coming strong.

Greenberg was sitting alongside me now. He had his .45 out, waiting calmly. I dropped one of the final three, which somersaulted into a twitching heap. The other two were at forty yards, still coming fast, teeth clearly visible, ropes of drool flying.

"I've got one round left," I said.

"I've got the world's supply," Greenberg said, brandishing a spare magazine. "You keep the ones up the hill honest."

I steadied the rifle back up to where the rest of the dog pack was milling around, not willing to run by the one gut-shot dog that was still screaming on the hillside. I sighted in on one especially big dog and dropped it with a hindquarters shot. It went down with enough drama to convince the rest of the pack to withdraw into the woods. I lifted my eye from the scope in time to see Greenberg sighting carefully from a two-handed grip right between the two oncoming dogs, whose growls were now audible. At the last minute, he fired, right and then left, shooting both dogs through-and-through. They tumbled into a single bleeding heap about ten feet in front of them, too badly hurt to scream.

I swung the scope back up the hill, looking for signs of humans in the tree line. There was a big boom next to my right ear as Greenberg dispatched one of the wounded dogs, which had begun to crawl toward us. When I looked back up the hill I thought I saw a face in the trees.

"Down!" I yelled, and we both ducked behind our rock just as a bullet blasted a spray of granite bits all over us. Three more rounds came down the hill, each one placed right where our two faces had been seconds before.

"Those the usual warning shots?" Greenberg asked with a grin, and I shook my head.

We executed a high-speed slither into the tangle of downed trees. When we came out the other side, I whistled up the dogs and we took off running again, keeping well into the woods, which by now were deep in shadow. We could no longer see the firebreak lane, but I knew in which direction the lake was and, by this juncture, all slopes headed down would end up in the water. There was no more shooting from up on the ridge. I was hoping that the dog pack had decided that we were definitely bad juju. We jogged for fifteen minutes and then took a breather. My thighs were hurting again, and I was glad for the momentary respite.

Until a huge dog came out of the woods from our right and lunged at my face. I ducked the snapping jaws by throwing myself backward hard enough to crack my head on the ground. The dog went over my head, landing in a heap, but then whirled around, jaws agape, only to be nailed by Frack, who seized it by the throat with a huge roar. The two dogs went down in a blurred tangle of feet, teeth, and flying hair. The attacking dog was bigger than Frack, but the shepherd had a death grip on its throat and it was already suffocating. Frick came by in a blur, went over a log, and attacked a second dog head-on, biting the attacker's right front leg off at the elbow and sending the amputee screaming back up the hill with Frick in hot pursuit, the dog's leg still in her mouth. Greenberg shot a third dog that had slid to a stop when Frick attacked, and then a fourth in midair as it launched itself over our position. I felt helpless without a close-in gun, but somehow I'd managed to get my knife out and was back-to-back with Greenberg.

The woods went silent except for the final sounds of the deadly struggle as Frack completed strangling the bigger dog. It was now down on it side, its eyes bulging and its rear legs kicking helplessly. Frick came bounding back to us, still carrying her bloody trophy. The air was filled with a sudden acrid smell of gunpowder and then dog manure as the big dog died.

Greenberg apparently saw something move out on the edge of his vision. He fired two snap-shot rounds in the general direction of the sound. There was a yelp in the woods, but I couldn't tell if it was human or canine. We got down behind some logs and waited. I reminded myself not to make any more assumptions. After five minutes, Greenberg took a deep breath.

"Chapter two," he said quietly, and we started running again, the shepherds bounding alongside, their hackles still up. Greenberg loaded his spare magazine and racked the SIG as we ran through the trees. I wanted to look back over my shoulder but had to pay attention to my feet, as the slope had steepened noticeably. Greenberg stumbled and went down in a heap of pine needles and furious language. Then we burst out into the open, picked our way across a wide strip of rocks and gravel, pushed through a ten-foot-wide stand of stubby, stunted pines, and slid down a rocky bank to the edge of the lake. Once down on the water, I tried to decide which way to go. A rifle bullet kicked up a waterspout ten feet out in the lake, and we both dived back to the base of the bank as the boom from the rifle arrived. I whistled the dogs over from the water's edge.

"Which way?" Greenberg said.

"If he's up high, he can't see us as long as we stay under this bank. Let's go that way as far as that point, see if we can spot the island."

We hunched over and went west along the lakeshore, making sure we couldn't be seen by the long-range shooter up on the ridge. We'd gone fifty yards when a goddamned dog started barking at us from up on top of the bank. Greenberg stepped out and fired once. He missed, but the dog jumped back when the ground next to him blew up. Another bullet smacked a waterspout into the air offshore, indicating that the shooter, taking his cue from the dog, now knew where we were and, more important, in which direction we were running.

"*Fucking* dogs," Greenberg said, prompting disapproving looks from the shepherds. We were still a hundred yards from the point, and, to make matters more dangerous, our friendly bank dissolved into a narrow, rocky beach at the point itself, creating a no-cover zone.

"We're going to have to wait until it's dark," I said. "We can't cross that open area with riflemen up there."

The dog returned, barking furiously at us from the edge of the bank. Then a second one joined in. They weren't making any effort to come down to the shore, but they were making it absolutely clear to anyone watching from the ridge where their quarry was holed up. I judged we had another hour at least before it would be dark enough to try to cross that open ground, and then we'd still have to deal with an unknown number of dogs. A third hound joined in the noisy chorus up above, and yet another heavy round punched a hole in the lake, followed this time by the distinctive boom of a black-powder rifle. A second round hit the top of the bank, blowing a spray of rocks and dirt out into the water and scaring the dogs, but only for a moment.

As long as we stayed down below the rim of the bank, we were safe from gunfire. But we couldn't get away, and, as more dogs joined the ones up on the bank, it was only a matter of time before the pack mentality took over and our pursuers would spill over the bank and come to dinner.

"How many rounds you got left?" I asked.

"Not enough for all that," Greenberg said, pointing with his head at the rim of the bank.

Another heavy bullet hit the top of the bank. The shooter was either trying to keep us pinned down until others could get down to the lake, or he was just showing off, I thought. A puff of wind blew in from the lake toward the shore, which gave me an idea.

"Got your lighter?"

Greenberg patted his pocket, nodded, and fished it out.

I took it and began looking around for a small, dried-out bush. I found one and ripped it up out of the sandy ground. The barking and snarling from up above was getting more enthusiastic. Greenberg took careful aim and dropped one of the dogs. Its body came tumbling down the slope, which seemed to just make the survivors hungrier. The two shepherds lay with flattened ears next to the water, for the first time looking worried.

"You gonna start a fucking forest fire?" Greenberg asked.

"A little one," I said. "Remember that gravel strip? That should act as a fire-break. Hopefully the fire will drive the dogs and the humans off the bank."

"But what if it gets loose?"

"We'll blame it on God," I said, setting the lighter to the dried branches. "There's precedent: It's a burning bush."

Greenberg rolled his eyes as I climbed up the bank and then whipped the smoldering bush around my head until it burst into bright flames. The dogs suddenly shut up. I threw the flaring bush up into the line of dry pines at the top. At first, the pack went nuts, but when the wind from the lake gusted and began to blow a flame-front down the lakeside strip of vegetation, the dogs decided enough was enough. I peered over the top just long enough to be sure and saw a satisfying brush fire with lots of useful smoke roaring down the beach line.

I signaled Greenberg. Time to go. When we got to the edge of the clearing, the fire behind us was audible, pushed along the lake margins by a suddenly interested onshore breeze. So far, the gravel strip was doing its job, but I didn't know how far that strip extended. Greenberg was right: I might have just started a major forest fire. But that beat being eaten by a pack of dogs.

"We gonna run for it?" Greenberg asked as we crouched under the last of the cover.

"Any better ideas?"

Greenberg took a deep breath and then nodded. We took off across the open stretch of beach, the shepherds running with us. Amazingly, Frick still had her trophy leg. There was no gunfire as we splashed through the shallows at the point of the rocky spine and then around it, where we were again sheltered by a high bank. The point with the island at the end was right ahead, and there appeared to be cover all the way as we were now on the back side of the ridge. The sun was finally setting, glowing yellow through the big cloud of smoke behind us and making it doubly difficult for anyone up on that ridge to get a good shot. The glow of the fire silhouetted the lower spine of the ridge as we moved out onto the island itself. I kept telling myself that the fire was diminishing, but that may have been wishful thinking. Now all we had to do was figure out how to raise those two canoes and get the flock out of there.

We made it back to my cabin at just after four in the morning. Greenberg had brought his stuff down to the lake in his personal pickup truck, which now had both boats strapped in the bed out in the lodge's lower parking lot. I made some coffee, and we dropped into chairs out on the creekside porch.

"Well, that was fun," I said. I wanted some scotch in my coffee, but my legs were too rubbery to get up. "So now what?"

"We witnessed a near murder, executed right in front of the Robbins County sheriff," Greenberg said, lighting up a cigarette. "Can't just let that sit."

"We witnessed an *apparent* near murder," I said. "While basically trespassing on private property and spying on private citizens, without a warrant or jurisdiction and, in my case, against the explicit orders of the local sheriff not to leave town. Then, let's see, we shot somebody's dogs, killed some wildlife, and started a forest fire in a national park. Can't wait to go in and tell local law all that good news."

"Or," Greenberg said, "we set off to take a perfectly innocent hike in said national park. How were we to know we'd strayed out of the park and into Robbins County? We rested under some rocks while we tried to decide where we were. Saw some shit. Left. Got chased by guys with guns and a pack of mad dogs. Defended ourselves, from them and the damned wild pig. One of the bullets fired at us hit a rock and started a *brush* fire, not a forest fire, and we had to escape by boat. Don't know who was doing all the shooting, or who that woman was who smothered that kid in front of the sheriff, but somebody should really look into that."

I looked at him. "Who would believe that bullshit?"

Greenberg squinted at me through a blue cloud. "What are you saying? We're just going to forget this all happened?"

"Hell, no. We just have to pick the right person to tell, that's all."

We both said the name at the same time: Carrie Santángelo of the North Carolina State Bureau of Investigation.

I looked at my watch. "It's Sunday. No, it's Monday morning. Let's get some sleep, call her later this morning. See what she makes of all this."

He nodded, rubbing his thighs.

"Told you down was harder," I said, trying manfully not to rub my own quivering thigh muscles. "You really okay going to state law with this?"

"Keep your friends close and your enemies closer," he said.

Over in a corner Frick still had her leg. I'd tried to take it away, but she'd given me one of those "I caught this leg fair and square and I am *not* going to turn aloose of it, friend" shepherd looks. I decided to go get some scotch after all.

"I know it's four in the morning," I said. "I need a drink. How 'bout you?"

"Thought you'd never ask," he said. "Down was a bastard."

6

In the event, Special Agent Carrie Santángelo did not make it up to Marion-burg until late Monday afternoon. Greenberg went back to his motel over on the Tennessee side after returning Mose's gear. I heard via the grapevine in town that there had been a brush fire over in the Crown Lake area, and that a Robbins County fire truck and bulldozer team had been needed to contain it. The cause of the blaze was unknown, but careless four-wheelers were suspected. I had checked in with the Carrigan County Sheriff's Office before going to dinner to see if anything was scheduled for the next day, but they had had no word back from Robbins County on the supposed fight victim or any warrants. They'd told me to check in again later.

Carrie had returned my call first thing Monday morning and said she could be up there by one or two. She arrived at the lodge at five thirty instead, having been delayed by the usual Monday morning crises in Raleigh. I called Greenberg over, went out for beer, and ordered in pizza, and then we debriefed her on our exciting excursion to Robbins County.

"How much of this have you told your bosses in the DEA?" she asked Greenberg immediately. He said he hadn't reported anything. Yet.

"And you?" she asked me. "Have you talked to Sheriff Hayes?"

I shook my head. The sheriff had been unavailable all day, and my status as a potential manslaughter suspect had apparently lost a lot of traction.

She popped the top off another beer and sat back in her chair. She was wearing a dark business pantsuit and looked older than when I had first met her, but still entirely streetable. Older is a relative term.

"Sheriff Hayes reported the business of the fight at the Creigh cabin to SBI headquarters," she said. "But less to indict you than to report the unorthodox way M. C. Mingo was handling it."

"Fireproofing himself?" Greenberg, the bureaucrat, asked.

She nodded. "As you know, we have standard procedures for dealing with incidents like this between county jurisdictions. Mingo's off the reservation on this one, so reporting to SBI was a smart move."

She turned back to me. "Hayes did tell you to stick around?"

"He did, but so far, nothing seems to be happening. What about our little adventure? What will SBI do with that?"

"Beats the hell out of me," she said with a bright smile. "But that's why my boss gets paid the big bucks. You guys sure that was Mingo standing there when she crumpled the kid?"

We both nodded.

"We can't exactly take this before a judge," I pointed out.

"But surely you can fold what we've told you into any ongoing investigation of Robbins County, right?" Greenberg asked.

She gave him a cool interagency look. "Assuming there is such an investigation," she said.

"Oh, c'mon, Carrie," I said. "This guy Mingo the governor's long-lost illegitimate brother or something? What's the big reluctance in Raleigh to just going in there and kicking over the anthill?"

Carrie appeared to choose her words carefully. "Because some senior people in the SBI think that the meth business is a cover for something a lot worse."

We looked at her expectantly, but she shook her head. "I can't tell you any more than that right now."

We groaned in unison.

"Look: Let me make some phone calls. In the meantime, don't tell anyone what happened up there this weekend."

"What if Mingo delivers up a corpus delicti between now and the meantime?" I asked.

"Call me if that happens. You do *not* want to be taken into custody in Robbins County."

"Then I should get out of *Carrigan* County," I protested. "If there's going to be an extradition hearing, I'd want that to be held back in Triboro, not here."

"Let me make my phone calls," she repeated. "I'll get back to you tonight."

After she left, Greenberg asked if me we could make some coffee.

"This is not the SBI I know and love," I said, as I fixed up a percolator. "When it comes to local sheriff's operations, they're usually more of a consulting organization. This definitely sounds like they're running an op of their own."

"Well, I'm not comfortable keeping my office out of the loop," he said. "Her boss calls my boss, catches him off base with this story, he's gonna want to know why I didn't brief him first."

"No longer having a boss, I don't have that problem. On the other hand, I'm all alone out here, so I may talk to Sheriff Bobby Lee Baggett back in Triboro."

"She told us not to talk to anyone."

"I don't work for her," I said.

Greenberg nodded. "Me neither," he said.

My phone rang at ten thirty that night. Greenberg had gone back to his motel a few hours ago to make his own calls, and I had talked to Bobby Lee, who'd suggested that I get the hell out of there as soon as possible, as in tonight. He'd pointed out that Sheriff Hayes had no evidentiary basis for holding me, I hadn't been charged or even arrested, and I could always drive back if they did produce a corpus, but this time with shyster in tow. Or, if I elected to turn myself in to the Manceford County Sheriff's Office back in Triboro, I could force an extradition hearing, which would be conducted back on my turf and not in Robbins County, where the magistrate was reportedly yet another Creigh.

After hearing about the events of the past few days and now this SBI mystery, Bobby Lee had been even more emphatic. "You did what your friend asked you to do," he'd said. "Now get out of there while you still can. Let the alphabets play their games."

It had all sounded perfectly reasonable to me. On the other hand, I was curious now, and decided to wait for Carrie Santángelo to call back. I had heard that curiosity killed the cat, but, of course, I wasn't a cat.

Carrie was on the line when I picked up. "You're a licensed PI now, correct?" she began.

"Yup. And also, let's see, president, CEO, chairman of the board, secretary, and chief hygienic engineer of Hide and Seek Investigations, LLC."

"Wow, all that. Listen, the SBI wants to hire you, as an operational consultant."

"We're terribly busy," I replied, Bobby Lee's good advice still echoing in my ear.

"If Mingo produces a body, Sheriff Hayes will have to act," she said. "If, on the other hand, you have been working for us, your status would be different. They'd have to come through us to get to you. Ultimately, of course, we'd have to produce you. Which, of course, we would, in the fullness of time. Emphasis on the 'fullness.'"

"Have been? As in, for some time now?"

"The start date may be left somewhat vague. Look, Hayes doesn't want to turn you over to Mingo, and he doesn't want to get into any more pissing contests with that crowd, especially if some black hats decide there's the possibility of getting a genu-wine mountain-man feud up and running."

"I'm really expensive," I said.

"We're really cheap," she replied. "But you get a badge *and* a secret decoder ring. And more importantly, you might be uniquely positioned to stop something really bad from happening."

"Which is?"

"Which will be the subject of a formal briefing."

"In the fullness of time?"

"There you go. And not on the damned open telephone, *Lieutenant*."

"How quickly one forgets," I said. "Okay, let me think about it."

"Take as long as you want," she said. "But once Mingo produces an arrest warrant, we can't make this offer."

"My instincts are to pack up and beat feet," I said. "As Bobby Lee Baggett pointed out earlier, I've done what I came up here to do."

"But aren't you just a little bit curious?" she asked.

The lady was a psychic. "Not fair," I said.

"Hee-hee," she said, and hung up.

Damn all women and their intuition, I told myself. I dumped my coffee and steadied up on the scotch. I called the shepherds in, and we all went out to the creekside porch. The night was clear and cool, with a waning full moon trying hard to light up the hills. The creek was shiny black and somewhat subdued because of the lack of rain. Frick sat watching the creek; she'd hidden that damned dog leg somewhere in the cabin and I had to find it before house-keeping did. Or worse, didn't. Frack curled up at my side and went back to sleep. He'd been limping a little after our noisy jog through the mountains, and I had given him a pain pill. I sipped my own version of one.

Bobby Lee was right—I was way off my home turf and would probably be a whole lot safer back in Manceford County. The manslaughter charge had to be bogus: I hadn't killed anybody that night, and that guy had been breathing when I walked away. He could have croaked after that, of course, but if so, why couldn't Mingo produce a body?

On the other hand: Carrie's proposition sounded a lot more exciting than running down writs and warrants for the court marshals. Baby Greenberg had surprised me up in the hills; for a city boy he'd carried his share of the load quite well. And, of course, I was intrigued by Carrie's guarded references to a crime beyond methamphetamine sales and service. That mean old woman had almost smothered a kid, much as one might wring a chicken's neck for Sunday dinner. That dramatic gesture with her arms made me think maybe she'd done that before. M. C. Mingo certainly hadn't seemed shocked; he and Nathan had dumped the child's unconscious body into his backseat like a sack of potatoes. The cuffing indicated that the kid wasn't dead, but she sure wasn't healthy.

I heard footsteps approaching out on the gravel walkway. Frick padded out to the front door. It turned out to be Mary Ellen Goode, of all people. She was wearing jeans and a light sweater, and she ran her hand nervously through her hair when I appeared at the front door.

"I know. I should have called," she began, but I waved off her apology.

"Come on in. It's always good to see you."

That got me a sweet smile. We settled on the porch after she declined the of-fer of a drink. She still looked very tired, and I wondered what it was going to take to pull her out of her depression. She told me that Janey Howard had finally made a full statement to the sheriff's office, confirming what the coroner had already concluded, namely, that the man in chains in the lake had been hanged. She'd also given a description of the two men she saw doing the hanging.

"Did you get to hear the description?" I asked.

"Yes. One was older and thin; the other she described as being a heavily bearded fat man. He's the one who beat her up, among other things."

"That sounds like the runner I saw taken down by the dog pack," I said. "Robbins County, taking care of business, perhaps."

She gave me a sad look. "It depresses me that the only things you and I ever talk about are murder and violence," she said. "I guess, well, I guess that's why I dropped by."

I waited, although I was pretty sure I knew what she was about to say. I think we'd both had high hopes in the past about a possible relationship, but time, distance, and some unholy memories had proved toxic.

She took a deep breath. "I think it best for my mental health that we don't see each other anymore," she said. "And I'm truly sorry about that. I had hoped . . ."

Suspicions confirmed, I thought. "I understand," I told her. "I wanted the same thing. But I worked a violent profession for many years, and now it looks like I'm right back in it." I told her that the SBI wanted to hire me to work a problem in Robbins County.

She nodded, as if not surprised. "And I'm the one who asked you to come up here," she said. "So my problem is partly of my own making. Not your fault at all."

"I don't feel like I'm at fault, Mary Ellen," I said gently. "My life was going pretty well until we uncovered the cat dancers. My ex and I were getting back together, I was leading an exciting and productive police unit, and life was pretty good even if I was just a cop. All that changed when someone started frying bad guys. If I made a mistake, it was getting you involved in all that."

"I thought I could handle it," she said. "Now I know better."

"You need to find a nice guy who's not wearing any kind of uniform," I said. "I think maybe you should get out of uniform, too. You have that Ph.D. Go back to the campus. Change your life. Run with some civilians for a change."

She smiled. "You haven't been around academia much lately, have you?" she said. She looked away for a moment and then swore softly.

I got up, took her hand, and pulled her up out of her chair. For a moment, I wanted to kiss her, just to see if this was all talk. But the look in her eyes signaled apprehension, not desire. "C'mon," I said. "I'll walk you back to your car."

When we got out to the almost empty parking lot, she surprised me with a warm embrace. I kissed the top of her hair and told her I'd miss her. I was surprised to discover how true that was. Frick had come outside with us and was hovering anxiously, ever sensitive to charged human emotions.

Mary Ellen recomposed her face, slipped into her car, waved, and drove off. As she neared the ramp back up to the hotel's main entrance, there was a flare of headlights and a rumble of tailpipes as Rue Creigh's pickup truck popped over the hump at the top and slewed down into the parking lot. Rue's window was open and her long hair was blowing in the breeze. Her wide-lipped coloratura face was clearly visible in Mary Ellen's headlights, and it was my turn to swear. Talk about lousy timing. Rue Creigh's late-evening arrival was precisely what I didn't need to happen just then.

Rue drove over to where I was standing with my shepherd and shut the noisy truck down. The engine was powerful enough to literally shake the truck when it stopped.

"Hey there, lawman," she said brightly. "Did I show up at a bad time?"

I shook my head. "Hello, Miss Creigh. What brings you out at this late hour?"

"Late?" she said. "This ain't late. This is about when I get goin'."

I almost thought I could smell alcohol on her breath. Her face was flushed and her pupils were unusually large. Then I wondered if maybe she was riding a meth horsey, since that was the family trade. I mentally chided myself for making a cop's observations. Out of the corner of my eye I noticed that Frick was watching this woman carefully.

"Well, it's my bedtime, Miss Creigh," I said, trying to keep it light.

"Works for me, honey," she said with a leer. "Best believe I know *all* about bedtime."

I kept a smile on my face. "I do believe," I said. Then I had an idea. "The problem is that first I'm gonna have to get on the phone with that young lady who just left and do some serious fence mending."

"Aw," she said. "Can't that wait? Besides, she didn't look none too happy to me. Y'all have a fight?"

"Something like that," I said. "We go back a ways, and the history has some bumps in it."

"So you're tellin' me that you ain't gonna invite me in for a drink?"

"Yeah, I'm afraid so."

She shifted herself in the truck and then opened her door. "You want to check out my outfit before you make up your mind, lawman?" She pushed the door wide open and stretched those long legs out into the night air, revealing that all she was wearing below her waist was a pair of panties that would make the girls down at Victoria's Secret blush. She raised one leg and ran her hands down its full silken length just to make sure I got the point.

I stared for a second. What man wouldn't—she radiated sex.

"We don't have to go inside," she said, her voice husky. "You could do me right here. More exciting that way. Somebody might even see us."

And then the moment was broken when Frick advanced and started barking. It was an urgent, rapid-fire, shepherd warning bark, and as Rue turned to look at the shepherd, I saw the knife on the seat right next to her. It was a long boning knife of some kind, with a wooden handle and a glinting, slightly curved blade nearly eight inches long. She moved her hand to push it out of sight, and Frick jumped at her. She quickly withdrew into the truck and slammed the door.

"Well, my goodness, lawman," she said breathlessly. "That there dog is downright im-po-lite. What a party pooper." Her voice was still teasing, but the look in her eyes was something entirely different. She knew that I'd seen that knife, and that I had to be wondering.

I cleared my throat. "That dog is telling me that you're a dangerous woman, Miss Creigh," I said. "I think you're gonna have to find another party tonight. Nice seeing you. So to speak."

She tried to laugh off being rejected, but there was a flash of pure hatred in her eyes. I waved and turned away to go back to my cabin. Frick put herself between the truck and me until Rue fired it up and drove off. On the way out of the parking lot she deliberately sideswiped a brand-new SUV parked in the lot, carving a nasty crease down its full length with the truck's rusty back bumper.

Well, well, I thought, *that would have been a ride.* Then I reminded myself of Bobby Lee's little maxim that served to douse any physical regrets at missed sexual opportunities: *If she'll do you, handsome, she'll do anyone and probably has.* Besides, I told myself, I had some serious thinking to do. And then, of course, there was that knife, right there on the seat. *Do me here in the parking lot,* she'd suggested. *And while you're at it, I'll plant this steely beauty somewhere between your liver and lights. If we can't get you one way, we'll try something a lot closer up.*

Mose Walsh was right—I hadn't appreciated the danger.

7

The phone rang at five thirty the next morning; I fumbled for a bedside table lamp and then answered. It was Carrie Santángelo.

"You need to get out of there," she said without preamble.

"I do?"

"Yep. I called Sheriff Hayes last night after I talked to you. I wanted to know what was shaking with the Robbins County beef. He said he was still waiting for Mingo to make the next move. I told him that you had a working relationship with the SBI and asked if he could keep me in the loop. He said he would."

"And?"

"I just got a call here in my room from Hayes's operations office. Mingo sent a telex in, saying he had a warrant for your arrest and would be coming down to Carrigan County at seven this morning to execute it, and would they please have a couple of deputies available to come along. The watch officer called Hayes, and he called me."

I was fully awake now. "How'd they get a warrant without a body?"

"Robbins County," she said. "Who the hell knows? But you need to get out of there, and now would be nice. I've got a place for you to go. Meet me out front in fifteen minutes."

She was in the parking lot in an SBI unmarked Crown Vic when I came out, carrying a hastily packed bag and accompanied by two yawning shepherds. "Follow me," she said, and I fired up the Suburban.

We drove through the predawn darkness to the Thirty Mile ranger station toll booth. There was a chain across the entry road, but plenty of room on both sides to get around it. We drove past the darkened Park Service offices and then down a paved road that led up into the park itself. The paved road became a hard-packed gravel road after a few miles, but that didn't slow Carrie down. I had to drop back just to be able to see through all the dust. Six miles up the road we pulled into a clutch of log cabins scattered around a woodsy playground area. There were cars parked at the darkened cabins, and it was a busy hiking and camping season if the overflowing trash bins were any indication. Carrie drove through the little village and up a steep side road to a single cabin surrounded by tall pine trees, where she stopped and parked her car.

"This is one of the Park Service ranger cabins," she told me when I got out.

"Except the DEA's had it requisitioned for the past year. Occasionally the SBI gets joint use."

"For that investigation that isn't going on?" I asked. The cabin was perhaps twenty-five feet square, with wraparound porches and a stone chimney at one end. The dogs ran around, Frick checking out the new surroundings, Frack insulting trees.

"Possibly. Come on inside."

"Presumably there's no one home right now?" I asked, as she unlocked the front door, barged right in, and started turning on lights. I half-expected a sleepy DEA agent to come stumbling out, gun in hand. There was a single large room, a small loft, and a kitchen–dining room combination occupying the left back corner. There was a bunkroom and a bath in the opposite back corner. A table was set up next to the fireplace, which was covered with wireless communications gear, cell phone chargers, and a desktop PC.

"There are basic provisions in the cupboards," she said, "and I'll bring you some fresh stuff once the stores open. But for right now, you're legally on a federal reservation."

"And theoretically, county cops have no jurisdiction here."

"Unless the Park Service accommodates them, which it won't once I get to someone at their district HQ over in Gatlinburg. You are going to play ball, right?"

"Only if you were serious about the decoder ring," I said, and she grinned. We both knew that, at the moment anyway, I had little choice but to take their deal.

"Great," she said. "Why don't you make us some coffee, and I'll explain what we need from you."

She went back out to her car to get her briefcase while I loaded a Mr. Coffee machine I found on the kitchen counter. Carrie came back in and produced a contract and some credentials she had had made up identifying me as an authorized operational consultant for the North Carolina SBI. Over coffee she explained what the SBI wanted me to do.

"We'd like you to go back into Robbins County, on foot, and do a few days' worth of physical reconnaissance."

"The Creigh place again?"

"No," she said. "The hollows around the Creigh place. There are several smaller communities up there—cabins, trailers, even some substantial homes, within five miles of the Creigh place. Some of those people have to be working for them, but there are other people up there who have nothing to do with the Creighs. Retirees on government or coalfield pensions, tenth-generation welfare rednecks composting in their trailers, good old boys with hunting pens."

"And bad guys, too."

"Oh, yes: the bootleggers, marijuana farmers, psycho-mushroom pickers, and, of course, the meth mechanics."

"You guys have a database for the area?"

"ATF does, but they know it's woefully deficient. Every time feds go up there, Robbins County deputies go along and, they suspect, call ahead. Everyone of interest just clams up. The regular citizens either don't know or are afraid to run their mouths, and sometimes they're just loyal to their hills and hollows and won't talk to outsiders, period. DEA has had the same experience, and the Bureau has flat given up."

"What makes you think I won't get the same treatment?"

"Outside law has always come in crowds; we are going to be a couple of hikers."

I put down my coffee mug. "We?"

"Oh, didn't I tell you?" she asked brightly. "I'm coming along." She started laughing when she saw the expression on my face.

"Oka-a-ay," I said. "But now you have to tell me what this is really all about, because it's obviously bigger than drugs."

"I have a better idea," she said. "We'll go up there and look around. After a few days, we'll back out, and then I think you'll be able to tell *me* what this is all about. That way I won't taint your conclusions."

"We're just going to walk the hills and dales, go knocking on people's doors, talk nice to the moonshiners when we stumble on their stills, evade any of Mingo's deputies who happen to live out there in some of these houses, and keep telling ourselves that Grinny Creigh won't find out we're up there?"

"Something like that, yes," she said. "Look: We've got all the aerial photography, topo maps, suspected smuggling routes, IR plume shots of supposedly abandoned shacks and trailers that go hot at night, arrest trends with links back to Robbins County, in other words, tons of data. What we don't have is any HUMINT—human source ground truth."

"But why not? The feds have certainly been looking."

"Basically, none of the alphabets has ever been able to get probable cause to do search and seizure because M. C. Mingo undoes their every attempt, one way or another. That's why the feds came to us in the first place. Plus, they've been totally unable to get anyone undercover because the bad guys, one, are all related and, two, have known each other since the Blue Ridge first turned blue."

"The feds want to break up a drug ring, and the SBI wants to clean out a dirty sheriff's office," I said. "Seems like a match made in cop heaven. Why not declare them all suspected terrorists and take them down to Guantánamo for a year or so? Hit 'em so hard they can't recover for a few generations."

"Because," she said patiently, "the government is already under siege by lawyers and civil rights activists over the detention of real live car-bombing, throat-slitting, Koran-thumping Muslim fanatics. These people are, for better or for worse, Americans."

"So are the Crips and the Bloods, but the feds walk all over those guys from time to time, if only to thin 'em out."

"The feds have people *inside* those operations. Real-time intelligence. Major deals they can rumble and then seize. Up here, these people are making the shit in caves and the tunnels of old mines. Everyone's kin. You piss off the boss and you get eaten by dogs, right?"

"And why me, again?" I asked.

"A couple of reasons," she said, finishing her coffee. "One, you've been up there and made it back. Two, you've seen some of the players up close and personal. And, three—well, I can't tell you that one. Yet."

I stood up and walked around the cabin's main room. "And, three, as a consultant, if things go really wrong, the SBI can deny me three times before sunrise and keep its bureaucratic skirts clean."

"Such a cynic," she said. "We're not that clever."

"Oh, right. Okay, try this: Three, I'm officially a fugitive from a warrant in Robbins County. So if things really go wrong, you can say that you were in pursuit of a fugitive, and that's why you were up there in the first place."

"Now you're talking," she said, again with a grin. "Consider yourself a target of opportunity. If you can get us what we need, great. If not, we're no worse off than when we started."

"Which doesn't necessarily describe where I'd be."

"That's one of the perks of going private," she said.

I smiled. "Damn, Carrie, you really know how to make a guy feel wanted."

"Oh, you're wanted, all right," she said. "Just call M. C. Mingo."

I had no reply for that, so I tried to change the subject. "You physically qualified to walk the high country?" I asked. "And run, if necessary?"

"Absolutely," she said. "And I can climb, too. Straight up rock walls, if I have to. Can you climb?"

"Only if the bear is big enough," I said. *Or the pig*, I thought, remembering our little scamper up the pine trees.

"Well, there you go, operational consultant. And if I choose to run, you know the bear rule, right?"

"Yeah, yeah, you don't have to outrun the bear, you only have to outrun me. Who's going to handle logistics? You're not proposing we tote a bunch of supplies, are you?"

"That's where Mr. Greenberg and his crew come in," she replied. "They're going to go 'camping' in the national park. We'll get up with them once a day to resupply and to report what we've seen."

"Can they act as cavalry if the need arises?"

"Not legally," she said. "Which isn't to say they won't come. But the whole idea is to put a small team on the ground, not a federal horde."

I sat back down in one of the chairs. "A whole grunch of questions come to mind here," I said.

"What can I tell you," she said, flicking her hair away from her eyes. "You said you liked to go camping."

We set out late that afternoon. Greenberg and his team had hired Mose Walsh to bring in their camping gear at noon by truck, and then they'd staged everything up to a fire-lane road in the park at the upper end of Crown Lake. From there we could walk down through a pass to a gentle valley that was two ridges over from the Creighs' home base. The plan was for the pair of us to set up a camp just below the ridge at the head of the valley that evening, and then begin our photo "hike" down the first valley and up the adjacent one, returning to the park boundaries by nightfall. Greenberg and his crew would maintain the base while keeping at least one agent in a position from which he could maintain line-of-sight communications with Carrie and me using DEA tactical radios. Mose would handle resupply on a daily basis.

Carrie and I wore civilian backpacks and field belts, and we each carried a shelter half and a sleeping bag rolled on packs supplied, once again, by Mose Walsh. I had a sport-fisherman's vest, under which I wore my SIG .45. Carrie carried a weapon I hadn't seen before, a nasty little number that she called a mamba stick. It looked like and served as a pool-cue-shaped walking stick but could fire up to six .223-caliber bullets with a flick of the wrist. It was part six-shooter, part rifle. To fire it, all she had to do was pick off the tip of the walking stick, ratchet the base end to the left to cock it, point it, and then press a small button to fire each round—basically a single-action bang stick.

I relaxed a little when I saw her decked out in well-worn outdoors clothes and boots. My gear was similarly well broken in; I spent at least two weekends out of each month somewhere in North Carolina either fishing, hunting, or just taking the mutts out for a spin. Once every two hours one of us would open the radio and ask *Can you hear me now,* aping those ubiquitous Verizon commercials and probably annoying the shit out of the duty DEA comms agent. We set up our first camp alongside a pretty stream in a high meadow. This put us on the eastern boundary of the national park. The entire valley spread out below us, and we hoped to see some lights below us when darkness fell.

It turned out that Carrie did not cook at all. "My father was an excellent cook and wouldn't tolerate women in the kitchen," she said. "At least not until dinner was over and there were pots to be washed."

"How do you survive?" I asked, as we unpacked our stuff.

"I'm a charter member of the nuclear age," she said. "I buy it, I nuke it, I eat it. Unless I can con some guy to do better."

"You could con me," I said. "But then I'm easy."

She smiled. "Good—you do the honors around the campfire, and I'll handle what has to happen in the creek."

"Deal," I said. I boiled up a cup of rice over the fire and then added a package of dehydrated chili and the required water. In the coals I made some biscuits in a collapsible Dutch oven and then set up a coffeepot on one side of the coals. The shepherds each got a cup of dry kibble, although they made it perfectly clear that chili would have been a much better deal. We ate in contented silence as we watched the sun go down behind the western mountains, throwing the valley below into deeper and deeper shadows.

"This going to be worth the effort?" I asked.

"I think it will, especially if you come to the same conclusions that we have. Then things might get interesting."

"That tells me a lot," I said. "I mean, how are we going to play this?"

"We're photojournalists," she said. "We're doing a photographic essay on life in the mountains on the edge of the Great Smokies Park. We meet the people, photograph them if they'll let us, their houses, their farms, their dogs, and then interview them as to what life's really like up here in what the maps label as game lands."

"Eventually we'll stumble onto one of Grinny's retainers," I said. "And then we're going to have some problems."

"There are more righteous people down there than you might suspect," she said, pointing down at the lights that were beginning to twinkle through the trees down the valley. "According to our aerial maps, a dirt road parallels this creek all the way to where it empties into a river. There are maybe two dozen cabins, houses, what have you, along that road. They can't all work for Grinny Creigh."

I fished around in my pack for a nylon windbreaker; even in late summer, the air temperature dropped like a stone once the sun went down. "It just takes one," I said. "And they'll recognize me, especially with these dogs."

"Then we do what we have to do," she said. "By the way, was that a flask I saw in your pack?"

I looked at her. "You're a pushy broad, aren't you."

"You gonna share?"

"Aarrgh," I said. "I hate sharing."

"I can talk all night, if you'd like. I can even sing."

"Of course you can. I'll get the flask."

The first place we came to the next morning featured an immaculate stone cottage surrounded by gardens and small alpine pastures in which sheep congregated. The people who lived there were both retired from the postal service and were refreshingly friendly. I noticed that the line of power company poles extended up the dirt road as far as their cottage, so these people were living comfortably in the twenty-first century. It turned out in the course of Carrie's questions that they had never heard of the Creighs or of any particular crime problem in or around Robbins County. They also seemed to have no problem accepting our photojournalist cover story.

The next three homes down were similar situations, retired people who had always wanted to live in the mountains and enjoy the privacy and rustic beauty of the Smokies. The closer we got to the bottom end of the valley, however, the less appealing the home places were. Log cabins and stone cottages gave way to trailers, and gardens to collections of junked cars and trucks. Up the valley the dogs had been friendly if alert; at the lower end they were chained to trees or old cars and inclined to drooling snarls. I kept the two shepherds on the creek side of the road; the last thing we needed was a dog fight.

The first two trailers we passed seemed to have no one home except for some angry dogs. The third one, an especially nasty pile of rusted metal, with loose trash, a hard-packed dirt yard, and a lone, scabrous two-year-old playing in an abandoned tire, was occupied by a man and woman of indeterminate age. Several dogs could be heard barking from behind the trailer, and they didn't sound very happy, either. There was an electric power pole in the yard, but the meter base was empty. Carrie sighed as if she'd seen all this before.

I held the shepherds over by the creek bank while Carrie unslung her pack and approached the yard to ask if they'd be interested in being "interviewed." The man, a paunchy, hairy, and paranoid-looking individual wearing blue-jean overalls and a filthy T-shirt told her to get on out here or he'd set them dogs yonder aloose. The woman, a stringy-haired stick figure whose dark-rimmed raccoon eyes indicated an end-stage addiction of some kind, hung back in the doorway of the trailer, a cigarette dangling from her lips and a vacant expression on her face. The child playing in the dirt never looked up during the entire interchange. Carrie waved and backed off to rejoin me on the other side of the dirt road. The man finally saw the shepherds and reached down to pick up an axe handle. He yelled something else at us, but whatever he said was drowned out by the barking dogs behind the trailer. I walked ten feet behind Carrie, and made sure the shepherds stayed between us and the hostiles.

The next two trailers appeared to be abandoned. The final place had beef cattle and a two-story nineteenth-century log house, but there was no one at home except for two small collies, who cowered when they saw the German shepherds. The steers looked well fed and the fences were in good order, so it was a working farm. By late afternoon we'd reached the lower end of the valley, where the stream joined a larger one in a pretty waterfall after crossing under a mostly paved one-lane road. There was a perfect campsite on the point formed by the juncture of the two streams, downhill from the paved road and partially hidden behind a stand of stunted pines. It had obviously been used before, based on the blackened ring of stones in the clearing above the streams.

We set up our tents and a small fire and then went to soak tired feet in the cold stream. Our campsite was on the high, western bank of the stream, and we could see a large tree that had fallen across the water about thirty yards upstream. Its top surface had been flattened and there was a single rope handrail, indicating a crossing point for a local footpath. The sun dropped below the ridges behind us at the top of the valley and darkness settled quickly, followed by the temperature. The dogs curled in as close to the hot rocks around the fire as they could.

We had seen fewer people than I'd expected, but there also had been some chained driveways leading back into the woods and slopes where we had elected not to go. I'd let Carrie call the shots as to where we tried and where we simply passed by. She seemed to have a good sense of which was which. I found myself warming to her—she was practical, carried her share of the load, laughed often, and was easy on the eyes. She maintained that quiet reserve I'd observed in many attractive women, who knew full well that men were likely to make assumptions about their character based on looks rather than competence.

That was fine with me. This was not exactly a romantic excursion in the making, and I was still worried about some of the people we'd seen. I kept thinking about that homing dog Nathan had fired down the meadow. I'd also begun to appreciate the problem law enforcement had in coming to grips with criminal enterprises in the mountains; short of bringing in an occupying army, there was no way even to tell how many people actually lived up here. Based on some of the signs we'd seen, the people who'd built homes here valued their privacy and were more than willing to defend it.

We checked our communications with the DEA base camp over on the lake and then heated some food. Afterward we sat around the fire and talked about our experiences in law enforcement. During the whole time we'd been down there, I realized, we hadn't heard a single vehicle up on the road above. The woods around us were extremely quiet, with no animal or even bird sounds. There was a dim moon, but the stars blazed above us in the crystalline mountain air.

"You know," I said quietly, looking around at the clearing, "this would be a bad place to be if someone were to come at us in the night. We'd be trapped with our backs against these two streams."

"You think those people in that one trailer recognized you, don't you?"

"It's possible," I said. "That guy looked pretty hungover, and he obviously didn't cotton to strangers. And that woman was in bad shape. I'm thinking maybe we should move our bags over across the stream, just in case."

"Leave the tent halves?"

"Yeah; bank the fire, leave the shelter halves, make it look like we're sleeping down here. I just think there may be more eyes watching these hills than we know about."

Carrie shivered. "That's a lovely image. And I suppose I have to cross that damned log up there? In the dark?"

I grinned. "It's been there a while," I said. "And there's a hand rope. Piece'a cake."

"Unh-hunh. For those of us who don't like heights, not exactly."

"I'll hold your hand," I said. "Let's see if there's some flat ground over there behind those big rocks."

Getting the dogs across the tree-trunk bridge turned out to be harder than getting Carrie across. We set up a bare-bones camp behind three large boulders. There was a thick carpet of windblown pine needles on the back side, which would make for more comfortable sleeping, but I still sprayed the sleeping bags with DEET before setting them down in hope of deterring the five billion or so ticks and spiders I knew were lurking in that aromatic piney carpet. While Carrie got settled, I went back across the log bridge and climbed up to the road. Using a small LED flashlight, I finally found what I was looking for, two serviceable if rusty tin cans. With my knife and some fine fishing line from my woods vest, I rigged a tripwire consisting of the tin cans with pebbles inside, to cover the approaches to the log bridge on the road side. We might not hear it if we were sound asleep, but the shepherds would.

Then I went down to the original campsite, added a few thick logs to the edge of the fire, piled the stone ring a little bit higher, closed up the shelter halves, and returned to our sleeping hide.

"I miss my tent," Carrie said from deep inside her sleeping bag as the evening dew began to draw the chill from the ground. I rolled my bag around in the pine needles, took off my boots, and slithered in. Frick came over immediately and curled up.

"Call one of the dogs over if you get cold," I said, looking over at her, fondly, I realized. All I could see of her was the pale oval of her face against the indistinct material of the sleeping bag. "If that doesn't work, you can always call me."

"In your dreams," she said sleepily.

"Well, yeah," I said. "Is that news?"

"That's your libido talking," she said. "Baby Greenberg tell you my nickname at work?"

"That he did."

"Well, I haven't been exactly successful in my relationships with men," she said. "I've about given up."

"If it's not lust at first sight, then the trick is to become friends and let the physical side come along when you least expect it."

She sat up on one elbow. "That the voice of experience?"

I told her about how I'd gotten back together with my ex-wife. How we'd operated as just friends until the night when our respective libidos had come up-scope in the hot tub, as sometimes happens. I also told her what had happened to Annie, and that while I wasn't avoiding relationships, I wasn't actively looking for one, either.

She was quiet after that, and I had to smile. Our conversation sounded an awful lot like the BS boys and girls say to one another so as to not be seen as taking that first, potentially embarrassing step. I thought she'd gone to sleep.

"You have that thunder stick ready in there?" I asked, just to make sure.

"Mmm-hnnh."

She drifted off to sleep, but for some reason I wasn't sleepy. Maybe it was just instinct, but I had a sense that the night wasn't over yet. It had been too easy, our little hike through the hollow. I reached over to my pack, retrieved the flask, and shucked the sleeping bag. I put my boots and jacket back on and tiptoed over to the one flat rock overlooking the junction of the two streams. The waterfall made a soothing sound as it plashed over mossy rocks and snags. The scent of mud, wet weeds, and dank stone wafted up out of the creek bed, and a few horny frogs sounded off from time to time, defying their reptilian thermostats. The fire flared briefly across the way as one of the larger logs rolled over in a shower of sparks.

I tried to figure out what it was she was waiting for me to detect among the hill people. They had been, all things considered, about as I had expected, an eclectic mixture of retirees, working families, and farmers, as well as layabout white trash. Tomorrow we would walk north along this larger creek and then head up the next valley to rendezvous with our DEA support team. I wondered what they were doing to amuse themselves; probably spying on Grinny Creigh's lair in the second valley over. The fire across the water looked inviting, and I wondered if I hadn't become a bit paranoid about nighttime attackers. I poured a second cap of scotch, tossed it off, and went back to my own bedroll. The shepherds were both curled around the indistinct form of Carrie's sleeping bag. *Faithless mutts*, I thought. It wasn't *that* cold.

I awoke to the sound of a large truck laboring its way up the one-and-a-half-lane road above the creek. I sat up, rubbed my eyes, and shivered in the cold air. The two shepherds came over and helpfully licked my face while I struggled to get my arms out of the sleeping bag. Carrie remained asleep. I unzipped my bag, got up, and reached for my boots and jacket. The truck sounded like it was about a half mile away, but it was definitely coming this way. The moon had gone over the mountains to the west, deepening the darkness. Even so, I could see fairly well in the starlight.

I checked my watch, and wondered why a big rig would be coming up the mountain at this hour in the morning. An owner-driver coming home after a ten-day cross-county stretch? I checked my SIG .45 and wondered if I should wake Carrie. She was certainly physically fit, but she was also an office rat, and all this mountain trekking had put her down like the proverbial log. I moved quietly down to the edge of the big boulders and tried to see across the creek. The fire had declined to a red glow, and the pines above were pitch-black. The truck kept coming. The shepherds had left Carrie and were tight alongside me, ears up.

Finally I saw it, or rather its marker lights. It was running without headlights and coming up in a low gear, the diesel working at high RPM. I could make out the cab lights, and the fact that there was some kind of trailer behind the truck. As it got closer, I could see something black and bulky behind the cab, but couldn't make it into a trailer. The dogs were fully alert now as they sensed my own rising tension. When the rig finally drew abreast of the campsite, some fifty feet up on the road, I realized it was a logging truck with a full load of huge logs. Even as I comprehended what I was seeing, the tractor veered over toward the edge of the road and then swung hard left as if trying for the dirt road we'd walked down earlier. But the trailer came much too far to the right and the wheels slipped over the road's edge. The entire load, several thousand pounds of logs, came right off with a thunderous noise, tumbling huge logs down the slope, smashing everything in their path, including our original campsite. One log hit the fire end-on, showering red sparks and embers into the creek in a spray of fire. Most of the logs ended up in the larger creek, and the trailer itself slid down the embankment for about twenty feet before finally stopping and then doing a slow-motion rollover onto its right side. The tractor cab remained on the road above, its engine still roaring, until the driver finally idled it. Carrie appeared at my side, the mamba stick in her hands.

"What the fuck?" she whispered, as the last of the big logs rolled over the bank and crashed down into the creek. Frick woofed at all the noise. I told her to shut up.

"Bad luck for the campers over there," I said. "Notice the truck didn't come down the hill with its trailer?"

"Which means?"

"Which means this may have been deliberate. He did something to the hitch and the tie-downs before he shed that load. I think we're supposed to be dead under all that stuff."

The trucker shut down the engine and doused all his lights. I motioned for Carrie to follow me into the jumble of big rocks. I chose a position from which we could see the tree-trunk bridge upstream.

"Now what?" she whispered.

"Let's see if anyone comes down there to admire his handiwork."

With the trucker's lights off, we could see the hillside across the way fairly well. Nothing happened for a few minutes, but then we heard another vehicle coming. This time it was a pickup truck, approaching from the right, also with no lights. The truck made a normal stop in front of the tractor, which told me the driver had expected it to be there. We could hear doors opening and closing, followed by the sounds of low voices. We heard and then saw four men pushing their way through all the wrecked vegetation and flattened pine trees to the area of the campsite. Two of the men were carrying what looked like shotguns.

"That what you bring to an accident scene?" I whispered. "Shotguns?"

Flashlights snapped on, and I pushed Carrie down behind one of the rocks as I ducked my own head. Moments later two white beams were probing the tops of our rock pile and then the creek bank on our side. I signaled the dogs to lie flat and stay there.

"Ya git 'em?" a familiar voice called from the road above.

"I believe that's Nathan Creigh," I whispered to Carrie.

"They ain't here," one of the men opposite called back. "Ain't nothin' here but some hot rocks."

"They *was* there," Nathan called. "Spread out and find 'em. Look down in that creek."

"Found a piece'a tent," another voice called. "Tore *all* to hell."

"Then look down in that water, under them logs," Nathan ordered. "Grinny's gonna want'a know we seen meat."

I motioned for Carrie to follow me. We crawled on our bellies along the back of the rock pile until we had a clearer view of the log bridge. Carrie wiggled up alongside me. "Get on the radio and see if you can raise Greenberg's boys," I said. "Tell them what happened. I'll watch the bridge."

"They're off the air until morning, remember?" she said.

"Try anyway; they may have left a radio on. Hell, they probably heard that crash. Then come back over here. I'll cover the bridge."

Carrie disappeared into the gloom in the direction of our sleeping bags. I could hear the men crashing around the banks on the other side of the creek below me, trying to see under the massive pile of logs. After about fifteen minutes, I finally saw a shadow moving up the bank toward the log bridge. Carrie still hadn't returned, so I pulled the two shepherds close to me, one on either side, and lay down with them. I put a hand gently over each of their muzzles and stared at the bridge in the darkness. The dogs went very still and watched where I was watching.

I felt them tense and I squeezed their muzzles again, reinforcing the command to not bark or growl. I stared into the darkness, offsetting my gaze to put my peripheral vision on the bridge. I never saw the man start to cross, but I did hear a tinkle of gravel in the tin cans and then a soft oath.

"Wait," I murmured to the shepherds, whose heads were alongside mine and whose concentration was absolute. I hoped Carrie had heard the tin cans, too, and remembered what that meant. I was flat on the ground a good thirty feet from the bridge. I still couldn't see anything against the stand of pines. I waited, one hand cupped gently over each dog's nose.

There. A thicker shadow. The man was alerted, which was probably why he wasn't using his flashlight. He was creeping, his footfalls masked by the thick blanket of pine needles. I felt Frick gathering herself, so I finally whispered the command: Take.

The dogs launched without a sound into the darkness like two furry torpedoes. I was suddenly blinded by the beam of a flashlight, which then shot into the air as Frick hit the man from one side in the knees while Frack hit him full-on in the chest going at the speed of heat. Two hundred pounds of determined German shepherd knocked the man flat in an instant, and Frack contained his target's cry by clamping his jaws around the man's throat and standing over him, growling quietly every time he moved. The flashlight had fallen ten feet away and was still on, pointing at a tree.

I got up and hurried over to retrieve the flashlight. I swept the area of the bridge to make sure no one else was coming and then pointed it down into the man's terrified face. I was pretty sure the men down in the creek bed couldn't see anything but the light's beam, but then I remembered that Nathan was up on the road. There were trees between where we were and the road, but I wasn't going to take any chances with a long gun. I switched off the light and then felt Carrie at my side.

"Nobody home," she whispered. Suddenly there was a strong odor of urine. I cupped my hand over the flashlight lens, pointed it down into the man's face, and switched it back on. Frack still had him by the throat but was looking up at me as if to say, *This still necessary?* The man's eyes were rolled back in their sockets and he was entirely still.

"Is he dead?" Carrie asked.

"Fainted," I whispered, and called Frack off. I ordered them to watch the man and went back over to the rock pile, where we could hear the other men still thrashing around down in the creek bed.

"Y'all got 'em?" Nathan called down from up on the road.

"They gone," one of the men answered. "Ain't no sign of 'em."

"Look across the creek, then," Nathan ordered. "That there fire was goin'. That's where they was."

"Tommy is doin' that," one of the men called back. "Hey, Tommy? Seen anything?"

I nudged Carrie to follow me and went back to where Tommy was still lying on the ground. He was short and thin. His open mouth revealed the blackened, rotten teeth of a meth devotee. His throat was already starting to bruise. I grabbed the man's legs and pointed Carrie to the other end.

"What're we doing?" she whispered.

"Throw him down into the creek where they are," I said. "While they deal with that, we'll boogie."

We carried Tommy over to the end of the rock pile and got into position to launch him.

"Hey, Tommy?" the man below called. "Where the hell are ye?"

On a silent three, we heaved the inert Tommy over the bank's edge and down into the tangle below. I switched on the flashlight and threw it after him. Tommy rolled down the bank in a clatter of stones and pine branches, while the flashlight hit the rocks and ended up in the water.

We ran for our bedrolls as we heard a commotion break out down below.

"Which way?" Carrie said.

"Cross that log bridge, head up the slope toward the trucks."

"*Toward* the trucks?" she asked.

"Last thing they'll expect," I said, grabbing my sleeping bag and pack.

"Last thing *I'd* expect," she said, but by then we were trotting toward the bridge, the shepherds right behind us. We crossed the log and moved as quietly as we could into the stand of pines below the road and then sideways up the hill. There were three flashlights going down in the creek bed and a lot of shouting between Nathan and his crew in the creek. We reached the road's edge about a hundred feet to the right of the pickup truck. It sounded as if Nathan had gone down the hill, so we slipped into our packs and moved out onto the road, where we began to jog away from the scene in the direction of the next valley.

After we'd gone for about ten minutes, I stopped and told Carrie to hold up for a moment. I caught my breath and then called in the dogs and told them to sit.

"Okay, guys," I said, and they looked at me expectantly. "Wanna sing? Hunh? Wanna sing?"

The shepherds started to pant eagerly. I threw back my head and let go with a mellifluous wolf howl for about twenty seconds. As soon as I stopped, Frack stuck his muzzle in the air and did likewise, followed by Frick. I did it again, and the shepherds really got into it this time, yipping and rooing for a good minute.

"Okay," I said, shutting off the serenade. "Let's go."

"What the hell was that?" Carrie asked, as we resumed our trot up the dark road.

"I wanted to spook those bastards," I said. "Especially when Brother Tommy comes to and tells his tale."

"Worked for me," she said.

By sunrise we were hiding out in a barn about three miles upstream. We made contact with the DEA team on the radio and agreed to rendezvous on the southern slopes of Spider Mountain just before sunset. I debriefed Greenberg on the attack of the night before. He agreed to send a vehicle around from Marionburg to see what remained of the logging-truck wreck.

The old barn was concealed from the road by a knoll of trees and was about a hundred feet above it. We had taken turns keeping watch in case Nathan and his boys decided to get their own dogs and do some tracking, but there'd been no movement or traffic along the road until well after sunrise. We waited until midmorning, then set off up the hill.

Our excursion up the second valley produced six home sites, but only one person, an elderly woman, had been willing to talk to us. The rest either ran us off or wouldn't come out of their trailers and cabins. When the old lady introduced herself as Laurie May Creigh, I'd been alarmed, but it turned out that Laurie May, although related, had no time for the likes of Grinny Creigh and all her evil works. She'd invited us onto her front porch, offered cold tea and some homemade muffins, and told us she'd be pleased to set a spell and talk. The porch was in shadow as the sun began its late-afternoon arc into the mountains.

She said she was eighty-and-some years old, and she looked it, although she displayed no visible infirmities beyond the measured movements of that great age. There appeared to be no electricity in the log cabin where she lived, but the place was clean and orderly, with freshly split firewood piled neatly all along the front and side porches and the yard free of the clutter we'd seen at most of the mountain trailers. There were three small outbuildings behind the cabin, one of which contained a dozen chickens. There was a curious circle of dense pines on the slope above the outbuildings. Her cabin was three-quarters of the way up the slope from the one-lane road and overlooked the crashing creek that had created the hollow in the first place. There was one more homestead above hers.

"'At woman ain't no damned good," Laurie May pronounced, banging her cane for emphasis. "We's kin, you know, but I don't own to the likes of her. She and that no-good son of hers, that Nathan, they's the reason folks 'round here call this hill back yonder *Spider* Mountain. Real name is Book Mountain. The onliest spider is over yonder in the next holler."

"We've heard some stories," Carrie said, trying to make it sound casual. I sat on the front steps with the dogs, while Carrie sat in one of the rockers on the porch. I'd decided to let Carrie do the interview, although the old lady seemed willing enough to talk.

Laurie May reached under her rocker for a small leather bag, opened drawstrings, and pinched some dipping tobacco into her lower lip. "They call her *Grinny* Creigh, but her real name's Vivian. Once her pap passed, she'n her brothers commenced to fussin' and feudin' over who was gonna run the 'shine business in these here parts. Years ago, that was. The brothers turned up dead, all but one, and that's when folks started callin' her Grinny. The live one became sheriff down in Rocky Falls, and he's of a stripe with Vivian."

"Who was Nathan's father?" Carrie asked.

"Some damn viper snake, spit itself out of a log," Laurie May said promptly. "That boy is downright crazy." She spat over the porch rail into a much abused flowerbed. "Goes around with a bag'a knives all the time. Nathan and his bag'a knives, folks say. They's an old gold mine buried in the hill behind her cabin. All played out, of course, but folks say Nathan does *things* back in there, and I believe it."

"What kind of things?"

Laurie May spat again. "Ain't no tellin'," she replied. "Bad things. Came around here back in the spring, lookin' for some man ain't no one ever heered of. I run him off, all right. I called him Dead Eyes right to his face, that's what folks call him, b'hind his back, mind you. So I told him, I says, you git the hell outta here. Had my Greener right inside the door, and he knew it, too. Him and them damned ugly dogs. Not like these pretty things. Scared my chickens off their layin' for a whole week." She pulled an ancient lace handkerchief out of her sleeve and wiped the side of her mouth. "Boy ain't right," she said, tapping her own forehead.

"We've heard the Creighs are running more than just moonshine," Carrie ventured.

The old lady looked at her over her glasses. "What kinda cops you say you was?" she asked with a sly, toothless grin.

I laughed out loud. "Told you," I said. The old lady positively beamed.

"We're state police," Carrie said, pulling out her credentials while finessing my status. "We came up here to talk to people who live around Grinny Creigh and her crowd."

"That ain't gonna happen," Laurie May snorted. "'Sides me, ain't nobody livin' this close to the spider's gonna say nothin', if they know what's good for 'em. That damn Nathan'll come creepin' in the night and burn 'em out."

"But you're not afraid of him?" I asked.

"Lemme tell ye somethin'," she said. "Once ye get my age? Don't need much sleep, 'specially at night. I watch. They know it, too. Any snakes come around here get they rattles shot at. They know that, too. 'Cain't hold that big ole Greener like I used to could, but I got me a Colt .44. Come out here in the dark, set down in this here chair, put that thing up on the railing there, I can shoot the nut out of a squirrel's mouth the long way, if you get my meanin'. Was that y'all they was after last night, all that mess over to the bottom'a Deep Creek?"

I shook my head in wonder. The hills were indeed alive. "Yes, ma'am," Carrie said. "We think they faked an accident with a log truck, turned it over right where we were camping."

Laurie May nodded. "That'll be Nathan," she said. "That's his style. Fixin' to mash ye. One night he came a'creepin up behind this old man's trailer, over to Benson Bluff? He went and sawed him a tree right down on top of that poor man's trailer. Wasn't no chain saw, neither. Did it by hand, quiet, sneaky like. Took'm all night, prob'ly. Used him an oiled whip blade, him an' one other boy. Patient damn snake, that Nathan. Mashed that old man flat. Folks thought they was gonna have to bury the whole trailer to git the job done right."

"And the sheriff?" I asked. "Couldn't he see that it was a murder?"

Laurie May spat again, and I noticed for the first time she was killing insects every time she spat into the flowerbed. "M. C. Mingo's a Spider Mountain Creigh. Sees what he's tole to see, that one does. Folks say Grinny's got somethin' on him, b'sides they bein' brother and sister. He come around here, what, a year ago? Stood right out yonder, giving me what fer 'bout talkin' to strangers, like I'm a'doin' right now. Didn't figger on my boys bein' home, did he. No, sir. I got four of 'em. *Big* boys. There's the twins, and then t'other two.

Worked them coal mines, over to *Tenn*-essee. Coupl'a them gittin' on, but just the same, they ran his potbellied little ass right off. He don't come back up thisaway no more, I'll tell you that."

"What about children?" Carrie asked. "I haven't seen many children at all up here in our travels."

Laurie May shook her head. "Mostly old folks up here these days," she said. "Ain't no work, no money 'cept the welfare. Young'ns around here, they pack up to town or one of them cities back east." She paused as if trying to remember something. "Folks do say they's a lot of children who flat run off in these here parts. Cain't blame 'em if they do. 'Specially if you see some of them mamas. No-good sluts and hoors, the lot of 'em. Go 'round with hardly no clothes on, then act all s'prised when they get a baby stuck on 'em, like they don't know wherever did it come from."

She stopped talking when we heard a truck engine drop into a low gear at the foot of the valley and begin climbing the dirt lane that paralleled the creek. Then we heard a second vehicle do the same thing.

"Y'all be gettin' inside, now," she said urgently, rocking herself up and out of her chair. "And bring them dogs, mister."

We went into the cabin, which was as neat and clean as the yard. I noted the antique double-barreled shotgun lodged near the front door. Its twin stood by the back door in the kitchen. Laurie May took us over to what turned out to be the pantry door and opened it. She motioned for me to get my fingers into a hole in the floor and then lift a five-foot-long trapdoor. She gave us a lantern and a match and told us to hide out down in the cellar until whoever it was went away. She passed the backdoor shotgun to me as Carrie went down the steps. Then she went back out onto the front porch.

I wedged the door open and lit the lantern. I pulled out the DEA radio, called Greenberg's radioman up on the mountain, and told them we were going into hiding in case whoever was coming was the Creigh gang. I described the location of the cabin and then shut it down when Laurie May stepped back into the kitchen and said to hurry, they was almost here. We went down the wooden stairs and I lowered the trapdoor. We could hear her slithering a carpet over the trapdoor and then walking back toward the cabin's front door, her cane counting time.

"There's a reason they call it a *trap*door," I said nervously. "If she's one of them . . ."

"I don't think so," Carrie said. She took the lantern and looked around. The cellar walls were made of stone, and the floor was packed earth. The shelves along one wall were filled with Mason jars of preserved foods, sacks of flour and sugar, and store-bought canned goods. There were a dozen burlap sacks of lump coal stacked along another wall; a third wall held all kinds of antique kitchen implements, soap, candles, and three more lanterns. There was a kitchen table and three wooden chairs out in the middle of the cellar. The air smelled of chalky dust and old stone. It certainly could have been a trap—there was no other way out of the cellar other than those oak steps. The shepherds sat down next to the steps and watched the shadows being thrown along the walls by the kerosene lantern.

"Why did you ask her about children?" I asked, easing myself into one the chairs. A fine halo of dust rose from the table when I sat down. We couldn't hear anything from the outside.

"We've seen a dozen or so places in two days, and exactly one two-year-old child," she replied.

"There could have been more," I said. "The people who didn't come out, or the ones who told us to get gone—there could have been kids in those places."

"Then there should have been toys, trikes, big-wheels, swings—kid clutter. I didn't see any, except at that one place."

"Well, like she said—there's no future in these hills for young people, and it's the young people who have kids. They go to town or just plain away. Makes sense."

Carrie sat down. "That makes sense for teenagers—I'm talking kids. Four-to ten-year-olds. There's one combined elementary and middle school and one high school in this county, all in Rocky Falls. They combined the elementary and the middle school three years ago because the elementary school didn't have enough new accessions to warrant keeping it open."

"The overall population dropping?"

"Not much change really, and that's part of the mystery. Now, the county people do admit they have some 'data holes' in the higher elevations."

"Probably more like bullet holes in their county vehicles," I said. We heard a door close upstairs, and then Laurie May was tapping on the trapdoor with her cane. I went up the stairs and pushed the door open.

"They done gone," she announced. "But they was a'lookin' for ye, all right. Nathan and his boys. I told 'em you and the lady done been here. Told 'em you said y'all was headed for Spider Mountain. That put 'em right off they feed, that did."

"They say what they were going to do?" I asked.

"Heard one say they was gonna go get the dogs, put a track on ye. Best leave now, and don't go nowheres near Grinny Creigh."

"We're going to go right up to the top of this valley, and then we'll probably head out," I said. "I've seen that dog pack."

"Ain't we all," Laurie May said. "But Mr. Samuel Colt works on dogs, same as men."

"Thank you for speaking to us," Carrie said.

"Most folks up here is decent folks," the old lady said. "But not on Spider Mountain. Folks knows, but they skeered."

"That's why we're here, Ms. Creigh," Carrie said. "We want to fix that problem real bad."

The old lady nodded. "'Bout time," she said. "Folks been a'wonderin'."

Baby Greenberg took a sip of coffee from a metal cup, winced, and threw the remainder of the coffee into the fire. "Goddammit, Rupe," he said, "if I wanted asphalt I'd have asked for some."

Special Agent Rupert Jones shrugged his overlarge shoulders. "Never said I could make coffee," he said. "Don't drink that shit, myself." Then he and one of the other agents left to take up their night watch positions on the slopes above Crown Lake. The other two agents had already rolled into their bags.

We were gathered around what was technically an illegal campfire on the edge of Crown Lake. The duty radioman had picked us up at the top of the valley after we'd left Laurie May's and driven us down the firebreaks to the DEA campsite. Dinner had consisted of cold pizza from Marionburg, courtesy of the agent who'd driven the lower valley road to see about the logging-truck accident. The logs had all still been down in the creek, but there'd been no sign of the truck or trailer.

"If you were a truly *special* agent," I said, "you'd have some scotch in one of those briefcases over there."

"Why, is your flask empty?" Carrie asked innocently.

"Very," I said, making a mental note to get her for that.

"Well," Greenberg said. "In fact . . ."

He got up and returned with a bottle, which duly made the rounds. My shepherds were curled up close to the fire. Once the three of us had properly equipped ourselves against the rapidly cooling mountain air, Greenberg threw another log on the fire and asked the essential question. "So: Now what're you gonna do?"

"I think we've established that this is definitely Injun country," I said.

"Gosh, you think?" he asked.

"With a damned good intel and surveillance network," Carrie said. "They knew we were up there and where we'd settled for the night. And they had no qualms about squashing their problem."

"So we have grounds for taking action," I said. "But even if you guys came in force, swept up all the black hats you could find, including Grinny and Nathan, would you have a case for court?"

We all knew the answer to that question.

"How about the old lady?" Greenberg asked. "Could she point us toward some concrete evidence?"

"I don't think so," Carrie said. "She knows what's going on and who's who in the zoo, but I doubt she ever comes off that place. Apparently she has sons who see to her needs."

"She said there are lots of decent people living up there alongside the Creigh nest, but what she's doing doesn't really affect them," I said. "And according to Laurie May, if they do poke their nose in where it doesn't belong, big trees fall on their cabins at night."

"Shit," Greenberg sighed. "We're nowhere. Again."

"I say you all quit creeping around the hills, playing their game, and take a federal crew into Grinny's place, have a look at that abandoned mine that's supposed to be under her cabin. I recognized Nathan as being in charge of what happened last night, so there's probable cause."

"They'd say it was an accident with a logging truck," Greenberg pointed out. "Shit happens. The guy who came across the creek looking for you was only checking for possible victims."

"With his shotgun? And with all the logs in the creek?"

"You know and I know, but think what a lawyer could do with that in front of a judge who may or may not love the government and all its works. I mean, that applies both before and after any search. I'd hate to find a ton of evidence at Grinny's only to lose it because the search gets tossed."

Greenberg's radio crackled into life. "Incoming," reported one of the agents on the hill.

"How many?" Greenberg asked.

"One vehicle. Stand by." Then he came back. "Looks like a sheriff's patrol car."

"Ours or theirs?" I wondered aloud.

By then we could hear a vehicle approaching along the shoreside dirt road. Its headlights pitched bizarre shadows on the boulder piles just above us.

"Some ranger coming to check out the fire inside the park grounds, maybe?" Carrie asked. Greenberg groaned.

The vehicle stopped about a hundred yards away. Its headlights switched off and a single individual got out, flipped on a flashlight, and started walking toward the fire. The shepherds were up and alert; I ordered them to sit down as M. C. Mingo himself stepped down the bank and into the firelight. He was in uniform and had his right hand on his gun butt. He turned off the flashlight, stared at me for a long moment, ignoring Carrie, and then addressed himself to Greenberg.

"You're Special Agent Greenberg?" he asked.

"That's right."

"And who are you, miss?"

Carrie didn't answer him. She sat back in her folding camp chair and gave him a bored look. I noticed that her right hand had drifted down to the side of her chair, where the Mamba stick was perched. I'd taken my SIG off earlier and put it in my tent with the rest of my gear.

"And who might you be?" Greenberg asked.

"You know damn well who I am, and so does this suspect over here. Why haven't you turned yourself in, *Mister* Richter?"

"Waiting for a warrant, Sheriff," I said. "Sheriff Hayes knows where I am, and then, of course, we're going to want an extradition hearing. In front of a real judge, even."

Mingo glared at me, then at Greenberg. "What are *you* people doing up here? You're DEA agents. Why wasn't this coordinated with my office?"

"I believe we're in the national park," Greenberg said, looking around innocently.

"Not all the time," Mingo said. He was tapping the flashlight against his right palm impatiently.

"Yes, all the time," Greenberg said. "Haven't strayed from the park since we've been here." His tone of voice was faintly mocking, and I could see that Mingo's temper was rising. The flashlight tapping became more intense, and the light actually switched on.

"You're required by your own regulations to inform local law enforcement whenever you're going to conduct an operation. Why wasn't this done?"

"We're just camping out here, Sheriff," Greenberg said. "You know—like an off-site? A time to kick things around, without being bothered by all that e-mail and phone calls. Talk about what we're going to do about the out-of-control drug problem in Robbins County."

Suddenly the shepherds turned to face the lake and began to growl. I turned to look in time to see three flat-bottomed boats emerging out of the darkness. Each boat held two men who were standing and pointing shotguns at us. A third sat in the stern and paddled until the boats grounded in the gravel at the shoreline.

That damned flashlight, I thought. That had been a signal.

"Now then," Mingo said in a much calmer voice, his anger melting away. He had his own sidearm in his right hand. My shepherds weren't happy with these developments.

"Everybody just sit tight," he said pleasantly. "We don't want any of my deputies here making any mistakes, right? Mister Richter, curb those dogs or they're going to get shot."

"You have to be shitting me," Greenberg protested. "Pointing weapons at federal agents? Those aren't deputies—they're just a bunch of Creigh riffraff."

"All sworn this very evening," Mingo said. "And they ain't pointing at you, Special Agent. They're pointing at this murder suspect here. Mr. Richter, walk towards me." The two agents who'd been asleep in their tents poked heads out and froze when they saw all the guns.

Mingo turned to Carrie. "You, too, young lady. You're both under arrest for assault and battery against one Tommy Weil, who swore out an affidavit in my office that you two attacked him with these two savage dogs right there."

I thought I knew what was coming next, so I decided to get the shepherds out of harm's way. "Frick," I called in a very clear voice. "Frack. *Hide!*"

Before any of the humans could react, both dogs bolted, going in different directions into the darkness. One of the men in the boats swung his shotgun, but his target was already out of sight. I could see that Greenberg was about to get into it in a big way, and I gave him a warning shake of the head before walking over to where Mingo stood pointing a gun at me. Carrie didn't budge.

Mingo holstered his weapon and then made me turn around and put my hands behind me so he could lock on a pair of plastic cuffs. "I said, you, too, miss. You won't like it if one of my deputies has to help you."

I wondered what the on-watch agents were doing, but I had this sick feeling that they were sitting up there somewhere on a rock with a shotgun at the back of their heads. These guys had come in off the lake without making a single sound, and that was hard to do, the way sound carries over water.

Carrie got up and walked over to the sheriff, who cuffed her with a second pair of cuffs. He stood back, drew his weapon again, and motioned for us to walk toward his cruiser, being careful to keep his distance while keeping us covered. He opened the back doors and made us get in, then slammed the doors. He turned to face Greenberg and the two agents who were still crouching in their tents.

"I suppose I should have told you I was coming," he said, it being his turn to indulge in some mockery. "You know, coordination? 'Cept I didn't know y'all were doing anything up in these parts. Y'all have a good evening, hear?"

He got into the cruiser and turned around to face us. "See that open cuff hooked to the center seat belt?" he asked. I looked down and then nodded. "Put your cuff wire through that. You, too, miss. Then close it. I believe you know the drill, *Mister* Richter."

I thought about just sitting there and making Mingo come back there and do it. But then, even if we took him out, all those so-called deputies were still there, no more than thirty feet away. There'd be some kind of violent conclusion to our efforts, so despite the fact that Carrie was staring at me with obvious telepathic intent, I turned sideways and did as I was told. She let out a long breath and did likewise.

Mingo started the car, turned it around, and headed back down the bumpy firebreak lane that encircled the lake. I looked back to see what the "deputies" were doing, but they had vanished back out into the lake. Greenberg and his two partners were standing with hands on hips around the fire, glaring at Mingo's vehicle as it drove away.

"Well now," Mingo said pleasantly, looking at us in the rearview mirror. "Young lady, you look familiar to me, but you never did say who you are. Got a name on you?"

Carrie looked out the window at nothing, completely ignoring the sheriff's question. We both had to sit partially sideways because of that center cuff.

"Aren't you going to give us our Mirandas, Sheriff?" I asked. "You know, the one that says we have the right to remain silent?"

"Consider them given, mister," Mingo said. "She *will* answer my questions, by the way. Or you can speak for her. I don't care which. She might care, though. Pretty thing. Be a shame to have to force the issue."

I decided to play Carrie's game and went silent. Mingo saw the expression on our faces and turned back around. "Okay," he said. "Easy way or hard way." He stared again at Carrie in the rearview mirror, as if trying to remember where he'd seen her before.

*   *   *

Forty-five minutes later I found myself parked in a county jail cell. The sheriff had called ahead, and two oversized uniformed deputies met us at the back of the county building in Rocky Falls. Carrie and I were separated, and I didn't know where they'd taken her. They didn't book or print me, which did not bode well.

I considered my predicament. I was the one in trouble here. Carrie could end her problem by simply telling Mingo she was with the SBI. More likely, Baby Greenberg had already contacted her bosses and Carrie was down the road and gone. But I had no such official protections. Then I remembered that I was officially an SBI operational consultant. So maybe I did have some top cover. Neither of us had had our ID or weapons on when the sheriff and his night boatmen had appeared. But why hadn't Carrie landed all over the sheriff with a ton of official SBI bullshit? Especially when she was a senior internal affairs Nazi. Why had she just gone along? Maybe there *was* something bigger going on here than she'd let on. I dropped onto the bunk and put my mind in neutral.

An hour later I heard steel doors clanging down the cell-block corridor, and then the two very large deputies arrived at my cell door. Shaved heads, six-plus feet high and about as wide, with professionally bored expressions and massive hands. Their fingers kept opening and closing. Name tags both read HARPER.

"Sheriff Mingo wants to see you," the Lurch on the left said.

"We need to cuff you?" the other one asked. He was slightly shorter than the first one, but still tall enough to worry about ceiling fans. They had to be brothers.

"As in, am I going to give you boys any shit?"

"Un-hunh."

"Can't see any future in that," I said pleasantly, as if we were just going out for a nice stroll around the grounds.

"Got that right," the first one said, sounding satisfied. His physical demeanor made it clear that even if I did try something, it wouldn't matter much. "Come on, then."

They escorted me down the cell block, but instead of going back into the central building, we went the other way and walked down to what turned out to be the back door of the jail. This led out into the sheriff's department parking lot, which was about two hundred feet square and protected by a high chain-link fence. A darkened single-story parking garage with two dozen vehicle bays closed in one side and the back. There was a much older wooden structure on the other side, which looked like it might have been the town's original jail. The lot was lighted by sodium vapor lights. There were few cars, and no one else seemed to be around.

I tensed as we walked out into the parking lot. The deputies were walking alongside me and were well inside my personal space, but neither one had put a hand on me.

"This ole boy here thinks we're gonna beat on him some," the taller of the two deputies said to the other.

"Relax, mister," the other said. "We was gonna whale on you, we'd'a done it in the cell with your cuffs on. But you can hold up right here now."

I stopped and the big deputies stepped away. The glare of the parking-lot lights put their faces in shadow. "Sheriff says you wouldn't talk to him," the first one said. "So he's done gone and got somethin' special for you. You stand right there."

They backed away from me, continuing to face me, with hands conveniently near their holstered batons. I couldn't figure out what was going on until I saw Mingo step out of one of the darkened garage bays. He had an enormous German shepherd on a leash. The dog locked on to me from fifty feet away, let out a single, impressive growl, and leaned into his harness.

"You the one likes to sic them shepherd dogs on folks?" Mingo asked, coming forward. The deputies were well out of the way now, and now they had their hands *on* their sticks. "Thought you might like to see how that feels. Ace here is fixin' to show you."

With that, he leaned forward and slipped the leash. Ace came at a run. I didn't hesitate: I dropped to my hands and knees, bent my head down to my chest, and froze. The huge dog came into me with a roar, but then stopped, practically on top of me. I could smell him and sense his enormous physical presence, but I kept my eyes on the ground and lowered my head even more, exposing the back of my neck. The shepherd came in tight and pushed his nose into my throat and then across the back of my head. I heard Mingo yelling at the dog to "git him." But Ace backed off and went into rapid-fire shepherd barking, not so much barking at me as showering me with dominance noise, just to make sure the submissive human in front of him got the message. I still didn't move, and the big dog finally shut up and sat down.

"Well, I'll be a sonuvabitch," Mingo said, walking up. "I was hopin' you'd run for it." He came over to where I was still maintaining my submissive position on the concrete. I could sense the dog relaxing and waiting for further orders.

"Okay, take him back to the cells," Mingo ordered, snapping the leash back on Ace.

The two giants came forward and helped me up, and then all three of us began to walk back toward the cell-block door. The sheriff disappeared with his dog back into the parking garage.

"How come Ace didn't bite your ass?" one of the deputies asked, as we paused by the back door.

"Shepherd rules," I said.

"But the sheriff was *tellin'* him to git ya," the other one said.

"A shepherd is an honorable dog," I said. "You come at the one he's protecting, he's going to tear you up. But if he's been trained and comes after you on command, *and* you submit, he's going to sit down. No matter what Mingo says."

"Sheriff wasn't too happy," the first one said. The other agreed.

"I'll bet the sheriff knows exactly what happened out there," I said. "You spin up a big dog like that, you have to play by shepherd rules. Otherwise, you don't have an on-off switch, do you?"

They thought about that as we went back into the cell-block corridor. They still hadn't cuffed me and seemed relaxed enough about that. "You really a sheriff's office lieutenant?" one of them asked me.

"I was; did my time in the Manceford County Sheriff's Office, then took early retirement."

They walked me to my cell and locked me back in. "You boys brothers?" I asked.

They nodded. "I'm Big Luke," the shorter of them said. "This here is Bigger John."

"Where's Mark and Matthew?" I asked with a grin.

They looked at each other, and then Luke said, "Mark's in Carson prison; killed a man when he was eighteen. He's gone upstate for twenty years. Matthew drownded in the coal mines two years ago. Just us now."

"How long have you two worked here in the sheriff's office?"

The Big brothers considered the question. They appeared to want to think about anything they said, which I considered a useful trait in policemen. They also seemed like pretty decent people, and not the kind who would associate with someone who threw unconscious kids into his cruiser like sacks of coal.

"Goin' on five years now," Big Luke said. Bigger John nodded. Five years it was. "We growed up in these parts," Luke continued. "Went off to the Army for a while, then did this and that, then came home."

"What's the sheriff have you doing?"

"Traffic, some patrol, sometimes the jail here," Luke said. "We didn't do so good in school. Mostly played ball."

I thought for a moment. They'd treated me well enough—no cell-block roughhouse or demeaning tricks. "Let me give you something to think about," I said.

"What's that?"

"Three words. You ready?"

They looked down at me patiently. John might have been counting.

"The three words are: federal task force."

Luke blinked. John frowned, then looked to Luke for guidance.

"Federal. Task. Force. Ask around, but do it outside the sheriff's office. Do *not* ask the sheriff what it means. But once you find out, think hard on it."

The door to the interior offices opened and another deputy called for the hulking brothers to come inside. I sat down on the bunk bed. I wondered what they'd done with Carrie and whether or not she'd identified herself yet as SBI. She might not. I'd seen her set that jaw.

I thought about escape. There were no other prisoners in this part of the jail. The big deputies seemed friendly enough at this juncture, but I certainly couldn't take them both down, even if I did manage to surprise them. And then what? The building's doors were operable only by mag-cards and a key code that I did not know, and getting out of the building would put me right back in the same concrete arena where I'd met the lovable Ace. The question was: If Carrie were to be sprung by her own people, would she be able to spring her "operational consultant"? I needed to get word to someone back in Manceford County. I decided to go to sleep and see what the morning brought.

8

The following morning Big Luke brought me a breakfast tray from the jail kitchens with a paper cup of coffee perched on top. He handed it to me through the food slot in the bars and then left. He came back an hour later.

"Y'all's lawyer is here," he announced as he retrieved the breakfast tray.

Lawyer? What lawyer was that? Not the high-priced esquire from Triboro, certainly. I felt the stubble on my face and wondered when I was going to get some clean clothes and a shaving kit.

Bigger John came down the corridor, followed by a man with a briefcase. He looked vaguely familiar. John unlocked the cell door and let the man in, re-locked the door, and stood patiently outside. The lawyer handed me a business card, but when I looked at it, all it said was *go with it.* When the looming deputy didn't leave, the "lawyer" looked pointedly at him. When John still didn't get the hint, he asked John to leave so that he could speak in private to his client. John said, "Oh," and then left us alone. I finally recognized the "lawyer" as one of the DEA agents from Greenberg's team. He was freshly shaved, his hair was cut, and he was wearing a suit and some lawyerly eye-glasses. He sat down on the bunk, opened the briefcase, and took out a legal pad. He patted the bunk and I sat down next to him.

"Got some documents you need to see," he said in a loud voice, pointing at the ceiling, and then showed me what was written on the pad. If anyone was listening to us, this guy wasn't going to give them an inch.

Basically the pad revealed that Carrie had been released when her boss and a team of SBI agents showed up at the sheriff's office that morning. Baby Greenberg had stashed Frick and Frack at my love-nest cabin. Mingo had pro-duced a bench warrant for my arrest and refused to release me, SBI consultant or no consultant. My hearing was tentatively scheduled for a week from today at the Robbins County courthouse.

Mingo was playing hardball because his cousin, the magistrate for Robbins County, was backing him up. The Manceford County Sheriff's Office had been informed of my predicament, as well as my real lawyer in Triboro. SBI had been unable to get Mingo to investigate the logging-truck "accident," once again because they could produce no evidence, the pile of logs in the creek notwithstanding. My Triboro lawyer was not optimistic on bail, given the rela-tionship between the sheriff and the magistrate, nor did he feel that a recusal motion had much chance of success. SBI was going to work that angle and also request a venue change. Greenberg was setting up a surveillance cell in town in order to make sure there were no late-night rides resulting in a shot-while-attempting-escape deal.

Any questions?

I took the pen and told the agent to get someone close to the two big deputies who ran the holding cells and explain what a federal task force was all about and how it might be to their advantage to switch sides before the roof fell in on Mingo.

What roof is that? the agent wanted to know.

Make one up, I wrote. *They're outside Mingo's criminal crew.*

You know *that?* the agent wrote. I hesitated, but had to shake my head. *What's Carrie Santángelo going to do?* I asked.

She's in hot water within the SBI because of this, he wrote. *Her boss couldn't explain to his boss what we were all doing out there. He's pissed. Carrie's pissed. Baby's beyond pissed.*

I need some clean clothes and bathroom gear, I wrote.

The agent shook his head. *They're going to book you and process you into the jail system today,* he wrote. *Jumpsuit city. Sorry.*

That evening I found myself the sole occupant of that small wooden building attached to the main sheriff's office headquarters. My theory that it had been the town's original jail apparently was correct, based on the interior furnishings. It was connected to the main jail wing by a breezeway across one side of the parking area. There were four cells, in a two-across configuration. Each cell had a metal bunk bolted to the floor, a seatless toilet fixture, a steel sink, and a tiny table and chair, also bolted to the floor. Unlike the main building, there were actually one-foot-square barred windows up high in the cell walls, which was fortunate because there was no other ventilation system. The front of the cell and the dividing walls were freestanding bars. The exterior walls appeared to be made of stone blocks. I half-expected to see Marshal Dillon coming through the wooden door leading out to the breezeway.

They'd booked me that morning after my "lawyer" left, taking my street clothes and issuing me a lovely orange jumpsuit, some really uncomfortable jail shoes, a blanket, a single sheet, a pillow, and some basic toiletries. I was allowed to shower and shave with a disposable razor, which Big Luke retrieved when I was finished. Then the amiable giant had escorted me to the annex, as he called it, and placed me in a cell.

"Sheriff said to put you in here on account of you bein' an ex-cop," Luke told me. "Didn't want no trouble from the other prisoners."

"What other prisoners?" I asked him.

Luke grinned and shuffled his feet. "Well," he admitted, "ain't none right now. Sheriff Mingo, he don't hold much with puttin' folks in jail, less'n it's real serious-like. The field deputies usually just take care of things, one way'n another."

" 'Taking care of business'?" I said. "That still the official motto here?"

I could see that Big Luke was just a bit nervous; perhaps it was because

John wasn't around. I decided to try a little probe. "You ever hear of a woman named Grinny Creigh?" I asked.

Luke's eyes flared in recognition. He looked around as if to make sure no one had heard that. "I gotta go now," he'd said. "Supper's down at five."

Supper had turned out to be a bag of limp greaseburgers from the town's one and only fast-food joint, which was definitely not one of the national chains. As darkness settled, I wondered why I'd really been moved out to this old building. If indeed there were no other prisoners, it would have made more sense to put me right next to the front office in the modern jail wing. The small building was appropriately gloomy; there was only a single overhead light in the aisle between the cells. Through the windows I heard a dog barking; it sounded a lot like Ace, who was probably out patrolling the parking lots now that night had fallen. It was no wonder the two brothers weren't too worried about any escape attempts, not with old Ace on the job. Anyone slinking around the parking compound at night would invoke a very different set of shepherd rules.

I looked into the bag. The fries had congealed on the bottom into a starchy mass. I ate one of the hamburgers, drank some watery Coke, and then pitched the bag through the bars into a trash can in the aisle-way. I missed my nightly scotch. My liver probably did not.

After a few hours I heard some vehicles entering and leaving the compound, which I surmised meant a shift change. It was nothing like the mass movement of private and official vehicles that took place in the much larger Triboro Sheriff's Office, but the noises coming through the tiny windows were familiar. Fifteen minutes later, all was quiet again.

I flopped down on the lumpy bed. The building was about as devoid of human comforts as a building could be. No radio, no television, no apparent ventilation or air-conditioning, no telephone, that single incandescent light, and the smell of old wood. There wasn't even a ceiling, just a maze of wooden rafters and beams from what had to be the nineteenth century, if not older. The floor was made of thick wooden planks of random width, with well-worn tread marks down the center. The door hardware looked to be made of wrought iron, and there was even a set of supports for an inside locking bar to keep lynch mobs at bay.

I got up and examined the cell door's lock, which was of the old-fashioned skeleton key design. If I'd had a coat hanger I could probably have worked it open. But to what end? That big oak door had to be two or three inches thick, and there was probably another one of those locking bars in place on the other side. Besides, there was no usable metal in the cell whatsoever; in that regard, it was an entirely modern jail. I sat back down, wondering if the light stayed on all night. I could see no light switch. I wracked my brain to think of some way of getting that cell door unlocked, but it seemed truly hopeless. They'd taken not only my clothes and shoes but my watch and, of course, my pocketknife; the jumpsuit had no belt and my prison shoes fastened with Velcro.

Face it, sunshine: They got you. I drifted off to sleep.

I awoke in near total darkness. Someone had finally turned out the light, and the reflected light from the sodium vapor towers around the parking compound provided the only illumination. Without a watch, I had no idea what time it was. I heard a sound coming from the end of the aisle nearest the door to the outside: metal scraping on metal. A key?

I got up off the bunk; I'd fallen asleep in my jumpsuit. I pressed my face to the bars at the front of the cell and tried to see the door, but it was too dark. Then I saw a thin vertical line of light appear and heard a hinge squeak. The line held steady and then widened until I could see a figure standing at the door. Then there were two, and from the size of them, I recognized the big brothers. Big Luke came in while Bigger John stayed by the door as lookout. Luke was holding something in his hand and, for a scary moment, I wondered if I'd been all wrong about the Big brothers. I backed away from the bars until I saw the ring of keys.

"Come on," Luke rumbled quietly.

"We going to play with Ace again?" I asked as Luke unlocked the cell door. John was no longer visible.

"Mingo's comin' with his mountain boys," Luke said. "Fixin' to burn this place. Come quiet, now."

That was pretty damned clear. I didn't look back. I followed Luke down the aisle, out the door, and into the parking lot, where John had a cruiser waiting in the shadow of the old jail building. Luke opened the right front and back doors. "Git in," he ordered. "And git down on the floor."

I slid into the backseat and Luke shut the door quietly. I then rolled sideways and got down on my knees behind the front seat. Luke got in and John drove the car forward. I heard gates sliding, then felt the car go down a ramp and accelerate into the street. I could see the top windows of the main office as we drove by. I didn't see anyone looking back at me.

It occurred to me that I might be going for a ride in the mobster sense. Being the sole occupant of the old jail building made it easy for someone to take me out of the complex. I began to think of my next move.

"Okay," Luke announced. I got back up into a normal sitting position as John took a couple of turns and then headed out of town up a mountain road. From the backseat the two brothers looked like a circus act, their huge shoulders almost touching in the front seat. I could hear the static of the patrol radio, but the computer screen wasn't on. That meant they were offline, and no one in operations should know that the car was out of the lot. I didn't know if that was good news or bad. I surreptitiously looked to see if the back doors had interior handles. They did not.

"So what's going down, boys?" I asked, casually, reaching for a seat belt as John sped up the mountain road.

"Like I said, Mingo's gone to git his Spider Mountain boys," Luke replied. "I heard one'a the front office deputies sayin' they was gonna be a *insurance* fire back in the old jail and that Mingo said not to pay it no mind till it dropped."

"This guy know I was in there?"

"Don't b'lieve so," Luke said. "Everybody thought you was still back in the holding pen. Ain't nobody been back that way since we took you out."

"Lovely," I said. "And if the old building burned down, nobody would care very much."

"Yup."

"You guys get a chance to talk to somebody about a federal task force?"

"Yup."

That explained why I wasn't cuffed in the car. I saw the dashboard clock; it was two fifteen. John took a couple of switchbacks fast enough to make the tires complain, and then we pulled over into a scenic overlook space. John nosed the car right up against the stone wall, switched off the lights, and got out. Luke opened the right back door and motioned for me to get out, too. Neither had his weapon out. I wondered if this was Robbins County's version of the Tarpeian Rock, Rome's original execution place.

From the overlook, we had a good view of the town down below. The main drag through town was clearly lighted, and we could see the river and the backs of the houses that perched on the hillside above the main street. The sheriff's office parking lot was visible because of the sodium lights. John produced a thermos of coffee and some paper cups. He poured all three of us some coffee and then pitched the empty thermos back into the front seat. Luke lit up a cigarette and sat down on the stone wall that framed the overlook. Down below in the town we saw an SUV of some kind starting up the same road we had just climbed, several hundred feet below the overlook. A second one turned into the road a moment later. I finally began to relax when they produced coffee.

"That them drug cops?" John asked.

"I reckon," Luke replied. Five minutes later a black Bronco pulled into the overlook with its headlights already off. Baby Greenberg and Carrie Santángelo got out. They were both dressed out in tactical gear. Carrie walked ahead of the DEA agent, carrying a camera with a long telephoto lens. The second vehicle, a 1500 series Suburban, pulled in behind them. The two men inside stayed in the vehicle. One was my "lawyer," who waved.

"Love your outfit," she said to me, giving the orange jumpsuit an amused once-over as she went to the overlook wall.

"Got your stuff in the Bronco," Greenberg said, and then turned to the brothers. "Gentlemen, well done."

John and Luke acknowledged the compliment without comment, while I went over to the Bronco. I was really pleased to see four sharp-pointed ears silhouetted against the glass in the way-back compartment. I opened the back hatch and the shepherds came out, greeting me effusively. Finally I told them to sit down and then climbed into the backseat of the Bronco to change. Greenberg came over.

"How'd you turn them?" I asked.

"Wasn't hard," Greenberg said. "Convinced Big Luke; Bigger John goes along with whatever Big Luke says. Carrie helped."

"I was afraid they didn't know what was really going on here," I said. "That they wouldn't believe it."

"Oh, they believed it," Greenberg said. "Or Luke did, anyway. I think they both have a pretty good idea that M. C. isn't playing by the rules. And they knew all about Grinny Creigh and her reputation up on Spider Mountain. Actually acted a little scared of her."

"Smarter than they look, then," I observed. I climbed back out of the Bronco and threw the rolled-up jumpsuit into the weeds.

"Your weapons and stuff are in the way-back," Greenberg said. "I also told them about what she did to that kid. They said something interesting, or at least Carrie thought so."

"Which was?"

"That Grinny Creigh is known for doing things to children. Like some damn witch, as they put it."

"They're coming," Carrie announced from the parapet wall. She had the camera out of its case and was looking through the telephoto. I grabbed my weapons and gear belt and joined the others at the wall.

Down below we could see a small caravan of four vehicles entering town from the mountain end, led by a police cruiser. They were moving slowly through the town, stopping at the two traffic lights that turned red against them even at this hour. When they got to the sheriff's office compound, the cruiser kept going. The other vehicles, three pickup trucks and another Bronco, pulled into the side street that ran beside the compound. Their lights went off as they drove down into the narrow street past the back of the parking garage. The cruiser continued down the main street, turned left, and left again on the street that ran parallel to and above the main drag. It stopped a block away from where the other vehicles had congregated.

The parking-lot lights put the entire area outside the fence in shadow, so we couldn't see anyone approach the old jail building. Carrie could, however, and she reported that they were placing a ladder against the outside wall of the old jail.

"One guy's going up the ladder," she said, staring through the lens and clicking the trigger. "Someone on the ground's handing him something. A can, I think. Yeah, a can. A one- or two-gallon gas can, I think. Yes, it's red. He's pouring it into the building through a little window. There goes another one. Think you'd have smelled that?" she asked me.

"For a minute or so, probably."

"Think anyone would have heard you yelling?"

"Probably not."

"Deputies, want to see what I'm seeing?"

The Big brothers shook their heads in unison. It was apparently bad enough that it was happening, and that no one inside the sheriff's office was doing anything about it. On the other hand, I thought, they also knew there was no trapped rat in the old jail screaming for help, not that that would have mattered much. Luke's expression was one of resigned dismay.

"Ladder's coming down. Wait for it—there she blows."

We could all see the sudden flare of orange fire inside the old building, first in one window and then through them all. Smoke started up from the eaves of the roof. But there was no alarm, and if there was an internal surveillance system on the parking lot, no one inside the main building would have seen anything out back because there were no windows in the old jail facing the compound's parking lot.

We watched as the fire took hold in the dry timbers and beams. We saw a man passing by on the sidewalk out in front of the main building stop and stare, and then saw two figures come out of the shadows, grab him, and pull him into the dark alley. *Bad time to be a witness*, I thought. The shepherds were glued to my side. Then we saw the arsonists' vehicles appear on the street behind the compound and head back down to where the cruiser was waiting.

"That Mingo's cruiser?" Greenberg asked. John looked through the camera lens and nodded. The fire was starting to break through the end walls of the roof. I actually thought I could smell it, but knew we were too far above the blaze. The four vehicles passed the cruiser without stopping and turned right back out to the main street, where the trucks went one way and the Bronco the other. Then we saw the front porch lights of a nearby house come on and people run out into the street, staring at the fire. A few minutes later the town fire department siren began to wail. Frack, who loved to howl, started to reply, and I had to tell him to stifle.

Carrie put the camera back into its case and returned to the Bronco. She called the Big brothers over. "You guys were officially off duty, right?" she asked. They nodded.

"Okay, go home. And that's where you've been all evening, no matter what. You keep your ears to the ground, and if you get any hint that Mingo knows how the lieutenant got away, you get yourselves over into Carrigan County and report to Sheriff Hayes."

"Shouldn't they just go ahead and do that now?" Greenberg asked.

"Not while Mingo's thugs are out driving around. Let the dust settle. You guys have a way to know what's happening in town, don't you?"

Luke said yes and, as usual, John agreed. Carrie gave Luke a cell phone. "Keep this with you. If you get into trouble, press this button right here twice and it will call one of us. Don't use it for anything else. Don't turn it off. If it rings, it will be one of us. And in any event, report to Sheriff Hayes's office by tomorrow night. Got it?"

"Yes'm," Luke said, apparently somewhat awed by the sight of a woman giving orders.

"You've done the right thing," Carrie said. "When this is all over, you boys will be entirely in the clear. Now, get going."

The deputies went to their cruiser, where Luke popped the trunk. He lifted out two tactical shotguns and an ammo belt. He gave one of the guns to John. Then they got in and drove off.

"How long before Mingo figures out what happened?" I asked.

We looked down the mountainside and saw that the darkened cruiser was still parked on the back street. The fire department had arrived, and now the back door of the main building was open, spilling light and deputies into the parking lot. The old jail building's roof collapsed into the stone walls with a shower of sparks, and then the fire truck's water streams began to take effect.

"He's probably been called on the radio," Carrie said. "So he'll move pretty soon. Their noses will tell them no one was in the building."

Greenberg made a face. "Then we need to boogie," he said. "He's gonna have black hats *and* white hats scouring the county for his 'escaped' prisoner."

"Can we make it to Carrigan County?" I asked.

Greenberg shook his head. "We could have, but probably not now. There's only one road, right through town there."

"Actually," Carrie said. "There are others."

We both looked at her in surprise. She shrugged.

"Okay," I said. "Let's do this. Mingo had to know you guys were in town. How's about you and your people take one vehicle and go down there, show up on the scene, and baffle them with some DEA bullshit. Carrie and I will take your other vehicle and head for the hills. We'll figure out next steps once we get clear."

Greenberg gave Carrie a questioning look. She nodded. "Good a plan as any," she said. Then she turned to me. "Laurie May's?"

"Yeah, that's what I was thinking," I said. "They'll expect me to run for Carrigan County, not toward the other side of Spider Mountain."

"Mingo's moving," Greenberg announced.

"Is that cell phone transponder still set up?" I asked.

Greenberg said no, but that he would put it back on the air first thing in the morning.

"Got any maps?" I asked the DEA agent.

"Don't need any," Carrie said. "I know these hills. I grew up in this county. Let's go."

I whistled up the shepherds, and we swapped gear and vehicles with the other DEA agents. Then Carrie got in on the driver's side. I settled the dogs in the back compartment and jumped into the front passenger seat.

"Ever see the movie *Thunder Road*?" Carrie asked, as she cranked the Suburban around and pointed it up the mountain road. I took one look at the grim expression on her face and cinched up my seat belt. For a supposed city girl from Raleigh, this lady was full of surprises tonight.

The Suburban was a federal seizure and forfeiture vehicle taken from a drug dealer. Even though it was the smaller of the two versions, it had a big V-8, four-wheel drive, tinted windows, and a beefed-up suspension system. Carrie drove it like a bootlegger, and all the questions I wanted to ask about her little bombshell back there definitely had to wait as she took paved road, dirt road, curves, straightaways, and hills at the same breakneck speed. The shepherds, who normally rode sitting up, were not visible in the way-back.

I had no idea of where we were until she skidded through a right turn down by what looked like the same creek where Mingo had staged the logging-truck accident. Suddenly we saw a police cruiser coming fast the other way, a few S-bends ahead of us, its light bar flashing blue strobe light through the trees.

"Duck down," Carrie ordered, flipping on her brights, and I bent over in the seat. I felt the Suburban twist left, accelerate, and then swerve hard right, its horn blaring angrily. Then I heard the sounds of a crash behind us as Carrie decelerated hard going into the next curve.

"Okay," she said above the noise of protesting tires.

"He get a look at us?" I asked as I straightened back up.

"He was busy," she replied. "Now he's wet. Hopefully, so's his radio."

We drove to the road leading up to Laurie May's cabin, turned into it, and then hid the vehicle behind an old shed barn out of sight of the dirt road. We watched a few more police cruisers go by down on the hard-top road, but no one came nosing around. We watched for half an hour longer, but traffic seemed to have evaporated. I let the dogs out for a quick runaround and to make sure no one was nearby. I put them on a long down near the vehicle and got back in. Frick started barking at some woods creature, and I told her to shut up or I'd cut her ears off. She was visibly terrified for a good five seconds. Carrie asked if they always yawned like that when I yelled at them. I told her it was a fear response.

"Okay, Special Agent," I said. "Explain, please."

"Baby asked me if I had a personal stake in all this," she said. "He said you'd asked."

"Yup."

"First I should tell you that I've resigned from the SBI."

"Whoa," I said. "What happened?"

"The operations director fanged my immediate boss pretty hard, with direct orders for me to back off," she said. "She was not happy with the fact that I failed to ID myself as SBI when Mingo made his move. Said that we needed to regroup on the Robbins County problem, get a federal task force going, get the big Bureau back into it."

"And you disagreed?"

"Hell, yes. I mean, we've done all that before. But she's a bureaucrat first and a law officer second. A task force means meetings in Washington, overnights at cushy hotels, and a new bullet on her résumé. Regarding the real problem, turns out all she really wants to do is kick the can."

"The real problem?"

"The one you're supposed to guess."

"Unh-hunh. And you're retirement eligible, or did you just up and quit?"

"Took an early out," she said. "Just like you, as I recall."

I didn't remind her that I had taken early retirement with a multimillion-dollar trust fund in the wings. Her bailing out of a good state job was a lot more significant a move than my leaving the Manceford County Sheriff's Office.

"So what's the personal beef here?" I asked. The sky outside was starting to lighten in a false dawn. The shepherds were curled into tight little balls. Sometimes they were useless as guards, unless a bad guy happened to step on their tails.

She took a deep breath and then told me the story. Santángelo had been her married name, which she'd kept after her husband, a state parole officer, had gotten himself involved with an eighteen-year-old waitress down in Charlotte. He'd called it a case of the seven-year itch but admitted that he was desperately in love. She'd called it grounds for divorce, and now he lived in a double-wide on half pay with his Waffle House queen.

Her maiden name had been Harper, and she had actually been born and raised in the town of Rocky Falls, right here in wild and wonderful Robbins County. She and her mother had left when she turned sixteen, not long after her father and younger sister had been killed in a road accident. Her mother had gone back to the Charlotte area, where she had family. Carrie had finished high school, gone on to college, and from there into the SBI. She'd begun as an intern during her senior year, which evolved into a full-time job offer when she graduated. She'd been in the professional standards division right from the start.

"This goes back to the so-called accident," she said. "My father was a state game warden. He managed the game lands that surround the Smokies National Park on the Carolina side. At the time, the accident was described as 'cause unknown.' After I'd been at the SBI for a while I made some inquiries through the North Carolina DMV. Turned out it had been recorded as a hit-and-run accident, involving a large truck."

"Like a logging truck?"

"Just like that," she said, looking over at me. Her eyes were shining with steely resolve. "Big enough to knock Dad's pickup truck backwards into a ravine from the *inside* lane. His truck went into a river. And, and this is the interesting part, they recovered his body, but not that of my sister."

"Any evidence that she had survived the crash?"

Carrie blew out a long breath. "My father's family came originally from the Carolina coast. Their ancestors were Portuguese fishermen for the most part. Harper was a name change way back when, we think. Very independent-minded people. Dad, for instance, refused to wear a seat belt. Just wouldn't do it. Rainey, that was my sister's name, *always* wore her seat belt. Dad probably died in the initial impact, based on what I saw in the DMV accident reconstruction report. But Rainey should have survived—there was virtually no damage on her side, even after going into that ravine. Her door was found open, *and* her school book bag was gone."

"As in, maybe she got out?"

"Or was *taken* out. But the sheriff's office report speculated she had been swept away in the river."

"How old was she?"

"Eleven. And she was very pretty. I remember being jealous of her looks."

"Don't know why," I offered, and she flashed a bitter smile.

"Who was the sheriff then?" I asked.

"Three guesses."

I remembered Mingo thinking he'd recognized her. "Did you come back up here, poke around a little?" I asked.

She shook her head. "Not until now."

"Okay, so what's your theory?"

She patted her coat pockets like a smoker does when he's searching for a cigarette. She saw me looking and smiled. "Quit five years ago, but . . ."

"Know how that goes, too," I said. She wanted to tell me what this was all about, but at the same time, she didn't. I suspected that the mystery of this accident was as much the reason for her leaving the SBI as any overcautious bureaucrat boss. She leaned back and continued her story.

"Dad told us one time he'd run into some people pushing a small mule train in the game lands. Thought it was odd, the first time. Then, a month later, he encountered another group. Same deal—three mules, fully loaded with packs, armed men, moving at sundown. He stopped them, showed his badge, and asked them what they were doing. They drew guns and he barely escaped."

"And then he went to the sheriff, didn't he."

"Yes, he did. Ten days later he was dead in the river. And a pretty young girl was missing."

It was then I remembered her focus on children in Robbins County, and suddenly I thought I knew what she was pursuing.

"Carrie," I said, "what are Mingo and the Creigh clan doing to children up here?"

She didn't say anything for a long moment. A morning crow on dawn patrol spotted our Suburban and set up a racket in the tree that covered the shed barn. I saw what looked like a lantern light come on up at Laurie May's house.

"I believe they're selling them," she said finally.

Well, now, that trumps a meth smuggling case, I thought. Baby Greenberg and I had seen Grinny Creigh almost smother a child as if she'd been stepping on a snail. If she was trafficking in children, suddenly there were lots of possible explanations for her doing that.

"How does she acquire the 'product'?"

"Gets hardscrabble women hooked on something, usually meth, and then trades what they owe for drugs for a suitable child."

"What mother would do that?" I asked.

"A mother wouldn't. An addict would. You saw one the other day. Remember the vampire at the single-wide? She would. And if she wouldn't, *he* would."

"And of course you can't prove this."

"I can't prove it because we've never been able to get inside," Carrie continued. "No one's been able to get inside, not us, not the Bureau, not the DEA—no one. Until you showed up."

"Hang on," I protested. "It's not like I got inside, either."

"You're the first person I know who's gone face-to-face with Grinny Creigh and Nathan and lived to tell about it," she said. "Look, I've been riding this hobbyhorse for a few years now. My cohorts back in Charlotte think I'm just a little bit OCD on this subject. I decided this was probably going to be my best chance to find out."

There were two lights showing now up at Laurie May's cabin. In a minute she was going to step out onto the front porch with that enormous shotgun and hurt herself. Carrie was looking at me expectantly, and I knew precisely what the unspoken question was.

"We need to go up there and announce ourselves," I said. "Preferably before she opens fire on us."

She kept looking at me. Those black eyes of hers were the closest thing to mental telepathy I'd ever encountered.

"Okay, I'll work it with you," I said. "But you're going to have to find me some scotch."

She snorted, turned around and heaved herself up on to the back of the seat, and started rummaging around in all the gear bags in the backseat. I could have taken some serious liberties, but I valued my life. She slid back down into the front seat and produced a bottle of Glenlivet. "Baby said you'd be going into withdrawal."

"Baby is an officer and a gentleman," I said. "Now—let's go pacify Grandma before she finds the ammo for that Greener up there."

9

We got to the front porch about the time Laurie May found her box of shells. I couldn't tell if she was disappointed at not getting to fire the shotgun or if she just hadn't had her coffee yet. She peered at us carefully through the cracked front door and then nodded. I think she recognized the shepherds and then us, in that order.

"I knowed someone was down there," she said. "Didn't see them dogs, or I'd'a knowed it was you two. Come on in. I got me some coffee makin'."

Carrie thanked her and we went in. I told the shepherds to stay on the front porch and to leave the chickens alone. They were visibly disappointed. Chickens could be real fun.

"Saw 'em cop cars a-flashin' on the river road early this mornin'," Laurie May announced from the kitchen. The cabin smelled of well-done coffee and wood smoke. The aroma could have been coming entirely from the coffee, too. "Was that somethin' to do with you-all?"

"Yes, unfortunately, it was," Carrie said. "M. C. Mingo and his crowd are looking for us."

"What'd y'all do now?" she asked, bringing two mugs of coffee out to the table.

"Came into Robbins County and asked too many questions," I said. "Went some places we weren't supposed to. He surrounded us down on Crown Lake and put me in jail." I told her what had happened after that. Carrie's eyebrows rose when I described meeting Ace.

Laurie May was studying my face intently. "You don't look like no outlaw to me," she said. "Are ye?"

"I'm a retired deputy sheriff, from back east in Manceford County," I told her. "Apparently M. C. Mingo doesn't care for outsiders poking around in Robbins County."

"Laurie May?" Carrie said. "As I told you, I'm a police officer, too. Why don't you sit down and let me tell you a story."

When she'd finished, the old lady nodded. "It figgers," she said. "Folks is always talkin' about runaways and such. Grinny Creigh's mean enough, too. But what about them mothers? What's God gonna do to a mother, sells her own child?"

"Burn her in hell until the end of time," Carrie said simply, and Laurie May was one hundred percent on board with that solution.

"I've been talking to some people in Washington," Carrie said. "There's a federal task force looking into child-trafficking rings. There's word that a 'shipment' is expected soon from this part of the state. We need to find them, and stop this mess."

"Where you gonna look?" Laurie May asked.

"We have no idea," Carrie said, looking across the table at me. *Pile on*, she was saying.

"I saw Sheriff Mingo bring a little girl to Grinny's cabin," I told Laurie May. "She stood there and yelled at her for a minute. Then she grabbed her and smothered her until she was unconscious. Then Mingo took her away."

Laurie May was shocked by this, but then a flinty expression settled on her face. "Don't surprise me too much," she said. "That son of hers, that Nathan? Folks say he killed a boy at school for laughin' and makin' fun of how he looked. Stabbed him through the mouth with one of them long knives he's got, folks say. Throwed the body in a cave. Ain't nobody ever seen him again. There's murder in them Creighs for sure. You say Mingo's lookin' for ye right now?"

I nodded.

"Where you gonna hide?"

We both looked at her, and she understood right away. "You wantin' to hole up here, is that it?"

"We need somewhere to set up a base while we look for those children," Carrie said. "You're the only person we've met so far up here who's not afraid of Mingo."

Laurie May smiled. I think she recognized the sensation of some smoke being blown. "Y'all listen here," she said. "I ain't never said I wasn't afraid of

M. C. Mingo. I act all the fool and bluster them boys'a his like I was a crazy woman, but if'n they wanted to, they could do as they damn please. They know it, and I know it."

"Okay," I interjected. "Then it's not right that we put you in any danger. If we can hole up here for the day, we'll clear out tonight."

"You hold your horses, there, mister deppity," she said, wagging a bony finger at me. "I didn't say y'all couldn't stay. You just need to know how things really is. Ain't no point in tryin' to fool folks, not at my age." She turned to Carrie. "Fetch my shawl over yonder, missy. I got somethin' to show ye."

We walked up the slope behind the house toward a circular grove of old pines occupying a wide swale. When we got closer we could see a tiny log cabin, perhaps twenty feet square, almost totally hidden by the sweeping pines. Based on the color of the chinking, the amount of moss on the foundation stones, and the lean of the stone chimney, I guessed it to be very old.

"That there's Jessie's cabin," Laurie May said, stopping to catch her breath. "It's got it some blood on the floor, but it's a beauty for a hidin' place. My granddaddy built it well more'n a hundred years back."

The cabin had two shuttered windows, one on either side of the front door, a small front porch, and the single chimney at one end. The logs were of random diameter and black with age. The roof was painted metal that had rusted badly over the years. But the path leading to the porch was clear of weeds and there was no clutter on the porch.

"Blood on the floor?" I asked.

"Jessie's my only daughter," Laurie May said. "First born. Came to her beauty early on, married up with a no-good son of a bitch. They had 'em two young'uns right quick, but he was no provider, that one. Liked his whiskey, and liked to beat on her more'n he fancied workin' for his keep. Right bastard, he was."

"What happened?" Carrie asked.

"One night they had 'em a big ole set-to," Laurie May replied. "Wasn't the first time, neither. He was drunk and beatin' on her some. Hurt her this time. Drew blood on her. She got the scattergun, told'm to clear on out. He said he'd kill her if she didn't put it down. That the only thing she'd been good for was them kids. That he loved them and hated her. Hateful talk like that."

She paused, staring hard at the cabin, remembering. A soft breeze stirred the big pines. Laurie May took a deep breath. "Then she went crazy, done somethin' awful. She turned that there ten-bore on them little kids. Kilt 'em both dead, right in front of him. She tole him there wasn't no reason for him to stay around anymore, was there. Then she walked out that door right there, and into them woods yonder. That was twenty-three years ago. Long time, but I remember it like it was last night."

"What happened to her?" Carrie asked.

"She done disappeared off the face of the earth. I got one letter, months on after it happened. Tole me what happened, what she'd done. How sorry she was. That Larry, that was the bastard's name, Larry, done drove her crazy. Said she knew she was damned forever. Said one day, she'd come back here and join 'em young'uns. They's buried back there, behind the cabin. Last time we ever heered from her."

"And Larry?" I asked.

"That no-count kilt hisself a week later. Took that self-same shotgun and blowed his head right off in his pickup truck. Did it right there on the main street in Rocky Falls. Took him near a whole bottle'a whiskey to work hisself up to it, but he done it, right there in broad daylight. They asked me if I'd bury him back there. I told them to burn his body, so's it could keep up with his soul."

"Damn," I said. Blood on the floor indeed.

"Yessir, that's a fact. But I been a'comin' up here once a week, seein' to the cabin. Said she was a-comin' back, so I keep it ready. Clean. Firewood in the box. Ain't no facilities, so you'd have to use my privy, but there ain't no snakes nor a lick'a dirt in it. And ain't no one goes near this place, neither, 'cause folks 'round here think it's hainted by them young'uns and they daddy, wailin' with the night wind for all they lost."

I felt a shiver steal across my shoulders. There were probably more stories like this told across these hills than we knew.

"Shall we go inside?" Carrie asked me. I could tell she felt it, too. But the place was a perfect hideout, and at the moment we were fresh out of options. By now Mingo would have even the back roads covered.

Inside, the cabin was spotless. It was darkish; the front windows and the one door offered the only daylight. There were basically two rooms, one which combined a tiny kitchen, which had a woodstove and a dry sink, with a living room area containing a surprisingly large fireplace, a long farmhouse table, and six antique handmade wooden chairs. A smaller table by the door held four kerosene lanterns and some candles. The other room was a bedroom, which had a four-poster bed raised high off the wooden floor and a single oak armoire. The bed was made up with quilts and handmade pillows. There was another dry sink in one corner, with a brass chamber pot stowed on a lower shelf. There was no ceiling on the bedroom, and, like the front room, it was open to the rafters. The room smelled of old sachet and older dust.

"It ain't fancy and there ain't nothin' modern about it," Laurie May said, "but it'll keep the rain off'n your heads. And looky here."

She pulled aside a handmade knotted-rag rug revealing a trapdoor in the bedroom floor. "This here goes under the cabin and out the back. Tight squeeze an' all, but somebody corners you up in here, you can sneak on out the back."

I could just imagine what kinds of things were living under that floor, but it was good to know there was an escape hatch. There was another one of those rag rugs placed off center out in the living room area, which I was *not* going to look under.

"Like I was sayin', I keep it clean and ready for when she comes home. I know it ain't likely, but a mama's got her duty."

And her hopes, I thought. Of course, if her daughter ever did return, Laurie May would have a whole new set of problems, given what the daughter had predicted she'd do if she ever did come back.

"This is very generous of you," Carrie said. "Are you sure it's all right that we stay here?"

"Been enough pain and hurtin' on young'uns in these hills," Laurie May said. "If'n you can put a stop to it, I'm pleased to be of aid. You gonna have to hide that big vehicle, though—they gonna be lookin' in barns like that one down there. That and them dogs, too."

We moved our stuff out of the Suburban and into the cabin in the pines. There'd been no sign of a major search going on down on the hardtop, and only a few other vehicles moving along the river road, but it was still early. Mingo would have to know I'd had inside help getting out of that cell, and that might have delayed a broader search as he looked to clean house.

The shepherds plopped down on the porch as if they owned it. They knew where I was, and that was the main thing, except perhaps for chow. We had a fine view of tree trunks, which meant that no one down on the river road could see the cabin, either. Carrie plopped herself down at the big table. "Now what?" she said.

I sat down opposite. "You're not wanted for anything. You didn't break me out of the jail. Why don't you take the Suburban, go to town, get up with Baby and his crew, make a formal report, and figure something out."

"Just drive out of here?"

"Yeah," I said. "Why not? There's no place to hide that vehicle."

"What if they stop me?"

"They can't know you've quit the SBI. Hard-ass 'em. It's obviously a law enforcement vehicle."

"Unless that deputy last night got a look at me before he went into the creek."

"I doubt it. You had your brights on and, like you said, he was really busy trying not to die. Don't go back roads—take the main road, right on into Carrigan County. Bold as brass. They won't dare mess with you."

She sighed. "I'm not as tough as you might think," she said.

"Santa Claws?"

She laughed. "Damned Greenberg. What will you do?"

"Spend some quality time with Laurie May. Find out what I can about the local geography, the neighbors, try to figure out a way to set up a better surveillance hide on Grinny's place. You think they have a clutch of children hidden somewhere?"

"Yes, I do. Probably right there at the Creigh compound."

"Okay," I said. "Then what we need is probable cause to go toss that place. That will be my job. Get a warrant. Make it and me official. You be my field director. Orchestrate support from the DEA and whoever else is willing to play."

She gave me a challenging look. "Don't want me along out here?"

"Hell, Carrie, I'm already in the shitter with the local law. You'll be a lot more useful running free in Carrigan County than ducking behind a tree every time a cop car goes by. Besides, there's only one bed."

She tried to stay mad but then grinned. "But it's such a big bed," she said. "Okay, I'll go to town. I'll come back after dark."

"Don't forget the brothers Big," I reminded her. "They should be making their creep out of Robbins County pretty soon." Then I had a thought. I told her about Mose Walsh. Maybe he could lend some local knowledge or help them figure out a better surveillance plan.

She thought for a moment. "I think I remember someone like that—Indian face? He was older than me, but the kids called him Big Chief. Something like that."

"That'd be him. Huge nose."

She suppressed a quick grin. "If it's the guy I'm thinking about, it wasn't about his nose."

"Wonderful," I said with a sigh. "Now you have two reasons to check him out."

I spent the day with Grandma Creigh and learned a good bit of useful information. A rocky spine separated her hollow from the other Creigh cabin, and there were two trails leading over that ridge, one high, one low. The people who lived in this hollow did not consort with the gang in the next one over to the north, with the possible exception of the one unfriendly couple we'd encountered down by the river road. They were considered officially no-count by the decent folks in the holler, in Laurie May's opinion, and thus they were unknown quantities. Someone had alerted Mingo and his troops as to where we'd camped that night, and I thought they were good candidates.

Grinny Creigh had a fearsome reputation in this part of the county, with the rumored powers and abilities typically ascribed to mountain witches and demons. I told Laurie May I'd experienced that second-sight ability when Grinny had somehow known we were watching from the ridge. She didn't think that was particularly unusual.

"Her mama had it, too. Grinny's big and fat. Her mama was thin and had her this long white witchy hair even as a chile. Green eyes. Sharp little teeth. Teachers was scared of her."

"And how about Nathan?"

There were apparently three constants about Nathan: He never spoke to anyone except Grinny, he was never without his bag of knives, and he obeyed Grinny Creigh with frightening dedication. As a boy, he had gone to the county elementary school for one whole day, during which the other kids had taunted him unmercifully about his freakish looks. One brat in particular, Billy Lee Ranson, had led the torment. At the end of the school day Nathan was seen walking down the dirt road in the direction of Book Mountain with a protesting Billy Lee in tow, literally. Neither of them had ever come back to school. Billy Lee's older brother had gone up on Book Mountain to see about Billy, and he hadn't come back, either. The sheriff at the time was not especially interested in bothering the clan up on Book Mountain, so the school authorities had decided to cut their losses and get on with the school year. The sheriff was known to be a sensible man, and the Ranson brothers were deemed to be no great loss.

At midday we saw a patrol car go past Laurie May's and up the dirt road toward the neighbors at the top of the hollow. I put the shepherds into the little cabin. Laurie May gave me some bread and tea, and I went to the cabin to hole up. I was able to hear the cruiser come into her cabin yard about a half hour later, and then drive away.

"Said they was lookin' fer a dangerous escaped prisoner," Laurie May reported. "Said he burned down the old jail and they's a'feared he kilt two deputies. I sent'm on his way. Ain't seen nothin', ain't heered nothin'."

I told her what had really happened, and that the two deputies should be alive and well over in Sheriff Hayes's office by now.

"I know them boys," she said. "They growed up 'round here, then went off to the army or somewheres. Came back, though. And I know that old jail. One'a *my* boys got locked up fer brawlin' in the town. I had to bring him his vittles, on account of because they didn't have no money to feed no prisoners."

"As best we could tell, it was Mingo's boys who set the fire, so he and I have a score to settle."

She wagged a finger at me. "Don't go talkin' about scores to be settled," she said. "That be serious business in these parts."

"So's burning a prisoner to death because he might know too much," I said.

I took a long nap that afternoon. The four-poster smelled faintly of pine needles, but it was very comfortable. Both shepherds had eyes on getting up on the bed, but I told them they'd die trying. More terrified yawns. Frack went over to that other rag rug and lay down. Moments later he snorted, got back up, and went to a corner of the room. *Blood on and* in *the floor*, I thought.

At four I took the dogs out. Laurie May was feeding her goats, and reported that there'd been one more cop car come by the place looking for that dangerous escaped prisoner. I took the DEA cell phone and went up the hillside to see if I could hit that transponder and get in touch with Carrie. I slanted my way toward the rocky spine between the hollows so as to avoid any eyes uphill from Laurie May's along the dirt road. I didn't need anyone seeing a stranger in the woods and calling Mingo's people.

As it turned out, I had to get right up on the ridgeline before I saw any bars in the cell phone signal indicator. I didn't like being right out in the open, silhouetted on a ridge, so I stepped down into a circle of man-high boulders. It being a DEA phone, the directory was locked, so I just kept hitting the call button and finally raised Baby Greenberg.

Carrie had made it out to Carrigan County without serious incident. She'd driven right through Rocky Falls without anyone so much as looking at the

Suburban. Just outside of town there'd been two sheriff's office cruisers parked along the road. She'd pulled over and talked to the deputies, asking them who they were looking for. They told her, giving her the clear impression that they believed the cover story Mingo had put out about my escaping and taking out the Big brothers. They asked her if she was in the county on official SBI business, and she told them that she was going to a meeting with some IRS officials concerning irregularities in the Robbins County pay and benefits system. Then she left.

"That word was probably all over the deputy force within an hour," Baby said with a laugh. "Anyway, the Big brothers made it in to Sheriff Hayes's office, where they gave statements about the fire. Carrie wrote up a report to be sent to SBI in Raleigh, in SBI-ese, and Hayes said he'd send it out under his signature."

"Well, hell," I said. "That ought to do it, right? Two of Mingo's own people testifying that Mingo orchestrated this whole deal?"

"Um."

"What do you mean, um?" The shepherds appeared to be watching something in the trees, so I moved down the ridge to make sure I couldn't be seen from the fields below.

"Well, Carrie's still entirely focused on this supposed child-trafficking business, but now that she's resigned from the SBI, she's been cut off on any current intel. And my bosses keep reminding me we're supposed to be rolling up a meth smuggling and production operation. The fire in the jailhouse and a crooked sheriff don't interest them very much."

"It should—he's the top cover for your meth crowd out here."

"And your *evidence* for that would be . . . ?"

"Hell's bells, can't you guys go to a grand jury with what you've got? I can testify, the Big brothers can testify, *you* can testify—how much more do we need to get something going here?"

"My bosses' say-so, for one thing," Greenberg said. "And, like I said, they've lost interest. In fact, we're being pulled off to work a possible drug homicide over in Andrews. My line boss, Jack Harrie? He says this thing in Rocky Falls is a genu-wine hairball, Carrie Santángelo's on a personal crusade, and we're outta there."

I didn't know what to say. Without backup like a DEA squad, there wouldn't be much I could contribute.

"Hey, I'm sorry," Baby said. "I'm going to forget to retrieve the transponder, so you'll have some comms until the battery dies. Carrie's been shut out, like

I said, so she has to figure out what she's going to do. I told her that her first mission is to get your ass out of Robbins County."

"They *are* watching," I said. And so were the shepherds. They were still staring into the tree line above me on the transverse ridge. What had they seen? I changed position again.

"Gotta go," Greenberg said. "I'll try to get back into it after this homicide deal. We'll put your stuff back in that sex pad."

"Thanks for that, and tell the lodge I'm still 'there.' Tell Carrie she can use the cabin until I can extract, if she wants. She can leave my Suburban there, too. Do you have her cell number?"

"Carrie Santángelo in the bridal suite," he said after giving me the number. "Now there's an image."

"With a gun," I reminded him. "Maybe two. And claws."

"There is that," he said. "Look, again, I'm sorry about this. I feel like we're abandoning you."

"DEA doesn't have a dog in this fight," I said. "Go solve your homicide. If these people are taking kids, we'll get 'em. And besides, I owe M. C. Mingo one fire."

I shut off the phone. My side of the slope was darkening into evening shadow. The shepherds were still watching up the hill but didn't seem as alerted as they had been. I sat down against one of the big rocks and took in the view. The stone was still warm. It seemed so peaceful up here. It was hard to imagine the gritty infrastructure of meth labs, midnight bootleggers, and especially the notion of impoverished women selling their children to the likes of Grinny Creigh. I leaned forward to stow the cell phone in my back pocket and probably saved my life.

The rock right behind my head exploded into a spray of razor-sharp granite shards, followed by the echo of a booming rifle up on the high ridge. The back of my neck felt like it was on fire as I rolled to one side and deeper into the rock pile. The shepherds came running, but I yelled them down as another round slashed down the hill, spanging off a rock and out into the hollow below. I made like a snake, wriggling between the bigger rocks, conscious of wetness on the back of my shirt. Another round came into the rock pile. This one ricocheted off about five rocks before passing over my head like a supersonic hornet. The shooter knew I was in there and was hoping for a lucky hit. I was looking for that fabled direct route to China through the center of the earth.

Finally it stopped. My neck still hurt like hell, but it was now dark enough on the hillside that the guy probably couldn't see us anymore. The distant boom of the rifle was still echoing in my ears, and I remained down on the ground for another thirty minutes until it was almost fully dark. Then I crept toward the edge of the rock pile nearest Laurie May's place. The dogs were whining above me, but I told them to stay down until I got clear of the rock pile. Five minutes later I was able to get into some trees and call them down. Crouching low, I trotted down the hill toward my not-so-secret-anymore cabin.

Somehow they'd found out where I was holed up. Laurie May must have said something or done something to alert one of the visiting cops. I didn't believe she'd intentionally done anything, but, either way, I couldn't hang out here anymore.

I waited at the edge of the woods that concealed her doomed daughter's cabin and watched her house for several minutes to make sure there wasn't a reception committee down there. I finally spotted the old lady through one of the windows in the lantern light and decided to go on down. Her front door was open and I called her name. She came to the door and asked if I had been doing all that shooting. Then she saw my collar and told me to come in right away.

That first round had embedded enough granite dust in the back of my neck to make a good piece of sandpaper, as I discovered when she patiently extracted every speck of it. I was gritting my teeth and wishing for my bottle of scotch by the time she was through. Then she smeared some foul-smelling ointment on the wounded skin that took a lot of the sting away. I was afraid to ask what was in it.

"How many was they?" she asked.

"I think just one, with a long rifle and a good scope. He had me pinned in a cluster of big rocks." I turned around to look at her. "I can't stay here anymore," I told her. "They'll figure it out if they haven't already."

"I ain't afraid of them no-counts," she said bravely, as she put away her tweezers and the cotton roll.

"You tell them when they come that I made you put me up. Tell them I had a great big gun and threatened to shoot your livestock. And we need to burn that bloody cotton—I don't want them to know they hit me."

She threw some sticks in the woodstove, shook the ash grate, pitched in the cotton waste, and then stirred the soup pot. "Where's 'at pretty woman?" she asked.

"Over in Marionburg," I said. "She managed to get out of Robbins County, but I don't think she can come back here while Mingo's people are all stirred up. I'm going to hike out." I explained some of what I'd learned in the phone call.

"I'll heat ye some soup," she said. She clanked the firebox door shut. "You know they gonna be out there in them woods. Prob'ly have 'em dogs with 'em, too."

"I can't let them take me again," I said. "Especially now that my allies have been backed out."

"Which way you gonna go?" she asked.

"I think the best route will be over the ridges toward Crown Lake. I think the roads will be too dangerous."

She stirred the soup some more. I realized I was really hungry. The back of my neck had settled down to a warm burn, which I hoped was not an infection getting under way.

"If'n it was me," Laurie May said slowly, "I believe I'd go t'other way. They gonna be lookin' for ye to run for Marionburg town. If'n it was me, I'd go up and over that ridge yonder and hide right in Grinny Creigh's backyard. Ain't none'a them gonna expect you to do that."

Including me, I thought, but she had a point. If that shooter had alerted the rest of Nathan's crew and the sheriff, the woods would soon be alive with the sound of guns being cocked and slavering dogs sniffing out trails. They would in fact never even think to look at Grinny's place. She saw me considering it and gave me a toothy grin.

"I'll show ye a shortcut through that backbone ridge yonder," she said. "Put you into Grinny's place sideways, other side'a them dogs. They's a little cave on the bottom side of her front field. Maybe you can hole up in there, watch and see where she's hidin' them poor young'uns."

And that was the objective, wasn't it, I reminded myself. Carrie had de-fanged herself when she resigned from the SBI. She had no legal authority to pursue Grinny Creigh. Neither did I, for that matter, but I was here and she wasn't. If I could watch the Creigh place undiscovered for a few days, maybe I could actually put some flesh on the bones of Carrie's theory about Grinny selling children. The transponder was still in place, for now, anyway, so, in theory, I could call out.

Evidence. We desperately needed evidence.

"Okay, I'll do just that," I said. "The cave big enough for me and the shepherds?"

She nodded and then told me to sit down and eat. I briefly wondered how she knew about a cave over on the other side of the ridge. On the other hand, she was old enough to know damn near everything about these hills.

An hour later we turned down the lanterns in her cabin, put them in the front windows, and then slipped quietly out the back door. I had my field belt, the spotting scope, a bedroll, water, and the SIG .45. Laurie May had fixed up a bag of bread and a couple of hard-boiled eggs. The shepherds seemed to sense our need for stealth; they were sticking close and moving in silence. There was a weak moon rising above the mountains, so between her knowledge of the path and a borrowed walking stick, I managed to stay upright as we climbed through the rock rubble toward what she had called the backbone ridge. We seemed to be heading right into the side of it as the ground rose, and I wondered if we were going to have to go straight up and over. But then we walked into a dense stand of gnarled pines whose branches were low enough to require constant swatting. Laurie May was moving surprisingly fast for a woman of her age, which hopefully meant she knew right where she was going. After about seventy-five feet of pine needles and bugs going down my shirt, we broke out in front of a crack in the ridge.

"This here broke clean through the 'bone long ways back," she whispered, pointing into a narrow defile, which was in total darkness. "They's water runnin' through it, comin' down off'n them sides. Foller it through to t'other side, go down to yer right hand, mebbe twenty rod, to the cave hole."

"Thanks, Laurie May. I'll try to come back out after dark tomorrow. If by any chance Carrie contacts you, tell her where I am. If she comes to your place, try to keep her there until I get back."

She nodded in the darkness, squeezed my hand, and started back into the pines. I approached the passageway through the ridge. Her description of it breaking clean through was accurate. I stepped into the crack and looked up. Sheer rock walls rose on either side of me, no more than six feet between them where I stood but getting wider toward the top, which had to be two or even three hundred feet straight up. The ground underfoot was loose stone and mud, and I could see thin dark streaks of moisture weeping down the sides of the defile. I'm not one to feel claustrophobic, but this passage through the heart of the ridge got me close to it. I tried to imagine what titanic forces could split and then open the whole ridge like this. I had to resist the temptation to keep one hand on the walls to make sure they weren't closing together on me.

The shepherds followed nervously, stopping when I did and picking their footing carefully.

The path through the crack led straight across for about a hundred yards and then slightly downhill, and the water took on some depth as I neared the other end. The air was dank and cold, and the looming rock walls seemed to amplify my every footstep, no matter how careful I tried to be. At the other end the crack narrowed down to no more than four feet, and it took all my willpower not to bolt the last fifty feet.

Finally I reached the other end and stopped just short of stepping out onto clear ground. The hollow containing Grinny Creigh's place opened in front of me, and I had a good view down the slope and overlooking the buildings and pens around her cabin. My vantage point was a good three hundred or more feet above the cabin in elevation. There was no cover on this side of the ridge except one lonesome pine tree, which was tapping the water seeping out of the crack. I hesitated to just step out there; there were dim lights on inside the main cabin, but all the outbuildings were dark. I was facing the south end of the cabin, so I couldn't see anything on the front porch where she'd been enthroned the night I'd been there. And might be tonight.

I stepped just out of the crack and sat down to watch for a while, mostly to get my night vision acclimated to the moonlight. Now that I was out of that sheer-walled split in the mountain, I could see much better. The tiny weep spilling out of the crack went straight downhill and disappeared into a brush-covered gully. I used the telescope to scan the compound, looking for any signs of humans or dogs, but there was nothing moving down there. There was a slight breeze blowing across the face of the ridge as cooler air from the upper back ridge poured downhill toward the road and creek way down to my right. Otherwise there wasn't a sound coming from the hollow.

The shepherds lay down on either side of me, and their warm, furry hides were comforting. I settled back against the rock, and my shirt collar reminded me of the rifleman who'd damn near laid me down on the other side. Which further reminded me of the cell phone. I took it out, turned it on, and checked for a signal. One lonely bar, and it wasn't entirely persistent. I switched it back off since I had no way to recharge it.

After a half hour my back was getting cold, so I decided to find the cave. Having no idea of how long a rod was, I elected to simply go sideways down the ridge, moving slowly and feeling along the rock wall for a cave entrance. I'd gone maybe fifty feet when I heard and then saw the headlights of a pickup truck coming up from the river road toward Grinny's cabin. I was well above their line of sight but decided to freeze in place and sit down again, trying to make myself small. On a full-moon night they might have seen me, but I figured I was pretty inconspicuous against the gray rock wall of the back-bone ridge.

The truck stopped in front of the cabin and shut down its engine and lights. I halfway expected someone to get out and haul yet another chained body out of the truck's bed. Instead I watched Nathan get out of the passenger side and go into the cabin. Even at this distance he was unmistakable, his stooped figure moving awkwardly up the steps and into the shadow of the porch. I saw a match flare on the driver's side. That was good—the match would destroy the man's night vision should he happen to look up in my direction. I was still pretty ex-posed and considered moving on down the hill. Then I remembered that motion wasn't the best idea if perchance someone was actively scanning the ridgeline.

Ten minutes later Nathan appeared out of nowhere at the back of the pickup truck. He had two large dogs with him, which he proceeded to heave up into the bed of the truck. I could hear their claws scrabbling for footing. One of them started barking, and I heard a rough voice yell "Shut up" at him. Nathan got back in and the truck started up. The driver turned on his headlights, and now it was my turn to lose all night vision as his brights swept across my position on the hillside. All I could do was hope like hell they weren't looking up here, because there wasn't a stitch of cover anywhere. In the event, the truck kept go-ing and soon was out of sight and sound down the hill. I stayed put until I could see again and then continued my way down the ridge in search of the cave.

About three hundred feet from the crack, I felt the rock wall give way to a narrow opening. I had a penlight on my field belt, but decided not to take any chances. I sent the two dogs into the cave instead. Hopefully there wasn't a six-foot-long rattlesnake denned up in there for the night, because if there was, we were in for some noise. Both shepherds popped out of the cave a minute later, so I decided it was reasonably safe for me to try it out. The opening was only four feet high and perhaps eighteen inches wide, so I had to duckwalk sideways into the cave. The actual cave curled to the right from the entrance. Once in-side, I turned on the penlight and checked the ground for snakes and the ceil-ing for bats. Nobody home.

The cave wasn't much of a cave—it was just a hole in the rock. It had a sandy floor and went back about ten feet, ending in a crack in the rock that was perhaps a foot wide. The ceiling started out at six feet but rapidly sloped down to no more than four at the back. I shone the light into the crack but couldn't see anything that resembled a passageway, just more gray rock. Fortunately the cave was dry as a bone. I switched off the penlight.

"Okay, mutts," I announced quietly. "We're officially here."

I shucked my bedroll and the field belt and then moved back to the entrance to see what kind of view I had. It wasn't terrific. Because of the way the cave entrance made that initial turn, I couldn't see much of the Creigh place without coming back outside. Fine for the nighttime but dangerous during the day. I went outside and sat down with my back against the rock again. The cave would be okay for holing up, but I needed a watching point that would conceal me and the dogs while giving me a clear view.

There was another problem. Nathan had come back to the cabin to get some dogs. If they were trackers, *and* if he went to Laurie May's, they might track me up to and through the crack. After the shooting earlier, somebody knew I was in the area, and probably where I'd come from. In which case, I didn't want to be holed up in any dead-end cave. They could just stick their shotguns into the entrance and leave the resulting gore to compost.

The cell phone slipped out of my pocket. I picked it up, switched on, and checked for a signal. This time there were two whole bars. I fished around for Carrie's number and called her. She answered on the third ring, and I moved back into the cave's entrance.

"Where are you?" she asked. Her voice sounded a bit off.

I told her and then asked her the same question.

"At your fancy cabin," she said. "My room at the main lodge was on the government's nickel, which is no longer on offer."

"Good, I'm glad someone's using it. I wish I were there instead of out here in this damned cave."

"You didn't tell me you had all this scotch here," she said. "I may have overindulged. Just a little."

That accounted for her voice and slightly slurred words. "Good for you," I said. "Having second thoughts about resigning, are we?"

"Yep," she said. "Standing on lofty principle usually means the next step is down. The loftier, the farther down. I should have eaten something. I've already got a headache."

"Regrets?"

"Well . . . ," she said, hesitating. "I've discovered that being in the SBI gave me most of my identity. Now . . ."

"Now you feel naked," I said. "No badge, no creds, no gun, no authority. And guess how I know all this?"

"Yeah, I suppose you do. I'm desperate to pursue this thing with the Creighs, but I'm no longer a player." I heard a hiccup. "May have fucked up."

"Would they take you back?"

"You know? I'm not so sure. My boss didn't try very hard to talk me out of it, now that I think about it. Of course, he was pissed over what we'd been doing here in the hills."

"Drink lots of water," I said. "Get some sleep. Everything looks better in the daylight."

"I won't," she said. "Daylight means mirrors. What are you going to do?"

"Laurie May suggested I hide out in Grinny Creigh's hollow because that's the last place they'd go looking for me. But Nathan just showed up to get some dogs, so my plan may have to change, and soon. There's no good cover where I am now."

"I should be out there with you," she said. "This is my beef."

"Right now you're more useful to me in Marionburg," I said. *Especially with a snoot full of scotch*, I thought. "I may yet need extracting if these guys get lucky."

"I suppose," she said. There was a moment of silence, a noise I couldn't identify, and then I heard her say "Oh, shit." Then the connection was broken.

I immediately called back. The phone gave me a canned system message saying it was no longer on the air.

What the hell had just happened? Had the Creighs gone after Carrie? In Carrigan County? I shut the phone off and restowed it. I looked at the shepherds, who were lying there alert, awaiting orders. Something told me to get out of that cave and to go in motion. I told the dogs to stay down and stepped out of the cave to reconnoiter. The more I thought about it, the more it seemed that Nathan and his dogs might be on my trail pretty soon, so I couldn't stay up here on the ridge, and it wouldn't be terribly bright to let them catch me in that crack in the rock.

Okay, we'd go down to Grinny's. If Nathan and his dogs had tracked me toward the cabin, he'd think his dogs simply wanted to go back to the pen. I hoped.

I roused the shepherds and we set out down the ridge. There was no cover until I got within a hundred feet of the cabin, and then we slipped into a tree line. I went downhill along the tree line until we got abeam of the cabin itself. I put the shepherds on a long down and crept to the house side of the trees, some thirty feet from the porch. This was where Nathan's black hats had been standing the night they brought me up to socialize with Grinny. The wind was slightly in my face, which hopefully would keep the dog pack behind the cabin from detecting us. Grinny's reputed second sight might present a more dangerous problem. There was some light coming through the curtained windows, but it was yellow and diffused, probably lantern light. I couldn't see anyone inside or on the grounds.

I was trying to figure out what to do next when I heard another vehicle coming up the pasture road below the cabin. It sounded like a modern SUV instead of one of the ancient pickup trucks these folks seemed to favor. Whoever it was knew where he was going and drove right up to the front of the cabin. I settled down in the pine thicket to watch as the vehicle, a dark-colored Chevrolet Tahoe, stopped and shut down.

For a long minute, nothing happened, and then the front door of the cabin opened and Grinny Creigh stepped out onto the front porch. A foreign-looking man got out of the SUV and greeted her in the lilting accent of Southwest Asia. He went halfway up the steps and stopped when she told him to wait there, and then she went back into the cabin.

I studied the man as he waited in the dim moonlight. He was perhaps five-seven or -eight and in his late thirties. He had a sharply outlined, close-cropped black beard that joined his mustache, and he had the prominent nose of Pakistan or perhaps India. He wore khaki trousers and a light windbreaker, under which I could see a cell phone and a pager clipped to his belt. He waited patiently on the front steps, looking around at the mountains and open fields around the cabin as if he'd seen it all before.

The door opened and Grinny Creigh reappeared, carrying a lantern this time and leading a young girl by the hand. The girl was between eight and ten years old and very thin, with flaxen hair and a pinched, frightened face. Grinny gripped the little girl's wrist as if to make sure she wouldn't bolt as she raised the lantern to fully illuminate the child. The man on the steps examined her carefully, asking her to turn around a couple of times, and then came up on the porch to lay his hands on her. Given what I was expecting, I was surprised to see that he wasn't touching her in a sexual manner, but rather examining her, the way a doctor might. He looked into her eyes and mouth, asked her to cough even though he didn't have a stethoscope, and felt her limbs as if to gauge how well fed she was.

I experienced a sudden urge to shoot them both and rescue the little girl. But for all I knew, this was a county social services doctor or PA making a house call of some kind, even if it was pretty late. The child was thin and frightened, although she didn't look to be ill. Grinny just stood there looking bored, but not letting go of that slim, bony wrist for one moment. I thought for just a second that I glimpsed another small, pale face peeking through the curtains at what was going on out front, but then it was gone, like a ghost on the move.

The man thanked Grinny and said that everything was acceptable. Grinny turned the child around and sent her into the cabin. Then she turned back to the man, who had stepped down to the walkway.

"If'n we had to, how many could you take in one go?" she asked.

The man thought about that for a moment. "No more than one per night," he said finally. "And that would be difficult. The airport security would notice."

"Ain't sayin' we'll have to, mind," she said. "But there's been some folks snoopin' around, and it ain't been the ones we usually see 'round here, them drug cops, I'm talkin' about."

"Who are they, then?" he asked.

"We don't know. M. C. had one of 'em, but he got away 'fore we could have a little talk with'm."

"Is it about the children?" the man asked.

"Like I keep sayin', we don't know. But if we git cornered up, you could take all of 'em, right?"

"The demand far exceeds the supply, always," the man responded. "It's the processing and transport that are tricky. For a sudden oversupply, the costs would be higher, of course."

"Unh-hunh," Grinny said in a sarcastic, suspicions-confirmed tone of voice.

"Let me get something out of the car for you," he said, and turned to go back to the SUV. Grinny stood there for a second and then reached down behind that oversized rocking chair and pulled a shotgun toward her, which she set down behind her against the door. Her huge bulk completely hid it from view.

The man came back from the SUV with something small and black in his hand, and for a second I wondered if he had a gun. Instead he handed it up to Grinny on the porch.

"This is a one-time pager," he said. "Use it once and I will come at the regular hour. Then throw it away. Never use it again because they are able to track such devices now." He pointed up into the sky. "From space, using satellites.

Imagine. If you must move them all at once, activate the pager precisely at noon on whichever day you use it. Otherwise, activate it at some other time, it doesn't matter when."

"All right," she said, keeping her right hand buried in her housecoat and close to that shotgun.

"I will be back in a few nights," he said. "I will let your Mr. Mingo know when to meet me."

She nodded curtly at him and went back into the house, shutting the big wooden door and locking it with some kind of metal bar, which I could hear thump down into place. The man drove off in his SUV. He'd been just far enough away for me not to be able to get the license plate number.

I sat back on my haunches. Some kind of a transaction had just taken place. The little girl had been approved for sale, confirming our worst suspicions about Grinny Creigh. And there might be more of them, either in the cabin with her or somewhere else, based on her question about having to possibly move more than one in a hurry.

But move them where and to what end? He had said something about airports, so maybe the theories about children being sold out of the hills into global sex-slave markets was accurate. I remembered Laurie May's question about what kind of mamas would do such a thing. What kind indeed.

Two dogs started to bark back in the dog pen. I decided it was time to get out of there. I checked the cell phone, but there was no signal down here at the cabin. The dogs finally shut up after five minutes or so. We moved away from the cabin and went back up the hill, staying in the trees for as long as possible, the shepherds plastered to my side. It was slower going up than it had been coming down, and I was puffing once I made it to the cave. I slipped into the black hole and rested for about twenty minutes, trying to decide what to do next. I kept coming up with the same answer—immediate departure. Then deal with the problem of the children. I tried the cell again. There was a single signal bar showing in the little window, so I told the dogs to stay and stepped back out of the cave to see if I could do better.

My heart sank. I should have heeded my own advice. There was Nathan, standing with two other men in the dim moonlight. All of them had shotguns. A fourth man was wrestling the tracking leads on the two big dogs I'd seen Nathan throw into the back of the pickup truck. I thought about calling out the shepherds, but there were simply too many shotguns.

Nathan swung the barrel of his shotgun toward the distant cabin and tipped his head in that direction. Clear enough.

10

They marched me down the hill to the cabin, Nathan leading, the other two gunmen behind me. They'd patted me down and relieved me of my field belt, the cell phone, and my weapon up at the cave. The man with the dogs was way ahead of us, being practically dragged back to the dog pen by those two big brutes. None of them had gone into the cave, which was a good thing because I don't know what would have happened if they had. They'd have probably shot the shepherds and then fed them to the big dogs. If they'd seen me coming back up the hill from the cabin, they weren't letting on.

Grinny wasn't sitting in her chair on the front porch like the last time. They took me to one of the side barn buildings and locked me into what had been either a horse or cow stall, I couldn't tell which. They chained a steel cuff to my right ankle and then barred the wooden stall door. The other end of the chain was made fast to a wooden beam that had to be twelve inches square. The floor was covered in dense straw that smelled of old manure. There were no windows and no lights. I could hear some kind of animals shuffling around in other stalls, but it was too dark to see what they were. The walls of the stall were about seven feet high, rough oak, and harder than any nail. The barn roof beams were a good fifteen feet above my head.

I sat down in a corner of the stall with my back to the plank walls, my leg extended to accommodate the chain. I could hear some of the dogs in the big pen, but no human sounds. The back of my neck was on a low burn.

I was in deep shit any way you looked at it. The shooter earlier had not been firing warning shots, which meant he'd been told to take care of business. I was now locked up in the enemy's camp. The fact that there was a chain shackle permanently mounted in a stall meant that they'd held people here before. And there was a fair possibility that my only contact with the outside world had also been compromised. Greenberg's crew had been pulled off to a project well south of the area, and no one in the SBI would be especially concerned that they weren't hearing from Carrie.

I had to get out of there. I began with the shackle. Like most cops, I carried two knives, a big one on the field belt and a much smaller penknife sewn into a pouch in the back of my trousers' waistband. I fished that out and went to work on the shackle's lock. The shackle was actually a work shackle, the kind used on prisoners in a chain gang to keep them from running. It was not tight at all. The lock was an old-style, bar key series lock, but the steel was as strong as ever and my knife not strong enough to make the mechanism move. I took off my field boot and sock and tried to pull my foot through the shackle. I have smallish feet for a guy of my size, but the ankle was a mite too big. If I had some grease it might just work, but I was fresh out of grease guns. I sat back and rubbed my neck. Where there was a thick smear of greasy ointment.

I wiped as much of the smelly stuff as I could on my bare ankle and heel and then pulled the chain out to its full length. I knew I'd have one shot at this, because the tissue would swell immediately when I really forced the issue. I set my foot at as flat an angle as I could, closed my eyes, and exerted a steady pull. It hurt, but it was very close. I took a deep breath, set my jaw, and then yanked hard on my left leg. The rim of the shackle felt like it was planing off the top of my foot, but the heel finally slipped through and I was free of the chain.

I opened my eyes. My instep felt like it was on fire, and I could feel a weep of blood starting up. The rest of my foot did not want to straighten out just yet. I could actually feel the ankle starting to swell. I rubbed more ointment on the raw, abraded skin, then put my sock and boot back on while I still could. Standing was harder than I had expected, and running was clearly out of the question for a while. What I needed was a nice cold creek, preferably a few miles from Grinny Creigh.

Now for the walls.

The stall walls were stacked oak boards, but they had warped over the years and there were finger and toeholds all the way up. I wondered if a one-footed guy could do it. Depends on how bad he wanted out of here, I told myself. I started up the wall, which wasn't that hard except for my left wheel, which could take almost no weight. At the top of the wall I found out that there were two rows of stalls facing each other across a narrow aisle. There was absolute darkness at one end and the barely visible outline of a set of double doors at the other.

The doors were not locked. They'd assumed that the chain would keep anyone from getting out of that stall. I could hear the noises of the dog pen to the right of the barn and knew that opening that door would rouse at least some of the dogs. That would bring Nathan or one of his helpers. Then I noticed there was a small room at the end of the aisle nearest the door. I opened that door and found a smelly freezer running quietly underneath a window. So they *did* have electrical power up here. I wondered how—maybe a hidden generator?

The window was dusty, but I could make out the open dog pen and, beyond that, the end of the porch on Grinny's cabin. There were no lights on in the cabin, and the dogs were lumps of shadow on the dirt floor of the forty-foot-square pen. I opened the freezer and found unwrapped chunks of frostbitten red meat, probably deer, stacked inside. I tested the window. It opened freely. I saw a couple of the dogs look over to the window with sleepy interest. I opened the window wide and threw out a lump of meat. Two dogs got up immediately and went for it. This awakened some of the other dogs. I began throwing meat to the far side of the pen, away from the side I'd be traveling. Soon the whole pack was up and chasing rock-hard pieces of meat around the pen. There was some snarling and growling, but I threw so much out there that pretty soon every dog had something. Then I slipped out the front door and limped toward Grinny's cabin porch. I was hoping that the noise from the dog yard would bring Nathan to the door, and I was determined to get there before he did.

It was close. I was up on the porch and sneaking as fast as my bum foot would allow, trying to get next to the cabin's front door. It opened and Nathan stepped through, trusty double-barreled shotgun at port arms. He was wearing long johns and was obviously not quite awake. I stepped in front of him, grabbed the barrels, and pushed them hard back into his mouth. He was stunned, both to see me standing there and by the sudden pain of getting hit in the mouth. Feeling the barrel still slack, I hit him again, this time on the bridge of his nose. He yelled in pain and tilted to one side, which is when I jerked the shotgun out of his hands, reversed it, and jabbed with the gun butt, the first time between his legs followed by a thump to his forehead as he doubled over. He collapsed with a whoof onto the porch, blood streaming out of his nose and mouth and his hands clutching air, not knowing what to grab hold of first because everything seemed to hurt. Hopping on one foot to get a few feet away from him, I then took a golfing stance and teed off on both of his shins with the gun butt, curling him into a grunting, gasping ball of agony on the porch. You want to keep a really tall guy down, the shins are always the best place to work.

Then I pointed the shotgun into the dark interior of the cabin and discharged both barrels, aiming high in case there were kids in there. I mostly wanted to keep any reinforcements from charging the door. The ten-gauge kicked like a mule, and the noise was terrific. The dogs, frozen meat forgotten, set up a barking frenzy when the gun went off. I heard breaking glass inside the cabin and something solid falling onto the floor. I glanced at Nathan, but he was still curled on the floor, mewling through bloody lips. I spotted the box of shells on the little table by the door and grabbed a handful. I stepped away from the door and over to one of the windows while I jacked out the empty hulls and reloaded. I fired two more rounds through the left-hand window and heard more debris flying around inside the cabin's front room.

I reloaded one more time and this time blasted two holes into the porch floorboards, one by Nathan's feet and the other right next to his head. He screamed in terror and scrambled through the front door back into the gunsmoke-filled cabin. I stuffed another handful of shells into my pockets and limped off the porch, reloading as I went. The dog pen was insane at this point, so I fired two more rounds into the enclosure, which sent most of the dogs yipping for cover. Then I hobbled my way down the front field toward the woods, using the warm shotgun to balance myself.

My ears were ringing with the sound of the heavy gun. I wondered if I should have killed Nathan, because if he ever caught up with me, he was going to want me dead. At the edge of the woods, maybe fifty yards from the cabin, I fired two more rounds up at the porch. At that range, I knew they wouldn't do any real damage, but the rattle of ten-gauge pellets on the front wall ought to encourage anyone inside to stay inside. Then I pushed into the trees and headed downhill for my favorite river road.

I wasn't afraid of Nathan coming after me, but Grinny, assuming she was there, might loose the dog pack. A tactical police shotgun could keep them at bay, but not an old double-barreled model, so I kept an eye and an ear over my shoulder for canine pursuit as I made my way awkwardly down the dirt road. There was just enough moonlight for me to make pretty good time, especially since I was going downhill. As the adrenaline from the fight with Nathan crashed, I realized how tired I was and that my foot was really hurting now. It was well after midnight, and I hadn't had any sleep since that brief nap in Laurie May's hideaway.

Laurie May. Had she told them where I was hiding? And where Carrie was probably staying in Marionburg? Nathan and his dogs had probably come through that crack, so they may have tracked me to the cave. On the other hand, what scent article did they have to set up the dogs? Something I'd left behind in her daughter's cabin? The blanket on the bed?

The jury was still out on Old Lady Laurie, although I had a hard time featuring her as being an ally of these bad guys.

I stumbled over something in the dirt road and went sprawling, doing my injured foot no good at all. *Time to take a break*, I thought. I was at least a quarter mile down the hill from Grinny's place, so I should be able to hear anything coming through the woods after me. I sat down on the ground with my back to a fallen tree trunk. My neck was still hurting, but it didn't feel like

I was battling an infection. My foot had been rubbed raw by my boot, and I wasn't looking forward to seeing my sock. The ankle was definitely swollen, so I wasn't about to take that boot off, either. I reloaded the shotgun and counted my remaining shells. Nine. At least I was armed again, as any human pursuers would find out if they crowded me.

After ten minutes, I hoisted my weary ass off the ground and began a high-speed hobble down the road. Getting off my feet for a few minutes may have been a mistake; my left ankle was bigger than it had been and very definitely not happy. I consoled myself by thinking about how Nathan felt right now.

Then I heard something coming fast through the woods behind me, and it wasn't of the two-legged variety. I swung the shotgun around and took a shooting stance, and then relaxed when Frick and Frack burst out of the trees. I chastised them for waiting to reappear until I'd escaped from the clutches of the Creighs. They went into heavy licking and panting mode anyway. As usual I felt a whole lot safer with my two furry friends alongside. They'd detect anything else coming through the woods long before I would.

In fact, they heard the vehicle coming up the dirt road before I did. My fatigued brain had been on the lookout for headlights, but this vehicle wasn't showing any. All three of us scuttled off the road and into the underbrush. I put the dogs on a down and hunched behind a briar bush until I finally saw Rue Creigh's pickup truck grinding up the road in second gear. There appeared to be two people in the truck's front seat. I couldn't make out their features but assumed one was Rue and the other—Carrie?

Yes, by God, it was Carrie, and she looked a lot like a prisoner. When the truck was not quite even with my hiding place, I stepped out of the bushes to the side of the road and pointed the shotgun at Rue's face. She stopped almost immediately, her brake lights painting the woods behind her with a red glow. Her window was open.

"Police officer," I shouted, out of habit, I guess. "Shut it down, step out, and let me see your hands!"

Rue surprised me, and she might have succeeded had not Carrie yelled a warning. Rue produced a shiny handgun seemingly out of nowhere and pointed it right at me, obviously preparing to shoot right through her own windshield. I pulled both triggers on the ten-gauge, and Rue's face and head disappeared in a bloody explosion of skin, bone, brains, and windshield glass. I felt something snap by my own head as the big shotgun bucked in my hands, and realized she'd actually gotten off a shot a millisecond before I sent her to see her Maker.

I slowly lowered the shotgun and saw Carrie piling out of the pickup truck, her face ashen and the left side of her blouse and jeans stained with gore. Her wrists were cuffed in duct tape and she was barefoot. Bits of windshield glass glittered on her clothes.

"Sorry about that," I told her, trying not to look at the practically headless torso canted over to one side in the driver's seat. "Cop training. See the gun, pull the trigger. Answer questions later."

"Jesus *Christ!*" Carrie gasped. "What a mess!" She was trying not to stare at the truck's bloody interior. My ears were ringing again, and the woods seemed to have gone very quiet after the double blast of the shotgun. I wondered if they'd heard that up at Grinny's cabin.

"I was hoping to spring you *and* take the truck," I said. "Now I think I'd rather walk."

"Got that right," Carrie said, a hand over her mouth. "Talk about wet work. God*damn!*"

"Was she the 'oh, shit' I heard you say before we got cut off?"

Carrie nodded. "I turned around and there she was, gun in hand. I hadn't locked the screen or the front door, and I was fresh out of shepherds. She had a roll of duct tape on her wrist like a bracelet and a look of pure, evil pleasure on her face."

Now she had no face at all. First Nathan and now Rue. Grinny Creigh and what was left of her clan would declare war over this. "We have to get out of this county," I said. I told her what I'd done to Nathan and how I thought he and his boys had been able to find me.

"Laurie May?" Carrie said. "No way."

"Either blood's thicker than water, or they may simply have scared it out of her. Or hurt her, for that matter. Nathan may have used those two dogs to make her talk, not find me." I took out my penknife and hacked away at the duct tape. Carrie's clothes smelled of the blood and bits splattered all over the inside of the truck.

"Where're your shoes?" I asked.

She nodded in the truck's direction. "In there, in the backseat," she said. It was obvious she wasn't going anywhere near the truck, and she was licking her lips as if she were fighting down nausea.

I felt about the same way, but she had to have shoes, and I also wanted that gun. I had to hold my nose and my gorge while I retrieved Carrie's shoes and socks from the floor of the back seat and also Rue's handgun, a stainless steel .357 Magnum. Big gun for a woman to handle, but she'd still managed to get one off *and* damned hear hit me with it. She hadn't hesitated one second, either, even while staring at eternity down the barrels of a ten-gauge. I saw her cell phone lying on the seat, but she'd bled all over it, and I wasn't about to touch it. There were two unopened and unsullied bottles of water on the floor in the back, and I did take those. The smell in the truck was horrible, and suddenly I just had to back out of there.

I called the shepherds while Carrie got her shoes on, and then we got going down the dirt road. I figured it'd be daylight in three hours or so, and we needed to put as much distance as possible between us and the Creighs while we could.

"You okay?" Carrie asked me after five minutes.

"I'll live," I said. "I've shot one other perp during my career, and I've witnessed a few more."

"Is it always that bad?" she asked.

"There's always a lot more blood than you'd expect," I replied, not really wanting to talk about this just now. I knew it had been purely a self-defense shoot, but I still had this cold pit in my stomach. It wasn't like on the television, where there was a medium bang and a foreboding stain. One moment I'd been looking at and talking to a living human being and, in her own blowsy fashion, an attractive young woman. The next second there was nothing but a pumping stump where her head had been.

She got one off, I kept telling myself. *Close enough for you to hear it go by, too.* The question was—had she been thinking self-defense, too? Or had she just been that hard-boiled? Someone else in my shoes, without police training and reflexes, might still have hesitated when she produced that gun. That .357 would have had about the same effect on my face.

"Don't torture yourself," Carrie said, as if reading my thoughts. "She told me Grinny had sent her into Marionburg to get close to you and then put a knife in your ribs—her words—but the shepherd alerted and you turned her down. Said you hurt her womanly pride. That most men most definitely did *not* turn her down."

"Her mother's daughter," I said, calling the dogs in closer now that we were getting nearer to the paved road. "How far is it to the Carrigan County line?"

"Eight, nine miles on the river road," she said. "What's the matter with your foot?"

I told her about getting out of the shackle in the barn. As we reached the pavement, I looked at my watch. Three thirty.

"Right is southeast, toward Marionburg. The road follows the river. I was going to suggest we start jogging, make better time, but if your foot's injured—"

"It's not like we have much of a choice," I said grimly. "Let's boogie."

* * *

We made pretty good time, but only because we were going downhill for most of it. We walked the few upgrades we encountered and stopped often to listen for vehicles. My foot made it clear that it was going to get even with me. At times I wished it would just go ahead and fall off. My main concern was that once Rue's body was found, they'd definitely get those dogs out. We'd left a clear track down that dirt road, and the pavement wouldn't disguise the scent very much. I thought about crossing the river to interrupt the scent trail, but the stream was getting wider as it flowed downhill, and I was afraid we'd lose too much time. We badly needed to get out of Robbins County.

About an hour before sunrise, we came upon a whitewater rafting outfitter's place situated between the road and the stream. There was a log lodge building, which advertised tickets and supplies, and a dirt parking lot with chains across the entrance and exit. We stopped to catch our breath and then looked at each other. A raft ride would be a whole lot easier than jogging down the road. And it would eliminate our spoor.

We snuck around to the back of the place and found canoes hanging upside down on racks and a row of inflatable rafts stacked on their sides, big ones, medium ones, and even two-man jobs, all attached to a large oak tree by a cable with a padlock. The wire and lock were mostly there for show, because the wire ran through individual rope handles on the rafts. I cut out one of the medium, eight-man rafts, and we pushed it down to the ramp. There were paddles strapped inside as well as life vests. We unstrapped two paddles, put on some damp life vests, loaded the shepherds, and pushed out into the stream.

"Ever done this before?" I asked.

"Once," she said. "In Colorado. Much bigger raft, with professional guides. I was just along for the ride. Never felt so helpless in my life."

"Those are big rivers. This stream shouldn't be too bad. I think we can mostly drift with the current."

"So is there a reason that place called itself a *white*water rafting outfit?" she asked pointedly.

"Probably in the spring when this thing is up and running," I replied, with more confidence than I actually felt. I'd been out a couple of times but would have to admit I knew next to nothing about navigating real rapids. Fortunately, it was late summer and there shouldn't be enough water in the stream to build any real rapids ahead. If there were, we could always get out and resume our cross-country marathon.

"Do you think this will slow up the pursuit any?" she asked, again mirroring my own thoughts. I was dragging my left foot, sock and all, in the cold water. It felt wonderful. Getting the boot off had not been wonderful. I'd cut away the laces and then let the weight of the water pull it off.

"If they use dogs, they'll know we hit the river with a raft. Then they'll have to search both sides to find us, and the dogs won't be of much use."

"Is that a yes?"

My mind was foggy, and my foot was getting a good start on becoming a block of ice. I realized that getting into the raft was mostly going to be a comfortable break in an otherwise precarious escape plan. Once M. C. Mingo got a look into Rue's truck, every cop in the entire country and all the black hats would be on our trail. And getting into Carrigan County wasn't necessarily going to solve our problems. Mingo could fax over some crime-scene photos to Sheriff Hayes's office and we might get rounded up and handed right back over to our nemesis. I ducked her question.

"What else did Rue reveal on the way to Grinny's cabin?" I asked. "She say what they planned to do with you?"

"Mingo knows I'm not with the SBI anymore," she said.

"Which meant he was worried enough to check."

"Yes, I suppose. I tried to bluff her, tell her there'd be consequences when I got back."

"And?"

"And she said something along the lines of 'Honey, it ain't like you comin' back.'"

"Well, there you are," I said. "Now she's dead instead of you."

"Thank you."

"Yeah, right," I said wearily. "It was still pretty awful."

"Worse because it was a woman getting shot?"

I had to think about that for a moment. "Yes, I think so. That's probably not PC, and I know she was a snake, but . . ."

She moved closer to me in the back of the raft. Under other circumstances it would have been a very pleasant ride through the soft night. The stream was about sixty feet wide, and the raft was just sailing along peacefully. We were both in the back, and the shepherds were at our feet. The raft would bump into the occasional rock or one of the banks, spin lazily, and rejoin the current. We'd stowed the two sweeps, and I'd shoved the shotgun into two nylon safety harness loops on the side. Large trees overhung the banks, and the dim moonlight peered in and out of the leaves. We'd seen no vehicles on the road above, and after ten minutes or so I think we both fell asleep.

Which is how the waterfall surprised us. I awoke to feel the back end of the raft coming up and the front tipping down dangerously. By the time I got my wits about me we were over the edge and dropping like the proverbial stone. I grabbed a safety loop with one hand and Carrie with the other about the same moment that we hit the water below with a surprisingly painful thump. Both shepherds slid forward to the bow of the raft and were catapulted back to the middle when the raft folded up into an inflatable sandwich for an instant. I think the only reason we all hadn't gone into the water was that we had been grouped back at the stern of the raft.

Carrie swore as the raft did a giddy three-sixty and we got a look at the falls, which fortunately were only about six feet high. But now we found out why they called themselves a whitewater rafting company. The river's banks were closing in, and the current was beginning to really assert itself.

"Reveille, reveille," I said, reaching for one of the paddle sweeps. I hauled the dogs back to where we were, and Carrie pulled out a sweep.

"What do we do?" she said, shouting because the water was getting noisy. The raft hit a big boulder and whipped around, sending us backward down the increasingly turbulent stream.

"Not this," I yelled, and began to sweep with the paddle to get us going bow first before we hit something again. Carrie copied what I was doing, and we fought each other for a minute before we realized what was happening.

"Get up front," I called. "Try to keep us from hitting anything dead-on."

She scrambled to the front of the boat as I finally got the damned thing across and then aligned properly in the current. The dogs were staying low and giving me reproachful looks. I wondered if shepherds got seasick.

Ahead was a long, straight channel of high, slab-sided rocks and whitewater. *This stretch must be really something in the spring*, I thought, as we went over another low waterfall neither of us had seen in the darkness. Carrie gave a whoop and then disappeared in a blast of spray and bad language. If it had been daylight this might have even been fun. The good news was that we were making good distance in the suddenly strong current. The bad news was that we were effectively out of control, since neither of us knew what we were doing. And it was starting to get light, which meant that soon there would be eyes on the shore trying to find us.

We were shoved sideways to one side of the main stream, and the boat hung up on something, which resulted in cold water pouring over one gunwale in alarming quantities. The dogs scrambled instinctively to the other side, and the weight shift dislodged the boat before either of us was ready. Once more we were rolling downstream backward. I didn't know much, but I knew that was a prescription for disaster, and I yelled at Carrie to pull hard on her sweep. She called back that she was trying, and then the damned boat lunged sideways and settled into a whirlpool, spinning us sickeningly in three complete circles before spitting us out into the main channel again.

And then it was over. The river catapulted us out of one final, narrow stone chute into a broad expanse of black water and went back to sleep. I didn't know how long we'd been in the rapids, such as they were, but it had seemed forever. The river widened out again and entered a long, deep curve, once more embraced by large trees on either bank. We were both wet and, even in the late-summer dawn, cold. Frick and Frack were disgusted at our ineptitude and wouldn't look at me.

The shotgun was sloshing around in about three inches of water, so I shipped the oar and extracted the heavy gun. I ejected the two sodden cartridges, reloaded with semi-dry ones from my pockets, and put the gun across my knees. Carrie crawled toward the back of the raft, laying her oar down in the bottom, but the current had thrown us to the outside of the big bend, and the raft crunched to a halt in some gravel. Carrie grabbed her oar, got up on her knees, and tried to push us off the gravel bar. I shifted to the port side to unload the part that was aground, and she got up into a crouch to put her body weight into the push.

Just as she succeeded in pushing us off, she grunted painfully and pitched headfirst out of the boat as the echo of a long gun came booming across the water. A second round slashed the air in front of my face, and then a third smashed a big waterspout at the bow of the raft as we swung back out into the current. I flung myself flat into the bottom of the raft and tried to see where the fire was coming from. Two more rounds came in, both raising waterspouts in the middle of the raft, which I realized was now filling with water and starting to sink. The shepherds were scrambling around in the rising water right beside me.

Then I saw them: two vehicles parked nose out on a high bank on the road side of the river, about fifty yards ahead. One a civilian van, one a cop car. I caught a muzzle flash from between them as another round ripped all the way through the fabric of the raft. The raft's forward motion had stopped. I couldn't see what had happened to Carrie and desperately wanted to roll out of the raft, but didn't dare expose myself. Then I realized I was still gripping the shotgun. I tipped the barrels to make sure there was no water inside and then fired both in the general direction of the vehicles. Even partially wet, both cartridges functioned as advertised, and the shooting stopped long enough for me to roll sideways out of the raft. The dogs jumped in with me, and we started swimming awkwardly toward the same bank the shooters were on. When my knees banged on some bottom rocks I realized I could make better time by scrambling through the shallows, which were now out of the line of fire from the vehicles.

I searched back upstream in the morning twilight for any signs of Carrie but couldn't see anything, and I knew it wouldn't take those guys long to figure out where I'd gone to ground. I crawled up the low, stony bank with the dogs, fumbling for more shells while staying low enough not to make a good target. I didn't like the idea of firing on police officers one bit, but had to assume that these were Mingo's people and that they had orders not to bring back any prisoners.

We crashed into some low bushes and reeds near the top of the bank. I downed the shepherds and reloaded the shotgun. My clothes were soaked, and the hulls of the shells were definitely wet. I could only pray that they would fire if I needed them. The raft had disappeared out in the river, either sunk or floating just beneath the surface. I had one boot on, one boot gone, and no longer cared if my foot hurt.

Carrie had been hit and was probably bleeding in the shallows back upstream. I had to decide: try to get back to her or deal with these guys first. Easy decision: I had to neutralize this threat before I'd be able to help Carrie. I decided to do the unexpected and started crawling *toward* the two vehicles. It was tough going through all the riverbank debris. I couldn't see the shooters, and there'd been no more rifle fire since the ten-gauge had spoken, but I knew that it was highly unlikely I'd done any real damage from that range. The shepherds came with me, staying right by my legs and crouching low.

When I'd gone about thirty feet the bushes started to thin out, and I lay down behind a hollowed-out sand embankment for a minute to see if I could hear the shooters. Then I realized they were just on the other side of the same snag-mound. I thought I heard one of the vehicles start up.

"Lucas got the woman," a voice said. "Got her good."

"What the hell do we do now?" a second, younger voice asked nervously. "I don't hold with shootin' no women, and besides, 'at bastard's got him a Greener."

"We wait," the first cop said. "Mingo'll be comin' on with the rest of Grinny's boys. Then we'll do a find-'em line and roust his ass out. He ain't goin' far, and she ain't goin' nowheres."

"Mingo gonna take 'em in?"

"Shee-it," the first one spat. "Mingo's gonna take care of business. You seen what they done to Rue?"

"I heard," the younger one said.

I could hear him adjusting his position. The embankment was at least five feet high. I was beneath it; they had to be crouching just on the other side. I settled down even deeper into the sand. These guys were deputies. Lucas, who-ever he was, must be one of Mingo's "unofficial" deputies. I was tempted to just stand up and blow them away. Tempted, hell—they'd shot Carrie without compunction or warning.

But then I hesitated. I was assuming the shotgun's shells would work, and they'd been awfully wet going into the barrels. And where the hell was Lucas? Had that been him going to fetch Mingo? Or was he circling behind my land-ing spot?

I eased the heavy shotgun around from underneath me and pointed it up-ward. Still I hesitated. They were cops with their blood up. As far as they were concerned, they were chasing two stone-cold killers, and God only knew what Mingo had told them. It was Lucas who'd shot Carrie, not these two. At this range, any part of a ten-gauge blast would be fatal. But I needed to do some-thing, especially if I was mistaken about Lucas leaving.

I took a deep breath, gathered myself into a one-legged crouch, duckwalked up the embankment until I saw the top of a deputy's hat, stood up, let go both barrels into the space right between them, and then set the shepherds on them.

They both went down in a tangle of yells and snarling German shepherds. I let the dogs do their thing for a few seconds while I reloaded, and then I called them off. The two deputies were in Robbins County uniforms, and they were utterly terrified. The dogs had scared the living shit out of them without taking very much meat, and now their worst nightmare was standing over them with a ten-gauge in their bleeding faces.

"Got her good, did you?" I yelled at the older one, a black-haired man with a square, scowling face. I pointed the shotgun down into his crotch, and he started whimpering like a puppy. The younger one had pissed himself and was trying to hide his face behind his hands while backing away from the gaping barrels of the ten-gauge.

I herded the both of them down into the river after relieving them of their handguns, which I threw into the river. I told them to start swimming and they did a vigorous job of it, splashing through the shallows and out into the deeper channel. I really did want to blow their damned heads off but then heard sirens in the distance. I looked again upstream, trying to see any sign of Carrie, but the curve in the river still blocked my view.

Got her good, the man had said about Carrie. That meant he'd hit her in the core, and she was probably already gone. Shit.

The two deputies were scrambling through the shallows on the other side. I pointed the shotgun at them and they dived for cover, so I called in the shepherds and hobbled over to where the cruiser was parked. The other vehicle was gone. Fortunately, they hadn't followed procedure and locked the doors or taken the keys, which were right where I needed them to be. I roared out of the overlook area where they'd set up their ambush and headed south down the river road as fast as I could make that puppy go. Two miles later I sailed into Carrigan County, wondering already if I'd done the right thing by not going back for Carrie. The tactical situation clearly dictated otherwise, but still . . .

I came into Marionburg fifteen minutes later and headed right for Sheriff Hayes's office. No point in letting Mingo tell his side of the story first. I was too early; the sheriff wouldn't be in for an hour, and the look on the sergeant's face when he got a gander at me wasn't reassuring. I went back to my abode of marital bliss, fed the shepherds, took a shower, and got some dry clothes. I bandaged my foot as best I could and put a slipper on it. Then I found a diner back in town and had breakfast. As I came back out to the Robbins County cop car, I noticed two holes in the left front fender and a star in the left rear window. Go, ten-gauge.

Sheriff Hayes looked his usual weary self. I wondered again if he wasn't dealing with a heart condition or some other serious illness. Certainly the stress and strain of the job up here in the western mountains could not begin to approach that of his urban brethren, but he sure had the look. He listened in increasingly concerned silence as I told my story, including my confrontation with Rowena Creigh. When I was finished he buzzed his secretary and asked for more coffee. I thought it was for him, but he said it was actually for me. I guess I didn't look so hot, either.

"This is what, the third time you've butted your fool head against Robbins County and bounced off?" he asked.

"In a manner of speaking," I said.

"In a manner of speaking," he repeated sarcastically. "And each time, there seem to be more goddamned bodies. What are you, some kinda angel of death?"

I just sat there, not knowing what to say. He had a point.

"You came up here originally because Mary Ellen Goode asked you for a favor. You obliged and, in fact, broke that little mystery wide open. Got the little girl to talk. Established that two guys were involved, and that they were probably both deceased by now. Good work. End of story. Except it wasn't. Why the hell didn't you just go home? You do have a home, don't you? You're not homeless or anything, are you?"

I shook my head. The secretary came in with the coffee. He stopped talking while she set things down and then left.

"Rue Creigh is going to be your problem, not mine," he said. "M. C. is going to want your scalp for that, even if she did throw down on you, which I absolutely believe. That girl was all grit, clit, and bullshit. But Carrie Santángelo? That's very different. I'm going to have to notify the SBI, and they're gonna send a posse, and those boys will want to talk to you. At fucking length, if you catch my drift."

"It was her beef that I was working," I said, using her expression. "She's convinced Grinny Creigh is selling children into some porn or slave market, probably in Washington. She felt strongly enough about it that she resigned. Took early-out from the SBI to go work it on her own, knowing what that meant, too. Financially and otherwise."

"And now? Where is she now?"

I hung my head. "I don't know. She went off the side of that boat like she'd been hit by a board. By then I was ducking rifle rounds and trying to hide behind an inflatable boat. I had to deal with them before I could help her."

"You say you didn't kill them when you had the chance. They were sure as hell trying to kill you two. So why not?"

I explained about overhearing them talk about "Lucas" doing the actual shooting. "I couldn't know what Mingo had told them about us. They were a couple of deputies, probably doing what they thought was right."

"That's bullshit. Deputy sheriffs arrest perps and bring them to justice. They don't shoot them down like wetbacks in a fucking river."

"Like I said, I think it was the other guy who did the shooting. I believe emotions are running high up there. If they saw what remained of Rue Creigh, and Mingo spun them up, well . . . cops. What can I say."

He looked at me the way a drill sergeant looks at a recruit who's shown up with a pink Mohawk. That was a look I remembered from boot camp.

"And now I suppose you think you're going back in."

"Thought crossed my mind," I said. "Carrie's still out there."

"So's Mingo and his mafia," the sheriff said. "This time they'll get you. You're in no shape to go anywhere. You look like you're ready to fold up right there in that chair."

He was right. I was suddenly very tired. My bones ached, I didn't want to look at my foot, and I was worried sick about Carrie. It had been her crusade, but I was the guy who'd made it out of the kill zone. I didn't look forward to the kinds of looks I'd be getting once the SBI crew showed up.

"You need to go offline for a while while I get some adult supervision into this mess," he said. "Go back to that French boudoir of a hotel room and wait for *me* to tell *you* what you're going to do next."

"I mostly need some sleep," I said. "That's what Carrie was trying for when Rue Creigh waltzed in and took her prisoner. Right here in beautiful downtown Carrigan County, now that I think about it."

He gave me a sour look. "Okay, okay, I'll put some people on your hotel. You still have that Creigh shotgun?"

"It's out in that Robbins County cruiser," I said. "I'd like to keep it, though—Nathan took my SIG."

He thought about it for a moment, then realized the shotgun would provide little ballistic evidence.

"All right," he said. "I'll have a deputy follow you back to the hotel. Then I think we'll park their cruiser back out by the county line."

"What if Carrie was right?" I asked. "What if Grinny Creigh's got a clutch of kids in a cave somewhere and is preparing to transport them to God knows what?"

"First things first," he said. "Let's find out what happened to Carrie. You're positive it wasn't the deputies who did the shooting?"

"They had handguns, the shooter had a rifle of some kind. I definitely heard one of them say, 'Lucas got her good.' Don't know who Lucas is. That's all I'm sure about."

"But they didn't prevent it, either."

"No, they did not. And at least one of them was looking forward to phase two."

"That's what makes this thing so tough," he said. "I have zero jurisdiction or authority over there, or *I'd* take a crew in and look for Carrie. So now I'm going to call in some cavalry. Like I said, they'll want to talk to you."

"Ducky."

* * *

I slept right through to five o'clock, even though I'd set a clock for three. I fed the dogs again and then limped up to the main lodge to get something to eat. My ankle was coming down a little bit, but my instep still hurt and I couldn't get a shoe on yet. When I got back to the cabin I found three large men with North Carolina SBI windbreakers waiting for me. The shepherds were watching them from inside the screen porch. They weren't barking, but they hadn't let them in, either. They showed ID, and I told the dogs that it was okay. I led the threesome into the living room.

The man who appeared to be in charge introduced himself as Senior Supervisory Special Agent Carl Gelber. He was not a happy camper. He looked like an enforcer for a mob loan shark, minus the big pasta belly. Of his two associates, one was young, maybe twenty-five, and the other was in his late forties. Both of them were big boys, too. *The SBI must have a goon squad hidden somewhere,* I thought, as I watched them try to fit into the cabin's lavishly upholstered chairs.

Gelber said he'd been briefed by Sheriff Hayes and now he wanted to hear it from me, beginning at the beginning. I asked them if they wanted a drink. Gelber just sat there looking like he was barely in control of his temper, and, no, they were not here to socialize. This was definitely a business call. His expression said that I was lucky not to have been hauled down to a dungeon for this little consultation.

I took them through it from the beginning, or at least from the point where Carrie had gotten involved. They did not take notes—they just listened. Gelber watched me the way a hawk watches a little bunny hopping across a big field, waiting for it to get equidistant from any possible cover. His stare was sufficiently hostile that I called in the shepherds and made them lie down next to my chair. If he got the message, he didn't let on. Finally, when I was finished, he told me to go through it again. That pissed me off—he was in fact treating me like some kind of suspect.

"No," I said. "I've told you what I know. I'll answer questions if you have some."

Gelber's face froze and he balled his hands into fists. *Big* fists. Frack sat up, staring at him. "Not your call, cowboy," Gelber said, leaning forward in his chair as if he were getting ready to come at me. Frick sat up now, and both shepherds were locked on, without a word or signal from me. Gelber finally noticed what was happening.

"You sic those dogs on me and I'll shoot both of them before they get off the first bark," he spat.

I sighed. "You make any sort of move just now and you'll lose both your hands and your face," I said quietly. "You need to settle down, Special Agent."

Gelber got very red in the face, and for a moment I thought he was going to try it. It would have been interesting. Bloody and noisy, but definitely interesting. Then the older agent intervened.

"Carl," he said in a voice of calm authority. "Get ahold of yourself. You're being unprofessional."

Gelber blinked, turned around to look at the older man, and then deflated. "Yes, sir," he said. "Sorry, sir." He relaxed fractionally in his chair, opened his hands, and put them on his knees. Both shepherds relaxed along with him.

"Lieutenant Richter," the older man said to me. "I'm Sam King, and I'm the western district manager for the SBI. As you might imagine, everyone's pretty upset right now. Why don't you and I have that drink. We'll just let these gents go outside for a cigarette."

It was my turn to blink, but I agreed immediately and told the dogs to lie down and watch. Gelber didn't much care for that word "watch," but he and his buddy stepped outside. Both shepherds followed them to the door and then sat down on the porch. Gelber's anger seemed to have been genuine, so I didn't think they were playing the bad cop, good cop game, but I decided to be on my guard. If this guy was the western district manager, he'd be looking to make sure that this situation didn't get any serious mud on the SBI's shoes.

"We went into Robbins County," King said once we sat back down. "I had one team looking for Carrie Santángelo, or her remains, in the area where you said the shooting went down. No sign of her, unfortunately."

"Maybe fortunately," I interjected. "No body might mean she's still alive."

"Or drowned and not coming up for the usual two more days," he said gently. "We did find the remains of the raft, hung up on a snag. Complete with bullet holes. And someone's nasty toy."

The mamba stick. *One point for me,* I thought.

"I took another team into Mingo's office in Rocky Falls," he continued. "We were rather, um, belligerent. But Mingo was prepared for us. According to him, two of his deputies were cruising the river road, looking for an escaped prisoner."

"That would be me," I said.

"Yeah. Anyway, the gospel according to Mingo: They heard shooting, stopped to investigate, saw a man they say they didn't know shooting at two unidentified people in a raft. They thought they saw one of said people get hit and fall out of said raft. When the shooter saw the cops, he took off. They called it in and went down to the riverbank to investigate because they thought there might be someone injured in the river. While they were down there, somebody grabbed their cruiser and also took off. Here endeth the lesson."

"The two vehicles were parked together when the shooting started," I said. "Side by side. The rifle shooter was firing from *between* the vehicles. Those cops are complicit in this. They knew the shooter's name."

"And we've asked Mingo to get them in for a lie detector test."

"He agree to that?"

"Hell, no, he wouldn't even ID them. I'm guessing they'll get their union rep in and then stonewall. Assuming they've advanced to that point in Robbins County. We looked at the site, and, yes, there are vehicle tracks all over it. Too many, unfortunately. We did find a couple of fresh-looking cigarette butts, which might indicate someone had been staked out, waiting. But we also found used condoms, beer cans, fast-food wrappers, so it's probably also a make-out spot. We've sent the ciggy-butts to our lab for a DNA take."

"Did they say anything about Rue Creigh getting her head blown off?"

"Not a word," King said.

"That's very interesting," I said. "I can show you where that happened. I'll bet there's some blood evidence on *that* dirt road. No mention of my taking Nathan Creigh down and 'borrowing' his shotgun?"

He shook his head and consulted his notebook. "They did say that the raft had been stolen earlier in the morning, so they suspected the guy in the raft might be their fugitive. They said you burned the jail and possibly killed two jailers during your escape. Anything on that?"

I told him of the events at the jail and that the Big brothers were here in Carrigan County under Hayes's protection and could back up my story. He nodded and made a note, which is when I realized he *had* been putting stuff into his notebook the whole time we'd been talking. Smooth western district manager.

"Mingo say anything to indicate that he knew it was Carrie who got shot?"

"News to him," King said. "He did make an oblique reference to the fact that technically, anyway, she didn't work for us anymore."

"Sending you a little message, maybe?"

"Maybe," King said. "We've been looking at Robbins County for a long time, but it's always been in connection with Mingo and his crew of 'unofficial' deputies protecting the meth trade."

"That's not what Carrie was after," I said.

"Yeah, I know. And you're probably wondering why we didn't go with it."

"I assume it was the same problem everyone has in Robbins County: no hard evidence."

"That's right," he said. "And there was a personal, somewhat obsessive angle, which tended to taint any theories she might have advanced. When she quit, I had some second thoughts, so I went to the Bureau in Charlotte and asked them what they had on any child trafficking going on in western Carolina."

"And?"

"And that got me an invitation to drive down to Charlotte for a face-to-face conference with their intel people. I was supposed to be there today, but then Sheriff Hayes called."

"What's Gelber's problem?" I asked.

"He was Carrie's immediate supervisor," King said. "He thinks she resigned because you talked her into it, and then you got her killed."

"He's got it exactly backwards," I said. "I was all done up here. She's the one who wanted me to go back in, to chase this kid thing."

"Well," King said, closing his notebook, "you're welcome to try to convince him. He might just be feeling a little guilty for not taking her theory seriously, too."

I sighed. I was still tired. "Look," I said. "I can't produce any evidence of children being abducted and transported for sale. I overheard a conversation that confirmed that theory for me, and we had one old lady say that there seemed to be a lot of kids who ran away up there, but there are lots of other possible reasons for that."

"What's your point?"

"These guys were chasing me because I know what happened at the jail and I've become a thorn in their criminal hides. But why did Grinny Creigh send her daughter to abduct Carrie here in Marionburg? For that matter, how did they know where she was? Why'd they want her?"

"Because she was getting close to something?" he asked. "Something more important than their drug operation?"

"That's my take," I said. "They've held off the DEA for some time now, with Mingo's help, of course, but suddenly they have two strangers causing problems."

"But how would they know Carrie was looking at this new angle?" he asked. "Did either of you talk to them or anyone else about selling kids?"

"No," I said, but then remembered that, yes, we had. "Wait—we did. We were helped by the old lady I mentioned, named Laurie May Creigh. Carrie did tell her about what she suspected."

"Creigh? You guys talked to one of *them?*"

"She lives in the adjoining cove. Hates Grinny Creigh. Related, but has nothing to do with her. Hid us from the black hats when we had nowhere else to go. Showed me the best place to set up a watch on the Creigh compound. I think she's all right."

But even as I said all that, I still wondered. Nathan had known exactly where to find me, and they had somehow found out about Carrie's quest. King saw my sudden doubts. Laurie May had either set a trap or was maybe now lying injured or worse in her cabin after a beating at the hands of Nathan.

"What?" King asked. I laid it out for him.

He sighed and made some more notes. "Well," he said, "our problem is just what you said. I've got an asset inside Mingo's office, but so far all we have is a bunch of stories backed up by zero physical evidence. Even now, all we got is a raft with some holes in it. We can't legally go busting in on any of the Creighs without court paper, and I don't think we'd get the paper."

"How about conducting a general, wide-area search for Carrie, then?" I said. "You have a credible report that she's been shot. Even Mingo says so, and I sure as hell say so. Search the whole damned county, and make sure you get into Grinny Creigh's compound while you do it. Urgently. That's what I'm going to do."

"You have no authority to do anything, here or over there. You know that. And Mingo would love to get his hands on you again. And if he does, this time you won't make it to any damn jail."

"I'll take my chances," I said, with more confidence than I really felt. "I'll get the Big brothers to help out. Carrie may be out there in the woods right now, waiting for help. And you can be damned sure Mingo will have people looking just as soon as he thinks you guys have given up."

The phone rang. King asked me who had this number, and I told him lots of people. I picked it up. It was the front desk in the main lodge. "Taking calls now, Mr. Richter?" the operator asked. For a moment I didn't understand him, then remembered that I'd asked them to block all calls earlier while I got some sleep.

"Yes, I am—who's calling?"

"No name, sir, but he's local and I'd guess he's been up in them thar hills for awhile."

"Give me ten seconds," I said, nodding with my head toward an extension phone on the kitchen counter. King understood immediately.

"On three," I said after hanging up. The phone started ringing again, and we picked up simultaneously.

"I gotcher woman," a rough voice declared.

I was about to say she wasn't "my woman," but finally my feeble brain engaged. "Prove it," I said.

"*Prove* it? Awright, I will." King had the handset jammed under his ear while he worked his cell phone frantically, probably trying to set up a trace.

I heard shuffling noises in the phone, the man's voice barking some orders, and then Carrie was on the line. "Hello?" she said in a weak voice.

"Carrie? This is Cam Richter. Are you injured?"

"Head hurts," she said. "Hair's all sticky. Hurts."

She wasn't entirely there for the conversation, which confirmed a head wound. I wanted to ask her where she was, but she'd have no idea and was probably wearing a duct-tape blindfold anyway. There was more noise on the phone, a grunt of pain from Carrie, and then Mr. Personality was back.

"Satisfied, are ye?"

King was making keep-him-talking gestures. "Actually," I said, "I'm not sure who that was. It might be her, but she's out of her head."

"Yeah, she is. Got her a real nasty hairdo, she does. By rights, she oughter be dead."

"And you would be—Lucas?" I asked.

"Ho-o-o-o!" he exclaimed, making an owl noise. "How d'ye figger that?"

"Your deputy buddies told me you shot her and you'd gone to find her body."

There was just a fractional pause before he responded to that. I saw King mouth an expletive and shake his head.

"I ain't Lucas and I ain't shot nobody and I don't have no truck with no damn deputies," he said. "You want yer woman back or not?"

"If it's her, yes, I want her back." *And I want you dead*, I thought. "What's the deal?"

"*Deal?* I ain't proposin' no *deal*. I'm a'tellin' ye what yer gonna do, you want this woman back alive."

"Okay, then, shoot," I said amicably. I didn't need to challenge this guy. *Remember the objective*, I told myself. *Get her back, then you can take other action.* King had closed up his cell phone. No go on a trace, but he continued to listen in.

"You'n me's gonna meet up," he said. "You gonna bring a bag'a money. *Cash* money. Five thousand greenback dollars, cash money. I get the money, I'll tell you where she's hid at. No money, I leave her there to die. Plain as that."

"Okay," I said. "That's plain, all right. I can do that. Meet where?"

"Where you was this mornin'," he said. "Where them cops was parked, a'waitin' for ye."

"So you *are* Lucas," I said. "You missed me this morning. How do I know you won't be sitting in the trees with that rifle, waiting to try again?"

"'Cause I want that damn money. I was s'posed to git paid for killin' the both of ye. Y'all got lucky. Then I figgered, hell, more'n one way to skin this here cat. But you gotta come alone, now."

He'd given up pretending he wasn't Lucas. "I don't know, Lucas," I said. "I come up there alone, carrying a bag of money, you shoot me down from ambush, then kill the woman, you get my money *and* your paycheck. Now why should I take chances like that?"

King was giving me a strange look, but he was back on his cell phone, trying something else.

"You looky here, lawman," Lucas said. "I don't need to go puttin' you down, or this woman, neither. Didn't know she was a cop, awright? Nathan and them're gonna git you for what you done to Rowena. Far's they know, this here woman's puffin' up in the damn river, but they ain't payin' me nothin' without no body, an' the way I figger it, they's all so stirred up right now, I take them a body and then it's gonna be *me* in the damn river."

"That doesn't solve my problem, Lucas," I said. "How about this—I come in one vehicle, my backup comes in a second one. We get there together, in the dark. The place where you said. Can she walk?"

A pause, as if he were thinking about it. "Maybe."

"Then we'll arrive together, two cars. One plain car, one cop car. You send her out of the woods, she gets in the plain car. My partner then gets out, puts the money out on the ground, opens it up in the headlights so you can see it's really there, and then we both drive away. You come out when you want to and we're done with it."

"How do I know ye ain't trickin' on me?"

"Because we want her back, Lucas. And we can get the five thousand— we're the cops. Five thousand doesn't mean squat to us. And we don't have to go to any bank to get it. Besides, our fight's not with you—it's with the Creighs. We're gonna have us a war, Lucas. You want to be part of that, or do you want five thousand bucks, cash money, right now, and the chance to get out of Robbins County for good? Who else but the cops can do that for you?"

There was a long silence on the line this time. I decided to wait him out. It was a simple enough proposition, and we each stood to gain.

"Midnight tonight," he said. "Mess with me, I'll cut her damn throat. Best believe that."

"I do believe it, Lucas. Like I said, our fight's not with you. You were just paid to do a job of work. Didn't pan out. So now we both get to make it right and get on with business. Midnight. We'll be there."

"Awright then," he said and hung up.

"Damned hotel PBX system," King growled. "Blocked the trace. Good work on your end, though."

"We can get the money from Sheriff Hayes's office," I said. "He'll have a buy-money stash. Then—"

"'We' is not the operative word," King said. "'We' means us, not you. It's our girl missing, and we will go meet this guy and get her back or bring him back in a rubber bag. You are still beat to shit from the morning, so you are going to stay put."

I sat back in my chair and just looked at him. I knew that what he was saying made sense. He had the authority to execute the swap, and the means to put up the proper surveillance and backup nets.

"You know I'm right on this," he said with a weary smile.

"Yeah, but."

"I understand. But let us do our jobs. We know she's alive, for the moment anyway, and if we can get her back for five grand, we will have dodged a large bullet. You stay put. We don't need any stray operators in the mix right now. We get her back, we'll call you and you can go see her in the hospital, okay?"

Much as I wanted to go along, Lucas wouldn't know me from Adam. He wanted his money, and probably wanted to put some distance between him and his prisoner now that he knew she was a cop. I agreed. "Can she have her mamba stick back?"

"No."

"Why not?"

"That belongs to the state; she no longer does."

King left to round up his team and make arrangements. I went out front and took the shepherds. We watched them go. Gelber still looked angry, but I now suspected he was one of those guys who always looks angry. I spotted the county cruiser Hayes had promised sitting out in a corner of the parking lot and walked over to shoot the breeze with the deputy. To my surprise, it turned out to be one of the Big brothers.

"I see you've got a new job these days," I said.

Bigger John grinned and stubbed out his cigarette.

"Does M. C. know you hired on over here?"

"Don't reckon," he rumbled. "But he will."

"I never thanked you guys for saving my bacon the other night," I told him.

"That done it for us," he replied. "Them Creighs is outta hand. They find that Harper girl?"

I had to think for a moment before remembering Harper was Carrie's maiden name. "SBI's got an angle, going to work it tonight," I said. "Did you know her before she left for Charlotte?"

He shook his head. "Wasn't born yet. But Mingo—he knew her. Said her old man had been a problem once upon a time, but not no longer."

He lit up another cigarette and blew a big cloud of aromatic smoke out into the night air. It momentarily made me want to go back to the noxious weed. A car came by us going into the parking lot, and two kids in the back were staring at us as they went past.

"We have a pretty good line on Agent Santángelo," I said. "Some guy named Lucas wants to trade her for cash money."

"Might be Lucas Carr," John said. "He's done some stick work for M. C. from time to time."

I didn't have to ask what stick work was. "Have you ever heard any rumors about Grinny Creigh and children in the county?" I asked him.

"Other than she cooks 'em and eats 'em?" he asked.

"Yeah, besides that. Something maybe worse."

He didn't say anything for a long minute, just kept puffing on his cigarette. It looked like a white toothpick in his massive paw.

"We did a road scrape once," he said finally. "You know, one'a them real messy MVAs? Old boy had drove himself into a tree on a bad curve. His bottom half was puddled up a coupl'a feet from his top half. The top half was still alive, talkin', like nothin' had happened."

"Adrenaline's amazing stuff," I said.

"Mm-hmm," he agreed. "So're seat belts. Boy couldn't see he'd done been cut right in half. He was goin' on, mile-a-minnit, sayin' he had to do surgery, that he was a doc, and he was late. He didn't look like no doc, more like one'a them ay-rabs. Wasn't no way we could move'm or help'm, so we let him talk, just kinda waitin' for him to bleed down. Couldn't've got'm out without a backhoe, you know what I mean? I asked him *where* he was goin' in such a damn hurry."

"And?"

"Said he had to git to the county hospital here in Marionburg. Kept jab-berin' on about how late he was. Other boy with me, he asked'm who was he cuttin' on. Said he had to do surgery on a kid. By now, he was nose down and goin' fast. Other boy asked him, what kid. Said one'a them kids over to Miz Creigh's place." John glanced up at me to see if I'd heard the important bit.

"Kids? As in plural?"

He nodded. "Kids. At Grinny Creigh's place." He ruminated on that notion for a moment before continuing. "Now, there ain't been no kids to go any-where *near* that Grinny Creigh's place for some time, not after hearin' the old folks around Robbins County talk about her boilin' babies by moonlight an' all. Anyway, M. C. shows up. Wasn't unusual—he always comes out when we get a bad MVA."

He took a final drag on the hapless cigarette and pitched it. "You know what?" he continued. "I b'lieve he knew that fella. M. C. got there just about the time this so-called doctor crossed Jordan. M. C., he tells us to go back on patrol, he's takin' over the scene. Called some other deputies in, called the fu-neral home over here in Marionburg. Last we heard of it."

"When was this?"

"Three years back," he said. "If there's any paperwork, M. C.'s got it in them private files of his."

"Fatality on the highway, the state cops do the investigation," I pointed out. "The state police reconstruction team comes in. They close the road, make a big deal."

"Not if they don't hear nothin' about it," he said calmly.

I leaned back on the left front fender of the cruiser and thought about this little story. One among many about Robbins County.

Stories. Unfortunately, that was about all we had. Stories and flashes of mor-tal violence in the night that seemed to evaporate in the cold light of day. What in the hell would a foreign doctor be doing up here? I'd seen one last night, but no locals would want an Asian or any other kind of foreigner working on them—they'd call in a woods healer first. But kids, plural, at Grinny's place? This would interest Carrie, along with what I'd overheard, a lot. I told him that Sam King would want to talk to them both.

Bigger John was watching two teenaged boys lounging around an expen-sive German car, trying to pretend they weren't checking out something inter-esting inside. John turned on the cruiser's headlights and caught them square. They put their hands in front of their faces, moved away from the car, and then sauntered back toward the main lodge as if nothing had happened. I heard the radio crackle into life inside the cruiser. John bent forward to listen and then grunted.

"Gotta go back in," he said. "You okay here for a little while?"

"I think so," I said. "I've got my buddies in the cabin. And Nathan Creigh's ten-gauge."

"How'd you get ahold of that?" he asked. I told him, leaving out the part about Rue Creigh.

"Hope you whaled on him real good," he said. " 'Cause that old boy won't rest till he gets it back. And you with it."

"I'll be happy to face him again if he's really interested," I said.

"Not his style," he said. "Think big-caliber ball, Reb rifle."

After he left I walked across the parking lot and up to the main lodge. I'd left the shepherds in the cabin, along with the ten-gauge. I might get away with carrying a handgun into the hotel, but a shotgun would definitely make the waitstaff nervous. For that matter, the remaining shells were now thoroughly soaked and probably useless.

The lodge had a nicely appointed cocktail lounge. I limped in and ordered a single malt and a hamburger, in that order, and tried not to think about long guns. It was ten thirty, and I was disappointed at not being able to go along on the ride to recover Carrie Harper Santángelo. Special Agent King was right, of course, but I was also ashamed of having just left her there. The hamburger came; if the bartender thought it was strange to be washing down this culinary extravaganza with twelve-dollar scotch, he certainly didn't say so.

The lounge was full and humming. They had a fusion blues trio in one corner, a small dance floor that allowed for as close a dance as you might want, and the usual collection of mildly desperate men and women looking for love or at least some company. Including one Moses Walsh, who was ensconced at a corner table with a woman in her late forties trying hard to look thirty-nine. He was dressed in a long-sleeved white shirt and clean, faded jeans and had some kind of Indian decoration in his hair and at his throat. With that face, he had the part covered in spades.

The woman got up to visit the powder room, so I grabbed my scotch and sauntered over.

"Big Chief on the road to glory?" I asked.

I got a sonorous western movie grunt and a squinty-eyed sideways look. "Big Chief on short final," he said. "He hopes."

"I think I would need some more scotch for that one," I said, watching her walk away from us. "Not sure that would be a good wake-up."

"Ain't never gone to bed with no ugly woman," he quoted. "But I have woke up with some. Where'd you hear about Big Chief? I haven't heard that since high school."

I told him and he smiled. "Didn't know her," he said. "She pretty?"

"Very," I said. "And a senior internal affairs inspector in the SBI."

"Oh," he said.

I laughed. We talked for a few minutes, and then the woman came out of the bathroom, headed back toward the table. She stopped to talk to another woman of a similar stripe.

"You gonna introduce me? See if she has a friend?"

"Paleface blow Big Chief's cover, he's gonna die."

"No worries," I said. "And what kind of Indian are you supposed to be tonight?"

"Chippewa."

"I don't believe they were ever in these parts," I said.

"No, but everyone's cherokee'd out up here, so Chippewa it is."

I got up, trying not to laugh out loud, and walked away, nodding at the returning lounge queen. Fifty trying for forty was more like it, but Mose was obviously a practitioner of the Go Ugly Early rule. He was also probably getting lucky a whole lot more than I was these days.

I went back to the bar and signaled for a refill. I was enjoying said refill when Sam King slid onto the adjoining bar stool.

"Those shepherds of yours aren't always friendly, are they," he said.

"Depends on what their orders are," I said. "They're *German* shepherds. Partial to clear orders. You guys all set up?"

"Better than that," he said, signaling the bartender for a whiskey. "We got her back. A motorist found her standing in the middle of the highway on the Carrigan County side of the county line. She was dazed and wearing duct tape across her eyes. Guy called 911 and then brought her into the sheriff's office. They took her to the county hospital, and they're holding her overnight for observation."

"How bad?"

"Big, ugly gash across the top of her head. Gonna be some stitches there. Possible concussion. Gonna have a sideways white streak in her hair for life, probably. Otherwise, unharmed. Filthy dirty, really damp around the edges, a lot of blood on her clothes, but it looks like she dodged a big one."

"I'll be damned," I said. "Just like that."

"Yeah," he said. "Just like that. No signs of Brother Lucas, either, which is a shame. We were looking forward to getting up with him."

"With luck he might even have resisted."

King nodded and sipped his whiskey.

"This cannot have happened without you-know-who being in the mix," I said. I was keeping my voice low as the bar was starting to fill up. "And I heard another story tonight, from one of the deputies who used to work over there."

"Another Robbins County story," he said. "Terrific."

"It supports Carrie's theory that Grinny Creigh is doing some damn thing that involves children."

"Would a judge act on it?"

"Probably not."

He looked at his watch. "Then I don't want to hear it. We came here to get her back. She's back."

"You didn't get her back. They *gave* her back."

"Whatever," he said. "She doesn't work for us anymore, and she's back. That's what we came out here to do. Forgive me, but I'm a linear sort of guy, kinda like those shepherds of yours."

"So now what—you guys just gonna back out?"

"Wouldn't you, if you were still a lieutenant in the Manceford County Sheriff's Office? Or did you people run around expending scarce resources on colorful rumors?"

King took my frustrated silence for assent.

"Look," he said. "We're the SBI. You know we never get too far out ahead of the line departments. We come in when there's a solid case to be built, and then only when we're asked in *and* we have assets to offer that a local sheriff's office doesn't."

"And you never run your own ops?" I asked.

He studied his whiskey.

"How much smoke do you need before you go looking for a fire?" I asked. "You know you have a problem with Mingo, and that's something the SBI does do on its own. DEA knows they have a problem with the Creigh clan and Mingo. You said that even the Bureau had something for you when you broke off to come look for Carrie. I've been shot at, jailed, kidnapped, and rescued by two of Mingo's own deputies, who then jumped ship and are working for Hayes now. Your own ex-agent was kidnapped and got away only because her kidnapper stumbled onto me on a dark road, threw down on me, and got her

head blown off. Then Carrie gets shot and kidnapped *again*? And then myste-
riously released? What the fuck does it take, Special Agent?"

My voice had been rising, and some people were looking at us.

"Outside," he said, throwing some money on the bar. We walked through
the main lobby in silence and out into the parking lot. His official car was
parked out front, with my very good friend Storm Trooper Gelber in the driver's seat. I got the familiar glare when he saw me. The man was nothing if not
consistent.

"Here's some advice, *Mister* Richter," King said. "This is *western* Carolina.
Eastern Carolina is mostly horizontal, densely populated with lawyers, and
urban-minded. Western Carolina is mostly vertical, sparsely populated altogether, and bloody-minded, especially when it comes to strangers poking around
in the woods. Now, here comes the advice: Go home."

I just looked at him. He must not have cared for the expression on my face,
because he became angry.

"We *know* there's something wrong in Robbins County," he said. "Believe it
or not, we might even be working on it, but since you are an *ex*-lieutenant,
emphasis on the 'ex' part, I'm not inclined to share, okay? Same thing goes for
ex-special agent Carrie Santángelo. Emphasis once again on the 'ex.' Chances
are, you stay out of Robbins County and you'll both be a whole lot better off.
Go the fuck home. Trust me, I'll be telling her the same damn thing in the
morning."

Gelber, who'd been listening, had a nasty smile on his face and was exuding agreement from the car. King gave me a curt nod and went over to get into
the car. I tried to think of some really clever retort, but by the time I did, they
were down the road and gone. As usual.

I walked back to the cabin. It was a pleasant night, although there was a
hazy ring around the moon presaging rain later. The shrubbery around the
creek smelled of late summer, and the pea gravel along the walk crunched re-
spectfully under my feet. A zillion insects were communicating in the woods
in the rising humidity. The shepherds were waiting by the front screen door, so
I let them go water the grounds for a few minutes. I sat down on the front steps
while they ran around and thought about what King had said.

Go the fuck home. Basically, this is our game and we'll play it out the way
we want to. Retirees, agents who resign, and other undesirables, especially
ones who blunder into one fix after another and who believe in rural legends,
need not apply. He'd been pretty convincing. M. C. Mingo and the Creighs
hadn't gone into business yesterday, and it would probably take years of careful

and methodical police work, as usual, to roll them up in a way that would stand up in our wonderfully liberal court system.

Much as I hated to admit it, Special Agent King might just be right.

Then the shepherds returned. They were escorting one bedraggled-looking Carrie Harper Santángelo. I sighed. From the grimly determined look in her eyes, I knew there was no way in hell that I was going to get home any time soon.

"Breakout?" I asked her as she shuffled up to the cabin.

She nodded and then staggered just a little. I realized she was probably still under the effects of sedation. Her balance was off, and she was having trouble forming words. I helped her into the cabin. It being a bridal suite, there was only one real bedroom and one enormous bed, and that's where I took her, the shepherds following with lots of concerned interest. She'd apparently found her dirty clothes and put them on *over* her hospital gown.

I sat her down on the edge of the bed and examined the top of her head. She rested her forehead on my chest patiently. Her scalp was a mess, albeit a professionally sutured and disinfected mess. She looked up at me, and then one eye wandered just a bit. Whatever pain meds they'd given her were definitely still onboard. I wanted to get her a bath, but right then and there she was bound for the arms of Morpheus.

I stretched her out on the bed and, as gently as I could, relieved her of her shoes, jeans, and shirt. The hospital gown did little to protect her modesty, but there was nothing sexy about undressing a woman who'd had the top of her head sliced open by a rifle. She made a halfhearted attempt to cover herself and then gave up when I rolled her into clean sheets and pulled up a light coverlet. Her body was slim, trim, and athletic, lovely and round where it should be, yet surprisingly light. Some genuine joy there for the right guy, I thought.

I went into the bathroom and returned with a warm washcloth. I washed her face as gently as I could and then her hands. She made little mumbling sounds. I brought her some water and she drank an entire glass. She said something about scotch and I smiled. Not tonight, dear heart. I fluffed up her pillows, made sure her arms weren't contorted, and turned out the lights. I think she was asleep before I got out of the room.

I thought about one final scotch and then decided to pass. I was turning out lights and appraising the couch when there was a quiet knock on the door. It turned out to be the other Big brother, Luke.

"She okay?" he asked. He was twisting his deputy's hat in his hands, and I could tell he was somewhat embarrassed to be there.

"Lemme guess: You failed door duty."

He nodded. "Big time," he said. "She pops out into the hallway, bottom in the breezes, says she has to get out of there. I tried talkin' her back in, but she wasn't havin' any. Said she'd seen Mingo. Said she'd go out the window, she had to. Said people *die* in hospitals, she was leavin', *and* she had a gun." He grinned, despite himself.

"She get herself dressed, did she?" I asked.

He blushed harder. "Um, no, sir, I had to help her with that, too. Couldn't see lettin' her go half-nekkid down the damn hall. Said she had to get up with you. Said I had to spring her, that they was people comin' to get her, same people as what cracked her head."

I had to wonder where the hospital staff had been for this little drama, but I was glad he'd gone along. "You did the right thing," I told him. "I think."

"She gonna be okay?" he asked. "I can take her on back, you say so. Them nurses is gonna be havin' themselves a hissy by now."

"They know you aided and abetted?"

"No, sir, don't believe so. They was busy bein' distracted, sorta."

I didn't want to know any more. I told him it was okay and that he should go back to the hospital and tell them she'd checked herself out. "If she seems off in the morning, I'll bring her back, but she's probably safer here than in the hospital. There still a county vehicle out in the parking lot?"

"One comin'," he said. "John was here, but he got called out. You got you a gun?"

I told him I had Nathan's ten-gauge, and then remembered that I hadn't baked out the shells. He grinned.

"John said you kicked his evil ass." Then his face sobered. "He's gonna do somethin' about that, you know. *They're* gonna do somethin', best believe it."

"So I've been told. Make sure the deputy in the parking lot knows about that possibility. In the meantime, it's been a long damn day and night. I'm going to bed. She's safe here with the shepherds. We'll reevaluate tomorrow morning, okay? If there's any shit, they can come see me. I'll keep you out of it."

He nodded, looking relieved, and left.

I secured the cabin, put the ten-gauge and the least soggy shells near the bedroom door, and then went in to check on Carrie. She was sleeping, or so I thought. I adjusted her covers, and then one small hand came out of nowhere and grabbed mine.

"Hold me," she said.

I considered it and then said okay. I got undressed and slid into the bed with her. She rolled onto her left side and I put my arm around her. She took my right hand and pressed it to her left breast and then began to snore quietly as her body relaxed into mine and she dropped off into real sleep, probably for the first time in forty-eight hours.

I hadn't been in bed with a woman since losing Annie Bellamy to the cat dancers mob. Carrie's hair smelled of Eau de Betadine and hospital soap. Still, it was a nice feeling. The wind came up outside, and a rain squall pattered on the windows. The shepherds abandoned their porch and snuck into the bedroom. I pretended not to notice.

11

The county hospital people were less than pleased about Carrie's checking herself out, but were pacified by some exculpatory paperwork from her via one of Sheriff Hayes's deputies. I'd awakened before she had. I took the dogs out for a morning walk in the lodge precincts, making sure to stay within visual range of my cabin while she was in there by herself. When I got back she was in the shower, which I thought was a good sign. I made coffee, and when she came out she looked a lot better. Over coffee, she told me about hearing a loud crack, seeing stars, then falling. The shock of icy water revived her, and she remembered crawling into the rocky shallows only to be grabbed up by Lucas a few minutes later and hauled into the woods. He'd used duct tape to blindfold and gag her, and some kind of clasp chain to pin her arms and hands.

"My head was on fire, I was soaking wet and bleeding like a stuck pig—you know, head wounds—and I couldn't see or shout. So he pulled and I stumbled along behind him. He put me into some kind of van, put a towel around my head, and told me to shut up or he'd cut me."

"I wanted to come back for you," I said.

"No sweat," she said. "I was only semi-conscious when I went into the water, but I still heard the gunfire. There was no way you could have done anything."

"Still," I said. "Your good buddy Gelber thinks I'm some kind of cowardly rat."

"Gelber?" she said, surprised. "When did you run into him?"

I told her about the SBI sending in a posse, my final little séance with King, and his pungent parting advice.

"Gelber hates everybody," she said. "Mostly himself, I think. He was involved in a bad ambush deal several years ago. He was the only survivor. Three other agents died. Screwed him up. They should have retired him, but he is one tenacious SOB. They call him Fang."

"An interesting boss?'"

"To say the least," she said. "He has no life, though, and when we normal humans wanted time off, he was eternally disappointed in our lack of dedication. So: Your turn—what happened to you after I went in?"

I told her. She nodded when I told her what Lucas had said about the Creighs wanting her brought in, dead or alive. She wasn't surprised at King's reaction to her theories about a child-trafficking ring in Robbins County. She did pick up on the fact that the FBI might have something on it. Then I told her the story Big John had told me about the foreign doctor, and what I'd witnessed at Grinny's cabin.

"Son of a bitch," she said, sitting upright and then wincing when the sudden movement pulled her stitches. She patted her scalp gingerly. "That's a direct tie. Children at the Creigh compound? Foreign doctor? Airport security? That old hag is probably having them sterilized before she sells them. Did you tell Sam King this?"

"I told Hayes," I said. "King actually didn't want to hear it. According to him, your theories are tainted by a personal angle, and he's sick to death of Robbins County legends. Like I told you, he invited both of us to go away. I think he regrets losing you at the SBI, but he as much as said that everyone up here would be glad to see the back of us."

"Screw that," she said promptly. "I need to talk to Big John and hear that story for myself, and then I want to find out what it was the Bureau was going to reveal to Sam King."

"And how the hell are you going to do that?" I asked her. "They won't talk to either one of us, and after what happened to Rue Creigh, we wouldn't last a day if we step back into Robbins County. Mingo didn't report Rue's demise, which means the Creighs are taking that on as a personal vendetta."

"Where's Sheriff Hayes in all this?" she asked.

I described our conversation. "But you know what? I still think he's not well," I said. "I'd bet on a heart condition. I think he believes me, but he's just not up to taking real action, especially if the SBI's not willing to get out in front."

"That pisses me off, too. Do you think Laurie May gave us up to Nathan and the rest of them?"

"If she did, it was under duress. Can't prove that, but that's what I think."

"Yeah, me, too. How about Baby Greenberg? Can he help us?"

"Not officially. I can give him a call, see what's shaking. Maybe he could find out what the Bureau has on Grinny Creigh."

She beamed. "Now you're talking. You have any real food here?"

"Um, I can get some. But look: Sam King hinted that SBI, and perhaps other alphabets, may have something working on this problem, and that the last thing they needed right now was interference from outsiders."

"Horseshit," she said. "I would have been told about anything SBI had going in Robbins County."

"But you're basically internal affairs, right? Why would you or your office have been in the loop for an undercover operation?"

She didn't answer that. I asked her about her oblique comments to Greenberg that there was an operation going down.

"I may have been posturing," she admitted. "He's a fed. But Sam King is a senior manager. He's got a full plate, just like everyone else, and he doesn't want another helping of trouble." She paused to take a breath. "You said yourself you think there are other kids up there. You heard her say she might have to 'move' the whole passel of them. I can't abide the thought of that."

"Because of what you think happened to your sister?"

"Partly, yes, of course. But more importantly, if there is some op underway in Robbins County, even if I wasn't privy to it, it won't happen any time soon. Most of headquarters knows when something like that's about to bear fruit."

"What if we lit a fire over at social services in Robbins County? Using the abused kids angle?"

"Against the Creighs? What was it that woman told you?"

I sighed. She was right. Now the question became whether or not I wanted to join this fight. Then I realized that, having taken Rue Creigh's head off, I didn't have a whole lot of choice. It was just that years of police experience had taught me how badly Lone Rangers could screw up a perfectly good police operation. King had said exactly the right thing to give me pause. Carrie saw my hesitation.

"You want to bail, I can live with that," she said.

"No," I said. "I did that to you once already. No, I'm just trying to think of a way to go at this. Let's get some chow and then I'll call Baby."

* * *

After a day of rest for Carrie and resupply for me, we met Baby Greenberg up at the main lodge dining room at six thirty. He listened to our tales of mutual adventure and said repeatedly that we were both insane. Carrie had put a headscarf over the wound on the top of her head, and of course Baby had to have a look.

"Damn, girl," he said as she was repositioning the scarf. "Another inch lower and you could be in DEA management."

We had dinner and he told us what he'd found out with a few calls to the FBI field office down in Charlotte.

"I had to tell a few lies about why I was asking," he said.

"I'm shocked," I said. "Shocked."

"DEA and the FBI lie to each other all the time," he replied. "It's our way of showing bureaucratic affection."

"They wouldn't talk to Sam King over the phone," I said. "They told him he had to go down there."

"That's just feds jerking state guys around, what can I tell you," he said. "I called in on a federal secure pipe and we got right to it."

"Which is?" Carrie asked. She'd had a glass of wine and seemed to be coming back to life.

"Apparently there's a medium-sized federal task force in Washington working on the exploitation of children. It's running under the so-called PROTECT Act."

"Whassat?" I asked. The feds used to drive me crazy with all their acronyms.

"Prosecutorial Remedies and Other Tools to End the Exploitation of Children Today Act of April 2003," he recited. "Or PROTECT."

"This PROTECT bunch have an intel branch?" I asked.

"They do," he said. The waiter brought our dinners, and we waited until he'd left. I attacked a bloody rare steak. Carrie looked over at my plate and asked if I didn't want that thing killed before I ate it. Once the waiter finished with his is-everything-okay recital, Baby continued. "And subject intel branch has identified western Appalachia as one source for children being sold into international sex-slave markets."

"Suspicions confirmed," Carrie said, with a hint of triumph in her voice. "But western Appalachia is a big place. Any specifics?"

"No, and there's a wrinkle," he said. There was enough background noise in the dining room to cover our conversation. "They can't tie any reported instance where children have been rescued from one of these human sewers to a source in *this* area. I asked. But: They did have one CI who told them that there is a 'florist' up here somewhere, and that what she, and he did say 'she,' produces is extremely valuable in subject markets."

"Any details?" I asked.

"That's when they went NFI on me."

NFI was intel-speak for no further information. It was the code word intelligence wienies used when they didn't understand what some snippet of information meant. But that reference to a "she" also supported Carrie's theory.

"He used that term?" Carrie asked. "A florist?"

"Yeah, and I asked about that, too. A florist produces 'flowers,' which is the street word for the product, as in little flowers, plucked for the disgusting pleasure of some seriously bent motherfuckers."

"And why Appalachia?"

"Because the children have little value to a certain stratum of the population. As in, she was a'lookin' pretty damn good for thirteen, but then she done got her a damn kid hung on her. And if it was her daddy who did the hanging-on, then the child become disposable."

"Did you ask them that question I had about a doctor's involvement?"

"I did. They said that if the flowers are sterile, they're more valuable, for obvious if repugnant reasons."

"And this is a Washington, D.C., game?" I asked. "That seems like a dangerous place for this kind of enterprise, especially these days."

"The key is a transport channel with diplomatic immunity," Greenberg replied. "Most of the diplomatic courier channels in the country terminate in Washington and New York. They are not subject to search. Think about it: A Saudi woman shows up at Dulles, all burka-ed up in her best twelfth-century haute couture. She arrives with a sleepy child in tow, similarly covered, made up to look Saudi and probably doped to the gills 'because she gets airsick.' They're boarding a Royal Saudi Air Force plane, and her husband's a prince, of course. That's a government airline, and nobody messes with them. They pass the metal detector test and the bomb dogs, and off they go."

"So if someone's going to bust this up, it would have to be on the way into Washington from Robbins County?" Carrie asked.

"If you just wanted to rescue one flower, then yeah," he said. "But if you're a bunch of feds trying to put together a case that can be prosecuted, then you need to roll up both ends of the pipe. That's hard, and it takes time. Lots of time. Especially on the diplomatic end—especially if you assume it's the princes who are buying the flowers."

"Based on what I overheard, we may not have lots of time," I said. "Somehow our probes have spooked Grinny. She's talking maybe unloading the whole hothouse."

"Jeez, I wonder why," Baby said. "Nathan grabs you up and then gets beat to shit, Rue Creigh gets her head blown off, a third of their lovely little dog pack is vulture bait up on Book Mountain, somebody inside Mingo's force gets you out of jail, and they're *spooked?*"

"The way to stop this is a laser-guided bomb into Mother Creigh's little house of horrors," Carrie said. Santa Claws was in the building.

"LGBs are good," I pointed out. "Unless, of course, that's where the children are collected prior to a shipment."

"My Bureau contact said there's another problem, which is that, so far, they have never been able to put a TV monitor or even an eyeball at either Dulles or Reagan airport on a mother-and-child departure profile that seems to fit the bill. And there are zero ties to Robbins County or any other part of this area."

We ate our dinner for a few minutes, trying to digest this information. Carrie finally broke the silence. "If Robbins County is the source in question, the 'she' would have to be the Creigh clan. Who else has a criminal enterprise of substance going up there?"

"One wonders," I said.

"What's that mean?"

"I'm struck by the fact that the people like Sheriff Hayes don't seem to be very excited about the Creigh clan and all their works in general."

"That's partially because *we're* here," Baby said. "Chasing druggies isn't a big priority for local law if the appropriate feds are in the area. But we've been looking at the meth problem, not anything to do with trafficking in children. And, actually, by the Code of the West, that would belong to the Bureau, not us scruffy narcs."

"But they might be related," I said. "Desperately poor mountain families, staggering under a meth jones, might be tempted to sell a child to either sustain their habit or pay down a drug debt."

"No mother would do that, not even an addict," Carrie said. Even as she said it, I could see that she was remembering that woman we'd seen at the trailer. It was, in fact, entirely possible.

"There are some so-called menfolk in these parts who'd do it in a New York minute," Greenberg said. "We've arrested some pretty sorry-assed dudes up in them there hollers. And when you see some of the kids . . ."

"What do you mean?" Carrie asked indignantly.

Baby threw up his hands. "I'm talking some truly damaged DNA here," he said. "Yes, they're innocent children. But their chances of succeeding amongst the human gene pool are minimal, at best."

At that moment, the lodge's duty manager approached our table. "Gentlemen, lady," he said, and then looked at me. "Mr. Richter?"

I said, yes, that's me.

"Last night the sheriff's office told our security people they'd have a patrol car in our parking lot at random intervals, for your protection?"

"Okay," I said. "Problem?"

"Well," he said, looking around and then lowering his voice. "One of our waitstaff came in for the night shift a few minutes ago. She said there was what she called an old muscle car out in the parking lot with some 'bad-looking dudes' inside. She thought she saw shotgun barrels. Said the car looked like something a moonshiner would run. Said they were just sitting out there in that car, like they were waiting for someone. *Bad*-looking dudes. Should I call this in?"

"You bet," I said. "Call the sheriff's office and tell them what you've got. Especially the part about guns. They might be setting up to do a holdup, okay? Call 911 and ask for deputies, plural."

His expression told me that I'd just confirmed his worst suspicions. I had also, hopefully, taken my name out of the equation. He hurried out to make the call.

"What do you think?" I asked Carrie. "Mingo's black hats?"

"Or you're right, they're out there working up the courage to rob this place," she said. "I can't imagine Mingo would be so brazen as to send a hit squad over here."

"Nathan might," I said. "Rue Creigh was special to him, probably in ways you don't want to think about. And Grinny has a motive, too." I looked around at the crowd of diners and bar patrons. "I'd feel a whole lot better with guns and dogs at hand," I said.

"I can help with half of that," Baby said helpfully, patting his suit coat. "But life would be a whole lot simpler if you both took Mr. King's advice."

"Funny how so many people want us out of here, isn't it?" Carrie said to me. We finished dinner, and I signed the bill. We went out to the lobby to see what was happening. The manager gave us a signal that he'd made the call.

"Where's the vehicle?" I asked.

He parted some heavy curtains and showed us. The lot was pretty full, and I actually couldn't make it out. But just then three Carrigan County cop cars came swinging into the main parking lot. They'd come fast, dark, and quiet, but now they lit up their light bars and at least one tapped his siren. They swept down from the main road and then made a beeline for what looked to me like an old Dodge Charger, which was sitting all by itself out in the lot. They were parked closer to my cabin than to the main lodge, I realized.

The cruisers went right at it. One stopped nose to nose with the Dodge; the other two swept along either side and screeched to a halt, one flat alongside, the other at an angle, thereby preventing anyone in the Dodge from opening a door. We moved to the front door and stepped outside to see what happened next.

What happened next was that all hell broke loose. The deputies in the side-block cars jumped out of their vehicles with guns leveled across their vehicles' hoods and started yelling at whoever was inside to show their hands. The nose-in cruiser had his high beams and door spot on, which surely should have blinded the guys inside. Instead, the driver of the Dodge, who'd apparently fired up his trusty 318 when he saw cops swooping in, slammed it into reverse and, tires screeching and smoking, backed up at about ninety miles an hour— smack into a forty-foot-high parking-lot light standard.

The collision was forceful, and the tall aluminum pole jackknifed onto the top of the Dodge. The sodium vapor light fixture exploded in a blue-white flare of sparks on the pavement, which in turn ignited the fuel vapors that were streaming out from under the Dodge's crumpled back end. This produced a brilliant carpet of fire, followed seconds later by a really big boom. Guy must have been running on racing fuel, because the second explosion was a real crowd-pleaser. The light pole had put a pretty big crease in the top of the car, enough to have given everyone in the Dodge a headache. And to jam the doors.

The deputies, who had been left standing fifty feet back, scrambled for shelter behind their cruisers when the gas tank went up. Finally one of them stood up and began to approach the burning Dodge. He quickly backed up when there were two loud booms from inside the fire as someone's shotgun cooked off. There was some more of this, but by now the vehicle was settling on melted tires and entirely engulfed in hot orange flames. A muscular column of glowing black smoke was pumping into the night air, and it was clear that no one was going to come out showing hands or anything else.

Baby started humming that tune with the refrain about "another one bites the dust," which provoked a horrified look from a woman who'd come out to gape at the burning car.

"Those were genu-wine bad guys, ma'am," he explained pleasantly. "Who just discovered the express lane to hell."

She put a hand over her mouth and stepped back into the hotel.

"You better boogie," I told him. "Sheriff Hayes is going to show up soon. No self-respecting feds would want to be here."

"You got a point there, judge," he said. "Thanks for dinner. And the entertainment. You think those were Mingo's people?"

"It's going to take DNA to find out," Carrie said, as the car finally bottomed out and fire engine sirens could be heard. "But I'll bet Sheriff Hayes will have an opinion."

It took Sheriff Hayes about an hour to discover that we'd been at least tangentially involved in the mess up front and come knocking on my door. He did have an opinion, as it turned out.

"This was because of you," he announced as soon as we let him into the cabin. He was carrying a briefcase and looking agitated.

"We were having an innocent dinner, Sheriff," I told him. "The manager thought those guys were fixing to rob the place."

"Who's we?" he asked.

"Carrie and I," I told him.

"Manager said there were three of you," he said.

"Oh, him," I said.

Hayes waited a moment for me to elaborate, and when he saw I wasn't going to tell him, he shook his head and sat down wearily in an armchair. He still didn't look well. We probably weren't helping with that.

"That car was registered in Robbins County," he said. "They had at least three shotguns, and containers of some kind of fuel or accelerant in the trunk."

"Any ID on the toasts?" Carrie asked.

"Are you kidding?" he said. "Humans. We think. But one of 'em had this." He produced a clear plastic evidence bag from the briefcase. Inside was a badly charred SIG .45 semiautomatic pistol. It wasn't impossible that a bunch of black hats would have a SIG, but it also wasn't the kind of gun they normally would use.

"Mine?" I asked.

"We'll soon find out. But didn't you tell me Nathan Creigh relieved you of one of these up in that cave?"

I nodded. He put the bag back into the briefcase and leaned back in his chair. "I think they were here to exact revenge for what you said happened to Rowena Creigh. They were probably going to shoot you with your own piece." He looked over at Carrie. "You well enough to travel, young lady?"

"Where am I going?" she asked.

"Away," he said, his voice rising. "The both of you. I want you out of here. Out of my county, out of the state if you can manage it. I've had enough death and destruction for one month. The Creigh clan won't rest until this is taken care of, and that just means more of the same."

"Why don't *you* stop it, then?" Carrie demanded, surprising the sheriff and me in about equal measure. "Why does Mingo and his gang have free run of Carrigan County? If you *knew* that trouble was brewing, why weren't your people alerted to look for just exactly what showed up in the parking lot here? Why was Rue Creigh able to drive in here and abduct me and then drive right back through the center of Marionburg with me in plain sight, adorned in duct tape?"

Hayes started to splutter, but suddenly Carrie Santángelo of the SBI professional standards investigations division was in his face and not backing down.

"*We're* not causing this shit. We might be provoking them, but that's because we've had the temerity to lift up the rock and see what's under it. You and your people, on the other hand, are doing nothing. *Nothing!* You think the Creighs aren't moving product here in Carrigan County? You think there's no meth problem in your piece of the hills?"

"You listen to me," Hayes began, but she shut him right down. The shepherds had long since crawled out of the room. I was trying to figure out how to join them.

"No, Sheriff, you listen to *me*. I'm beginning to think that I need to call my *ex*-boss in my *ex*-organization and tell him they need to take a look at the *Carrigan* County Sheriff's Office, that the sheriff here is either hopelessly ineffective or he's part of the Creigh organization. Or maybe I should go find the local newspaper and write a little op-ed piece. I'm a citizen now, not a state employee. I can say whatever the hell I please. And if that's not okay with you, then get off your fat ass and get to work. Find these bastards. Arrest them. Harass them. Fucking *do* something! And in the meantime, get the hell out of here before I get pissed off."

The sheriff was red in the face by the time she'd finished, and I was suddenly concerned about his heart condition. But then, to my utter amazement, Hayes grabbed his hat and briefcase and stomped out of the cabin. I went to the window and saw one of his deputies hotfooting it up the path to the parking lot with the sheriff behind him, his hat jammed low over his forehead. I suspected the deputy had heard an earful and was anxious to get to the safety of his cruiser. I pulled the curtain closed.

"Well, now," I said, and then stopped when I saw there was still fire in her eye. "Want a drink?"

She shook her head and went out onto the porch overlooking the creek. I fixed two scotches and went out after her.

"I chase bent cops," she said, "but I have a positive hate-on for do-nothing cops."

"I'd've never guessed," I said, handing her a drink. She took it without looking at it, but she didn't refuse it. A waft of leftover smoke from the front parking lot blew down in our direction. "That the car or the burning bridge?" I said.

"Fuck 'em if they can't take a joke," she said. "You're either with the good guys or you're not. Hayes has been doing the ostrich act for too damn long. Time somebody braced him up."

"If he does have a heart condition," I said, "it tends to sap the do-something right out of a guy."

"Then he should retire and let someone else do the job. Right now the Creighs are walking all over him."

"So you don't think he's dirty?"

She shook her head. I agreed with that assessment. "So how the hell do we prove this business with Grinny Creigh and children in Robbins County? And do that all by our lonesome?"

She grunted defiantly and sipped some of her scotch.

"We still have Baby Greenberg as at least a passive ally," I said. "I don't know about Sam King—he tried to make it look like he was washing his hands of this mess, but I'm not sure I believe that."

"Whatever they're doing, they won't tell me," she said.

"Right, so we have to figure out some way to blow this thing open. We need to find the children."

She looked over at me in the darkness. "No shit, Sherlock," she said, somewhat more amiably. "And how do we do that? You got a plan?"

"I got the glimmer of one," I said. "What's the very last thing the Creighs would expect us to do right now?"

She thought for a moment. "Come back at them?"

"Bingo," I said. I explained what I had in mind. "So that's what we'll do," I concluded. "But first we'll need to execute a little cover and deception. And for that I need to go see Sheriff Hayes and eat some serious crow."

I went out to my Suburban and drove out of the lower lot and up into the main parking area. One fire engine was still there, along with a state police crew, wading through three feet of white foam as they began the fatality investigation. The remains of the Dodge were covered in yellow rubber drapes, surrounded by several yards of police tape. There were a few gawkers out in the lot, but not very many, courtesy of the nauseating vapors exuding from the charred wreckage. I got a whiff as I drove by, and I drove over to the sheriff's office in Marionburg with all the windows open.

Hayes's office was still going strong after the incident at the hotel. I walked into the main reception area and told the sergeant on duty that I needed to see Sheriff Hayes.

"This is not a great time for visitors," the cop said.

"Why don't you tell him that Mr. Richter is here to apologize."

"Richter. Right. Heard that name earlier. You sure you want to do this?"

"It can't get much worse," I said. He gave me a look that said, *Oh, yes, it can*, but went into the sheriff's office. Five minutes later a deputy I didn't recognize came out to reception and called my name.

"Sheriff says you can have three minutes," he announced. He looked both ways and then said, "You sure you want to go in there?"

There's an echo in here tonight, I thought. "Can't wait," I said, and he rolled his eyes. I was most definitely in deep shit with the Man.

Hayes was sitting behind his desk when I was ushered into his office. Gone was all the previously sympathetic friendliness. In its place was a steely glare, backed up by all the authority a southern county sheriff can muster, which is considerable. For a moment I thought maybe I had made a mistake coming over here. I noticed a small yellow prescription bottle next to his in-box. I skipped the pleasantries.

"I came to apologize and to tell you that we're leaving," I said. "Sam King advised the same thing, so we're going to get out of Carrigan County and leave you in peace. I think Ms. Santángelo was out of line with what she said, and neither she nor I nor anyone at SBI thinks you're involved with the Creighs or anything going on in Robbins County."

"That's nice," he growled.

"Well, it's true," I said. "And how you handle the situation here is, of course, your business. We'll need the morning to get our shit together."

"That harpy going, too?"

"It's Harper, but yes, sir. And I'm sorry for that mess at the hotel tonight. I don't *know* that that was the Creighs, but I suspect it was."

He relaxed fractionally. His face was no longer dark red as it had been in the cabin. In fact, he looked a little gray around the edges. "I had our people call Mingo's office once we ID'd the car," he said. "The license plate came up Robbins County and listed the registered owner. Mingo sent a deputy over, and he gave us a tentative ID on the owner. The occupants are all stumps, of course; they'll require dental identification."

"Let me take a guess on the owner," I said. "A guy named Lucas Carr?"

His eyebrows went up. "How the hell did you know that?"

I explained the background. "He said he'd made the Creighs' shit list for screwing up the hit on Carrie and me in the river. My guess is they gave him one chance to redeem himself. They sent along two helpers to keep him honest. He's the one Sam King was setting up on to get Carrie back."

"Should have left that little witch over there," he said, starting to spin himself up again. "Who's that goddamned woman think she is, anyway?" Then he stopped, his eyes narrowing in suspicion. "You say you're leaving. Where are you going?"

"Away?" I said, echoing his earlier words.

"How far away?"

"Far enough to be out of your hair."

"That's not an answer," he said.

"I know it isn't," I replied. He just stared at me for a long moment. He started to say something but then sighed and set his jaw.

"You told us to go, and we're going," I said. "Why not just declare victory?"

He leaned forward in his chair. "If you guys get yourself into any kind of crack up there with Mingo or the Creighs, do not, repeat, do *not* expect me or any of my people to come bail you out, understand?"

I nodded.

"And for the record, I'm telling you *not* to go back there. Let the appropriate authorities work the Robbins County problem. Neither of you fits that category anymore, right?"

I nodded again.

"Okay, then. We're done. We're still cranking out paperwork on your latest mess. Out."

Back at the cabin I found Carrie busy sorting out her equipment. The two shepherds were in attendance, watching with their usual interest. Everything is a great adventure to a shepherd.

"He buy it?" she asked.

"No," I said. "And he made it pretty clear that if we do go back there, there will be no cavalry from Carrigan County."

"Never expected any," she grumped. "Guy's lost his nerve. He's afraid of Mingo, and that's the long and the short of it."

"We have until noon tomorrow," I said. "Time enough for us to get what gear we need and then to make our move. I'll call Mose Walsh."

"Go in daylight?"

I sat down on the edge of the bed. "The Creighs and Mingo own the night in Robbins County. I think if we just drive in there, go straight to Laurie May's, we've got a pretty good chance of remaining undetected. Her place is nowhere close to town."

She plopped down on the bed. "What we don't know is whether or not she'll let us hole up there again," she said. "Or if she's even there. They may have done something to her."

"Or worse," I said. "She might be part of it. That's one loose end we need to work out. But that's the only place I can think of to base, now that we're been thrown out of here." As I said that, though, I had another idea.

"What?" she said.

"We could base up in the national park," I said. "Remember that cabin we used? The one that's been requisitioned by the DEA?"

"That's a long hike from where we want to go," she said. "And the last time we had permission."

"But it wouldn't depend on Laurie May Creigh. Plus, I doubt the Park Service people know about your leaving SBI."

She sighed. "That would mean I'd have to basically impersonate an SBI agent," she said. "I don't want to do that. Look: We need to break open this child-smuggling ring. We can't do that from the safety of the national park. We have to fight the Creighs on their own turf."

"Taking on your enemy on his home ground is not usually a prescription for success," I said.

"Mingo has to know he's got Sheriff Hayes buffaloed," she said. "He's been there a long time, and he's used to getting things his way. So's Grinny Creigh. If we're going to do this thing, we have to do what they least expect. It's the only hope we have."

They least expect it because it has the smallest chance of success was what I wanted to say.

"I guess I really can't do this alone," she said. She'd put a rueful smile on her face, and for a moment she reminded me a little bit of Mary Ellen Goode. A woman who'd been beat up now screwing her courage to the sticking point. She had to know what the odds were, and she was still determined to go back there and uncover the Creighs' secret. I looked over at the two shepherds, who were still watching from the doorway. They were game, but then again, they were always game. Being game wasn't the same as being smart, though.

"Okay," I said. "Let's figure out what we're going to need."

12

We spent the morning doing logistics, checking out of the fancy lodge and into a much smaller motel closer to the Robbins County side of Marionburg. I called Mose Walsh late in the morning and then met him at the outfitter's shop. Instead of maintaining their own individual shops, most of the local guides were associated with one of the two storefront outfitters in town. Mose met me at the one on the main street of Marionburg. He was chatting up one of the young salesladies at the register counter when I walked in. There were maybe a half dozen customers in the store, most of them just looking at all the woodsy stuff. Mose said something quietly to the girl that made her giggle and then came over to meet me at the front door.

"Don't you ever quit?" I asked him. The girl at the register looked like she was maybe fifteen.

"Woman once told me," he said, in his most dignified Big Chief voice, "that I was so damn ugly that women would be either repelled or attracted, but they'd all be just a bit curious."

"Like your granddaughter over there?"

"She's twenty-six, married, but not serious about it, God love her." He looked around to make sure no one was listening to us. "What're you guys doing, fucking around with Grinny Creigh and her demon spawn?"

"Us?" I said, pretending total innocence. "We're just going camping."

He nodded with his head in the direction of the pack racks, and we walked back there. "Word is," he said, pretending to examine the pack selection, "that the auto-da-fé down at the lodge parking lot last night was a hit squad of meth mechanics from Robbins County."

"Really," I said. "What else does Mr. Word have to say?"

"That your lady friend is wearing a headscarf because one Lucas Carr creased her headbone with his thirty-ought, on orders from Nathan, who is, word says, somewhat indisposed up there on Spider Mountain."

"Big Chief's jungle drums are fairly well informed in these parts," I said.

"All sorts of people go to bars. People go to bars, they drink. They drink, they talk. Big Chief doesn't talk and actually doesn't drink a whole lot anymore. Big Chief listens. So then they feel they have to fill the void. It's fucking amazing, sometimes."

"Heard any stories about the late Rue Creigh?" I asked.

His eyes widened. "That *was* you?"

It was my turn to pretend to be interested in the packs. I tried out my version of the Indian grunt. Mose wasn't impressed.

"God *damn*, man, and you're going back up there? Why don't you just go find a hornets' nest, pluck it down from the tree, and strap it on like a gas mask?"

I took him by the elbow and steered him to a back window where there were no other people. I told him what had happened with Rue and why we were going back in there, and all the wise-ass went right out of him. He stared bleakly out the window for a full minute, digesting what I'd told him. Then he shook his head resignedly.

"Try as you might," he said wistfully, "you can't get away from it. *Kids?*"

I nodded, then had a thought. "What can you tell me about Bill Hayes?" I asked. "Is he possibly in bad health?"

Mose shook his head. "It's not him. It's his wife. She's dying of some bad-ass bone disease. Docs told him to call the hospice. It's fuckin' the guy up, to hear the deputies tell it. What're you and the SBI lady planning to do about this?"

"At the moment, I have no freaking idea," I said. "First we have to find them."

"You've got that bassackwards," he said.

"I'm talking about the children, not the Creighs. Look, maybe you could help."

He gave me a wary sideways look. "Help?"

"Yeah—you hear stuff. You say people talk to you. Push that process a little bit. Anything about exploiting children in Robbins County."

He stared out the window again. "I told you, I gave that world up when I came back here," he said. "Bad for the soul."

I didn't say anything. Let him fill the void this time.

"Okay," he said finally. "Against my better judgment, such as it is. How can I find you?"

"We'll find you," I said.

Carrie and I had lunch in Marionburg, went back to the motel to make sure we had everything we needed, and then launched for Robbins County. I'd half-expected to see a Carrigan County cop car follow us out of town, but they apparently had bigger fish to fry. We'd divided our stuff into things to leave behind and gear we'd need up there, and left the excess in the motel room. We took my Suburban. I had Nathan's shotgun. Carrie's nasty little mamba stick was back in SBI custody, so now she had a nine in a belt holster.

She'd asked me to check her head wound, and to tell the truth, I wasn't pleased with what I saw. The sutures were red and a little puffy-looking, and she admitted that she had a headache that wouldn't go away. I asked her if she'd like to go back to the hospital for a quick checkup and maybe an antibiotic shot or at least another Betadine paint job, but she was adamant about getting on with it. I'd told her what Mose had said about Bill Hayes, and she seemed relieved.

It was midafternoon when we crossed the county line. We passed the usual tourist traffic on the two-lane main road as people came back from rafting trips and other excursions into Robbins County. We saw one cop car parked for a late lunch or coffee at a roadside eatery, but no other law enforcement activity on the road. If Mingo was expecting us, he wasn't being obvious about it. The thought had crossed my mind that Hayes or someone in his office might tip off Mingo and his people, but I discarded the notion. Hayes might be afraid of the hard men in Robbins County, but I didn't think he was part of their operation. He was preoccupied with problems closer to home.

We got to Laurie May's place without seeing any of the local residents, and we hoped none of them saw us. I wasn't worried about the honest citizens, but we hadn't seen any people out in their yards or along the road leading up to her cabin. We stopped in front and waited for someone to come to the door. I saw Carrie playing absently with the stitches on her scalp and wondered how bad that mess hurt.

When no one came to the door, we decided to drive the vehicle around to the back so that it could not be seen from the river road or the lane coming up into the hollow itself. Carrie got out and went to the cabin's back door and knocked. Nothing happened, so she knocked again, at which point I saw a shadow move behind the door's curtain. I was still in the car and began easing my right hand down to the shotgun. The door swung open, revealing a short but large and densely bearded man standing in the doorway pointing an equally large shotgun in our general direction.

I probably couldn't do anything for Carrie just then, not with a shotgun two feet from her chest. Frack saw the man with the gun and began growling. I told him to be quiet.

The man was staring at Carrie, who had frozen in place. "Who're you?" he asked in a low voice. "What're you-all doing here?"

"I came to see Laurie May," Carrie replied, still not moving. I admired her poise—the muzzle of that gun looked like the twin tubes of the Holland Tunnel. "She knows us. Is she all right?"

He took a step backward into the kitchen and summoned somebody inside with a jerk of his head. A moment later his twin appeared in the doorway, holding another shotgun by the receiver, its barrels pointed down at the floor. Then I knew who they were—Laurie May had said she had twin boys, coal miners. The one who'd come to the door was looking over at me, and I nodded pleasantly. The other one slipped back out of sight. He returned after a minute and said something to his brother, who lowered his shotgun. Carrie turned in my direction and told me to come in.

Laurie May was in her bedroom, and when I saw her I swore out loud. Two black eyes, bruises on her face, and her badly bruised broomstick of a right leg stuck out from under the covers and rested on a quilt.

I looked over at one of the twins. "Nathan Creigh?"

He nodded.

"They made me tell 'em," Laurie May said, blinking back tears. "That be-damned Nathan, he come in here and beat on me with my own walkin' stick."

Carrie approached the bed and took the old lady's hand. "We know, Laurie May," she said. "We know. And we know you're no betrayer."

"I ain't," Laurie May said with surprising vehemence. "I ain't no betrayer. He beat on me. He done cracked my shinbone. He pushed me down, God damn his eyes."

I introduced myself and Carrie to the twins. They weren't tall, but they sure as hell were wide. Coal miners. One of them introduced himself as Bags, the other as David. They'd apparently changed their last names to Jones some years back, because neither one of them could abide the Creighs. Bags seemed to be in charge, so I decided to tell him why we were there. The twins listened in silence. Carrie apologized to Laurie May for bringing misery to her house, but Laurie May was defiant.

"My boys here, they fixin' to go over there and clean out that rat's nest," she declared.

"They certainly need that, and more," I said. "But let me tell you-all why we're here. Maybe we can join forces."

Carrie indicated with a nod of her head that I ought to take this back to the kitchen. She stayed behind with the old woman while I went out to the kitchen with the twins. There was coffee brewing, so we sat down around the table to talk. I noticed that there were four more shotguns and a few rifles stacked against one wall, and boxes of ammunition on the kitchen counter. They'd been planning a small war, from the looks of it.

I walked them through the background of why Carrie and I were up here, what Laurie May had done to help us, and what we thought was going on over in the next cove. The brothers listened in stony silence. At first, I got the impression that they were just being polite, letting me tell my story, and then they were going to proceed with whatever it was they'd planned. When I brought up the business of abducting and selling children, they drew closer. They were flinty individuals, toughened in the dark danger of the mines. They had thick shoulders and chests, bony faces, black beards, and gnarled hands that would never be entirely white again. But this talk of selling children visibly disturbed them.

It turned out that their plan was to go through the crack in the middle of the night and then walk down to the Creigh compound and slaughter every living thing, men, women, dogs, pigs, and chickens. It sounded good and traditional, but when I pointed out to them that they'd probably be shot down by snipers before they got within a quarter mile of the Creigh cabin, they were taken aback.

"There's no more just driving up to the front porch, rolling down the windows, and going to town with shotguns," I said. "They're alerted over there. They may have spies in Marionburg who know we've left town, and they might even be coming here tonight. I got away from Nathan's little jail cell, beat him to his knees in the process, and then I had to blow his sister's head off because she threw down on me. The Creighs are not sitting over there watching television."

This news really sobered them up. Carrie joined us from Laurie May's bedroom and asked if she'd been seen by a doctor. They said no, but a healer she trusted had come by, and she'd prescribed bed rest, an herbal remedy for the pain, and immediate revenge. I had to smile.

"What's your notion on all this?" David asked. His brother looked on with squinty-eyed interest.

"If that woman is selling children to perverted sons of bitches," I said, "then we first need to find the children, and then take care of her and all her people. Keep in mind, if it is true, there are some mothers out there who've done a terrible thing, turning over their children to the likes of Grinny Creigh."

"Some ain't got no choice," Bags said. "I've heard something about this before. Way I hear it, Grinny gets 'em hooked on that there meth. Do any damn thing to get some more. Sell their damned souls, they have to. Sellin' they kids? Ain't nothin' to the likes of some of them poor sonsabitches. Goddamned zombies, after a while. That shit even eats their teeth."

"The kids don't get a vote," I said. "Now: Let me tell you where the law stands on all this, because it's important that you know who we are and who we are not."

"Let me," interrupted Carrie, sitting down at the kitchen table. She explained who we were, that the Carrigan County sheriff had told us to get out of the county, and why she, personally, was pursuing the matter. It was this last bit that seemed to make the biggest impression. I guessed it was because she was hunting satisfaction for what had happened to her father and sister. These men weren't especially interested in the legal aspects of any of it, but a family feud—well, that was different.

As she was talking, I watched her unconsciously rubbing her temples. Whatever was going on with that wound, it wasn't getting any better. Then she touched the top of her head and came away with pink fingertips. Bags saw it, too, and looked over at me. That did it.

"This little war's going to have wait one more night," I announced. "We need to get a doctor to take a look at that, Carrie, before it gets really infected."

She gave me an annoyed look. "That means getting back out on the roads," she said. "That's dangerous."

"There'll still be tourists out there, finishing up their day's vacation. We can come back after dark."

"It can wait," she said defiantly.

"No, it can't," I said. "Look, you're going to be useless if you wake up tomorrow morning with a raging infection. Go get a damn shot. The Creighs aren't going anywhere. Bags, can you get someone to come stay with Laurie May?"

Bags said he could get his wife's sister, who volunteered over in her local county hospital, to come over from Gatlinburg. I told him I'd take Carrie back into Marionburg and that we'd come back after dark.

"You think 'em Creighs gonna come over here tonight? Lookin' for y'all?"

"They might," I said. "Nathan knows we hid out here once, so he may well check it out." I could see what he getting at: We might drive back into an ambush of some kind. "Let's do this: You guys stay here until we can get back and work up a plan. If there's any reason you think we should not approach, put a single lantern in a front window. If you think it's all clear, put two lanterns, one in each front window."

"Them Creigh boys show up here, we goin' to get to it," David said.

"How's Nathan looking?" I asked.

"He's limpin' some, according to Ma. Still well enough to put the hurtin' on a defenseless old woman, though, the piece'a shit."

"They come, you guys thin 'em out then," I said. "Make it easier for later on."

They both grinned at that prospect. I gathered up Carrie and we went out to the car.

"I still think this is an unnecessary risk," she said, but I saw her wince when she put her head back on the headrest.

"I meant what I said in there," I replied. "I need you operational, not delirious with a fever, which is about where you are now, yes?"

She nodded and winced again. "Even my hair hurts," she admitted.

"Okay, then. Let's wait at the motel until dark, then go into the ER and see what they say."

At eleven I was sitting out in a corner of the parking lot behind the Carrigan County hospital. I'd taken Carrie into the emergency room. The triage desk nurse told her it would be an hour's wait, at a minimum. That had been two hours ago. When Carrie had mentioned "gunshot wound," the nurse immediately wanted to notify the sheriff's office, but Carrie talked her out of it, saying that she'd already been treated here for this same injury and the incident was already in the system. I had decided to wait in the car. If there were bad guys looking for us, they'd be looking for the pair of us. Carrie was relatively safe inside the hospital, at least from any marauding Creighs. *Staph. aureus* was another matter.

I'd made a couple of phone calls back to Triboro. The first was to my office, where I left a message for Tony, telling him what I was up to. Then I put a call in to Bobby Lee Baggett's office. I wanted to brief him on what we thought was going on up here, but he wasn't available. His executive assistant promised that he'd return my call in the morning. I called my defense lawyer at home and brought him up to date on the growing list of charges against me in Robbins County. He once again advised me to get back to Triboro as soon as possible, as in, tonight would be good, and warned of lots more fees if I kept at this. It was good to know he kept his focus, but I acknowledged that it was good advice. The problem was that I was in much too deep to back out now. Or so I kept telling myself.

I had parked in the darkest corner of the hospital parking lot to wait. The Dumpster alley was behind me, and I had a terrific view of the back of the Laboratory Services building, which apparently also housed the Pathology fun house. The hospital was a single-story affair stepped in layers along a hill. It consisted of several wings, with a small parking lot up front for the docs and the meat wagons. For ordinary humans and patients there was a larger lot behind the complex, which sloped down the hill, getting narrower as it went. Carrie was supposed to call my cell phone when they were done with her. It was cool enough to open the windows and not be eaten by mosquitoes. Fall was definitely coming on. I was ready.

At some point I must have dozed off, because I was startled awake by the sound of an argument somewhere in the parking lot. The voices were male, urgent, and, strangely, familiar. It sounded like they were trying to keep their voices down. I couldn't make out what it was about, but when I finally found the source of the racket I sat right up.

And then I slid right back down again. I was in one corner of the narrow part, in the last and lowest row. The argument was in the other corner, and the noise was coming from two police cars, parked nose to tail so that the drivers could talk. They'd parked under a light, so I could see that one of them was Sheriff Hayes. His verbal antagonist was no other than M. C. Mingo.

My blood went cold. Hayes and Mingo meeting in a dark parking lot? Good Lord, was Hayes a part of the criminal matrix in Robbins County? I really, really did not want to believe that. I saw brake lights flare at the back of Hayes's cruiser, and then backup lights. I slid all the way down below the dash, hoping like hell he wouldn't recognize my Suburban. Once I heard his cruiser leave the parking lot, I raised my head again in time to see Mingo's car approaching the back doors of the Laboratory Services/Pathology wing. He stopped, put a phone up to his ear, and talked to someone. Two minutes later, outside landing lights came on and the back double doors opened. A middle-aged man who had a neatly sculpted beard and wore a white coat came out, pushing a gurney. I stared hard, trying to see if it was the same bearded guy I'd seen at Grinny Creigh's, but the building floodlights were shining in my eyes.

Mingo got out of his car and went around to the right rear door of his vehicle, which was out of my line of sight. The two men transferred a blanket-covered something to the gurney, and then they both rolled it back into the hospital. Whatever it was, they handled it gently, as opposed to the way they might have handled a body. A few minutes later, Mingo came out. I went down-periscope and waited for him to drive away. The floodlights near the door went out.

I waited a good five minutes to make sure that there weren't any other cop cars in or near the lot and that Mingo hadn't swung back through to check his trail, and then I drove over to the wing into which they'd gone. A smaller sign near the door read LAB/PATH SERVICES ENTRANCE. The doors had small windowpanes, but the hallway behind them was dark. I was tempted to get out and try the doors but decided against it. If they were unlocked, then what? Go inside and snoop around? I didn't think that would work out. Then my cell phone chirped; Carrie was waiting at the front entrance.

"Was that fun?" I asked her when she got in. Her face was pinched and she sat down gingerly, being careful not to let her head touch the headrest this time.

"Loads," she said. "They had to remove the stitches and debride it, and then they gave me a shot with some kind of elephant syringe. Now I have seven days of these." She rattled a pill bottle at me.

"Good thing we came in, then," I said cheerily. I wasn't positive, but I thought "debride" meant scraping the wound. Not fun. I drove away from the entrance with all its bright lights and turned back down into the parking lot.

"What's this 'we' shit, paleface?" she grumped, still shifting from side to side in the seat.

"Actually," I said, and then I told her what I'd witnessed. She exclaimed in disappointment when I mentioned Hayes. Then she asked what had been on the gurney.

"I couldn't see, other than a mound under a blanket," I said, knowing what was coming next.

"Was it the right size to have been a child?"

"Yes."

"Mingo with another unconscious or drugged kid in his car? What the *fuck*?!"

"I don't know that it was a child, and they were being more careful than that time Baby and I saw him handle that other child."

The rest of the lower lot was empty, so if Mingo or even Hayes did come back, we'd be pretty obvious. I parked the car next to a delivery truck that I hoped wouldn't be moving until the next morning to give us a little cover.

"We've got to report this," she said. "You saw them take a child down at

Grinny's. You watched while she showed a guy who's probably some kind of back-alley abortionist the latest merchandise. And now here they are, Mingo and Hayes, delivering a child to a pathology lab where some bastard with a degree from Burundi U. is probably sterilizing an eight-year-old girl."

"Um," I said, "report to whom?"

She thought for a moment. "Mingo and Hayes collaborating? That has to go to Sam King."

"Sam King? He'd blow you off, say this is just another interesting tale out of Robbins County. Plus, they were arguing."

She stared at me. "So?"

"Hayes may have been running him off, not collaborating."

"But that's not what Mingo did, is it," she said, angrily. "They talked, and *then* Mingo made the delivery."

"All I'm saying is—"

"What—we do nothing?"

I held my temper. I was pissed off, too. Hayes and Mingo. Not good. "No," I said, "but let's see what happens next. If we're right, somebody will come back and pick up the flower."

"Mingo might just be disposing of a body," she said.

"He'd have Nathan take care of that, Carrie. They wouldn't bring an inconvenient body into town, especially outside of Mingo's territory, not when they have all that empty country available. They give you any pain meds?"

She nodded.

"Put your seat back. Close your eyes and let that shit work. I'll keep watch. I got a nap while you were partying in there."

She let out a big sigh of exasperation but didn't argue. In fifteen minutes she was asleep. I got out, rummaged in the backseat, and found a car coat to drape over her. It wasn't really cold, but she was obviously uncomfortable. Her breathing was shallow and her forehead was warmer than it should have been. If we were going to do anything about this tonight, she wasn't going to be a player, not until that infection was knocked down.

Twenty minutes later, the driver of the delivery truck showed up, got in, and drove the thing away in a clatter of diesel engine noise. We were now sitting out there all by ourselves, and there was no other place to park the vehicle where we could also watch the lab entrance. The truck's departure woke Carrie up, and I pointed out our predicament. We decided to get out of there before Mingo came back. If he and Hayes did have some kind of understanding, we'd be fair game in that empty parking lot.

"Well, damn," Carrie said wearily, as we went back into town. "Now what?"

"We go somewhere and get this all down in writing. Then we mail a report to someone who'll listen."

"Like who?"

"Like the Bureau? Or maybe that federal task force in Washington Baby was talking about—that PROTECT outfit."

"And then what—sit back and wait for our government to get off its enormous inertial ass and do something?"

"No, then we join forces with some other interested citizens and see if we can catch these bastards in the act. But first, we obey the old fire department rule: See a fire, tell the fire department, *then* go see what you can do."

She looked so down I decided to try a little humor. I leered at her. "Hey, little lady: Wanna go to a motel, fool around a little?"

She smiled despite her frustration. "I've never done anything like this before," she said. "Will you mind if I throw up in the middle of it?"

"Kinky," I said approvingly. "I love kinky."

My lame attempt at humor didn't really work, though, as neither of us could get our minds off what might have just happened in that lab. As I drove back to the motel, I could just imagine that bastard giving an unconscious little girl some kind of deep sedative and then going to town with scalpels or sterile knitting needles. And somewhere up there on Spider Mountain, was Grinny Creigh keeping a whole stash of potential flowers, which she might want to dispose of in a hurry? From a practical standpoint, I knew we couldn't do anything for the kid in the lab. But somehow, somewhere, we needed to light a fire under one of the alphabets.

13

I did get her back to a motel room, but kinky it was not. That big blast of antibiotics sent Carrie into the bathroom for a double-ended purgative siege lasting an unpleasant hour. She was miserable, and so was I in not being able to do a damned thing for her. Plus, I was out of scotch. Even though it was past midnight I spent the time drafting a report of everything that had happened up here since I answered Mary Ellen Goode's call for help. I named names and told it like it happened, being careful to protect Baby Greenberg as much as

I could. I laid down our theory of what the Creighs were doing and delineated
the events supporting that theory, especially what we'd seen tonight.

Normally a government report ends up with a list of recommendations, and
there I hit a brick wall. Regrettably, I couldn't just say bring in a section of
F-18's and wipe Grinny and her entire establishment off the face of the Smokies, although that would have improved the Smokies immensely. I finally gave
up, deciding that a summary of the facts would prompt better brains than mine
to some kind of effective action. I fervently hoped.

Carrie emerged from the bathroom several pounds lighter and pale as an oys-
ter. She flopped onto one of the beds, told me not to go in there, and asked if I
had any whiskey. I told her no and she groaned. Both of us knew she did not
need to be drinking any alcohol, but I sympathized with the idea. I did the cold-
washcloth routine on her face and arms for a few minutes, but she was still fighting an infection, and what should have been soothing began to irritate her. Then
I had a stroke of genius, something that happens about once in a good year. It
was nearing 2:00 A.M., so I turned on the television and found a channel where
the station was off the air. The beam of white noise where the signal had been
was still on the air, so I turned that up, doused the lights, lay down beside her,
and held her hand. She was off to sleep in about ninety seconds. I soon followed.

I was awakened by a gentle tapping on the motel room's door. It took me a
few seconds to gather my wits and realize that it was bright daylight out there.
The knock came again, gentle but insistent. I got up without disturbing Carrie
and went to the peephole. It was Bigger John, or at least one of the shirt but-
tons on his chest. I was still dressed except for shoes, so I opened the door and
stepped out, extending the deadbolt so I wouldn't lock myself out. I checked
my watch. It was nine thirty and it was indeed broad daylight. A crew of happy
Hispanic ladies was clattering housekeeping carts down the sidewalk.

"How'd you find us?" I asked, wiping the sleep from my eyes.

"Said you was moving to a motel here in Marionburg," he rumbled. "Made
me some calls. You always sleep in your clothes, Lieutenant?"

"One of the benefits of being an *ex*-lieutenant," I said. "Plus, I was up late.
Ms. Santángelo isn't doing so well after that head shot."

He nodded sympathetically. "Word in the office was that y'all had left
town," he said.

"I told Sheriff Hayes we were leaving town, but her injury flared up, so we
had to go back to County last night. Infection." I looked around the parking
lot. I saw his cruiser but no others, which I thought was a good sign. "Anybody
in particular asking?"

"Ain't nobody asking," he said, shuffling his feet. "But we get the ER report every morning down at the sheriff's office?" He smiled. "Professional courtesy sorta thing?"

I nodded. We'd managed something similar down in Triboro at the sheriff's office. Quite often the violent events of the previous night and some of the people flopping around in the ER were related.

"Luke saw mention of Ms. Santángelo being treated, so him an' me, we kinda figured y'all might still be around."

"Is there news?"

He nodded solemnly. "Big trouble last night up in Robbins County," he declared. "Big trouble. Seems Laurie May Creigh's two boys, them twins? Made 'em a blood feud on Grinny Creigh late last night."

"Oh, shit," I said. I'd forgotten all about our promise to go back up there. "Nathan and his boys roughed up their mother," I told him. "They said they were going to go do something about that."

"Might you recollect when they said that?" he asked. As in, how do you know that?

I told him we'd gone up there on our way out of the area to check on Laurie May because, given how quickly Nathan had caught up with me that night, we figured she'd been coerced.

"On your way out of the area?" he asked. Bigger John wasn't missing much this morning. Of course, he'd probably had his morning coffee, something I desperately needed.

I shrugged. "So: How'd it come out?"

He smiled ruefully and shook his enormous head. "Word is, they rode in on Grinny in that there old Bronco they drive and started shootin' up everything in sight. The cabin, the barns, some'a them dogs, winders, doors, everythin' and anythin' what couldn't take cover."

"Let me guess—then they ran out of ammo."

"It's possible," he said. "'Cause what happened next was that Grinny and *her* boys did one'a them Bonnie and Clyde numbers on the Bronco. Then somebody, ain't nobody knows for sure who, of course, went over to Laurie May's place and throwed a bunch'a gallon bottles of gasoline into the house."

"With Laurie May inside?"

"It's possible," he said. "Leastwise, that's what it smelt like when the fire boys got to it."

"Lovely," I said. The same house where we had been planning to lay up while we figured out our next move. Bigger John was watching me and probably reading my mind.

"Sheriff Hayes know about this incident?" I asked.

He nodded.

"You suppose he knows we were out there earlier, before those boys went for their final ride?"

"Don't believe he does," he said. "Yet. He did ask this morning if y'all was still in Carrigan County, though. Called you the death angel."

"All he has to do is read his own ER report," I said.

"He will," John said patiently. He was looking at me, as if he were waiting for me to get something important. I really needed my coffee.

"You telling me we should get our asses out of Carrigan County while the getting is good, Deputy John?"

He smiled. "There you go," he said. "Sheriff's in court until noontime. Then he'll go to dinner, then back to the office."

"And do his paperwork," I said. "Okay, got it. We'll get down the road directly. Now, let me ask you something. Did the sheriff mention having any kind of run-in with M. C. Mingo last night?"

He shook his head. "I ain't heard that," he said. "Why you askin'?"

I almost told him. I trusted the Big brothers, mostly because they had played fair and square from the git-go—and saved my ass from being burned up like Laurie May Creigh. But since I suddenly had an inkling of why Hayes might be consorting with the likes of M. C. Mingo, I changed my mind.

"You should mention to him, when and if he gets around to asking about us, that you did some checking after seeing that ER list. That you located us, talked to me, and urged us to get a move on. It'll show initiative, and he'll like that."

He eyed me from that vast height. "And what else should I be tellin' Sheriff Hayes?" he asked. *Not missing much at all,* I thought. Like many really big guys I knew, this one kept his brains quietly out of sight, a tactic that probably allowed him to surprise lots of people.

"Just that we *are* leaving the area," I said, and then I paused.

"And?" he prodded.

"And that I was in the parking lot last night," I said. "Behind the hospital."

"Aw shit, what y'all gettin' at now?" he asked.

"I do believe he'll know what that means. Now: We will leave town, but not until I'm sure Ms. Santángelo can travel safely, okay? No more Marshal Dillon games. She was in a bad way last night and she's still out. We'll leave as soon as possible, but the more time we have for her to rest, the better, okay?"

He said he understood and asked if I needed him to get anything from the store or pharmacy. I told him I'd take care of it and he left. I poked my head back into the room, but Carrie was still out for the count. I went down to the motel office and cadged some coffee and a complimentary greasy doughnut. When I got back to the room she was sitting on the edge of the bed, looking shot at and missed, shit at and hit. I told her so and she thanked me sincerely. Then she swiped my coffee, so I figured she must be feeling better. I went back for more coffee. She was dressed and had both eyes open when I got back. I told her about my conversation with Bigger John. She was alarmed when she heard the part about telling the sheriff we'd been in the parking lot last night.

"Was that wise?" she said. "If he's Mingo's partner, we might get to do our own Bonnie and Clyde scene right here in this motel."

I didn't think so. "I guess it's possible he might sic Mingo on us, but I think he's mostly interested in getting us the hell out of here. I didn't say we saw Mingo and his pet quack in the hospital doing their thing. Just that we were in the parking lot last night. He'll have to wonder what we saw. That way, I've got leverage on him, just like he's got leverage on me. That's a good reason to just let us go away."

"I don't know, Cam—you might be outsmarting yourself there. These mountain people favor direct action most of the time."

"I outsmart myself all the time," I admitted. "So if you are ready to roll, let's get out of Dodge."

She sat down on the edge of her bed. "I'm physically better. I think my fever's down if not gone. But I'm not ready to be run out of town or this county. I want to get those bastards, Mingo, Nathan, Grinny Creigh, and the honorable Mister Hayes if he's really part of this. And I want to save as many of those kids as possible from what probably happened in that lab last night. I still want to know what happened to my baby sister all those years ago. I am determined on that point."

Lots of I-wants there, I thought, but her expression evoked some of the more thunderous stuff I'd read in the Old Testament. You can take the girl out of the mountains, but you can't take the mountains out of the girl. I did have the sense not to say that out loud.

"I ran out on you once already," I said. "I'm not ready to do that again, just yet. Unless, of course, you start fooling around with other guys."

She softened her expression for a moment, but then shook her head.

"You're the one who's technically a fugitive from Robbins County," she said. "The one who's got bench warrants out, and the guy who removed Rowena Creigh's least useful part. You're the one who needs to get out of here. Hayes could solve his problem by handing you over to Mingo, and it would be perfectly legal, if not his sworn duty."

I picked up the pages of my handwritten report. "I'm Fed-Exing this to the Bureau's Charlotte field office today. I think you should do one, too, if you're up to it."

"Fine," she said. "I will. And if I get into trouble, I'll make sure Hayes knows that you've done that. But lemme tell you what: I want *personal* satisfaction here. And now I don't have a career or anything else standing in my way anymore. I should have done this years ago."

"All of us, you, me, Greenberg and his crew, *all* of us have bounced off every time we've gone into Robbins County," I said. "Speaking from personal experience, I don't recommend any more frontal attacks."

She nodded. "You're right. I'm going to send my report to a couple of television stations in Raleigh," she said. "The legislature's still in session, so that ought to stir up some noise. Really, it's time for you to get out. You've done more than your share."

It was my turn to smile. "Okay, Carrie. I get the picture. You don't love me anymore."

She made a rude noise and looked around for something to throw. Then she grinned.

"Okay," I said. "I'll leave you to it. You've got my cell number."

"Where will you go?" she asked immediately.

"What you don't know can't be forced out of you," I replied, semi-facetiously, "but probably back to Triboro. My lawyer keeps telling me to get back to civilization or his fees are going to double."

"Smart lawyer," she said.

I went over to her. Removed the coffee cup. Sat down and gathered her into my arms. "You're okay, for a girl," I said. "You're smart, gutsy, and easy on the eyes. If I'm slow on the uptake, it's because I'm a guy."

She folded into me and put her hand on my face. We sat like that for a while.

We spent the rest of the morning resorting all our equipment between our two vehicles. I still had Nathan's ten-gauge, and Carrie had her nine. I went to a nearby grocery store and brought her back some light food from their salad bar, and then we said good-bye. She said she'd find another place to stay, and one perhaps not quite so easily available to police inquiries.

As I drove off, the whole thing, of course, felt wrong. Part of it was my own sense of duty telling me not to abandon a fellow cop, even if neither of us was officially a cop anymore. But she was tough and she had no illusions about what she was doing, even though I didn't think much of her plan or her chances. The same arguments that she'd made about Hayes solving his Richter problem applied to her, and she had to know that. But for the life of me, I couldn't figure out any way to go into Robbins County and do something to or about the Mingo-Creigh Axis of Evil. Mailing in my report to the Bureau would either provoke something or it wouldn't, and I had no leverage there, either. Her idea of throwing some sensational stuff into the media pipe might be more effective than my sending in a report to the boys in the seriously gray suits.

I stopped by Marionburg's version of a mail store, looked up the Charlotte field office in a federal directory, and fired off my saga of battle against evildoing in the Carolina mountains. I'd addressed it to the special agent in charge, whom I knew by name, in hopes that at least an executive assistant would read it. Otherwise it would go to the mail room and into the Letters-from-Santa pile. Which provoked a thought.

I called Carrie on her cell phone and got voice mail. I told her to make sure she said in her submission to the Raleigh media that a report had been filed with the FBI in Charlotte. If my magnum opus did get lost in the mailroom, there'd be the scramble from hell to find it down in Charlotte once that tidbit came out in public.

As I came out of the mail store I was nearly run over by a Park Service Jeep backing out of a parking place in the crowded lot. The driver was Mary Ellen Goode, who was, somewhat to my surprise, glad to see me. She looked much better than the last time I'd seen her. The circles under her eyes were much diminished, her expression was sunny, and she was well on her way to regaining her status as one of the brightest objects in Marionburg again. Since it was getting close to lunchtime I suggested we go grab a bite. We ended up in one of the tourist cafés along the main drag, surrounded by lots of flatlanders with aching feet. We took a table in a back corner and ordered lunch.

"You look terrific," I said. "What's changed?"

"Believe it or not," she said, "this is my last official day with the Park Service. I was actually in there mailing a box of my desk stuff to Wilmington."

"Wilmington."

"A new chapter in my life, I hope," she said. She'd resigned from the Park Service and accepted a faculty position at UNC Wilmington down on the Carolina coast. No more unruly tourists, guns, pepper spray, grouchy bears, budget cuts, lovesick bosses, and other adventures in the western mountains.

"That's great," I said. "As I remember, we talked about this back when, well, you know."

She nodded. "I resisted the whole notion at first," she said. "But then, just for the hell of it, I went online and took a look. My first application was accepted immediately. Pay raise, my federal retirement transfers, and totally new surroundings."

"And no more cat dancers, mountain lions, or ex-cops ripping up your life, either," I said.

She frowned for just a second, and I mentally kicked myself. Then she waved it off. "That's all in the past," she said. "Besides, I took a look at the faculty picture gallery. I do believe I might do some damage down there amongst all the women's-studies, post-post-deconstruction sisterhood."

I laughed. This was more like it—she was a beautiful woman in the prime of her life, and she absolutely ought to go break some hearts. Our food came, and she asked what I'd been doing since we'd last met. I told her not much, not willing to resurrect all the Sturm und Drang of the last few days. I could just imagine how the rest of lunch would go if I described taking Rue's head off on that dirt road, or how I was actively avoiding not one but two local sheriffs who were interested in arresting my interfering ass, if not worse. This wasn't the kind of place cops would frequent—I hoped, anyway—but I'd noticed that the courthouse was only a few blocks away.

Then I remembered something. I asked her how things were going at the ranger station and, as casually as I could, whether or not the DEA still had that cabin up in the park. Turned out that, yes, they did. I moved the conversation on to other things while wondering if I could find that cabin again.

We said our good-byes in the parking lot, after which I drove over to the local supermarket. From their parking lot I put a call into Baby Greenberg and, for once, got him. No, they were not using the cabin, and, to his knowledge, neither was anyone else. He said that I was, of course, *not* authorized to use that cabin, and I promised him solemnly that I would never do such a thing. He was glad we had that cleared up. I told him that I'd been ordered to get out of Carrigan County, but that Carrie Santángelo planned to stick around and I was nervous about leaving her alone. He immediately wanted to know why she was staying, and I suggested he might want to come by said Park Service cabin this evening. I promised him a steak and some scotch, which he said sounded appealing, even if it did involve my being in the very cabin I was not authorized to be in. I asked him if he was working anything over on this side of the park, and he said no.

"For the moment, anyway," he explained. "We've basically been told to stay out of the various goings-on over there in Robbins County. Did you really ice Rue Creigh?"

I told him that, yes, regrettably, I did.

"In that case, dinner is going to be well offline."

"You'll be on federal turf, not Robbins County," I said. "Checking to make sure there aren't any squatters abusing your hideout."

"Sounds good. You find out what the hell that old woman is doing with children up there?"

"How do you like your steak?" I asked.

"Rare."

"Define rare," I said, mostly to see if he knew the formula.

"Cut off its horns, wipe its ass, and bring it to the table," he recited.

"Good. Now I don't have to buy charcoal."

He showed up just after sundown in an unmarked Crown Vic. He might even have thought that no one would have ever suspected it might be a cop car, but as I watched his progress through the tourist campground from on high, I could tell that every teenager down there who saw the car knew precisely what it was.

He was calmer than usual—no wide-open eyes, rapid-fire speech, or twitchy hands. I gave him some scotch, briefly seared two steaks, and then debriefed him over dinner. He didn't seem too surprised about what the Creighs were up to, almost as if this was what he'd come to expect from the Appalachian lowlife. The news about Hayes did dismay him.

"I suspect it's not about personal gain," I said. "His wife is apparently desperately ill, and I'm guessing their health plan has run out. Something like that. Or it could be that what we saw was just Hayes hassling Mingo for being in Carrigan County."

"But you don't think so?"

I shook my head. "I think he knows what Mingo is up to and is probably on the payroll, if only to look the other way. That's when I decided it really wasn't safe to be there anymore. Carrie wouldn't leave, though—which is why

I telegraphed the fact to Hayes that I'd seen him and Mingo in the parking lot. Once that gets back to them, I'll be their main problem, not her."

"How chivalrous," Baby said. "But in the end, if they're partners, they'll whack you both if they can. That report you sent in to the Bureau—*that's* going to stir up a shit storm, I think."

"*If* it gets through the mailroom and the SAC's palace guard," I said. "You know how that goes. They get a lot of crank mail."

He sipped some scotch. "Yeah, but I got a call from Sam King at the SBI, after those hillbillies did their Buddhist monk interpretation in the parking lot? He confirmed the Bureau had something going on this kid thing, although not specific to Robbins County. Said he'd told the both of you to get out of the way before you really fucked things up."

"Well, then," I said. "My report ought to just corroborate their suspicions. Maybe now they'll move in force."

"I wonder, Cam. You know those guys—they don't play well with others. I used to think it was really good operational security. Now I think it's because they want the option of saying, 'Hey, everybody, that wasn't us,' should whatever they try happen to go south. If they do know about this alleged child-sex-slave deal, my guess is they're probably working the other end."

"Meaning?"

"Meaning, they're trying to find out who the *buyers* are. You mention your theory that it's going overseas?"

I said I had, but that of course I had no real data. "It isn't likely they're selling into the U.S. in places like Washington," I said, "New Orleans, now, I'd believe that, although Katrina might have slowed that down a little. But D. C.? That town's one big piece of flypaper for anything like this these days."

"I'm with you on that," he said. "Too many tripwires in Washington right now. This has to be an overseas deal, and I like your theory on diplomatic immunity channels."

I cleared the plates and threw steak scraps to the two fuzzy piranhas hovering discreetly near the table.

"I'm kind of conflicted on this whole gig," I told him. "As an ex-lawman, I can see perfectly well how we could screw things up for some operation we don't know about. Sam King is right—we should knock it off. On the other hand . . ."

"On the other hand, you're a civilian now," he said. "These animals are in your face. Remember all the times when you were on the Job that you wanted to pick up a club and invoke Father Darwin on some walking pustule? Well, now you can, as long as you do it right and don't get caught."

"You ever get that urge in your business?'

"I rarely harbor such thoughts, or at least no more than hourly," he said, pouring some more scotch. "At least you took that bitch Rowena Creigh off the boards."

"That was pretty awful," I said. "I acted instinctively and, trust me, I felt that .357 round with my left ear. But still, a double-ten to the face makes for some vivid memories."

"Don't trouble yourself," he said. "That skank compromised one of my guys. Got him all hot and bothered, went to some no-tell motel in Rocky Falls, took him around the world, only she was making movies the whole time. Had to transfer the guy out of the area *and* his wife found out. You did the world a service."

"And stoked the Creighs' revenge ethic," I said. "We're not going to have any more polite conversations on the front porch."

"Hell, that just clarifies your position," he said with a grin. "See a Creigh, pop his ass. Self-defense, a priori. Guaranteed clean shoot. I'll testify for you."

"What do you think about all this?" I asked.

He sniffed. "I'm at the stage in my life where I'm focused on getting off this bus with enough money to be comfortable, the Neanderthals up in the hills notwithstanding."

"They're selling kids, man. To kiddie porn monsters."

"You know what?" he replied. "That's probably a better fate for them than dying of worms in their front yards."

Both shepherds, who had been listening raptly to our conversation and hoping for more scraps, got up suddenly and went to the front door, ears up. Baby had all the lights out and I had the shotgun in hand in about the same five seconds. We each took a window. It was full dark by now, but the campground lights down below the cabin gave us a good look outside. The shepherds weren't growling, which I finally realized meant that they might know who or what was outside. I couldn't see the area right in front of the door.

Then I remembered who'd brought me to this cabin in the first place.

"Lemme guess, you're desperately seeking some decent scotch," I said softly.

"Open the freaking door, please," Carrie said from the other side. "It's getting cold out here."

Baby, his gun pointed down at the floor, opened the door and she stepped through, both arms full of gear. "Having a nice chat, boys?" she asked as she dumped her stuff on the floor. The shepherds greeted her warmly. "You're lucky I wasn't a creeping Creigh, with all those lights on and a clear shot right through my window of choice."

"This is a federal reservation," Baby declared self-righteously, putting away his gun. "A national park, even. A treasured heritage. A Vanderbilt tax write-off. They wouldn't dast."

She snorted and asked where the glasses were. In our haste we'd forgotten to hide the bottle, so, unfortunately, we had to share. We sat back down at the table.

"So what's the plan, Stan?" she asked no one in particular.

Baby made a by-me gesture with his hands. "I was just invited over for dinner," he said. "You know, just passing through the neighborhood?"

Carrie looked over at me expectantly. She was wearing jeans, a sleeveless blouse, and a too-large ball cap, presumably to cover up the new sideways part in her hair. But her eyes were clear and she seemed to have regained some of her normal spunk.

"Beats the shit out of me," I said. "I was just taking the night off."

"He lies," Baby said helpfully. "He didn't want to slink away back to beautiful downtown Triboro and leave you alone up here with all these black hats looking for you. Watch yourself, Carrie—it might be true love."

I gave him the finger and Carrie started laughing. That was a pretty sight, actually.

"You write up something to send in?" I asked, trying to change the subject.

"I did," she said. "Between naps. It's over there in that pile of stuff. You mail yours?"

"FedEx overnight to the Stick People down in Charlotte," I said. "Baby here thinks it's actually going to stir up some shit."

"Like the subtle message you sent along with Bigger John this morning did?" she said.

"Somebody get upset?"

"Sheriff Hayes has apparently disappeared."

"Disappeared?"

"Deputy John came back by this afternoon. Said Hayes left his badge and a letter of resignation on his desk, citing personal reasons."

"Did Deputy John confirm he'd given him my message?"

"He did. Said the sheriff got a funny look on his face, closed his door, and made a long phone call. Then he came out, told his secretary he had an urgent meeting, took his cruiser out of the sheriff's office lot, and drove away. She didn't find the resignation letter for another hour, by which time he was long gone. No sign of him since. No radio contact. No nothing. And he kept his weapon."

"And what was this little love note you sent the sheriff?" Baby asked. I'd neglected to tell him that part earlier, and when he heard it, he whistled. "That old boy may be sucking on his Glock as we speak," he said.

"If he's been involved in a scheme to sterilize young girls and then sell them to Arab potentates, that's the least he could do," I said.

"Or," Carrie said, "that really was an argument we were watching, and now Hayes has gone to settle something with Mingo."

"Like what?"

"I don't know. He may have been operating under the assumption that impoverished young women in Robbins County were getting abortions and Mingo was the gatekeeper, using a moonlighter at the Carrigan County hospital. Once you told your story about seeing Grinny handing over a child, and then talking about kids and airports, well, that may have been an epiphany for Mr. Do-nothing Hayes."

"That would explain the way he turned as hostile as he did," I said. "Up to that point it was him and us against the face of evil in Robbins County. Then all of sudden it was *Get out of my county.*"

"Whatever, they can't find him, and they're worried."

"Did you tell John that you were coming here?" I asked.

She said no. "I told him I was checking out this afternoon and let him draw his own conclusions. He does have my cell number. Oh, and he said that Laurie May had been moved before her boys went to war and the Creighs burned her cabin down. One of the other brothers came and got her. She's alive and well over in Tennessee at his place. There were two old dogs that did not get out."

"You know what?" Baby said, getting up. "You guys are starting to scare me. I'm going to go back to the relative safety of chasing down homicidal druggies."

"Okay if we camp out here for a while?" Carrie asked him.

"Oh, hell, yes," he said. "We're not using it, and after what I've heard tonight, none of us peace-loving narcs are going to get anywhere near this or the neighboring county. If the Park Service rumbles it, you're on your own, though."

"Can you help with that report I sent in to the Bureau?" I asked. "Like maybe call someone down there, tell them to be looking for it?"

He nodded. "Yeah, sure," he said. "I can give the ASAC a heads-up. But he'll invite me to butt-outsky, and for once, I'm going to oblige with a smile. You two really ought to take a vacation and wait for the heavies to get into this."

We both looked at him and he shook his head, knowing that probably wasn't going to happen. "All right, at least keep your cell phones on, then," he said, as he slipped into his windbreaker and headed for the door. He stopped before opening it. "No way I can talk you out of this crusade?" he said. "Either of you?"

"They're selling children, for Chrissakes," Carrie said.

He looked like he was going to argue with her, but then waved and left.

Carried stared at the closed front door. "What's the matter with that guy?" she asked in visible exasperation.

"Baby doesn't think very highly of the people up here," I said. "He acts like this isn't the worst thing he's seen some of these people do."

She sat down and rubbed her head. "That getting better?" I asked.

"It's itching," she said. "That's supposed to be a sign of healing. I think this scotch is helping a lot."

"Better go easy," I said. "Remember your seven days of pills."

"You just don't want to share," she said.

"That, too," I said. "Let's see if this fireplace works. Maybe fool around a little?"

She gave me one of those you-gotta-be-shitting-me looks. I'd seen those before. I grinned at her. I went to get some firewood and water the shepherds. At least the cabin could be warm.

I got a fire going. It really wasn't all that cold outside, but the fire was nice, just the same. I pulled up a chair and sat down, ready to just watch the fire burn. Carrie was doing something behind me, so I sort of zoned out.

Then she handed me a wee dram and sat down on the floor, her shoulders between my legs. She rested her head back on my lap. The ugly scar was right there, but somehow, it seemed like an intimacy I wasn't supposed to see. I put my hands on her temples and pressed gently in a massaging circle. She made an appreciative noise.

That's how we fell asleep. It wasn't about sex. It was all about being close, sharing affection, trust, togetherness against the night outside and the terrible world of the mountain Creighs. I was disappointed with Baby Greenberg. All he could offer was a repeat of the Greek chorus we'd been hearing from everyone else: Go away.

14

We spent the next morning going through her version of the report to make sure it generally correlated with what I had said. We didn't want them to be identical, but we didn't want to leave any big discrepancies through which work-averse civil serpents could slither out, either. We kicked around several ideas for going after Grinny Creigh & Co., but none of them sounded like a winner. Just after noon, however, Carrie got a call on her cell from Bigger John. It seemed that Sheriff Hayes had contacted him and wanted a meet with Carrie at the Hayes family home place up in the mountains above Marionburg. She said she'd do it as long as both John and Luke came along. John relayed that stipulation, and Hayes apparently agreed to that. She said she'd meet John in town at four that afternoon.

I asked her if she wanted me to come along, too. She did, but not actually with her and the two deputies. "How's about you play backup?" she said. "Follow us up there but stay out of sight. If we get into trouble, you ride to the rescue and cover yourself in glory."

"You don't mean try to tail you on a mountain road, do you?" I asked. I still remembered her version of a casual night drive in the mountains.

"No; you drive too slow. I'll tell the brothers Big that you'll be in the backfield. I trust them. I'll keep you advised of what we're doing and where we are, and maybe you can even get a tactical observation spot on us when we meet with Hayes."

"Hopefully it's just Hayes," I said.

"Either way, it would be good to know you're out there, and Hayes, of course, doesn't have to know you're there unless things get tense."

"You know, you don't really have the authority to deal with Hayes," I said. "I mean, suppose he cops to being involved in this kid thing—it's not like you can bring him in, or make any promises."

"The Big brothers are sworn officers. They can bring him in," she said. "Besides, I have a feeling he's not calling to make any kind of a deal. I think he wants to get right with God over what he and Mingo've been doing."

"I don't know, Carrie," I said. "I know you *think* that about Hayes. On the other hand, it could be a nasty setup, with Hayes on the porch and Mingo and his crew waiting in the weeds."

"Why?" she asked. "You're the one he thinks saw him at the hospital. You didn't say anything about me being there, did you?"

"No, I didn't, but he knows you were there being treated, and we've been operating together. If he thinks I've blown town, you're the loose end at hand, so to speak."

"I'll chance it," she said. "We're not going to bust Mingo and his operation on our own, and so far the heavies, as Baby calls them, aren't doing squat. If Hayes wants to repent, maybe he can get us in. I still have this terrible feeling there's a clutch of children being held somewhere for one final 'harvest.'"

On that happy note, we stopped yapping and made our preparations. I followed Carrie into town in a loose tail. She met up with John and his brother at the sheriff's office, and she followed their cruiser out of town. I had the dogs, my Remington rifle, Nathan's ten-gauge and a whole box of extra-dry shells, the spotting scope, and enough rifle ammo for a fair-sized firefight. I felt better that both the Big brothers were coming along. Carrie called me on my cell phone as we left town.

"We're proceeding to the Hayes home place," she said. "It's about ten miles out of town in the direction of the Robbins County line. Apparently there's the original house, a modern cabin, and an abandoned mine on the property."

"Have you talked directly to Sheriff Hayes?" I asked.

"No," she replied. "John called him and told him we were starting up."

"And they know I'm in the picture?"

"The brothers do, Hayes does not. Luke and John were cool with that. They said they're not expecting trouble."

"That's when trouble usually rears its ugly head," I said, and hung up. She'd been an SBI bureaucrat for most of her career. I, on the other hand, had been a street cop and an operational major crimes detective for most of mine. She was expecting a civilized meeting. I was expecting an ambush. I would really have liked to be able to do a prebrief with the Bigs, but they were in a separate vehicle, so off we went.

On the way up I got a call from Mose Walsh. He wanted to know if I'd heard about the sheriff going walkabout. I said yes.

"I was sitting next to some off-duty deputies last night for supper," he said. "One of 'em said this supposedly had something to do with M. C. Mingo and Grinny Creigh."

"That's not news," I said.

"Yeah, right," he said. "But if people are talking like that, it's gonna get back to Robbins County. And if this *is* about selling kids, whoever's holding the product may just panic."

"Good point," I said. "Things are in motion, so, please, keep listening."

I followed them up into the actual mountains, and finally they turned off onto a well-maintained dirt road. I lingered on the main road for about five minutes, assuming there was only the one road going up. I assumed wrong, as usual. A quarter mile into the woods the dirt road diverged into two branches, one going right and up, the other going left and down. I quickly tried to call Carrie. No signal. I got out and played Indian, trying to see where the fresh tire tracks were. I failed Indian. The shepherds were no help—they had no scent to focus on. I stood there, listening for the sounds of vehicles, but heard only a few crows laughing at my Indian act. I remembered why I used to like shooting crows.

It was a dirt road, I kept telling myself. There had to be tracks. The shepherds were pretending to look for something, but I knew they were mostly just confused. I walked up the hill on the right-hand track, assuming the home place would be on high ground. The surface of the road was actually hardpan, with lots of shattered flat rocks and even some shale. It was showing zero tire tracks, and I was getting antsier by the minute.

I walked back down to the dividing point, listened again to make sure no one else was coming up the road from the two-lane, and then tried going down. Fifty feet in I found a wet spot where a tiny creek was soaking through the dirt road. I finally passed Indian–tire tracks at last. I went back to the Suburban and called in the mutts, and we headed down, going slow with all the windows open. After another half mile it looked like the trees were thinning out ahead. I didn't like being below whatever it was I was going to be watching, but this branch of the road had gone ninety degrees away from the upper branch, so it was going to be low ground or no ground. I parked the Suburban, hiding it as best I could behind some bushy pines. I rousted out the shepherds, the rifle, and the scope and headed into the woods on the left-hand side of the dirt lane. About three hundred yards in I stepped over a small creek and could finally begin to see the Hayes home place through the trees.

I discovered that I was approaching from below a long earthen dam, behind which there was a three-acre pond, formed in the valley cut out by a creek. At the other end of the pond there was a very pretty log cabin, which looked to have been one of those modern kit jobs, as opposed to an original rustic. There was a detached frame garage, behind which I could see Carrie's vehicle, the brothers' cruiser, and presumably Sheriff Hayes's vehicle parked on one side of the cabin. To the left and slightly above the cabin was a graying, narrow, three-story house made of rough-hewn timbers. It was pretty obviously long since abandoned, with a slumping roof, gaping window frames, and a front porch that was down on the ground. There were several old outbuildings surrounding the house in similar states of ivy-draped decomposition.

Above and beyond the house, cabin, and pond, the land rose steeply on either side of the creek that supplied the pond, and I could see a mound of tailings halfway up the hill to the left, along with some rusting machinery stands and a few disintegrating mine carts. I was too low to see the actual mine entrance, but it had to be up there by those tailings. The mine was probably three hundred feet higher than the cabin and the house. There were no pastures or any other signs of farming, and the enveloping mountain forest was slowly but surely reclaiming the entire place.

I moved to the left along the grass face of the dam until I had a better view of the vehicles and the slopes to my right, where presumably that other road came out. We were miles from the Creigh place over in the next county, but not very far from the county line, as best I could tell. The Hayes place was on an eastern slope, and the late-afternoon shadows were beginning to creep down the higher ridges as the sun began to set. Unfortunately, there was absolutely no cover where I was crouching, and the slanting sunlight was full in my eyes. I had to move.

I signaled the dogs, and we went back down the dam face to the outflow creek and then down the long gulley below the dam until I could no longer see the cabin or the falling-down house. Then we cut directly south, into the woods. My objective was to circle the whole place until I came out up at the level of the abandoned mine. From there, I should be in the shadow of the setting sun and able to see the cabin, all the vehicles, and anyone coming down through the opposite woods.

It took me almost a half hour to get in position, as the woods on the south side of the property were thick with wait-a-minute vines and stands of hawthorn. I didn't make any decent progress until I crossed a narrow track that presumably led up to the old mine. There were railroad ties and a badly rusted cog rail on one side of the track, so I followed that up until I reached a small plateau cut back into the face of the hill. The mine entrance was a rectangular black hole, framed in large timbers and cut into the side of the hill, with rusting narrow-gauge tracks coming out toward the tailings dump. The hill rose above the mine entrance two hundred feet or so.

There was more extinct machinery littering this area, and the flattened remains of a sorting shed to one side, which is where the cog line terminated. The little plateau was higher above the house and cabin than I had estimated, but the position was a perfect place to watch the cabin. The setting sun was behind me now, and the light was strong enough to penetrate the woods on the other side of the pond. We had maybe two hours before the virtual sunset caused by the mountains.

I used the scope to make a visual sweep of those woods and the hills above, but saw no sign of any creeping Creighs. The shepherds went exploring, which I figured was okay because we could not be seen from the cabin. Frack poked his nose into the mine entrance but came right back out, while Frick went rat hunting along the remains of the sorting shed, whose metal roof was now only about two feet off the ground. I wondered what had happened to the mine, whether it had simply played out or flooded, which was what usually shut these smaller operations down. There was enough old machinery scattered around the entrance apron to indicate there'd been a fairly good vein down there.

I crept over to one side of the tailings pile and set the scope up on the cabin itself. The front porch overlooking the pond was in shadow and out of my direct view, but the side and back porches were fully illuminated by the bright yellow setting sun. There was a lot of firewood stacked along the back porch. All the windows were covered with curtains, so I couldn't see anything inside the house. The immediate yard was neatly tended, and there was none of the junk and trash I'd seen decorating all too many of the places in these hills. I envied the sheriff and his tranquility up here, although he probably wasn't enjoying much tranquility right now.

I swept the scope back over the far slopes again, cruising optically over all the good hiding places. Frack came over and sat down next to me. If I was watching, he would watch, too. It was what he did best, sit down and look at things with those amber wolf eyes, which was why he saw the problem before I did. He gave a small woof, and I looked over at him to see what was up. He was staring down at the pond, so I swung the scope over to the pond and the dam and landed the lens right on the face of a man. He was lying prone on the face of the dam, just his head showing as he swept the cabin area with binoculars. I thought for a moment we were looking right at each other, but he was focusing on the cabin. His lenses flashed in the setting sun, while mine should have been in deep shadow. I told Frack to lie down and backed away from the rim of the tailings apron so that just my scope was sticking out into the black hat's field of view.

I'd assumed they'd come from the high ground because that's what you did if you could. Instead, they'd probably come up the same damned road I'd walked. Assumptions were kicking my ass this afternoon. I wondered if they'd found my Suburban.

I refocused the scope for longer range and swept it through the trees and underbrush beyond the pond, and finally caught a metallic glint through the leaves. After a minute of study, I concluded that it was probably a slick-back Crown Vic. That meant Mingo's crew was here. I pointed back onto the dam, but the watcher had disappeared. That had not been Mingo looking though the binocs, so I had to assume at least two potential shooters, maybe as many as four. I swept back up to the far slope just to make sure there weren't twenty of the bastards out there, and then remembered there was a fair-sized hill above me and the mine. I rolled slowly over onto my back and traversed the scope up along the ridge above the mine entrance. Nothing visible, but I realized I was pretty exposed out there.

I called Frick quietly, and then the dogs and I moved underneath the ruins of the trestle over which the tip cars had been dumped onto the tailings pile. A rusting mine car was growing into the ground at the base of the trestle, and that should protect me if Mingo got a shooter up there on the ridge above the mine. I still had a good view of the pond, but I'd be more exposed to fire from down there than I'd been when lying flat on the ground at the rim of the mine plateau. Keeping the scope pointed downhill, I began to use my boots to gouge out a shallow foxhole in the tailings debris. Then I saw the head again, rising like a round periscope above the top of the dam, binocs glued to its face. I slid the Remington over and tried its scope. I had the sudden urge to pop this guy, but it would have been a tough shot, downhill on about a twenty-five-degree slope, at an unknown range, and over water just to make things harder. I bolted a round into the chamber and the dogs moved away—they hated the noise of gunfire.

I put the rifle down and went back to the spotting scope. The head was gone again, but I caught a quick glimpse of a rifle barrel about twenty feet to the watcher's right. Okay, at least two. I did another sweep of the opposite hill and then checked my back. Nobody visible, but that didn't mean there wasn't another tactically capable shooter up there who was waiting for the same shot I was waiting for. Then I heard a vehicle coming, and whoever was driving was making no attempt to be stealthy about it. A moment later another cop car eased into view on the lower road. I recognized it as M. C. Mingo's personal car. He drove right up to the point where the dam melded back into the front lawn. He turned his car around to point back down the road, shut down, got out, took a quick look around, and then walked up onto the porch and out of my line of sight.

Coming the way he had, he had to have seen those shooters plastered against the face of the dam, which confirmed that those were his people. No big news there, but it also meant that when he was done with his visit, he'd be signaling those guys to either back off or get on with an attack of some kind once he was deniably clear of the scene.

I tried my cell phone again, but the right-side signal panel was blank. Useless damn things. Now I had to figure out how to warn the people inside without giving away my own position. I could try to sneak down there, but if the guy with binocs went up-scope at the wrong moment, he would warn Mingo and whatever was going to happen would start inside the cabin. Not a good plan. I did my scope sweep of the surrounding area again, and this time spotted a figure moving through the trees high on the opposite ridgeline above the cabin. It looked like he was trying to get into a position to cover the cabin's back door. Then Frick gave a low growl and stared hard behind me.

I rolled over slowly to the left, making sure both dogs were down on the ground with me. I peered around the nearest trestle post and saw a fourth man half-sliding, half-walking down the hill above the mine entrance. He was carrying a rifle, and he was paying close attention to where he was putting his feet, which was probably why he hadn't spotted me. It looked like he was aiming for the mine entrance as a hiding place. He would have been in full view of the cabin had anyone been looking, but my guess was that Mingo was keeping everyone inside fully occupied. I mentally chastised the Bigs for not posting a lookout.

I rolled back the other way so that I'd be out of sight when he finally got down to the plateau, and then the dogs and I crawled up toward the lip of the tailings slope right where the dump trestle projected out over the pile. We watched from the edge, hopefully well out of sight of the men hiding down on the dam. The shooter finally reached the plateau in a shower of loose dirt and rocks, which dumped him unceremoniously on the ground twenty feet to the right of the mine entrance. He got up, dusted himself off, and then walked over toward the lip of the plateau, where he stood out in full view for a moment. He waved his rifle, then turned around and walked back toward the mine entrance. He was wearing jeans, a light denim jacket, and, bless him, a black hat. I waited until he was out of the sight line from the dam and the cabin and almost to the entrance to the mine, and then I fired the shepherds at him.

They went in at a dead run, ears flat, tails out, back legs pumping hard, and hit him simultaneously in the back of the legs and the small of his back. He went down like a trapdoor, with a shepherd tugging hard on each shirtsleeve and in opposite directions, totally immobilizing him. I got up and sprinted across the plateau, trying to minimize my time in the open. When I got to the man I relaxed because he was so obviously petrified I knew he wasn't going to be a problem. I kicked the rifle away from his reach and stabilized the dogs. Keeping my own rifle on him, I told him to crawl into the mine, where I secured him on the ground with his own belt, socks, and shoelaces, the belt for his hands behind his back, his socks and shoelaces to tie his feet together. Then I knelt down beside him and pushed his face into the dirt.

"Listen to me," I said, as calmly as I could. "You keep still. No matter what happens outside. If I see you move, I'll send these dogs back in here to eat your face, and then I'll cave this sucker in right on top of you, got it?"

He whimpered something, his eyes still squeezed shut. It was unlikely that the shepherds would eat the guy's face, unless there was a really good sauce. But he didn't know that. He was heavily bearded like most of them were, but he couldn't have been more than twenty years old. Thin, bony face, bad complexion, snaggled, yellow, meth-rotted teeth. And so scared I could smell urine. I left him ten feet back into the mine itself, which was a square tunnel hewn out of the rock and supported by heavy side beams pushing up corrugated tin sheets on the roof. The tunnel went back and down as far as I could see into the dusty gloom, and I had no inclination to go any farther in. It smelled of damp rot and chalk, and the floor had about a two-inch layer of fine dust covering the two rails running down the center.

I took his black hat with me and picked up his rifle on my way out. I put the hat on, downed the shepherds at the entrance to watch my prisoner, and went far enough out on the plateau for my hat and rifle to show if the guys down on the dam took a look, which they did about two minutes later. I could see the binocs flashing up my way, so I tipped my head forward, hopefully showing the hat and rifle the guy down there was expecting to see.

But my original problem was still there—how to warn the good guys inside that Mingo was having them surrounded. Then I had an idea: send a messenger.

I scuttled back to the entrance of the mine. The dogs were sitting on either side of the black hat, who was being very still. I walked over to him and cut off his bindings. He opened his eyes. Then, standing behind the guy, I flashed my teeth at Frack, who flashed back and growled. It was just a thing he'd learned to do, but it was really impressive. Frick just watched. I did it again and the guy in the dirt whimpered. I told him to stand up, carefully, with no sudden moves. He got to his feet and it looked like it was taking everything he had not to bolt—*into* the mine.

"I have a job for you," I told him. "Mingo's down there at Sheriff Hayes's cabin, right?"

He nodded, while trying not to stare at Frack. When he did look at Frack, I flashed my teeth again over his shoulder and got a truly gratifying response from the big black dog.

"I want you to go down there and tell Mingo that federal cops are on this hill. I'm not the only guy out here watching you people, understand?"

He nodded again, still keeping an eye on Frack, who was waiting to play some more. "Yessir," he croaked.

"You go down there and tell him to get his people off this land or there's going to be a war, and the guys with the machine guns are going to win."

He blinked. "Machine guns?"

"I've got one right out there under that trestle, so when you walk down this hill, you remember that."

"Yessir."

"I can put a hundred rounds through your spine in ten seconds," I boasted, and he nodded. He glanced down at his feet.

"Shoes?" he asked, and I told him no. Based on the looks of him, I figured he'd been barefoot for a good part of his life already. I gave him his hat back, but not his rifle, and he limped his way across the slag debris and the gravel and then started down the hill. I resumed my position under the trestle, and he did not look back. The dogs watched him go. Frick seemed a little disappointed. Maybe she *would* have eaten his face. Perhaps it was all the food bits in his beard.

I surveyed the dam with the spotting scope and finally saw the binocular man again, then saw him start when he caught sight of his barefoot buddy making his way down the hill from the mine. I wondered if they'd shoot him. If they did, that would be a warning, but I preferred getting my little message in front of Mingo if that was possible. He might or might not believe it, but his posse would.

My messenger made it up onto the porch, took his hat in hand, and disappeared around to the front door. A few minutes later he came out with Mingo, who went down the front steps at a quick walk, his erstwhile shooter hobbling behind him. Neither Carrie nor the Big brothers were visible, but I could just see Sheriff Hayes standing on the edge of the front porch, watching Mingo go. I swung the big scope around to follow Mingo, who had reached his car. He said something to the barefoot man, who nodded repeatedly, and then Mingo got in. I could see him pick up his radio mike. He said something, dropped the mike, and drove off. The barefoot man walked after the cruiser, hopping from one sore foot to the other on the stony surface.

I could just imagine what Mingo had said to him. I swung back to the far edge of the dam and pretty soon saw three, not two, men slink off into the underbrush. Then I heard a screen door slam and looked back at the cabin. Carrie was standing out on the back porch, looking up at the mine. I waved from my hide under the trestle. She waved back and then indicated I should come down there. I flashed my hand, five fingers extended, at her twice, indicating ten minutes. She understood and went back into the house. I saw Bigger John out on the side porch now. He had his gun out and was watching the area in front of the house while sucking up a quick cancer stick.

I waited for the full ten minutes. If those guys were leaving and not just repositioning, I wanted time for them to get gone so they couldn't see that the "army" of revenuers consisted of one guy and his dogs. I spent the entire time searching with the scope for any signs of humans in the underbrush who could achieve a line of fire when I came down off this hill. I didn't find anybody, which of course wasn't the same as saying there wasn't anyone up there in all those tall weeds. Then I finally went down there.

They were all gathered on the side porch by the time I walked up. I put the dogs on a long down in the yard along the side of the house and the scope on the steps leading up to the porch. Then I walked up onto the porch, my rifle in my left hand. I was focused on Hayes, whose face was haggard. I walked right past Carrie and the brothers and stopped in front of the sheriff.

He looked like he half-expected me to hit him. Perceptive man.

"You part of a conspiracy to sell little girls to offshore perverts?" I asked, not realizing I'd cocked my right fist.

He raised his own hands in a defensive gesture and said he could explain.

"Cam," Carrie said from behind me. "Let's take it inside. Those people may still be out there."

"Answer me," I said to Hayes. "I saw you and Mingo at the hospital the other night, where he was delivering what looked like an unconscious child."

He looked down at the floorboards and took a deep breath. "It was Mingo's scheme," he said finally. "I was paid to look the other way."

"What were you two arguing about?"

"Mingo had always said that these were kids who needed an abortion. Teenagers who'd been abused by their father or their uncles. Said he didn't need no more incest monsters in Robbins County. There was never any talk of selling them. The abortions were illegal, 'cause they were underage. But they were necessary. We've got mongoloids and worse up in those hills. He paid me to keep the county hospital's involvement quiet."

"What was the argument about?"

"You and the DEA guy told me you'd seen Grinny Creigh almost smother a kid. Then you said you'd overheard her talking about selling them. I was asking him what the hell was really going on in there."

"And the answer was?"

"He laughed at me. Told me I was in it up to my neck anyway, so what'd it matter. Then he told me to get out of there before someone saw us talking."

"Someone did," I said. "And I've described it all in gory detail to the FBI down in Charlotte. You come up here to eat your gun?"

Carrie said my name again in an indignant tone. Hayes stared at me. His face was not a pretty sight just then.

"Well, get to it, you bastard," I said. "If you need some help, I'm your man."

"Okay, that's enough," Carrie said. "There's more to it, and we're wasting time. Right now we have to stop Mingo from killing those kids at Grinny Creigh's. She has *six* of them up there, goddammit."

I continued to glare at Hayes for a moment, and then decided it was time for a deep breath. The look in his eyes made it clear that he was desperately ashamed. We went inside, leaving the two embarrassed deputies to keep watch outside. We sat down in the cabin's living room. I asked Carrie what Mingo had had to say.

"We never found out," she said. "He didn't expect the rest of us to be here, so there was some hemming and hawing, then he got mad, started making threats, and then that barefoot man banged on the door. We heard him say there were cops with machine guns on the hill and Mingo had to pull his people out of here. That was the first we knew that his people were out there."

"I think he came here to kill me," Hayes said from the couch. He seemed to have shrunk in the past few minutes, and he looked a hundred years old. "Those other people were just for insurance."

Before either of us could reply to that, I heard the shepherds start barking, and then Big Luke stuck his head through the front doorway. "Car comin' in fast," he reported.

We went to the front door and looked out. A police car was coming up the lower driveway, coming so fast that the driver could barely maintain control. It was a cruiser, and it looked a lot like the one Mingo had been driving.

"Inside," I yelled. "Everybody inside!" Then I called in the dogs and grabbed up my scope.

We backed away from the doorway and the two deputies piled in, followed by the two shepherds. We slammed the door and took up position by the front windows, weapons ready. Hayes went to the fireplace, took down a large double-barreled shotgun from a gun rack, and began feeding it shells.

The cruiser blasted up past the edge of the dam and then headed straight for the cabin. We could only see one person inside the car, and, at the last moment, he swerved to the right and drove the vehicle up onto the lawn in front of the cabin, tearing huge ruts into the soft ground as he got it stopped.

It was definitely Mingo, and the expression on his red face was murderous. Before we had a chance to react, he reached to his right and produced a Bushmaster M4. He stuck it out the window and opened fire on the cabin. We all spent the next few seconds getting flat while a hail of gunfire blew out all the windows and reduced the front door to splinters. I yelled at the deputies to get to the back of the cabin, and they made a high-speed crawl through all the racket and flying debris back into the kitchen area and out the door. The shepherds fled into the kitchen with them.

Carrie, like me, was down on the floor taking shelter behind the largest base logs while bullets blew hunks of chinking into white dust all over the room. I glanced behind me and saw Hayes, also on the floor, starting to inch toward the front wall with the shotgun cradled in his arms like an infantryman. An instant later, the shooting stopped, and I chanced a look through one of the bullet holes in the chinking. Mingo was reloading a new magazine, so I took the opportunity to poke the rifle into the hole and take a single snap-shot at the cruiser. I think I hit a nearby tree, but Mingo wasn't impressed. He brought the Bushmaster back up and we all went back to imitating pancakes. The noise was incredible, and the chinking was filling the room with a choking cloud of white dust. Framed pictures were being blasted off the back walls, and even the dining room chandelier was blown off its ceiling hook. Whatever else happened, this place wouldn't be waterproof for years.

By the time Mingo got through his second magazine, Hayes had reached one of the front windows. He didn't hesitate but rose up into a sitting position and let go both barrels at the cop car outside. He rolled away from the window, got two more shells into the gun, and rolled to the remains of the front door, where he stuck the gun through the thoroughly splintered wood and fired two more loads in the general direction of the cruiser. Then he flattened himself behind a two-foot-thick base log just as Mingo opened up again.

I was beginning to wonder just how much damn ammo that crazy bastard had out there, but then realized he'd shifted his aim to that big stone fireplace, because now there were rounds ricocheting all over the interior and there was truly no place to hide. All we could do was to stay down and hope. Then I heard three booming gunshots from the side porch, and the hail of automatic weapons fire stopped suddenly. One of the Big brothers had apparently crawled around the porch and momentarily put Mingo's head down.

The silence was a pleasant respite. Carrie's face was dead white, with fear, I thought, until I realized it was chinking plaster. She had her nine in her right hand, but no way to shoot without exposing herself to that Bushmaster. Hayes, on the other hand, was crawling through the crunchy white dust on the floor toward the front door again. Then we heard Mingo yelling something from out front. I was still a little bit deaf from all the shooting, but he was using the loud-speaker from the cruiser.

"Hayes, you weak bastard, this is between you'n me. Tell them other ass-holes to stay down and get your yella ass out here."

Hayes kept crawling toward the front door. He held two ready shells in the splayed fingers of his left hand, and for the first time I saw that his head was bleeding. The blood running down his white-dusted face made him look like he'd put on war paint.

Mingo kept yelling more taunts. I tried to figure out where exactly he was. My best guess was that he was down behind his cruiser. Hayes kept crawling.

"What're you doing?" I asked him.

"You people get out the back," he said quietly. "I'll take care of this prob-lem. Keep your eyes peeled—he never goes anywhere alone."

"You can't go up against a Bushmaster," I said, but even as I said it, I knew he could and would. The look on his face said as much, and I realized then that what he had in mind was unofficially called suicide by cop. That worked for me, considering what he'd been party to. I signaled Carrie to start backing away from the front-wall logs toward the kitchen and the back door.

"If you've got another shotgun in here, I can cover you," I offered.

He shook his head. "This is my problem. You go get those kids away from that witch."

Mingo was shouting some more trash out front, and I was beginning to wonder if he had any more ammo for that M4. Just then one of the Big broth-ers popped off three more rounds at the cruiser from the other side porch and received an impressive blast of automatic fire in response. It sounded like the rounds were chain-sawing the corner-overlap logs out on the front porch. And the answer is—why, yes, he does. The world's supply, apparently.

Hayes had stopped crawling across the floor and was pulling the edges of the front-hall rug back, revealing a trapdoor in the floor. He looked over at me and jerked his head toward the kitchen. Carrie was already halfway there, so I cradled my rifle and started moving back. I had to leave the spotting scope. Hayes was disappearing down into the crawl space below the cabin as Carrie and I made it to the back door. Mingo fired another burst at the front of the cabin and yelled more obscenities. By the time the rounds reached the kitchen area they were flying high, but the air was still pretty thick with bullets. They're not big bullets—.223 Remington—but they are propelled by a powder cartridge that's about a half mile long, so when they come, they come seriously energized.

Carrie and the shepherds slipped out the back door and down the back steps, putting as much of the stone foundation between them and the nutcase out front as they could. I went sideways along the back porch until I could signal the deputies, who backed away from their positions at the porch corners. I was really glad they were along for this little adventure, both as witnesses and shooters. We gathered at the back steps, staying down at the level of the foundation, trying to keep the stone steps between us and the hillside where Mingo had put shooters earlier.

Using the rifle scope, I began to scan the tree lines behind us, looking for his backup, although I didn't think he'd brought any this time. His little posse of assassins might still be waiting down on the dirt road for the gunfight at the OK Corral to be done with. We could hear Mingo still ranting away on the loudspeaker, but nothing from Sheriff Hayes. I told the Bigs that Hayes had gone down a hole into the crawl space.

"What's the plan, Stan?" Carrie asked me, taking her own nervous look around at the surrounding hills. This cabin had not exactly been situated in a defensive position. The woods came down to within a hundred feet of the steps, directly behind us, and that was the obvious way out.

"I've got the rifle," I said. "You guys and the dogs make a run for that tree line. If there's a black hat up there, I'll deal with him. Keep the cabin between you and Mingo's sight line."

Then we heard the cruiser's engine crank up. It sounded like he was backing up. "Change one," I said, and the four of us bolted around to the left side of the cabin as we heard Mingo put it in drive and gun the cruiser around to the right side of the cabin, where he proceeded to let go a blast of enfilading automatic weapons fire through the side windows this time. We gathered at the left front corner of the cabin, still trying to keep as much of the structure as possible between us and that Bushmaster. Then he gunned the cruiser again, swerving it around to the back of the cabin.

"The dam!" I yelled, and we took off on a dead run down the front yard, tripping over all the tire ruts in the lawn, until we made it to the dam and slid down the grassy face. We could hear Mingo yelling over that damned loud-speaker and then firing some more into the house as he drove around it like an enraged Apache. I felt naked out there on that exposed face of the dam, espe-cially if Mingo's guys were down there in the trees below us, but at the moment there was nowhere else to hide. As long as Mingo stayed focused on the cabin, we'd be relatively safe. I glanced at the deputies, who were calmly reloading their clips. Big Luke saw me looking and grinned; the big galoot was enjoying all this. Then we finally heard Hayes yell something from inside the cabin. I crawled back up to the top edge of the embankment.

Mingo had somehow managed to turn the cruiser around so that it was fac-ing the backyard on what from our current position was the right side of the cabin. He had the Bushmaster stuck out the window, and I could hear him slam another magazine into it as I watched. He yelled back at Hayes, and then I saw, down low on the ground and behind some shrubbery, the double barrels of Hayes's shotgun sliding slowly out a hole in the foundation, pointing up at about a ten-degree angle. Mingo couldn't see it because he was busy leaning out the driver's window and firing another burst into the side windows of the cabin. Those black barrels kept emerging, now pushing through the bush it-self. Mingo stopped firing and was reaching for the speaker mike when the shotgun let go.

At a range of no more than twenty feet, I could see the loads punch two big, dimpled, dinner-plate-sized holes in the door. Mingo was knocked side-ways back into the car, taking the carbine with him. The shotgun barrels tipped momentarily, leveled, and then Hayes fired again, lower this time, punching two more lethal-looking, multiple-holed indentations into the door panel. I actually saw upholstery explode inside the cruiser. Something dark sprayed all over the inside of the windshield.

The other three had poked their heads up when they heard the shotgun. Hayes pulled the shotgun back into the crawl space, and the sudden silence made me nervous. We could smell the gunsmoke drifting down across the front lawn. Mingo still had that Bushmaster in there, even if he was probably wounded. I became aware that we were clustered very close together. The last light of evening was dwindling fast, but our little band made much too good a target.

"Spread out," I said. "In fact, why don't you guys move across the dam and into those trees in case he's got a rifleman down there behind us." The deputies moved immediately, probably glad to head for some cover.

Carrie stayed put. "What are you going to do?" she asked. Damned woman just couldn't take orders.

"I'm going to keep this rifle on the car until Hayes shows himself," I said. "Mingo may be playing possum."

"Why?" she asked. "A little while ago you were ready to help Hayes kill himself."

"Still am," I said, watching carefully for any signs of Hayes. It was getting hard to see anything up by the cabin. "But I think he wants to take his ex-partner there with him, and I'm in favor of that."

"Cam," she began, but I cut her off.

"Hey, Carrie: What we need now is not to get surprised from behind—that's where Mingo's people went, remember? Let me work this situation, and you make sure no one is setting up on us."

"You shoot either one of those duly elected sheriffs, it'll be a whole new ball game," she warned.

"I know that," I said. "Now, please—get back under cover. Look: Hayes is coming out."

She peeped over the rim of the dam and saw the sheriff crouching by the corner nearest the back porch, which put him in front of the cruiser. I couldn't see anyone in the cruiser, and obviously neither could he. He carried the shotgun low and pointed at the car. Carrie slid back down to make sure she was out of the possible line of fire and duckwalked across the face of the dam to join the deputies. I moved left to the swale where the dam intersected the front lawn and then set myself down into the prone position. I made sure my rifle barrel went up into the air before settling in on the cruiser, so that Hayes would know I was out there. He stopped for a moment when I made the move, but then continued his creep toward Mingo's cruiser. There was a long cone of shadow in front of the cabin.

I scanned the vehicle through my rifle scope. It was getting dark fast, but that definitely looked like blood on the windshield. There was no visible sign of Mingo. I assumed he was either down in the front seat or perhaps in the space between the seat and the dashboard.

You'd think I'd learn something about making assumptions, because what occurred next happened in a blur. Somehow Mingo had managed to get into the *back*seat of the cruiser. The moment Hayes arrived at the driver's-side window, stood up, and looked in, Mingo rose up in the backseat and shot him three times in the chest with a black handgun that produced quite a muzzle flash. Hayes sat down on the ground with a painful grunt and a stunned expression on his face. Mingo popped the left rear door open and started out to finish the job. I settled my rifle on him, but that was when Hayes let go both barrels of the shotgun through said door and blew Mingo ten feet backward into the grass. Based on the angle of his neck as he lay motionless on the ground, he'd been dead before he landed. All my efforts to keep the fight even had been overtaken in about three seconds of gunfire.

I got up and trotted over to the cruiser, rifle at the ready, pausing only momentarily next to Mingo's body to make sure he wasn't acting like far too many snakes I thought I'd killed. When I saw the bloody crater in his lower abdomen, I stopped worrying about M. C. Mingo. Sheriff Hayes, on the other hand, was not dead when I got to him, but he was definitely preparing to depart this vale of tears. I knelt down beside him, trying not to put my knees in all the blood literally pouring out of him. He focused his eyes on me and blinked several times.

"Never knew," he whispered.

I waited.

"Never knew she was selling them."

"Yeah, that's what we figured," I told him, trying to give him some small comfort now that he was about to die.

"Took the money, though," he said, and coughed. It made an ugly, wet sound in his throat. I heard Carrie coming up behind me. She stopped at Mingo's inert form.

"Why?" I asked.

"In-surance ran out before Helen's cancer did," he said. "All for nothing. She isn't going to make it."

"We'll tell her this was line of duty," I said. "She doesn't need to know the rest."

He gave me a grateful look in the dim twilight and tried to reply, but then he coughed again and went slack. I stood up slowly. Once the SBI or even the FBI got into it, the whole horrible deal would come out, but maybe there was a way we could shield the widow, especially if she was terminal.

"He's alive," Carrie said, and I whirled around, pointing my rifle down at Mingo across the yard.

"No way," I muttered, but she was kneeling down beside him, her back to me. Then, to my astonishment, she suddenly hauled back and slapped his face as hard as she could.

"Carrie!" I yelled, but she was fixed on Mingo's pasty face. By the time I got there, he had one eye open and an evil sneer on his face. I stared down at him with disgust, trying not to look at what was uncoiling out of his abdomen.

"He admitted killing my father and taking my sister," Carrie spat, her fists clenched.

"And now he sells little girls into a lifetime of slavery," I said. "A true life of accomplishment."

"Wrong," Mingo croaked, revealing bloody teeth. "Better."

"*What!*" Carrie shouted. But Mingo's eyes rolled up and this time he was really gone. I pulled her away before she lost it again. There were tears in her eyes, and not for the first time I remembered the old rule about being careful what you go looking for.

"Let's go," I said. I wanted to hold her, but she was much too angry for consolation. "His people may come back now that the shooting's stopped."

I could see the Bigs standing up now at the other end of the dam. I pointed my finger at Hayes and then made a thumbs-down sign, and did the same thing with Mingo. I collected Hayes's shotgun and some extra shells from his pocket and then signaled for the deputies to come back to the cabin. I went back inside and retrieved my scope, while Carrie got her coat.

The brothers stood there around Hayes and Mingo for a few minutes, surveying the carnage in the grass. Carrie had walked over to the edge of the pond and was staring at nothing. John had retrieved the Bushmaster. It was a variant I hadn't seen before, with a flat folding stock and, of course, the modification to make it go full auto. The muzzle brake still looked too hot to touch.

"Reckon we should call this in," Luke said, indicating the two dead men. John looked over at me.

"If we do," I said, "Grinny Creigh will get word and she'll know someone's coming for her. We'd have no chance of rescuing those kids."

Carrie walked back, looking hopefully at the lighted panel of her cell phone, but then she put it away with a disgusted sound.

"Cain't just leave 'em here like this," Luke said. "Ain't right. Meat birds'll be on 'em directly the sun comes up. Them'n the night dogs."

That was a lovely thought, and he was right: We couldn't just leave them to the scavengers. I told the brothers that I thought they should make the report, but make it to their supervisors back in Carrigan County. Then they should stay there at Hayes's place and await the first responders.

"You're still both technically sworn officers in Carrigan County," I told them. "This is your duty. Let your bosses call Robbins County, but this way, you'll be at the scene so none of Mingo's people can sneak back and screw things up here."

"They may be out there now, just waiting for us to leave," Carrie pointed out.

"Okay, so you and I will leave," I said. "Once the brothers here get on their radio, the black hats will fade away into the woods, assuming they haven't already done that."

"Why wouldn't they come back and check?"

"Because I told that one guy we had a squad of machine guns up here. That's exactly what they heard."

"Once someone calls Robbins County, Grinny Creigh's going to know," Carrie said. "Live kids are going to become a real liability to the Creighs."

"Okay, so make sure your people in Marionburg know that, John," I said. "Ask them to get people over here, secure the scene, and *then* call Robbins County in—just don't tell them who's been shot until they get here. That way we might have a chance to get to the Creighs' place and do something."

Bigger John gave me a bemused look. "Like what, exactly?" he asked.

"I have no frigging idea," I admitted. "But something. We have to do something, and so far, the federal people who'd normally roll on this won't touch it."

"You don't think they'll come in now that Mingo and Hayes have killed each other?" Carrie asked.

I was getting frustrated. We were standing here talking when we should have been on the move. "Look," I said. "Mingo's people are either out there in the woods somewhere or on their way to report back to Nathan that there was a small war out here and nobody came out. Get the local cops into it, explain what we think is happening, and let them pull in the feds. I'm not willing to wait. Grinny Creigh won't wait, I guarantee it."

The two deputies looked over at Carrie to see what she thought, and she nodded agreement. "Join up with us as soon as you can turn over the scene," she said.

"Awright," John said, and Luke agreed. If John was happy, Luke was happy.

"Okay, then," I said. "Give us ten minutes to get out to the highway. If you don't hear any more shooting, you can assume we're clear of the woods." There I went again, encouraging people to assume.

It was fully dark by the time we made our way out onto the paved road. We'd gone carefully, lights out, guns poking out of the car in all directions, in case Mingo's crew had set up an ambush. Carrie rode in the back right seat while I drove; the shepherds were in the way-back. Nothing happened on the way down, so once we got to the paved road I put the hammer down toward Rocky Falls. It was almost seven as we came into the outskirts of town, and I suddenly realized I was starving. Carrie said she was, too, so we pulled over into the town's version of a fast-food joint and hit the drive-through for greaseburgers all around.

I parked the Suburban in a back corner of the lot where semis would usually park, and we attacked the food. Both shepherds were partial to the No. 2 Combo, which they dispatched with a gusto that gave new meaning to the term "fast food."

"What did he mean right there at the end?" Carrie asked. "That 'wrong' and 'better' stuff?"

"Delirium of the dying," I said. "I don't think it meant anything."

There were no other vehicles parked back where we were; the one semi that had been there when we went through the drive-through left. I was wondering whether or not we were being just a mite conspicuous when I saw a Robbins County cruiser pull up into the drive-through lane. There were two deputies riding, but they didn't seem to be actively looking for anyone. They stopped at the order box, placed their orders, then started around to the pay window. Halfway through the turn, their brake lights came on, followed thirty seconds later by their blue light rack. Hamburgers forgotten, they swerved out of the line, turned left out of the parking lot, and sped off in the direction from which we had come. The girl in the pay window stuck her head out and stared after them.

"Word's out," I said.

"Yup," Carrie said. "Too soon. Now what?"

"Now we go up there."

"You're just going to drive into the Creigh compound and, what? Demand they turn over the children?"

"Exactly," I said. "Tell 'em Mingo's dead. Tell them the game's up and that a whole herd of feds are on the way. We don't want them, just the children. Give them up, we leave, and you sick fucks have maybe an hour's head start. Like that."

"And I suppose I get to go up on the front porch?"

"You're the peace officer," I said.

"You seem to forget: I resigned, just like you did."

"Actually, I don't think you did. I think you just told everyone you did. And while we're at it, I think the Big brothers are SBI, too."

She cocked her head sideways. "Really."

"Yeah, really. Brother King told me he had people in Rocky Falls. Baby Greenberg supposedly had a cell on watch when I landed in the pokey, but it was the Big brothers who showed up to spring my butt. And even more miraculously, they switch allegiance from Mingo to Hayes's office, *and* get hired in a single day, after you told them to execute that little move. And back at Hayes's cabin an hour ago? When I was suggesting that they stay there? John didn't agree until you gave the okay."

She wasn't looking me in the eye anymore. "Well," she said. We saw another cop car go roaring past, lights ablaze, in the same direction the first one had gone.

"Yeah, well—nicely done, actually. It's not like I'm pissed or anything, and of course I can't make you do anything you don't want to. But enough's enough: I'm going up there. If you won't pitch the deal, then it'll be harder, but I'm not going to sit here eating some fries while the clock's ticking on when Grinny Creigh decides to cut her losses. How about it?"

"I have to make a quick call," she said, pulling out her cell phone and opening the car door.

"Quick's the operative word," I said and got out myself to run the dogs for a moment while she conferred with whoever was running her little operation, probably King. I was telling the truth when I told her I wasn't pissed. I'd sort of figured it out when I thought about how easily the Big brothers were moving through the various jurisdictional lattices. And then up at Hayes's cabin those boys had looked to her more than once, even when I was the one yelling orders.

I got the dogs back in the car and readied Hayes' shotgun. I was wishing I'd snatched up the Bushmaster, but I hadn't seen any more magazines lying around. Carrie got back in the car.

"Okay, let's do it," she said. "King said all hell's breaking loose in the Robbins County Sheriff's Office right now, but he doesn't think the Creighs have been alerted yet."

"That something he *knows*?"

"Nope. Not at all. I think we have to assume the opposite."

Assume, I thought, and started laughing. I don't think Carrie appreciated why.

15

The closer we got to the Creigh compound, the less confident I was. I couldn't tell if Carrie felt the same way, but I could not for the life of me think of any different move. Nathan might get one look at me and come screaming off the porch with a handful of knives, as might Grinny herself, over Rowena if nothing else. It was fully dark, so they might have to wait a few seconds to see who or what had showed up. Carrie kept trying her cell phone to establish comms with someone, anyone, but the signal evaporated once we left Rocky Falls. I looked at my watch—it was seven thirty. I hadn't seen any utility poles going up to their cabin, so, even if they did have a generator, they might not have telephone service. The trees looked larger than life as our headlights swept over them along the river road.

"If the kids are there, where would she keep them?" Carrie asked.

I told her about Baby's theory that there was a cave or some other underground structure behind or below the cabin. "And I thought I saw some little faces inside that time I was taken there at night," I said. We were approaching the turnoff to the dirt road.

"You really think I should go up on the porch?" she asked.

"Hell, no," I said. "We'll drive up there, honk the horn until someone shows up, and conduct our discussion from inside the car. In fact, you should be in the backseat with a shotgun instead of over there on the passenger side. That way you can give me some cover if they come out shooting."

"What if they don't come out at all?" she asked. Good point, I thought. But I had a plan.

"Then I'll find some way to set the place on fire and we'll burn 'em out. Like they tried to do to Laurie May."

"Listen to you," she said. "Eye for an eye—you're starting to sound like you're the one who came from here, instead of me. Stop and let me get into the backseat."

We were approaching the entrance to the field that lay out in front of the cabin. I stopped and she switched seats, taking Hayes's shotgun with her. There were no lights showing up above around the cabin. I decided to drive right up there, the way Mingo had done. I turned the headlights on bright to make it tougher for anyone inside to see who was coming and gunned it up the front field, half-expecting gunfire as we made our approach.

Nothing happened. I pulled up in front of the steps and lay on the horn. Carrie was crouching in the backseat with the shotgun barrels resting on the left rear windowsill. I had her nine in my lap. It felt like a toy. I hit the horn again, waiting for lights inside.

Nothing. Silence. Not even a dog barking. Then I realized there should be a dozen or more dogs barking.

Nothing but the sound of my engine running.

"Where are all those damned dogs?" I asked.

"They've run," Carrie said quietly from the backseat.

I decided to shut down, get out, and look around. It felt like there wasn't anyone there. Carrie got out, and I asked her to cover me with the shotgun. I left the dogs in the vehicle, just in case Grinny's pack appeared suddenly. I walked down across the front of the cabin, the nine in hand, until I got to the dog pen area. It smelled as rank as before, but it was definitely empty. The moon was rising in the east, but it was still pretty dark up there. A small breeze stirred the pines, bringing a draft of clear, cool air down from the big ridge behind the cabin.

I opened the door to the barn where they'd cuffed me in the stall, and it, too, appeared to be empty of any animals, four- or two-legged. Carrie had moved halfway down the covered breezeway with all the firewood in order to keep me in sight.

"Anything?" she called quietly.

"Nope," I said, walking back to where she was standing. As I examined the cabin for any signs of life, I thought about going inside. Even the side windows had bullet holes in them, courtesy of my temper tantrum with Nathan's shotgun.

"No way," Carrie said, reading my intentions. "She probably has it booby-trapped."

"Get the car keys," I said. "Then let's go around in back."

About the time she opened the Suburban's front door a match flared on the front porch, and we both spun around, guns coming up. Grinny Creigh was standing in the front doorway, turning up a kerosene lantern. We hadn't heard a sound until she lit the lantern.

She didn't even look at us until she got the wick where she wanted it, dropped the glass, and then lifted the lantern with one hand and picked up her own shotgun. She held it by the receiver. It was an old-fashioned, heavy steel double, and she held it as if it were a willow wand. She didn't say anything, just looked at us. Her massive body looked like a small silo with a human head on it.

"Police officers," I said, loud enough to be heard in the house. "We've come for the children."

"What damn children?" she said calmly.

"Mingo's dead," I said. "Hayes killed him. There's a couple dozen feds in Rocky Falls right now. They'll be here soon. Give us the children and we'll leave you alone."

"What children?" she said again.

"The ones you have for sale," I said. "Like the one you showed that doctor the other night, when you asked him if he could take more than one should you need to unload the whole mess of them."

She studied my face in the lantern light. If she was impressed with what I'd just said, she gave no sign of it. "How's Brother Hayes?" she asked.

So she knew what had happened. Two could play this game. "Where's Rowena?" I countered.

Her face twitched. "Away," she said. She turned to Carrie. "You that Harper girl, went off to work for the state?"

Carrie said, yes, she was. Her shotgun was still pointed in Grinny's general direction, but not right at her.

"I recollect your little sister," she said. "Pretty little thing. Went missing in the river with your papa. Real shame, that was."

Hold on to yourself, Carrie, I thought. *Don't go doing what you want to.* "She's trying to provoke you," I muttered to her. "Watch out for creepers." She grunted through clenched teeth but started looking around at our perimeter. The shotgun was still pointed in Grinny's direction, however.

"Just give us the children, Grinny," I said. "We don't want you. The feds do, but it'll be an hour before they get here. Give us the kids and we're out of here."

"You the one shot down my Rowena, ain't you?" she asked, holding the lantern a little higher.

"She kidnapped Special Agent Santángelo here and then pulled a gun on me. I shot her before she could shoot me."

"Blowed her head clean off, didn't ye," she said. "Had'ta plant her in two pieces, we did."

Carrie raised the barrels on her shotgun to point at her. "That's what shotguns do," she said. "Want to see?"

Grinny looked first at me and then at Carrie's gun. Then she did a curious thing: She smiled. It was a twisted, faintly triumphant smile. Then she raised two fingers in a **V**, mumbled some words, and spat between them. I felt Carrie stiffen beside me.

"There now," Grinny said. "Count the hours, missy."

"I'm so very not scared," Carrie said.

"You should be, missy." Then she turned to me. "Ain't no children here," she said. "Everybody in these parts knows I'd eat 'em if they was. Boil 'em in oil and then eat 'em for breakfast, so everybody says. You people get on outa here. Them revenoors want to come in here, they better bring 'em a warrant."

"Count on it, Grinny," I said. "And pack your bags. You're going away."

"No," she said, "You the ones going away." She carefully set the shotgun down on its butt against the wall, reached sideways, and pulled on a chain that was attached to something in the floor of the front porch. We heard what sounded like a trapdoor dropping, and a moment later every damned one of her dogs was piling through the latticework under the porch, unlimbering a yard of slavering canine ivory each, and coming our way.

We both scrambled into the Suburban with maybe one second to spare before they were all over the vehicle. I zapped my window up and started the engine, while behind me I heard Carrie's gun go off as three snarling dog heads appeared in the left rear window trying to get in. One dog lost its head while the other two went screaming, earless, for cover. Grinny had disappeared and her front door was closed.

I backed up in a hurry through a sea of snapping, snarling, growling beasts. My shepherds were very wisely keeping their heads down in the way-back. I illuminated the front of the cabin with my brights again, but there was no sign of anyone else getting ready to take action. Carrie had rolled up her window and was reloading the shotgun.

Nathan had taken the children somewhere. I was sure of it. Grinny didn't care if the feds did come; they wouldn't find anything. I was also sure she didn't keep meth or any other drugs here, so her cabin would reveal nothing. I'd been bluffing about feds coming, anyway. Most of the action would be in the two sheriffs' offices, in both counties, for some time. I backed the car up some more and then turned to head back down the field. All that bravery and we'd flat-ass struck out. Bounced off, once again.

"Now what?" Carrie asked. She was getting good at asking that. And then it occurred to me that Grinny might have been simply lying. They were all in there, kids and Nathan, down in the basement or in that cave or whatever it was behind the cabin. Short of going back and shooting every last dog, there was no way we could to force our way in there. The dog pack continued to surround the vehicle, making more noise than ever, as we drove off. They were everywhere, snapping at the tires, trying to jump up on the hood and the back door.

"They could be in there," I said. "I'm not taking Grinny's word for fuck-all. Let's lose these dogs and then come back."

"Lose these dogs?" she said. Two of them had locked their jaws on the bumpers as we rolled down that field.

"Well, hell, at least thin 'em out," I said. I kept the Suburban rolling down the field in first gear and half-lowered my window. I shot the first mouthful of teeth that jumped at the window and then the next one after that. They backed away then, but still followed us down the field, raising absolute hell and lunging at the vehicle from every direction. Carrie lowered her window and blasted two more with the shotgun as we finally made it into the tree line. The dogs quit at the edge of the field. We rolled up our windows, and I turned on the vents to clear the gunsmoke.

"Let's go over to Laurie May's," I said, putting the vehicle onto the dirt road leading down to the big creek. "We'll come back through that crack in the ridge."

"And do what?" she said. From the sound of her voice, the dog pack had unnerved her. To be honest, it had unnerved me, too. That had been very close.

"There's that cave on this side of the ridge, right down from the crack. We get to that, make noise, and attract the dogs. Then we kill every one of them. We've got two shotguns and my rifle. *Then* we walk down there and get close to that cabin."

"The stealthy approach, hunh?" she said.

"They know we're back. If the feds do show up, all the better. If not, I still want those kids. She knows we know, so maybe she won't kill them all out of hand."

"Or she already has," Carrie said. "Or Nathan's gone and taken them up to some hole in the mountains where he'll bury them alive."

"Gone where?"

"Shit, take your pick. To any one of the hundreds of hideouts, caves, old mines, sinkholes, you name it, up there in that ten thousand acres of blank space on the map the state calls game lands."

"First things first," I said. "Let's go do what no one else has ever been able to do."

"What's that?" she asked.

"Get inside that cabin."

"Why not wait for backup?" she said. "Get the Bigs here, at least."

"Time, Carrie, time. You know what might be happening in there, now that she knows someone's rumbled their operation."

"I can just imagine the kinds of things Grinny Creigh will have in her house," she said. "Can't wait to go inside."

I turned to look at her. "What's the matter—that witchy-twitchy bullshit didn't get to you, did it?"

She looked away. "No," she said, most unconvincingly.

"Aw, for God's sake, Carrie," I said. "Focus! There might be a half dozen little girls in there, and they've absolutely got something to be scared of. Let's not give her any time to think about this. We need to go back there, eliminate the dog problem, and get inside. No one else is going to do it."

She didn't reply.

"Okay, look," I said. "Watch your cell phone. You get a signal, tell me to stop, call your boys, get 'em out here."

It took us an hour to get over to the cave. We hadn't spent too much time around the remains of Laurie May's cabin, which was indeed all gone. Even in the moonlight, the pile of blackened rubble was a desolate sight among all the pretty flower beds and the fenced yard.

Carrie had been unable to reach the Big brothers. Our problem now was that the Creigh dogs didn't show up when they should have. Carrie figured Grinny had retrieved them and put them back under the house. It was one thing for us to hole up in a cave and shoot them as they attacked. It would be another thing altogether if we were creeping Grinny's cabin and they all appeared at once like the last time.

"We shouldn't have left," I said. "We could have dispatched that whole pack right there from the car."

"And if those kids are there, Grinny would have been down in the basement cutting throats while we were eliminating attack dogs," Carrie said.

The field leading down to the Creigh cabin was just as bare of cover as before. I'd brought the spotting scope and spent some time scanning the whole compound, but that wasn't helping us get any closer. It was nearly midnight, and we needed to either back out and get some help or get down there and start some shit.

"Cam—look," Carrie said, pointing down the hill. I looked. A child was walking out of that tree line that ran down alongside Grinny's cabin. I swung the scope around. She was blond, almost white-haired, wearing a long dress that reached to her ankles. Her face was pinched and scared, and she was somewhere between eight and ten years old. And she was coming right up the hill toward us like a diminutive ghost.

16

"My God," Carrie said. "They *are* in there."

"And can you tell me how she knows we're up here in this fucking cave?" I asked.

Carrie had no answer for that and neither did I. If ever I wished for a working cell phone it was right then, which is when I remembered that the cave was a signal point. Nathan had captured my ass when I stepped out to improve the signal.

"Cell phone works here," I said. "Call the Bigs."

She looked at her phone, swore, and called the Bigs. I watched the little girl climb the hill, and then remembered to put away the guns and to make the shepherds lie down. She looked scared enough as it was. I heard Carrie talking to someone, so I stepped out, without the guns, to wait for the child to make it up the long hill. I hoped she wasn't a stalking horse for some guy with a long gun down at the cabin, but she was coming purposefully, as only a frightened child could. I cursed M. C. Mingo, Hayes, Grinny, and all their works.

Carrie snapped the phone shut behind me. "Zoo city in Marionburg," she said. "Sam's there with an SBI squad, and there's real goat-grab under way. Bigger John says he's heard talk of the Bureau coming in. I told him to back out and meet us at Laurie May's."

"Look at her," I said, and Carrie looked. The child knew precisely where we were. She was almost there, and we could hear her puffing with the exertion of climbing the hill.

"You go out there and talk to her. She'll be scared of me."

"Right," Carrie said, and went partway down the hill to meet the child. I went back to the spotting scope to make sure there wasn't some Creigh snake-in-the-grass setting up on Carrie. A moment later, the two of them came into the cave. The child recoiled when she saw the shepherds.

I told her it was all right and brought each dog over to lick her hands. She relaxed, but only a little, so I took the dogs to the cave entrance with me, where I went back to the scope and Carrie sat down to talk to the little girl.

"What's your name, sweetie?" she asked.

The girl put a grubby fist in her mouth for a moment before answering. Her eyes were pale blue and just the slightest bit out of focus. "Honey Dee," she said. "I'm Honey Dee."

"Well, Honey Dee, what are you doing out on this big old hill so late at night?"

The girl closed her eyes for a moment, as if she were recalling a rehearsed message. She was wearing a long white shift and had a frilly little bonnet on her head embroidered with crude yellow bees. She continued to nibble on a knuckle; then she got the message out.

"Grinny says y'all have to leave us alone, or we all goin' in the glass hole."

I stopped breathing for a moment when I heard that. Out of the corner of my eye I saw Carrie stiffen.

"Who else is down there with Grinny?" Carrie asked.

The little girl had to think about that. Then she began to count on her fingers and name names. She named five more names.

"So there's six of you in the house?" Carrie asked.

That provoked some more heavy-duty brow wrinkling. Somehow I didn't think Honey Dee was operating with a full deck, not with that partially vacant expression I'd glimpsed earlier. Vacant? Or partially blind? I couldn't tell. Then she counted laboriously on her fingers to six this time and nodded.

"What is the glass hole, Honey Dee?" Carrie asked gently.

Honey Dee shrugged. She didn't know.

"But it's a bad place?"

She nodded vigorously. Bad place.

"Do you know *where* it is?"

More head shaking.

"Is it downstairs, under the house?"

Another shrug. Fist back in her mouth, and then a yawn.

"Keep her here or send her back?" I asked quietly, still sweeping the area with the scope. I was looking for dogs.

Carrie sighed. "I think we have to send her back. We keep her . . ."

"Yeah." Then I saw movement on the front porch of the house. It was too dark to see what it was, but the shape was big enough for it to have been Grinny. I told Carrie, and the child perked up. Interestingly, she seemed more eager than fearful.

Carrie took the child's hand and walked back out into the open. She pointed down the hill and told her to go to Grinny. Honey Dee giggled and then positively ran down the hill and into the trees. I focused the scope on the dark porch and saw movement again, a bare glow of yellow lantern light, and then just shadow.

"Think she'll let those dogs out again?" Carrie asked.

"Actually, I don't," I said. "She knows we could take them all down from inside this cave. No, I think the dogs will come out if and when we get a lot closer to that house. Then we'd be the ones in trouble."

"How did she know?" Carrie asked. "And what in the hell is a glass hole?"

"Not sure I want to know," I said.

"There was a signal a few minutes ago," she said. "I say we call Sam King and tell them there are six hostages in there and Grinny's threatening to kill them. Maybe that will finally stir up the feds. Big enough posse, that dog pack's no threat."

I couldn't think of anything else to do, and we didn't have much of a chance of getting into that cabin, not if she let that dog pack loose again. "Try it," I said.

She stepped back out into the night air, opened the phone, looked at it for a second, held her arm out, and then began to move it around, searching for the ever-elusive signal. The dog came out of the dark at about a hundred miles an hour and went right for her extended hand. She yelped as massive jaws snapped down, and then she jumped back into the cave, tumbling over my shepherds as they lunged for the cave entrance. But the beast was gone into the night. And so was her phone. I recalled the shepherds before they got sucked into some kind of canine ambush.

"He get you?" I asked, backing slightly into the cave with the shotgun ready.

"Didn't break the skin, but not for lack of trying. God *damn*! Hand really hurts."

I searched the dark hillside for a glimpse of the cell phone. The dog had gone for a nice juicy hand, not the phone, so I hoped it would be where we could retrieve it. Depending, of course, on how many more of those bastards were waiting out there. Assumptions again, biting me in the ass and Carrie in the hand.

"Can you cover me?" I asked. Carrie was holding a penlight on her hand, which was already swelling.

"For the moment I can," she said. "I think."

I handed her Hayes's shotgun and told her to stay in the cave entrance. I stepped out with my own gun ready, Frick and Frack alongside. I remembered to check the hillside above the cave, but I didn't see anything. That damned dog hadn't made a sound, so maybe there was just one of them out there in the darkness. It had come in fast, low, and hungry, and I knew I was taking a big chance stepping away from the relative safety of the little cave. But we had to have that phone, as mine was in the Suburban. If we couldn't find it, we'd have to back out and return to Marionburg.

I kept the shepherds close by my side and searched the ground in the general direction that the dog had run, while trying to watch as much of the hillside as I could. I pulled the hammers back on the shotgun and walked in a series of small, continuous circles, looking down and then out into the darkness. The shepherds would be my first line of defense, but I didn't need them getting torn up right now, either.

There was a small breeze nudging cooler air across the slope, but not enough to stir the grass or make any noise. The only sound came from my boots as I crunched through some of the loose gravel. Carrie was down on one knee at the cave entrance, her shotgun resting on her thigh, while she held her injured hand under an armpit. I knew about dog bites—they hurt. A big dog could exert hundreds of pounds of pressure with its jaws. It was like having your hand run over by a car with studded tires.

I finally stopped to take a careful look all around. The phone was one of those small silver numbers. It should have been visible out there, assuming the dog had dropped it when he realized he couldn't eat it. Or maybe he did eat it; he'd looked mean enough to eat a car. And where the hell had that fucker gone? The nearest cover was either back in the crack through the ridge or down in that tree line near the house. The four hundred yards in between was just a wide open space.

I decided to make my way up toward the defile through the ridge. It was a hundred feet or so above me and maybe seventy yards away. I could make it out as a darker shadow against the gray rock face of the ridge. I kept circling as I went—I couldn't turn my back on any sector with that thing out there, but the closer I got to the crack, the more I wondered if that dog wasn't in there, waiting. So I sent my shepherds ahead, aiming them at the opening.

Big mistake.

The moment they got fifty feet away from me, I saw out of the corner of my eye something coming at me from the downhill side. I vaguely heard Carrie call out and just had time to whirl around and raise the barrels of the shotgun as the dog leaped at me. I ended up stuffing both barrels down its throat, and then the gun was wrenched out of my hands before I could fire, sending me tumbling backward into the grass. The dog landed five feet away and tried desperately to disgorge the shotgun with its paws and by shaking its massive head. Then Frack pounced and seized it by the throat, followed by Frick, who grabbed the dog by its muzzle and started pulling, which had the effect of dislodging the shotgun. It tried to get up but it was too late, as Frack clamped down on its windpipe until the thing shuddered and then lay still.

I got myself up, grabbed the shotgun, hit the inert beast on the head as hard as I could with the gun butt, and then walked back in the direction from which it had sprung. The shepherds followed, excited but visibly pleased with themselves. I told them they'd been a little slow off the mark.

I finally found the phone, which had been crunched almost in two. It was obviously inoperable. I thought about Carrie's hand being in there and decided she didn't need to see how badly the phone had been mauled. I waved her over, and we headed for the exit out of this unhappy valley. We walked through the sliver of a canyon, Carrie facing forward, me facing Grinny's, in case there were more of them around. When we got down to the ruins of Laurie May's cabin, I was grateful to see that the Suburban was still there.

I checked my cell phone, but there was still no service, so we decided to wait there for the Bigs. Leaving the headlights off, I moved the vehicle to a better concealment position alongside some trees. Carrie was still holding on to her injured mitt, so I found some aspirins in my glove compartment and gave them to her. I told her I'd take the first watch, but she said no, her hand hurt bad enough that she'd never be able to sleep. I put the dogs out fifty feet away from the car in different directions, lowered all the windows, set up the guns, and then reclined my seat. Carrie kept her seat upright.

"I can't think of any way to get into that cabin," I said. "Not with all those damned dogs out there. We'd get some of them, but then they'd get us."

"One already did," she said. "And that was actually a near miss. Those things could amputate a limb."

"So can those guys right outside," I said, "But right now, we're stymied."

"We've got help coming, hopefully with radios," she said. "They can get word to the county cops in Marionburg that we have a confirmed hostage situation involving children. That should do it."

"I'm thinking I should go back and keep watch on that cabin. See if she moves the kids, or if Nathan comes back. The brothers show up, signal me and I'll come back here."

"Signal you how?"

"Gunshot? That sound ought to carry over the ridge."

"And what about those dogs?"

"I'll stay in the canyon. I can hold off the whole pack from in there."

"Unless they get behind you," she said. "It might be Nathan who's running the pack. Hell, he could be on this side by now. Get you on your way up to the canyon."

I sighed. We were stuck. The situation was getting away from us with every passing moment. But she was right—what if Grinny had turned loose three or four more of those savages and they'd tracked us through the canyon? These Creighs were pretty damned good at deploying those animals, as Baby and I had discovered during our run down the mountain. I was used to surprising people with my two furry torpedoes. The Creighs had taken that notion to the next level. I heard a little sound next to me and looked over at Carrie, who was now fast asleep.

Well, so much for that plan, I thought. *We tried.* I made sure the shepherds were where I'd left them, one a tawny shadow in the grass to our left, and the other two amber eyes on the right. Then I poked my shotgun out the window and settled down to try to stay awake.

17

The Bigs showed up an hour later in a Carrigan County cruiser. They drove right past our position and didn't stop until the shepherds ran up to their vehicle. My guys love cop cars. I saw that Carrie hadn't heard them arrive, so I pulled the keys and slipped out of the Suburban. The Bigs got out and Luke, bless him, handed me a cup of takeout coffee.

"Y'all havin' fun?" he asked.

"About as much as you," I said. They were looking around for Carrie. I pointed to the Suburban and folded two hands to my cheek to tell them she was asleep. Then I told them what we'd learned.

"Mr. King's gone into Rocky Falls with his people," Luke said. "Old boy named Ken Harper is acting Robbins County sheriff now."

"He a Creigh ally?"

Luke shook his head. "Older guy. Longtime cop. May even be kin to Ms. Santángelo over there. Took Mr. King into Mingo's office and was tryin' to explain how things worked in Robbins County."

"That'll take some doing," I said. "In the meantime, we need to get those kids safe." I told them what we'd run into in our latest unsuccessful attempt to breach the Creigh compound. Big John spat into the grass and suggested we go get us some antifreeze. I knew what he was talking about. Farmers who had a problem with feral dogs would often put bowls of antifreeze out in their fields and keep their livestock up for the night. Animals simply couldn't resist lapping it up, and then died horribly. The problem was that you got everything, not just the target pest.

"We also don't know where Nathan is," I said. "He might be there, he might be up in the hills, he might be watching us right now. This is going to take a crowd."

"Got one'a them at the sheriff's office right now," Luke pointed out.

"Your radios work out here?" I asked.

It took two more hours to get said crowd to the Creighs', and gaining entry turned out to be a cakewalk. The bad news was that there was no one there. No Grinny, no kids, no Nathan, not even any of the dreaded dogs. As I had suspected, there were also no drugs or other evidence of any criminal enterprise. Carrie and I got to sit out on the front field side while a host of heavily armed deputies from both counties tossed the place. They found the dead dogs we'd shot, which helped to corroborate our stories, but that was about it. The cabin itself was unremarkable, with furnishings and supplies typical of the people who lived up there. If there ever had been children there, the cops could find no sign of them.

They'd brought an EMS truck along, and one of the medics treated Carrie's hand and gave her a tetanus shot just to make her arm feel as good as her hand. We both gave formal statements to one of King's people, but the stark fact remained that the Creighs, the important ones, anyway, had vanished. Along with their flowers. We were nowhere. Again.

King himself wandered down into the field at about sunrise. He looked to be as tired as we were, and not at all pleased to see the two of us. I kept looking for Storm Trooper Gelber to complete my day.

"I told you to go home," he said.

"Why, good morning to you, too," I said. "You know more now than before I interfered?"

He started to answer that but then changed his mind. He asked Carrie how her hand was and she shrugged, which must have made the tetanus shot really happy. Her hand was bandaged and looked to be twice the size it should have been. Big, *bad* dog.

"There's nothing in there of any use whatsoever," he said, nodding toward the cabin. "Maybe in the daylight we'll do better."

"Any signs of children being there?" I asked.

"Not a thing," he said. "Not a damned thing."

"Well, we know there was at least one in there," I said, "and she said there were five more. Did you find out what was behind the house? That mound leading out of the hill?"

"The guys are working on that. There's no evident door or tunnels or anything like that, or at least not so far. I'm thinking of having them dig into it from the top."

"Be careful," I said. "The whole damn crew might be hiding in a tunnel or an old mine under there."

"Don't tell me my business, Mister Richter," he said. Just then there came the double booming report of a shotgun from inside and a flurry of activity up in the house. King swore and trotted off to see what had happened.

"What do you think?" Carrie asked.

"Booby trap? A lurking mastiff? Why don't you and I blow this pop stand, go get some breakfast and then some sleep."

"He did tell us to go home," she said.

There were two queen-sized beds in the motel room, and we each collapsed into one the moment we got to the room. It was daylight outside, so I forced myself to get up and put up the DO NOT DISTURB sign. Then I remembered I had to feed the muttskis, and then I had to take them for a walk. By the time I got back, Carrie was almost an hour ahead of me on the sleep marathon, and I was in that fugue state where I knew I needed sleep but wasn't actually sleepy. I also knew that somewhere along the line I'd go sideways and crap out, big time. The shepherds, damn their eyes, had no such problems and crashed on the bathroom floor.

I made sure I had my room keycard and went down to get some coffee. I took my cell phone and then sat in the Suburban and called the Bigs. I asked what that shotgun discharge had been all about.

"Nasty little trap," Luke said. "They found a false wall in the basement that led into that hump behind the house. Guy broke the lock, pushed opened the door. Felt something tugging when he opened it. He'd been to Iraq with the Guard, so he hit the deck about the time a twelve with a string trigger laid both barrels into the doorway."

"He get hurt?"

"Mostly scared," Luke said. "Another guy in the basement got one pellet in the back from a ricochet, but he had his vest on."

"And what was behind the green door?"

"Possibly the nursery," he said. "But completely empty. No furniture, toys, clothes—nothing. Empty. They found the remains of a recent fire behind one of the barns, but there's still no evidence of children here yet."

"Well, do we have Christian believers now?"

He paused before replying. "King keeps saying it's possible, but he'd be happier to find a toy chest or some other evidence that there were six kids kept here."

"Evidence again."

"Well, they're kicking it around. They've got your various statements, and that thing about Grinny being a florist. We just don't have any Creighs or any kids. Lots of discussion about that problem. Feds in the wind."

"Good," I said. "About goddamned time, too."

"Where's Santa Claws?"

"In her tree, fast asleep. One claw's a lot bigger than the other."

Luke was quiet for a moment. "You be nice to her, you hear?" he said. It wasn't any kind of direct threat, but more an expression of proprietary concern, as in, you mess her up, we'll mess you up. I'd also noticed that most of the homespun dialect had disappeared.

"It's not like that," I said.

"You lookin' at still waters there, Lieutenant," he said. "You might be the last to know."

"Okay," I said.

"And she's the one keeps getting hurt."

"You're absolutely right."

He didn't say anything, but I was now sufficiently fascinated that I wanted to keep it going. "So: You think I ought to be on point a little more," I said. "And Carrie in the rear with the gear?"

"Might not be a bad idea."

"You want to be the one who tells her that, Big Luke?"

"Um."

"Un-hunh. Because I don't. I might start getting hurt, you know what I'm saying?"

He started laughing. It sounded like a bear with a digestive problem.

"Look," I said. "I could have bailed, all the way back to beautiful downtown Triboro, where my terribly satisfying paper chase awaits. Instead, I stuck around."

He laughed some more. Now I wanted to whack him, but it would be embarrassing to whack somebody in the thigh.

"They're wrappin' up here," he said. "King says he has to 'frame' the sheriff shootout problem with the media. See if they can convince the feds to go chase Grinny and whatever troops she took with her just based on that incident."

"Tell King to remember that Grinny has a plan to unload all the merchandise, and if she can't do that, the merchandise is going to end up in someplace called the glass hole."

"What in the hell is the glass hole?"

"Something bad, according to a little girl we met, and I'm NFI beyond that. But the truth is, Grinny's capable of slitting all their throats if finding her with kids poses a threat, and of course it does."

"Mr. King's been up all night," he said. "He's a little testy right now. I might have to wait on suggestions from you for a bit."

"Just so somebody reminds him. We're in that same motel, but I plan to take Carrie out of here and back to civilization, assuming I can talk her into letting go for a day."

"You know what they say about assumptions, Lieutenant."

"You should hear me on that subject," I said, and then I had an idea. "Any chance Carrie and I could get into Grinny's cabin once the crowd subsides?" I asked.

"I'm pretty sure they'll seal it and put a deputy on it. Keep it pristine for our federal betters, assuming they're coming in."

"There *you* go assuming," I said. "Any particular deputy?"

He caught on right away. "I'll give y'all a ring if it works out that way," he promised.

Carrie apparently heard me trying to sneak in and sat up in the bed. She used both hands to do it and instantly regretted doing that. I'd brought a second cup of coffee back with me and offered to share. She shook her head and flopped back down. Her bandaged hand made it look like she was wearing a white oven mitt, and her face made it evident that using it was still out of the question.

"Anything I can do for that?" I asked her.

"Always wanting to play doctor," she said, closing her eyes.

I bent her head forward and examined the rifle wound, which looked scaly and horrible. That probably meant it was healing. "And some people call *me* a shit magnet," I said.

"You've just learned to duck faster," she said.

I took her other hand, and she opened her eyes again. "You found out what you wanted to know," I said. "We've failed every time we've tried to get our hands around the Grinny Creigh problem. Both sheriffs involved are headed for the cold, cold ground. Is it maybe time to let the big boys do their thing?"

"They'll cap it off," she said. "There's no way in hell they're going to find Grinny and her crew in those mountains. And the Bureau will *not* want a reprise of their Rudolph debacle. They'll ride in, take over the case, announce they broke up a ring of child peddlers and the two principals are dead. Victory."

"But we've both told them there are six kids in her clutches."

"We've told them lots of things," she said. "And they've done squat."

"I want to go back out there when all the cops are gone," I said. "We're missing something."

She sighed and closed her eyes again. "My hand feels like a bus ran over it," she said drowsily. "Let's sleep on it instead."

I hadn't let go of her hand and she hadn't let go of mine, so I lay down beside her. I gathered her in and she snuggled willingly, warm and sweet.

"You are beginning to affect my better judgment," I said to the back of her neck.

"Like you have any choice in the matter," she murmured.

I laughed. Even with all the coffee onboard, we both went out like that proverbial light.

18

We slept in until almost six o'clock, and both of us awoke feeling logy. The cell phones had been silent all afternoon, but neither one of us could quite wake up. I was suddenly conscious of this warm female in my arms.

"Hey, girl," I said. "Wanna fool around?"

"I have to go potty," she said.

I started laughing. So did I. Reality intruding.

"How's the mitt?"

"Aches, but it's better. Those medics were generous with their drugs."

"I can almost get my eyes open," I said.

"I think I saw a swimming pool," she said, a few minutes later.

It being the end of the summer season, the motel wasn't full, and, as the sun set, most of the guests were downtown going to dinner. We took turns changing in the bathroom. Carrie came out in a reasonably modest two-piece, while I wore my khaki running shorts, having failed to pack a real bathing suit.

I wouldn't have done that on a beach, but the pool was situated behind the motel and out of view of any windows or walkways. There was a six-seater hot tub in one corner of the pool enclosure with its own privacy fence to deter demon spawn from playing in it.

The pool's water was downright cold, but we both started to wake up after a few minutes of pretending that the pool's temperature was "refreshing." I decided to see if that hot tub was working. It was, and the water was still warm from the last occupants. I fired up the jets and submerged my aching body in the swirling waters, trying not to breathe in too much chlorine.

Carrie came over and sat down on the side of the hot tub. She'd taken off the bandage. Her hand was swollen and reddish. Her black hair was wet and hung down in a sleek, sculptured mat, nicely framing her pretty face. She extended her legs out over the water and looked them over. So did I. She caught me looking and gave me a teasing smile.

"You a leg man, there, Mr. ex-lieutenant Richter?"

"Actually, I'm a whole-foods kind of guy," I replied, wondering how far she might take this. Naturally, I was hoping for the best.

She raised one leg and then the other like a dancer, still appraising. Then she glanced down at her front. As slender as she was, she had a small if pleasing superstructure. She clicked her lips as if disappointed in what she was looking at.

"Don't tell me," I said.

"Tell you what?"

"That you have small breasts."

"Afraid so," she said, putting on a sad face.

"Well, that does it," I said. "I mean—small breasts? That's a total disqualification. You can hardly be a woman in America if you have small breasts. Everyone knows that. My goodness, what a total disaster."

She propped her feet close together on the edge of the tub and eyed me over her knees, which she began to bump gently together. Since I was directly in front of her in the water, the motion did interesting things to those slick wheels of hers.

"*Everyone* knows?" she said. "Really?" Bump. Bump.

"Totally," I said, wanting to clear my throat.

"What a shame," she said. "And just when I was thinking I needed— something."

"Something?"

"Don't squeak like that."

"Um."

"I had it a moment ago," she said with a dramatic sigh.

Bump.

"I know I did. Right there on the tips of my toes." Lift. Look. Down. "But that disqualification business—well, I didn't know that. But I do appreciate your telling me."

Bump. Bump.

"Um."

"Um? That the best you can do?" She reached forward and scooped up some warm water, and then began wetting her legs and thighs. I couldn't see her face anymore, probably because I wasn't looking at her face. An achingly familiar physiological short circuit between my brain and my nether parts had been firmly established.

"Well, really," she said. "How 'bout it there, Mr. Um? Are you up for a little nonintrusive massage work or not? Girl with a problem here. Got a groove in my head and a paddle for a hand. And, I almost forgot, small breasts. But, well . . ."

Finally, clarification. I submerged and resurfaced with my head and shoulders between her knees. I rose to lean over her disqualifying breasts. Her thighs were tense, and I began rubbing my face on the front of her bathing suit, just below her breasts. When I felt her start to relax, I put my hands on her hips, eased her halter top aside with my chin, and then went to work on her qualification problems to see if anything could be done.

Anything could be done, as it turned out. But all my plans for a leisurely exploration evaporated when I lifted first one knee and then the other onto my shoulders, leaned forward, and kissed her on the mouth. The next moment she was in the water with me, sans top and bottom, and telling me to go fast.

Go fast? No problem. For once, we went up the mountain and didn't bounce off. She clung to me like hot, wet silk, and this time it was the two of us taking care of business.

We relaxed into the foaming, hissing water, holding each other close, soaking up the heat, both inside and out, for several lovely minutes. She had her head on my chest, and I got a close look at what was going to be a very interesting scar.

Then we heard the unmistakable sounds of teenaged girls in the passageway between the motel and the pool enclosure. We moved apart. I helped put her suit together and then hiked my own trunks back up.

"You're supposed to say something," I said.

She thought for a moment and then said, "Thanks, I needed that."

"It was all that peek-a-booty that did it."

She giggled. "A hard man is good to find," she said softly. "You seemed to get the message quick enough."

"Hard to miss," I said, and she gave me a mock glare. "The message, that is."

Three preteens emerged onto the pool deck and immediately jumped in, followed by lots of brightly squealed oh-my-Gods. They happily ignored the two ancient adults huddled up in the hot tub.

"Like, I mean, it's time to, like, you know, go?" I said.

"Like, totally," she said.

We hit a corner bistro for dinner, where we encountered Mose Walsh. He was decked out in his evening hunting kit and sitting at the bar looking suitably inscrutable. For once there were no women hanging around. We invited him to join us at a table. I ordered drinks.

"So where's all the action tonight, Chief?" I asked him.

"It's early," he said, looking around just to make sure he hadn't missed anyone. "You guys connected to the big shootout over at the sheriff's cabin?"

"Us?" Carrie and I said, almost simultaneously.

Mose chuckled. "Yeah, you," he said. "All of sudden we got feebs and state guys right here in River City and some pretty dramatic rumors flying. Too bad about Bill Hayes, though. He was a good guy." He saw me frown and asked why. Carrie gave me a warning look.

"Bill Hayes got himself entangled with some of the shit M. C. Mingo was into," I said. "He kind of redeemed himself at the end, but there are some desperately loose ends still out there."

The waiter brought us our wine and Mose another scotch. "Not what I'm hearing," he said. "What I heard was that it all was over. Bureau suits on the courthouse steps declaring that the incident was wrapped, strapped, and ready for transport. Robbins County has an interim sheriff, the Carolina SBI is shoveling shit as fast as they can, and we're due for an interim election pretty soon."

Carrie gave me an I-told-you-so look, silently reminding me of her cynical prediction that the feds would cap it off and declare victory. I drank some wine, then told Mose what had happened out there at Hayes's cabin and detailed our most recent séance with Grinny Creigh.

"So you're sayin' that Nathan Creigh is out there in the backcountry somewhere, with six little girls? And the Bureau is aware of this?"

"I can't speak for what the Bureau knows and doesn't know, but I sent them a background report, as did Carrie here, and the SBI sure as hell has been informed."

"Then why aren't they acting on it?" he asked.

"I give up," I said. "Maybe they are, and we're just out of the loop."

"So you guys are gonna do the reasonable thing and step aside, right?" He was looking at Carrie when he said that. There was more than just a glimmer of direct male interest in those dark eyes, and I actually felt a momentary pang of jealousy. With that face and his determination to score at least once a night, I'd wager he had himself quite a track record. Carrie shook her head.

"No fucking way," she declared quietly. "We are most definitely not letting go, not until I know those kids are safe—or dead. That's why we're going back to that cabin. In fact, I was just thinking: You must know that backcountry pretty well. Care to take on an unscheduled guide job?"

Mose raised both hands in a gesture of surrender. "No, ma'am, I do not," he said immediately. "You're talking about getting on the trail of Nathan and possibly Grinny Creigh in the deep woods of Robbins County."

"That idea make you nervous, Mose?" I asked. I was going to rain on his parade, too.

"Tracking them?" he said. "No. It's what might happen when we caught up with them that worries me. To quote the lady at the table, no fucking way."

"Six little girls, Mose? In the hands of that monster?"

He shook his head again. No way meant just that.

"You really have lost your taste for it, haven't you?" I said. Carrie patted her pockets and then produced a vibrating cell phone. She got up to go find a better signal.

He gave me a neutral look. "I absolutely have," he said. "I lost my taste for it when I finally realized that there's an unlimited supply of evil assholes out there. Unlimited. Unending. A storm surge of them. And for some unknown reason, they're being allowed to breed. Their spawn comes out worse than they were. I gave that shit up over ten years ago. Working homicide was like standing at the outflow of a city waste treatment plant and putting your fist in the pipe—about the time you got used to the idea that your hand was eternally covered in shit, the tank would overflow on your head."

"So that's it?" I asked. I couldn't really justify goading him, but I was. Maybe it was the image of six little girls in chains in some damned cave. Or the way he had been appraising Carrie. Or the way she'd seemed to not mind all that much.

"So now you're down to sitting in bars, chasing loose women, and taking the occasional walk in the pretty woods?"

He sat back in his chair and folded his arms across his chest. He really did look like those pictures of Sitting Bull when he did that.

"Down to?" he said. Then he smiled. "You can't provoke me, Loo. I have fully clarified my life. I work an honest and productive job during the day. Then I go out at night, have some scotch, and chase those terrible loose women, as you called them. The chase is always fun; catching them is usually fun but always comforting. Having a cup of coffee with a new and totally relaxed woman in the morning is pleasant. Knowing that she's gonna go home in an hour is a daily relief. I've never married, because I don't think I'll live long enough to need the care of a good woman when I start to drool. So, yes, it's one day at a time, and for the most part, every one of them is both wonderful and ten times better than my best day on the Job."

He looked like he was getting ready to push back from the table. I reached out and held his wrist. "Six little girls," I said. "Sold by their so-called mothers to a pig-eyed Gorgon on Spider Mountain, who packs them into Marionburg at night, gets them spayed, and then ships them into a life of slavery in some fucking Arab's tent? Six little girls? Who are now happily ensconced in something called the glass hole?"

His eyes widened when I said the words "glass hole," but then he looked pointedly at his wrist, which I realized I was gripping pretty hard. I let go and sat back. He wouldn't look at me now.

"Unlimited supply," he recited. "Endless. A fucking red *tide* of evil bastards. And I never made even a dent in it, and neither can you. The difference is, I already know it."

Carrie was coming back to the table, so I gave up. "Okay, Mose. Sorry I pushed. Go get lucky."

He got up, gave me a quick, sad grin, shot me with his thumb and forefinger, and went back to the bar. Carrie sat down.

"What was that all about?" she asked.

"I was hoping to shame him into helping us find Nathan up there," I said. "Because, otherwise, I think we're dead in the water."

She shook her head. "We're only dead in the water if we quit," she said. She took a deep breath. "First," she said, "I need a nice big rare steak. Then we're going back out there to the Creigh place and we're going to take another look."

"Tonight?" I said.

"Yes, tonight. In about two hours, to be exact."

"We can't do that, Carrie—they've got that place secured. They'll run our asses right out of there."

She patted the pocket with the cell phone. "Not according to Bigger John," she said.

19

Deputy or Special Agent John—I wasn't sure which—greeted us when we drove up to the Creigh cabin. He'd been reading a book in his cruiser. Bobby Lee Baggett would have had his ass for that. Anyone could have snuck up on him in the dark. It wasn't until we'd gotten out of the Suburban and walked up to the cruiser that we saw the second cruiser, with Big Luke inside, shotgun and all, artfully concealed in some trees. Luke waved.

The cabin itself was not decorated with miles of crime-scene tape as I would have expected. Perhaps this was because no one had detected any crime there, unless you wanted to count the shotgun booby trap.

"Where's everybody gone to?" I asked John. The moon was up, so there was ambient light in the front yard, but the cabin was dark. I left my shepherds in the Suburban.

"Bureau showed up this morning," he said. "Made Sam King's day, long about nine. Been downhill since then."

I could just imagine. The place seemed eerily quiet without the dog pack. I kept glancing over to the cabin's front porch, expecting to see the two of them sitting there in their rockers, shotguns at hand. "And none of them is worried about six little girls?" I asked.

He shook his head. "There was nothing in the cabin, 'cept that little business with the door gun. No evidence of children. No drugs, no money, no nothin'."

"And no Grinny and no Nathan," Carrie said.

John nodded, patiently.

"We'd like to go inside and look around," Carrie said. "If there was no evidence of criminal activity, and I don't see any scene tape, then I don't think we'll be disturbing anything of value here."

"What're y'all looking for?" he asked her.

"Anything that might tell us where they went. And *how* they went."

"I'll have to come with y'all," he said.

"Great," I said. "And I mean that."

He stared down at his oversized feet. "Something ain't right," he said, speaking to Carrie. "No offense intended, but the bosses seem to be skatin' on this one."

Carrie went up to him and hugged him. He absolutely did not know what to do. Then we went up to the front porch and picked up some lanterns. John lit them for us and we went inside.

"I'd like to see that hidden room," I said.

John took us downstairs to the basement. It was earthen-walled and -floored, with a dressed stone rim that formed the cabin's foundation. The dirt was hard packed and had been there a while. There was a stack of shelves that had been pulled to one side, behind which was the opened hidden door. The left edges of the door were badly damaged.

The shotgun trap had been confiscated, so we went in, holding our lanterns high. The room was perhaps twenty feet by ten, and there was nothing inside but a single wooden chair and more dirt walls and floor. The ceiling was formed by the floor joists and floors of the cabin above.

"Okay," I said. "The shotgun was wired to that chair, and a trigger mechanism was made to the *inside* door handle."

"Yessir," John said.

"So how was that done from *outside* this room?" I asked.

This question provoked the expected silence. Carrie walked to the back wall of the room and began to thump the wall with her good hand, testing for a hollow area. Then we heard a car horn out front.

When we got back outside, Luke was standing in front of the cabin with a young woman who was so thin you could almost see right through her. Luke was holding a lantern so we could get a look at her. She had a bony, pale face, a strangely receding hairline for a young woman, and pale blue eyes. She was wearing a white, often-patched dress that barely made it to her knees, and her legs looked like white sticks with red bumps on them. She had blond hair so white that it made her look young and old at the same time. I'd seen hair like that recently. The girl wouldn't look at any of us. She stood there, twisting one grubby fist with the other.

"Whatcha got there?" John asked his brother.

"Says she's a'lookin' for her child, name of Honey Dee?" Luke replied. "Came walkin' out of the woods. Lieutenant's dogs told me she was comin'."

I nudged Carrie and she took over. She took the lantern from Luke and went over to the obviously frightened woman and began to talk to her. She told her that we'd seen her child earlier, and that she'd seemed to be all right.

"Where she at, then?" she asked, looking at each of us for an answer. Her teeth were dark brown, and her cheeks twitched when she spoke.

"We don't know," Carrie said. "That's why the sheriffs are here."

She put a hand over her mouth and began to tremble. I looked over at the Bigs and indicated with my head that we should leave Carrie to it. We backed off and listened from a distance. Carrie coaxed the story out of her with gentle questions, while the poor thing cried silently through closed eyes.

Baby Greenberg had been right about what was going on up here. She'd traded her child to Grinny to pay for her boyfriend's meth habit. It was obvious to me that she had one of her own, but Carrie finessed that problem. Grinny had finally cut them off, kept the child, and turned them out of the network. The boyfriend was, of course, long gone, and the young woman was now at her wits' end, starving, and crushed by guilt for what she'd done. When all we could tell her was that little Honey Dee was probably with Grinny Creigh, she folded into herself, squatted down next to the lantern, and began to beat her breast.

"Oh, God," she sobbed. "Oh, God Almighty. I'm a'lookin' at the fires of hell."

I figured that for once in her miserable life she was absolutely right, but held my tongue. Carrie asked Luke to put her in one of the cruisers, and then we took the lantern and went back inside.

We stood in the middle of what we suspected had been the kids' bunkroom. The lantern threw flickering shadows on the earthen walls and floor. The damaged door hung by a single hinge, and the basement beyond was dark as a tomb. The place was cold.

"Back to your question," Carrie said. "I thumped the walls all around and didn't hear anything that sounded like false wall. The floor is obviously hardpacked dirt."

"Which leaves the ceiling," I said, looking up at the floor joists and planks above our heads. Not, I noticed, very far above our heads. I wondered aloud if this room was lower than the basement. "Let's go find some water," I said.

We retrieved a large pitcher of water from the hand pump in the kitchen and went back downstairs. I stood at about four feet back from the entrance to the bunkroom and poured the water onto the floor. As I'd hoped, it immediately streamed across the floor and down into the bunkroom, where it puddled against the far wall.

"The ceiling it is," Carrie said. It took us fifteen minutes to figure it out, and it was pretty ingenious. Pulling down in the middle of one floor joist at the left end of the bunkroom opened a trapdoor in the ceiling. The trapdoor had boards nailed across it to serve as step risers, and at the top was a narrow black rectangle. We went back upstairs to tell John what we'd found and got ourselves a second lantern.

I went first, discovering that I had to crawl on my hands and knees once I got into the tunnel. It, too, had been cut out of hard-packed earth, and it seemed to drift slightly upward in a gentle left curve. The air was reasonably fresh, which made me think that it led to the outside.

After crawling for about a hundred feet I was finally able to stand up, albeit in a crouch. Carrie was right behind me. Ahead was a rough-cut wooden door, around whose seams I could feel air moving.

"Remember that nasty secret surprise the guys found when they opened the bunkroom door," Carrie said quietly. I nodded and examined the door. It was locked on our side by a large bolt-and-hasp arrangement. I tried the bolt and it moved freely.

"Let's get flat and then open it," I said, and that's what we did. There was no resistance when the door swung open on well-oiled hinges. Beyond there was an alcove of sorts, from which another tunnel led off to the left at about a ninety-degree angle to the one we'd been in. We stood up and stuck the lanterns into the alcove. The tunnel going left was wider than the original tunnel, and its ceiling had been reinforced with wooden beams and sheet metal. On the right-hand side of the alcove was a stone wall. Whoever had built the wall had been no mason, but it extended from floor to ceiling and felt solid. What cracks there were around the edges were dust-filled and looked undisturbed. As if to make the point, there were three solid beams standing in front of the door at regular intervals, one on each side and one in the middle.

"That may one of the abandoned mine tunnels," I said. The air was coming in strong from our left. "If they used this to bug out, then the outside is thataway."

"Outside would be good," Carrie said. Apparently she did not care much for tunnels. For that matter, neither did I.

"Left it is," I said, and we soon found ourselves walking up a moderate incline for about three hundred feet until we encountered another hard left turn and some crude wooden steps nailed to a plank going up to a small hole at the top. There was a fine trickle of water seeping down the side of the steps. When we pushed our way through the hole we found ourselves standing under that lone pine tree at the entrance to the Creigh-side crack in the backbone ridge. We left the lanterns down in the tunnel and climbed out.

We stood next to the tree and instinctively looked around for attacking dogs. I put my fingers in my mouth and whistled for my shepherds, who came at the gallop across that big open space between the crack and the cabin. It felt good to have them nearby. I saw Carrie massaging her injured hand, remembering.

"Okay, so now we know how they got out," she said. "But not where they went."

"I'm having a problem visualizing Grinny Creigh getting through that first tunnel," I said. "Nathan, maybe, the kids, no problem. But Grinny?"

"What're you saying? She's still down there somewhere?"

"Yeah, I think that's a real possibility. They've had a hundred years to dig out all sorts of tunnels and chambers down there—just look at this tunnel. It had to have taken months to cut this thing by hand."

"There was that one stone wall, at the junction," she said. "Maybe we—"

"Hold up, there's a vehicle coming," I said, pointing down toward the cabin. We watched the Big brothers join up to see who was arriving. We could only see headlights until it stopped in front of the cabin, so we started down the hill. It turned out to be the Big Chief himself, Mose Walsh, driving a pickup truck with a cap on the back.

He was apparently on good speaking terms with the Bigs, who were talking to him when we made it back down to the cabin. He gave me a sideways look as we walked up, but greeted Carrie with a big grin.

"The glass hole," he said. "I found out where that is."

"Great," Carrie said. "But *what* is it?"

"Well, actually, I've never seen it," Mose replied. "Guy I know, likes to do cave diving? He says it's the one vestige of volcanism in the Great Smokies on our side of the Tennessee line. According to him it's on the edge of the park, right inside the boundary with your favorite county. The scientists who've seen it say it's an ancient collapsed lava bubble."

"Can you take us there?" I asked.

He hesitated. "I've got directions, so I can take you there. I don't want to, because this involves the Creighs, but you said there are kids at risk. So . . ."

"How long would it take to get there?"

"Actually, we can drive most of the way, then it's a five-, six-mile hike in and mostly up."

"Is it someplace you could hide six kids?" Carrie asked.

"I wouldn't think so," he said. "According to my guy, it's under water."

20

We left in two vehicles early the next morning, Carrie and I in the Suburban, and Mose in his pickup truck. We'd shown the Bigs the escape route out of Grinny's place, and they promised to pass that on to any further investigators, assuming there was going to be any further investigation.

Luke took Honey Dee's bereft mother back to Rocky Falls. He promised to get a statement from her before the county social services system swallowed her up. We let them know where we were headed and why, which they duly noted. Neither of them seemed very encouraging. We told them that Grinny might be lurking in one of the abandoned mine tunnels, and all John could say was that meant we had her where we wanted her—underground. Carrie had wanted to explore that walled-off tunnel, but the kids were a more pressing issue.

I'd apologized to Mose for harassing him in the restaurant the previous night, but he waved me off. "When you mentioned the glass hole and captive kids, I knew I was screwed," he'd said.

"You really think you never made a difference during your career?"

"I worked homicide," he'd replied, with that wry grin. "By definition, my 'clients' always died."

"How many killers did you put away?"

"Killers? Real killers? Maybe a half dozen. Mostly it was husbands who lost their tempers, druggies, gangster kids, like that." He shook his head sadly. "Endless supply."

"Well, this clan falls into the 'real killers' category. They might as well be killing these kids, considering what happens to them."

He nodded. "I'll take you up there," he said. "But I'm not going to fight the Creigh clan for you. I really am too old for that shit."

And by implication, so was I. We followed Mose out of Marionburg and into Robbins County. It felt strange not having to be on the lookout for cop cars and black hats now that Mingo was gone. I still couldn't get his final words out of my mind, though. *Wrong. Better.* Had he been just babbling as his brain shut down? Or did those words mean something? And where the hell was Grinny Creigh?

Carrie had spent an hour on the phone with Sam King earlier, and it sounded as if her predictions of a Bureau-managed shutdown had been correct.

The escape of Grinny and Nathan Creigh had been shunted off to the Bureau's fugitive program, so there would be the standard manhunt—sometime real soon. The fact that there might be children being exploited had been passed to the federal PROTECT task force, and the SBI had been left to dig through the wreckage of Hayes's and Mingo's administrations. In other words, the law enforcement bureaucracy had portioned out all the interesting bits to its various constituencies and settled on a PR strategy, so all was right in the world. Grinny Creigh had been designated a "person of interest," but that was about it.

King had also offered Carrie her job back, but she'd been reluctant to make any decisions about that until she'd exhausted every lead we had or thought we had. She was still convinced that we were the only ones who truly believed there were six little girls out there in the woods somewhere. Personally, I figured they were out there, all right, but not necessarily alive and well. I think she sensed that was how I felt, but she was determined to press on. Having left her behind once and injured twice, I felt obligated to go with her. Besides, underneath all that hard-core internal-affairs armor, she was a sweet, intelligent woman who was valuable in her own right. That was reason enough.

About three miles into Robbins County, Mose pulled over onto a dirt road and stopped. He came back to the Suburban when I pulled in behind him.

"We'll take this dirt track for about five more miles and then we'll come to a Forestry Service fire lane. This thing got four-wheel drive?"

I told him it did, and he said okay. "We'll end up around four thousand feet," he told us. "The weather's supposed to be okay today, but there's a cold front coming in tonight, which might produce a little snow up high. I don't think it'll amount to much at this time of year."

"Where are we actually going?" Carrie asked.

"To a mountain pass. Then we'll park and hump it the rest of the way up to a small lake with no name. We'll camp above that tonight, and see what we see the next morning."

"Do you think the Creighs are out there?" I asked.

"If they went to the glass hole, they could be. Nothing to say they haven't been here and gone."

That comment produced a sudden chill in the Suburban. If they'd left, the chances that the kids would be found alive were small and shrinking with every hour.

*　*　*

We reached the ridge overlooking the no-name lake at just before sundown. It hadn't been a bad climb, other than it had been relentlessly up for two huffing and puffing hours. The scenery was spectacular in all directions, but Mose had been right about a cold front. The northwestern sky was darkening, and the wind had backed around ninety degrees as the front gathered to assault the western mountains.

I'd suggested that we spread out on the hike up to prevent concentrating a target in case the Creighs had left sentinels on their trail. Mose was unhappy with that thought, but agreed. He led the way, then Carrie, and I took up tail-end Charlie with the shepherds, who ranged between Mose and me for most of the trek. We kept each other in sight but generally maintained a hundred yards or so of separation. An hour before we reached the campsite, both dogs had gone to investigate something on the edge of the fire lane. The something had turned out to be a pile of dog manure. There were some boot prints in soft ground a few feet away, headed up. This occurred twice more as we made our way up the slopes.

I told Mose but decided to wait to tell Carrie. I took it to mean that someone with dogs had come this way recently. It could have been anybody, because this area was either national park or state game land. I'd asked Mose if there was another way up to this lake, and he said sure—any direction would do. But this was the route you'd take if you'd driven a vehicle as close as you could get. One thing I knew: Grinny wasn't up here. She couldn't have climbed that slope in less than a year.

We made camp at the edge of a steep, rocky slope that led down to the lake itself. Mose had us set up two shelters using downed tree limbs and the living ends of pine tree branches, under which we rigged our tents and bags. He situated our camp just inside the tree line and faced the shelters into the woods, toward the east and away from the oval-shaped lake below. We'd packed enough gear and supplies for three days, in and out, with the plan being to spend tomorrow exploring the area around the lake and the so-called glass hole. If it was indeed under water, I wasn't sure what we'd do.

We didn't build a real fire for security reasons, using a spirit stove instead to heat our food and water for coffee. Mose warned us to set out warm clothes for the morning, as the temps were going to drop pretty fast once that front arrived. He was right about being careful not to show light, as it would have been visible for miles around. We didn't know who else was out there, but those dog droppings indicated we were probably not alone. Men with dogs meant Creighs in my book.

I had my Remington 700P and a handgun; Carrie had her trusty nine. Mose carried a pepper-spray canister like the ones the park rangers used, as well as a little .25-caliber boot gun. I'd brought my pocket monocular. The spotting scope had been too heavy to carry this far in—and up—with all the rest of the gear. We left our cell phones in the vehicles; up here they'd just be excess baggage. Mose showed us one useful electronic item he'd brought along.

"This gizmo here is called an EPIRB, which stands for emergency position indicating radio beacon. If we end up needing rescue, you fire this little jewel and a satellite picks up the signal. A report goes to the U.S. Air Force. They always wait for a second satellite hit, so don't turn it off once you energize it. Then you'll have an Air National Guard helo overhead in about two hours. Most of the guides out here carry one."

As the sun went down, the surface of the lake was bright orange. Carrie asked why we hadn't gone down to the lakeshore to camp.

"Because to see the glass hole, you apparently have to be above the lake," Mose said. "Like I said, I've never been here before, but my buddy said to camp up here and wait a couple hours past sunrise. The light has to be just right to see it."

"Well, if this is a submerged feature, what could that kid have meant when she said Grinny would put them in the glass hole? She was gonna drown 'em in the lake?"

"By me," Mose said. "All I know about the Creighs is to steer clear of 'em. Everybody says they're bad to the bone, and after what you guys have told me, I believe."

We drank some coffee, laced with a contribution from my trusty flask, and then got ready to secure for the night. Mose said we weren't quite done yet. He hung the food bag high in a tree against bears and marauding German shepherds, and then went out into the woods with his camp axe. He returned with three ten-foot-long, two-inch-diameter pine branches and told us we were going to make us some bear sticks. He handed us each a branch.

"I give up," Carrie said, making an icky face when the pine sap got all over her hands. "What's a bear stick?"

"We're going to peel the bark off at both ends and then sharpen one end into a spear point," he replied. "Then if a bear shows up in the middle of the night, we blind him with our flashlights, use the pepper spray to disorient him, and then jab him with these suckers to make him back out of his problem. Beats a gun every time."

He showed us how to sharpen one end and cut ridges into the other for hand traction. I'd never made one of these, but it certainly made sense—especially since it would provide a silent defense option. The finished product was about eight feet long and heavy enough to make even a bear feel it. One of my buddies had shot a bear that rousted his camp—and shot him and shot him and shot him, mostly managing to piss him off. Pepper spray works much better: Anyone can outrun a blind and choking bear; outrunning a pain-maddened bear who can still see or smell you is something else again.

Carrie and I shared one shelter; Mose took the other. My mutts bedded down next to our pine-branch hooch. It was full dark when we hit our bags, and we'd been careful to keep our flashlights pointed down. We parked our spears next to the bags, along with our flashlights. Carrie, as usual, went down in about thirty seconds. I envied her ability to do that. My feeble brain always decided to review the day's happenings and then all of tomorrow's potential perils before finally switching into sleep mode.

The first dogs didn't attack until after midnight, right about the time the cold front swept in over the western ridge and came across the lake looking for us. After our long hike up the slopes, both of us were sleeping pretty hard when I heard the first bursts of rain and wind come up the slopes from the lake to stir up the trees. It was a comforting sound, actually, as we were snug in our bags with the shelters' backs to the wind, but all that changed when I heard a vicious dogfight break out in front of our shelter. I bailed out of my bag with a gun in one hand and my Maglite in the other in time to see Mose stabbing vigorously down at something between the two shepherds with his bear stick.

I threw the gun back into the shelter, grabbed my own stick, and swept the campsite with the light, illuminating two green eyes behind Mose. I just managed to get the stick pointed before the second dog came through the air and knocked me down. Fortunately he ended up impaling himself, so all he could do was lie there and bleed. I threw him off me, left the stick in him, grabbed Carrie's stick, and moved to help Mose. I caught a brief glance of Carrie's white face looking out from our shelter, but, heads-up girl that she was, she had my gun in her hand.

Mose no longer needed help. He had the big beast stuck to the ground with his bear stick while my shepherds savaged its face and head. I called them off and stabbed the thing once in the throat, which stopped most of the noise. My dogs circled it for a few seconds, then went over and began to tear up the wounded one. I dispatched that one, too, and then the rain came in like a solid wall and we all jumped back under our shelters.

"Are you okay?" Carrie asked.

"Got knocked down, but I don't think he bit me," I said. We used the Maglite to make sure that was true. I wanted to ask Mose if he was okay, but the wind and rain were coming in strong and there was no way we could talk. I finally got his attention, and he gave me a thumbs-up sign through the sheeting rain.

I looked at my watch. It was two thirty in the morning. We'd been asleep since about eight thirty, so whoever had dispatched the dogs had either been watching us and was really patient, or had just turned them loose in the area and told them to go feed. One thing was for sure—we were back in Creigh country.

The initial storm line blew over in about an hour, with more wind than precip. Then we got a brief epilogue of some stinging sleet, a half hour of flurries, and then just cold. I crawled out to retrieve our sticks and tried to listen for any signs of more dogs, but there was just enough wind up to make that impossible. Carrie was awake, too.

"You think they knew we were camped right here?" she asked. I told her my theories, emphasizing the one that had the dogs running loose in the area. It had been a noisy thirty seconds in the camp, but the wind had been up, and if the Creighs were west of us, or across the lake, they might not have heard the ruckus.

"If they have a base camp up here, they might just turn some of the pack loose at night. The dogs would come back to them for food, but in the meantime, they're bred to attack strangers. They might just have blundered onto us, or smelled the shepherds."

"We have to assume they know now, though?" Carrie said.

"Be a good bet," I said. "They'll be short two dogs, if nothing else." It was an uncomfortable assumption, but probably a valid one for a change. The sky was clearing, but the wind was still blowing low-flying scud clouds across the mountaintops, which meant that they came right through the camp, like fat ghosts, accompanied by blasts of sleet. Between squalls I could see Mose sitting like the proverbial Indian in his shelter, stick in hand, staring watchfully into the darkness. It was going to be a long damned night.

21

W e disposed of the two dead dogs in the morning by throwing their stiff carcasses down the slope. The sky had come out deep blue, and the air temps hovered around forty. There was a light dusting of snow on the slopes leading down to the lake, whose surface was steaming due to the sudden drop in temperature. We had coffee and some rewarmed biscuits, fed my dogs, and waited for the sun to hit the magic angle. We had a clear field of view down the slope to the lake's shores, so I put the shepherds out in the woods where the cover was thickest, just in case there were more incoming Creigh-dogs out there.

"I think that's what we're looking for," Carrie said, pointing down into the lake. Mose and I stared down the hill but couldn't see anything except the lake itself, which was about a half-mile-long, almost perfect blue oval surrounded by a gravel margin and dense stands of pine on all sides except ours. A nearly vertical spine of rock stood out over the right-hand end, dropping some two hundred sheer feet into the water and looking like the prow of a ship frozen in stone. Then we saw what she was pointing at: a deeper shade of blue in the water at the base of that rock formation, which extended out to encompass the right-hand quarter of the lake. The water was obviously much deeper there, and if our eyes weren't deceiving us, the hole in the bottom was in the shape of a giant cone, perhaps four hundred feet across and perfectly round. As the sun rose higher it became better defined until we could see it very well.

"It's like one of those old Victrola record-player horns, only under water," Carrie said. "It looks like it goes down under that rock formation."

I pulled out my monocular and scanned that axe-head-shaped cliff from bottom to top. I don't know what I was expecting to see, but nothing jumped out at me. There was a tiny level space at the top, and you could imagine one of those Mexican acrobatic divers doing his flying Maya thing from there. The slopes of the surrounding hill framed the rock spine like a house gable all the way up to about the same elevation where we had camped. I couldn't see any signs of human disturbance, but the dense pines could be concealing a multitude of bad guys.

"I think I'm going to take the shepherds out on a little scouting expedition," I said. "There might be enough snow on the ground to get an idea of where those dogs came from last night."

"And what happens if you succeed?" Mose asked.

Good question, I thought. "I'll back the hell out and regroup," I said.

"They may come up with a different plan," he said.

"We can't just sit here and soak up another night like last night," I said. "Besides, we're looking to retrieve some lost kids before they get really lost."

"Shouldn't we scout together?" Carrie asked, obviously uncomfortable with the idea of me and the shepherds leaving. I wanted to do this alone. My dogs worked better if they had only one human to protect.

"There's the glass hole," I said, pointing down into the lake. "I think that bears watching. I'll be back in an hour, hour and a half. If I get in trouble I'll start shooting. I'm going to go back into these woods right here and circle around to the base of that rock formation."

Mose shrugged and said okay. I knew he didn't want to mix it up with any Creighs, but Carrie still wasn't happy. I left her my handgun and took the rifle.

The shepherds and I slipped into the pine forest, moving methodically to get a good stand of trees between us and any watchers who might be down on the lake. The forest was filled with little clumping sounds as the pine branches dumped snow on the ground beneath them. The forest floor was covered in pine needles with a thin, crusty blanket of snow that was disappearing fast. I had hoped to track the dogs that had attacked us last night, but the snowfall hadn't been substantial enough here in the pines to help. I stopped from time to time just to listen, but all I could hear was the wind through the pines and the shepherds snuffling ahead of me.

When I thought I'd gone far enough into the pines, I turned left and began to make my way toward that rock formation. I didn't need a compass—as long as I kept the downslope to my left, I had to be working my way around the lake's rim, albeit a few hundred feet above it. We'd been gone from the camp about thirty minutes when I heard the all too distinctive sound of a large-caliber rifle booming through the trees back to my left. The dogs and I stopped in our tracks and listened to the echoes of the shot reverberating across the nearby ridges. I couldn't see anything but the trees around me, but the one thing I did know was that it hadn't come *from* our camp.

The question was—had it been fired *into* our camp? I had to go back.

I took my time making the final approach out of the dense pines to the camp itself, not wanting to blunder into an ambush. The shepherds didn't appear to be wary or alarmed, but all that meant was that there was no one hiding close by. A distant rifleman would pose a different problem. I kept looking for landmarks, although I knew I was retracing my steps, because I could still see them faintly in the rapidly melting snow crust. Finally I moved behind a large pine tree from which I could see most of the camp.

What I couldn't see was Carrie or Mose. Were they hiding undercover somewhere after that shot?

I sent the dogs down the hill and into the camp, where they ran around in circles. No one appeared. Then Frack started yipping excitedly, his face pointed into one of the tree-branch shelters. I hurried down there, afraid of what I might find. If Frack was that upset, I knew it wasn't going to be good news, and it wasn't.

There was a blood trail in the thin film of snow. It came from the edge of the trees toward the lake and ended in the shelter. I got low and scuttled over to the shelter. Mose was inside, curled up on his side with both bloody hands holding his chest. He was still breathing, short and shallow, but his eyes were closed and his face was an unnatural shade of white. It looked like a very bad wound, but it was hard to tell with his bulky jacket.

As I knelt by the side of the shelter, I looked around for Carrie but saw no signs of her. I looked at the snow, which was obliterated by many footprints. Ours? Or theirs? There was no way to tell. Mose groaned and opened his eyes. The shepherds sat five feet away, watching carefully. They knew when something was seriously wrong in the human world.

"What happened?" I asked him.

"Long gun," he whispered. "Two guys took Carrie."

"Which way? I asked.

"Down. Hill. Don't know."

"Okay—where's that EPIRB?"

But he shook his head. The effort cost him as he winced with pain. "Save it," he whispered. "You might need it for the kids."

"I need it right now to get you to the hospital," I said. "I'll find Carrie, but first—"

"No," he said. "I'm wearing a vest. I'm not bad hit. Bruise from hell, bullet tore a crease. Can't breathe so good, chest hurts like a mother. But it's not serious. Go find Carrie. Save the EPIRB."

"Let me check you out," I said. "You're bleeding pretty good."

"Like being hit by a truck," he said. "They've got Carrie, man. Get on it."

He closed his eyes and concentrated on getting his breath. I noted no blood in or around his mouth, so he was probably right—the round hadn't penetrated.

"Okay," I said. "I'm on it." Then I saw Carrie's nine in the snow by the side of his tent. I made sure it was chambered and gave it to him. "In case they come back."

He nodded. I knew he wasn't afraid of the men coming back. A couple of those big dogs, though . . . He'd been holding his little boot popgun. I took it with me.

I found him a canteen, pulled his sleeping bag over him, and stood up. The shepherds backed away from the shelter, as if afraid they were going to be blamed for something. I wondered if the shooter had thought he'd bagged me instead of a stranger. A man and a woman had been causing the Creighs all kinds of trouble, and there was a camp up on that hill above the lake with a man and a woman visible. Drop the man, take the woman. Clear mountain logic.

I backed into the trees with the dogs, got out the monocular, and spent the next fifteen minutes surveying the opposite shore of the lake and the big rock formation at the right-hand end of it, all the while absorbing what had happened to Mose. I felt like a complete shit-heel. Mose had done his level best to say no to us, and I'd shamed him into getting involved. Now he was down, probably with a cardiac tamponade at least. And Carrie was gone, too. I took another sweep with the spyglass. Nothing had changed. Pristine wilderness. No smoke from a campfire, no tracks or trails.

Tracks? If they took Carrie, they might have left tracks.

I circled the camp and found a second faint trail of boot tracks pointing diagonally across the slope leading down toward the lakeshore. I went back to our shelter and found Carrie's light jacket. I pressed the shepherds' faces into it and then gave them the find-it command. Off they went. I made sure my rifle was ready to work and followed the dogs down the hillside, being careful to jink and jive a little to make a long-range shot more difficult. The muttskis were hot on the trail, noses down, tails up, and doing their own zigzag search pattern in pursuit of lingering molecules of scent in the frozen grass with those amazing noses.

Down by the lakeshore there was a final barrier of scraggly pines, where the shepherds had a harder time of it. They seemed to be generally headed for that impressive rock formation, so I began to pay attention to that as we closed in on its base at the end of the lake. From here at the water's edge, there was no sign of the fabled glass hole. I stayed in the tree line to avoid making an easy target, and trusted the dogs to alert me to anybody or thing lying in wait. The sky above the trees was a deep blue, and the water reflected that color. It was now early afternoon and the sun was strong at four thousand feet, even through the canopy of pine trees. I could feel the sunburn coming on.

When we got to within a few hundred yards of the ship-shaped rock formation, the shepherds lost the trail. They circled and circled, returned to me several times, and then flopped down on the ground. I found a clump of boulders
and sat down among them, still trying to make it hard for any long-range shooters. The rocks were warm in the sunlight, and the snow and sleet of last night
seemed like a dream. But Mose was wounded up there on the hillside, and
Carrie was once again in the clutches of the goddamned Creighs.

I studied the sheer cliffs for several minutes. It seemed to be a different kind
of rock from a lot of what I'd seen in the Smokies. I wondered if it was basalt,
the weathered remains of an ancient lava plug, in which case the whole lake
was a crater. I kept looking for a cave or any other feature that might admit humans, but all I could see was sheer blackish rock, with a lone hawk soaring several hundred feet above it, on the prowl for prey.

There was a crash in the underbrush and, as I took the monocular away
from my eye, I caught just a glimpse of a doe, all pumping, tawny motion with
a flashing, oversized white tail, blasting its way up the slope, followed immediately by my two shepherds. I whistled for them, but it was too late—instinct
had overcome training, and they disappeared up the slope in hot pursuit. All
too aware that my eyes had just deserted me, I unlimbered the rifle and looked
around. Something had spooked that deer, and it hadn't been the dogs. Or at
least not *my* dogs.

A moment later, four of Nathan's dogs appeared out of the underbrush,
noses down, intent on the deer's trail. They stopped and milled around about a
hundred feet in front of me, happily unaware that I had them in my rifle sights,
and then set off in the same direction my shepherds had gone. I wasn't sure
that was good news until I heard a voice in the woods in front of me. A scruffy-
looking and extremely thin man dressed in black coveralls and a tattered Army
jacket appeared out of the woods, holding a single dog on a leash. This dog was
following the trail of his buddies, and the man was having a tough time restraining him. The pair stopped in the same place the other dogs had stopped
while trying to sort out all the scent. The man encouraged the dog to get on
with it, and finally it lurched to the left and followed what had to be by now a
virtual parade of scent up the hill. Then a second man appeared, holding a
shotgun in one hand and a walking stick in the other.

Unlike the first guy, this one was looking around, so he was quick to spot
me sighting down the barrel of my rifle at him. He was almost as tall as Nathan
and had an enormous black beard that covered his entire lower face. He
pulled up short and called the first man, who turned around and was then

nearly yanked off his feet by the big dog, which was still intent on getting that deer. For a moment, we formed a tense tableau, the bearded guy standing in midstride, the dog handler wrestling with his anxious beast, and me ready to perforate the both of them with as many .308 rounds as I could load before they hit the ground.

"Hey, now," the dog handler said, finally pulling hard enough on the leash to make the dog behave. It struggled for a few seconds and then caught sight of me. It barked once and started pulling in my direction.

"Where's the woman?" I asked, aiming my question and the rifle at the dog handler, since he seemed to want to talk. The other guy was leaning on the walking stick and staring at me, but he'd made no move to bring that shotgun up. Yet.

"You lookin' fer that woman, is that it?" the handler said. The dog was growling now and making it clear that he knew what his new mission was. I thought I saw the bearded man's hand begin to move, so I swung the rifle over to cover him. He had the shotgun, which made him the far more dangerous adversary here.

"Tell me where you've got her, or I'm going to shoot fuzzy-wuzzy and then you, in that order."

"Well, hey now," he said again. "Ain't no need for that. We'll tell yer, won't we, Jacky. Take it easy, now, mister, everythin's gonna be okay."

The handler looked pointedly over at Jacky, as if for corroboration of what he'd just said, and Jacky, never taking his eyes off me or the rifle, nodded once in slow, deliberate fashion. I almost fell for it. What that nod had really meant was for the handler to turn loose his baby-killer, which he did with a bare twitch of his hand. The dog lunged forward even as Jacky began to swing the scattergun.

I didn't hesitate. I fired one round at Jacky, which spun him around and sent him rolling down the slope with a howl of pain. I jacked in a reload and shot the dog through-and-through when it was no more than twenty feet away, and then I drew down on the handler, who was still, amazingly, standing there with his mouth wide open and a shocked expression on his face. I worked the bolt and took aim at his face. I was vaguely aware that the bearded one was flopping around down there in the weeds, still yelling, and made a mental note to put eyes on that shotgun. Just in case, I moved to the right, putting a boulder between me and where I'd seen Jacky fall, and then asked the man again where they had put Carrie. The dying dog began to cry miserably.

"Y-yonder," he croaked, staring almost cross-eyed at the muzzle of my rifle.

"In the glass hole." He pointed behind him in the direction from which they'd come.

"You lead me to her," I ordered. "Now! Move it!"

I knew I had very little time. Those gunshots would bring Nathan and whatever other hired help he'd brought with him, and they'd probably be a little more competent than this scarecrow trembling in front of me. The problem was that they would probably be coming from the same direction I needed to go.

"Awright—awright, I'll do her," the man pleaded. "Anythin', mister, just don't shoot me. That there woman's Nathan's bizness, none o'ourn. He's the one shot that other fella, too."

"Where's the hole?" I asked.

"T'other side that there big rock," he said, glancing sideways toward where Jacky had disappeared. He pointed with a trembling hand in the direction of the formation, which rose over the trees like a big black cloud. "Yonder it is."

I'd obviously hit Jacky, but I had no way of knowing how badly. The problem was that I couldn't see him anymore, or, for that matter, hear him, and a quick look revealed that he hadn't turned loose of that shotgun, either. Although even a flesh wound from a .308 would pack a hell of a punch, he was still out there in the weeds with a shotgun.

"You," I said. "Go find your buddy. Haul him out here where I can see him."

"Me?" he squeaked, looking around as if to see if there was anyone else out there. I had a bad feeling that there might be, but if somebody was going snake hunting in close quarters, it wasn't going to be me.

"Yeah, you. Or how about I shoot you right where you're standing and then go find him myself? Now do it, and keep those hands where I can see them."

He kept his hands out in front of him, as if ready to be cuffed. He started moving down the hill toward the lake. I remained in the boulders until he was within a few feet of disappearing into the dense underbrush, and then, perforce, I had to follow him. Behind me I heard the dog expire with an ugly noise.

My tactical situation wasn't terrific: As soon as that guy figured out that I couldn't see him, he'd run for it. Or he'd miss Jacky entirely, and then Jacky'd get a shot at me as we walked by wherever he was hiding. *If* he was hiding—he might have taken off, too. As I entered the thicket, I put my rifle on safe, slung it over my back, and got out Mose's little pocket gun. The rifle wasn't of much use in dense underbrush. Jacky's shotgun, on the other hand, was just about perfect.

I could hear the other guy pushing his way through the branches and bram-
bles in the general direction of the water's edge. I kept a lookout for any blood
trails and cursed my own dogs for taking off. I heard a rustling in the bushes
ahead and stopped to crouch behind a tree. As I strained to listen, a shotgun
boomed in the underbrush, and I heard the dog handler make a mortal noise.
I hit the deck and lay very still. Apparently Jacky hadn't taken kindly to being
fingered, or he'd mistaken the handler for me. I could hear the handler groaning up ahead, and he couldn't have been that far ahead of me.

The tower of black rock rose above the trees ahead, and I guessed I was
maybe a hundred yards from its base. I tried to imagine my previous line of advance and then began to crawl off in a direction at right angles to that line. It
was awkward with the rifle slung over my back, but I needed my hands free to
push bushes and branches out of my way quietly while I tried to work around
Jacky's position. I was pretty sure he was wounded and maybe even down, but
he was obviously not in such bad shape that he couldn't fire a shotgun, as his
ace buddy had just discovered. I got as flat as I could, pushing through grass,
gravel, briars, and baby trees. I kept stopping to listen, but all I could detect
was the sounds of the dog handler groaning.

Was Jacky moving, too? My cheek brushed up against a softball-sized rock,
so I picked it up and pitched it as high as I could over the bushes back in the direction from which I'd come. It made a satisfying thump, but unfortunately it
sounded just like a rock had been thrown into the undergrowth. So much for
my deception plan. Then I heard something coming from behind me, and the
something was making zero effort to hide its approach.

Dogs. *Oh, shit,* I thought. Nathan's four-pack had come back and were hot
on our trail. No, *my* trail.

I looked at the little .25-caliber peashooter and briefly considered using it
on myself rather than face the prospect of being torn to pieces by four big
beasts.

Except the furry face that finally broke through the bushes was Frack, who
was very happy to see me. Frick came through right behind him and took advantage of the fact that I was on the ground to do some serious licking. The
problem was that they were making a lot of noise, and if Jacky was near, that
shotgun was training around on us. I grabbed a stick and threw it high in the
general direction of where I figured the handler was lying, and they took off to
retrieve it. They went crashing through the bushes, so I took that opportunity
to squirm thirty feet farther to the right under cover of all their noise.

By now I had the rock formation at my back, which meant that Jacky and his erstwhile buddy ought to be between me and my original trail. The dogs were still thrashing around out there, and then they started barking. I winced and waited for the shotgun, but nothing happened. They continued to bark, and they weren't moving. I decided it was time to close in.

Jacky was propped up against the base of a tree with his back to me. He was trying to bring the shotgun to bear on the shepherds with just his left arm, and he wasn't doing too well. I could see a pair of boots sticking out of a clump of hawthorn bushes some ten feet in front of him. The shepherds were very aware of the shotgun and kept darting in and out of the line of fire, continuing to bark at Jacky. I was able to creep right up behind under cover of all that dog racket and grab the shotgun out of his hand before he could pull the trigger. He yelled in pain when I did that, and then pressed his left hand over his right arm, as if trying to hug himself. His left hand was covered in blood.

My snap-shot had managed to hit him in the right hand. It wasn't anything like the old western movies. That .308 round had essentially exploded his right hand, to the point where there were jagged bits of bone protruding everywhere his palm used to be. He was distinctly gray around the gills, and there was a baby lake of blood under his legs where he'd been hunched over, holding his right hand under his left armpit. His mouth was open and he was taking short, gasping breaths through all that beard. Keeping an eye on Jacky, I checked out the dog handler, but he was either unconscious or dead. Jacky had managed to put a blast of some large-caliber shot into the man's chest, and he was probably gone.

I turned back to Jacky, shut down the barking shepherds, and squatted down a few feet away from him, keeping the .25 pointed in his general direction. His whole face was gray now, and his lips were trembling as he slid deeper into shock. I was amazed that he could have fired the shotgun, given the recoil of a ten-gauge. I broke open the action and found two new shells, so he'd also been able to reload after shooting his own man down. He was glaring at me through a haze of pain. I was very aware that Nathan was out there somewhere, possibly with more of his black hats. They had to have heard all the gunfire.

"Where's the woman?" I asked.

He just looked at me, his eyes squinting with hate. There was fresh blood trickling down between his fingers as he continued to hold his shattered hand against his body.

I repeated my question. He made no reply. I unlimbered the .308, opened the bolt to make sure there was still a round in there, and then cycled it closed. I stood up and pointed the rifle at his face. As I pulled the trigger, I twitched the barrel a tiny bit high so that the heavy slug smacked into the tree instead. Even so, he felt the wallop and cried out despite his defiant expression. I jacked in another round and this time lowered the barrel to point at his belly. I asked him again: "Where's the woman?"

"Go 'head, do it," he gasped. "Won't do you no good, anyhow. She gone."

"Gone where?" I asked. I lowered the muzzle so that it pointed at his genitals. He watched it as one would watch a snake between his legs.

"In the hole, by now," he said. "She ain't a'comin' out, neither."

"Did you bastards kill her?" I asked.

An evil sneer crossed his face. "Naw," he said. "Hole does that. Takes a while. Go look, you want to. You'll see."

"Where is it, this hole?"

"Yonder," he said, pointing with his enormous, frizzy beard toward the rock formation. He coughed, and for the first time I saw blood in his mouth and at the end of his nostrils. It was only then that I saw the hole in his shirtfront and realized I'd hit him twice with the same round. He was a big guy, but he was also mortally wounded, and I think he knew it.

"What'd you do with those children? Are they in the hole, too?"

He got a blank look on his face, then understood. He shook his head. "Wasn't but one young'un up here," he said. "Grinny got the rest."

He closed his eyes and his breathing became more labored, as if the effort to speak had winded him. I lowered the rifle barrel. The shepherds were nosing around the motionless dog handler but keeping their distance. I thought I heard a sound over in the direction of the rock formation, but the dogs weren't reacting. Still, I knew I had very little time left.

I knelt down again to get closer to his face. "I'm here for Nathan Creigh," I said. "Where is he?"

He started breathing in even shallower gasps, as if building up enough oxygen to speak again. "Camp's yonder, by the hole. Nathan tole us to find the third man, after he shot t'other one. He'll be a'waitin' fer ye. You that lawman what kilt Rue Creigh?"

I said yes.

"Be damned, then. He said you'd be a'comin'. That Grinny would point the way. He'll be a'waitin'. You a dead man walkin'."

"Right now I think *you're* a dead man talking," I replied. I pulled his injured hand out from his armpit just to make damned sure he wasn't holding a pocket gun. He groaned with pain when I moved his wrecked hand. Then I got up. His hat was lying in the grass. I retrieved that and his shotgun, then called in the dogs. I walked fifty yards toward the rock formation and then gave the dogs the hat as a scent target. No dummies, they promptly headed back to where I'd left the bearded man. I called them back in and sent them in the opposite direction. They cut a trail pretty quickly, and we started down the hill to find Nathan, hopefully before Nathan found us.

22

It turned out that the Creighs had set up a permanent camp just around the corner of the landward end of the big rock formation. All my efforts to be tactically discreet came to nothing when the dogs and I blundered out of the woods and there it was: two ancient, crude log cabins, a fire pit, cages for their dogs, the obligatory junk piles, a privy, and Carrie, sitting with her back to a small tree, a grimly determined look on her face and the end of a rope in her hand. She had her injured hand back under her armpit again. The rope had two turns wrapped around the tree. The rest of it led right to the base of the rock formation.

"Knew you'd show up sometime," she said. "You have yourself a nice war up there?"

"Where's Nathan?" I asked, shotgun ready. The dogs did their usual running around after greeting Carrie.

"Oh, he's hanging around," she said, indicating the other end of the rope. I walked over to where the rope disappeared into a stand of hawthorn. I pushed through the tangle and finally got to see the glass hole.

It was indeed an ancient lava tube: It looked like a long funnel, perhaps twenty, thirty feet across at the top and necking down to twelve feet across about a hundred feet down. The sides were polished basalt, and I could see why they called it the glass hole. At the bottom was a pool of dark blue water. At first, I thought the water was reflecting the sky, but then realized it couldn't be—the tube went down at about a sixty-degree angle, so that water had to be connected to the main lake on the other side of the black tower. At the bottom of the rope, halfway down, was Nathan, hanging on with both hands and swinging gently from side to side.

"Okay," I said. "How'd you manage this trick?"

"He got a little hands-on after he'd sent his boys out to find you," she said wearily. "So I lay back and let him. Once he was distracted, I head-butted him, kneed him, whacked his limpy leg again, stuck an elbow in each eye, and then cold-cocked him with that tree branch over there by the fire." She looked up at me. "Is Mose—?"

"Mose is gonna be okay, I think. He had his old police vest on under that coat."

"Thank God," she said. "I heard that round hit him and he went down like a tree. I saw all that blood while those ugly fucks were tying me up, and I just knew . . ."

"They were there already?"

"Apparently," she said. "Nathan positioned them outside our camp, waited for his shot, and then they piled in and got me before I could get to a weapon."

"That's our Nathan," I said, looking down at the hanging figure in the hole. "I managed to surprise his helpers. The bearded guy shot his buddy by mistake, and I took him and one dog out. The only problem we still have is that there are four of his dogs out there somewhere."

"What do we do with Nathan?" she asked.

"Cut the rope," I said. "Or not—let him hang down there until he dies. Except—"

"What?"

"First I want to talk to him. The bearded guy said they brought one of the kids up here, but the rest were still with Grinny."

She became immediately alarmed. "I haven't seen her," she said, and then looked over at the hole.

I helped her tie off the rope, and then we both went back over to the edge of the glass hole. There was shrubbery growing right up to the lip, and woods creatures had probably been dying in that thing for centuries. Those shining sides looked entirely alien among the bushes and rocks at the top. There was absolutely no way anything could climb back out of that deadly funnel, especially if the climber was wet. It reminded me of one of those pitcher plants that trap insects. The light reflecting in from the tube's other end in the main lake made the hole look almost infinite in depth.

I had thought that Nathan was holding his end of the rope, but when I looked closely, I could see that she had tied a noose around his two wrists. He was literally hanging from the rope by his hands, which looked larger than they would normally be. I shouted down the hole and heard my voice reverberating off those glasslike sides. Nathan raised his head but could not open his swollen eyes. Carrie had apparently grown tired of being abducted by Creighs; he looked positively battered.

"Hey, Nathan, can you swim?" I said.

I thought he muttered something, but he was too far down for me to hear it. "Let's pull him up some," I said, and so we did. We got him to within ten feet of the lip, but the sides were so smooth he might as well still have been a hundred feet down. He was, in fact, positively battered.

"Where's the child, Nathan?" I asked.

He cracked one eye and glared up at us. The rope had pulled him into an elongated bow shape, and he was probably having trouble breathing. Broke my heart. He'd dropped Mose without a qualm with a long-range rifle shot and then taken Carrie back to his camp so that he could throw her into this alien geographical feature, where she would absolutely never be found. After he had gratified himself. The fact that they had a semi-permanent camp up here meant they'd done all this before.

"Where's the little girl, Nathan?" I asked again. I kicked the rope, which had the effect of squeezing his purple hands.

He grunted with the pain. "Ain't no girl," he said, finally.

"Your bearded buddy said you brought one up here—he's dead, by the way, along with his pal who had the big dog on the leash—so where is she? You throw her down this hole?"

"Y'all go to hell," he said, closing the puffy eye.

"Cam, look," Carrie said. She was pointing down into the lava-glass funnel. Way down there, in the water and at the edge of the lava walls, a tiny white object had appeared. It looked like a piece of paper, but it wasn't. I suddenly had a very bad feeling.

"What's that down there, Nathan? Down there in the water?"

Nathan tried to look down but couldn't. His arms had to be just about screaming by now, but I had zero sympathy.

"Get on the very end of that rope," I told Carrie. "Belay it around that tree right there, and then I'm going to drop this bastard."

Carrie did exactly as I asked. I took up the tension on the rope, she wrapped the very end of it around the tree, and then I let go. Nathan slid down the side of the tube like a luge rider, yelling all the way. He hit the water below with a clumsy splash and disappeared until the rope snapped taut, and then he burst back up to the surface. Without hands, he couldn't swim, so he went right back down again. I let him do this three times and then hauled in on the rope until his arms and head remained above water. I gave him a minute to breathe and then told him to go get the white thing that was floating about ten feet from him. He looked small and helpless all the way down there, which I thought was just about perfect.

He refused to move, so I tied off the rope to keep his head above water and then went and got my rifle.

"Cam," Carrie began, but I waved her off.

"I want him talking, but he needs some encouragement," I said. I knelt down at the lip of the lava tube and put a round three inches from his face. The sound effects were interesting, as was the knifelike slash of the bullet into the water right next to his face. I fired two more rounds, each one a little closer, and he finally yelled, "All right."

I gave him some slack with the rope, and he crabbed sideways with his body and then reached down to pick up the white thing. It became obvious that his hands weren't working anymore as he kept dropping it. I yelled down for him to grab it with his teeth, and, when he did, we both pulled on that rope with all we had. Nathan wasn't a little guy, but the hole wasn't vertical, either. Being wet, he slid up that glassine surface with very little friction. When his face got to the top, framed by his two straining arms, I stared at the white thing he held in his teeth.

So did Carrie. She began to curse him in a low monotone, using words I hadn't heard since the Marines. Then I saw what it was: that frilly little cap that Honey Dee had worn when she came up to the cave and brought us the message from Grinny, the one with the crude yellow bees embroidered on it. This evil motherfucker had thrown her down there to her death. And she hadn't been the first, as I kept reminding myself.

Nathan heard our reaction and for the first time looked afraid. I had trouble framing the words. "What—have—you—done?" I said through clenched teeth.

"She was a bleeder," he said, spitting out the bonnet. It stuck to the lava wall like a piece of wet toilet paper. "No good to us. Grinny said trash her, so that's what I done."

"So it's true?" I said. "You make those poor goddamned women pay for their drugs in kids? And then you sell them as sex objects?"

He gave a long sigh, as if he knew it was all over and there was no more point in playing the role of tough guy. He looked up at us with that one working eye, and I'd have sworn he was laughing at us.

"Better," he said.

Better? That's what Mingo had said.

"What the hell does that mean, better?"

"We sell 'em for parts."

I heard Carrie gasp, and then she was reaching for her knife to cut the rope. I grabbed her hand and yelled "No" at her. She fought me, reaching by me to cut that rope. She almost succeeded. The hell of it was I *wanted* her to cut that rope.

"He needs to die," she snapped.

"Sure he does. But think about it: Think about the evidence that has to be down there in that water. They've been using this place for years."

Nathan had closed his eyes again as the pain of being hung by his hands reasserted itself. Carrie glared down at him with a face like Medusa.

"Look," I said. "The one thing we've never been able to get is physical evidence. Down there is the mother lode. They'll convict this bastard, and then he's going upstate, where they'll lock him up for life as a child killer. Think of what the cons will do to him. Especially if his hands don't work any more."

"Some goddamned lawyer will get him off," she muttered, but she had lowered the knife.

I sat back on my haunches and looked down at yet another minion of hell. "That so-called doctor will talk," I said. "The doctor who took those kids into a lab at night and cut them up like stew meat. And we'll make sure the story's out there, so no bureaucrats can pull any more rugs over this mess. But first we have to find Grinny and the rest of them."

"Prison's not good enough," she said.

"Yes, it will be," I said. "If he gets life, they'll have to box him up so the rest of the cons can't get to him. He'll live in an eight-by-six concrete room for the rest of his life. And if he gets the needle, he still gets to live in that box for a decade or so, only this time in the death house. Our killing him would be a mercy, and this bastard doesn't deserve mercy of any kind."

I stood up and pulled her back from the lip of the lava tube. "What are we going to do right now?" she said.

"We're going to go back to our camp and check on Mose. Then we'll fire that EPIRB. For this mess, we need a crowd."

"And him?"

"Let him hang for a while."

We lowered Nathan back down to midway in the tube and then tied him off.

A crowd was what we got. The first helicopter arrived right at the end of the two-hour response window, as advertised. He couldn't land, but he did put down a rescue paramedic. While the bird flew around in lazy circles overhead, we explained what we had on the ground and that we needed Sam King and his SBI team here in a hurry, preferably before dark. Carrie did most of the talking. The medic checked Mose out and said he was stable and qualified for air transport. The helo came in and they did a rescue hoist. Mose was shocky from that big whack in the chest, but he managed a grin at Carrie, who held his hand until the hoist was ready.

Then the shepherds and I went back to the ambush site to mark the location of the two bodies there. Carrie stayed back at our camp. The paramedic had left her a radio, and she briefed the rescue pilots as they flew back to the nearest hospital on what to tell the cops. Then, while we waited for the SBI, we went back down to Nathan's camp near the lava tube.

We debated bringing him out of the tube. Carrie really liked the idea of letting him just hang there, but his hands were now a dark purple, and I didn't want him going off to some hospital to fight gangrene for a month. She, on the other hand, had this interesting theory of how his hands might just come off, and she wanted to watch. In the end we hauled him out of the glass hole and tied him to a tree. I left the shepherds to watch him, and then we trudged back up to our original camp to wait for the circus.

The enormity of it all swept over us while we waited for the helicopters to come back.

Better, Nathan had said. Just like that snake Mingo. They hadn't been sterilizing these little girls at that path lab—they'd been harvesting organs. Very fresh pediatric organs. That's what had been going overseas. Coolers filled with body parts. Couriered to an airport by one of Mingo's deputies, probably.

Then it occurred to me that if this story got out, Grinny would absolutely be forced to kill the remaining children. Once the swarm began here, Carrie and I would be wrapped up in it for a few days at least. I made a decision not to let that happen. I told Carrie that I was going to go back down to the glass-hole site and check on Nathan and the dogs. I asked her to remain at the camp to greet King and his people and to see if she could find a landing site. The radio blasted into life, and while Carrie was dealing with the first wave of questions from King, the mutts and I slipped out of camp.

I went back down to the tube. Nathan was still tied to the tree, and it didn't look like he'd made any efforts to get himself untied. He was exhausted from his excursions on the rope. His hands were still purple, he was having trouble breathing after being semi-crucified like that, and, more important, I think he'd given up. If there had been any more black hats up there, they'd probably melted away into the hills once all the shooting started. Even so, I wrapped a canvas bag around Nathan's head so he couldn't see, retrieved my rifle and the shepherds, and then quietly took the dogs around the crater lake the long way as a convoy of helicopters appeared up on the ridgeline.

I hated to just abandon Carrie to the arrival of the authorities, but she'd be the more helpful of the two of us, familiar as she was with SBI forensic and scene procedures. She knew as much as I did about what had happened there and would be more than able to describe Nathan's revelations. I, on the other hand, had zero official standing and, therefore, none of the legal inhibitions that would constrain the SBI when they finally swung into motion against Grinny Creigh.

Besides, I really, really wanted to get that woman. Mingo and Nathan had been players in their grisly business, but the real monster in the cave had always been that supremely evil old woman. They'd get Nathan into a courtroom, but I knew Grinny would die before she ever let that happen to her. I didn't think she'd run, either. For one, it would be physically difficult for a woman that fat to move fast. Two, these were her hills, her territory, her fiefdom. She would defend it to the end. That was fine by me. And by not telling Carrie what I was up to, I reasoned, all she could honestly say to the rest of the cops was that she didn't know where the hell I was. In a sense, I was doing her a favor. Sounded good, anyway.

"C'mon, mutts," I told the shepherds. "We have to get to that truck before it gets really dark." *And before Carrie finds out we've bugged out and comes down to fang our collective asses,* I thought.

It took the same two hours going down as it did coming up. Going down was still harder on the leg bones than climbing. The shepherds ranged ahead most of the time except for when we had to traverse some thick scrubland, and then I called them in as protection against any lurking Creigh-dogs. Which is why they didn't spot the man sitting on the front bumper of my Suburban smoking a cigarette as we walked up to the parked vehicles. I was unlimbering the rifle when I recognized Baby Greenberg. He flipped the butt out onto the ground and got up as we approached.

"So, sport, who won the war up there?" he asked. The dogs greeted him warily—they didn't like surprises or cigarettes.

"How'd you find us?" I asked.

He grinned, knelt down, and pulled the tracking transmitter from under the front wheel well. "Would you believe, federal voodoo?" he said. "For your own safety, you understand." He put the thing back on the frame and stood up, dusting off his hands. "And where's the rest of 'us'?"

I put my stuff in the back and then sat down on the back bumper to tell him what had happened up there, and what we'd learned from Nathan about their child-trafficking business. I'd expected complete shock, but this only seemed to fulfill his worst expectations for the mountain criminal crowd.

"Parts? Human parts? From *kids*? A new low."

I nodded. It was getting dark, and I was suddenly tired. We could hear the drone of another helicopter going over the ridge. I knew I needed to beat feet if we had any chance at all of saving the rest of the kids.

"There should be a fresh one in that glass hole or lava tube, whatever you want to call it," I said. "Carrie's up there leading the SBI through it. Assuming that they can retrieve a child's body from that formation, and that Nathan is ready to come clean, they'll finally have some physical evidence."

"A body in something like that might never be found," he said. "You know—bodies sink initially and then gas up a couple days later. But if that tube goes way down, it may not be possible to get it back. From what you're saying, that thing could be several hundred feet deep."

"I don't think so," I said, and explained about the light coming in from the main lake. "But it will take time and some specialized equipment, which is why I cut loose from the goat-grab up there."

"What's your plan?"

"I'm headed for Grinny Creigh's. There are five more kids still adrift, if Nathan was telling the truth."

"Why not wait for the cavalry?"

"Same reason as last time—she hears Nathan's in custody, she has to make those children disappear, and I'm betting they have other places where they can make that happen. Or she might run."

He shook his head. "She'll never run. Never in a million years."

"Well, good, then I look forward to getting up with her," I said.

He thought about that for a moment. "Want some backup?" he said finally.

"Where's your crew?" I asked.

"I'm solo on this," he said. "We're not supposed to know you anymore, so I can't involve my guys. They brought me up here when I found out that Mose had taken you into the hills. I actually came up to talk you guys into leaving this mess alone, but . . . *kids*?"

"We tried to tell people," I said. "I'm not especially comforted by my government's reluctance to jump into this with both feet. And from what Carrie found out, the federal response is being dictated more by turf boundaries than any sense of real urgency."

"I know, I know," he said, kicking a clump of grass. "I talked to my boss. At length. But he's a fucking wimp. Keeps saying: Where's the drug-enforcement angle in this? If she's kidnapping children, then call Charlotte. If she's moving meth, go catch her at it."

It was my turn to think. Then I had an idea. "I was told there's a hundred pounds of crystal meth in the escape tunnel behind the Creigh cabin."

He looked over at me with visible skepticism. "Told? By whom?"

"Can't say," I said. "Have to protect my sources. But it's a hundred pounds, all wrapped up for sale in the big city. Sounds like she's moving meth to me."

"That's laughably weak," he said. "My boss would throw you out of his office for bullshit like that. For bullshit less than that. Nobody wraps meth."

"But your boss is a wimp," I pointed out.

"Why, yes, he is," Baby said.

"So: You want to go along? Explore this anonymous hot tip? Make it official?"

"Duty calls," he said.

23

It was close to eleven that night when we reached the north end of that ridgeline crack above the Creigh place. Our vehicles back on the mountain had apparently not been disturbed, so I'd left a note for Carrie saying I was going to Grinny's to find the missing kids. I left out any mention of Greenberg's participation. I was counting on their not going back to retrieve Mose's vehicle until they'd settled the various scenes up on the mountain, because once they did, and found the note, they'd have people all over Grinny's. I wanted to have our one shot before that happened. I thought Baby was right: She'd corner up and fight, not run.

The night was cool and clear, and there was enough of a moon up to see pretty well. The shepherds were ready for some work, and so was I. We hunkered down in the Creigh-side end of the crack and scanned the cabin and buildings below. They were all dark, as usual, and there were no police vehicles there anymore, or none that we could see. That didn't mean there wasn't a deputy parked up under a tool shed down there, but the only police presence I could see was the occasional glimpse of a new tape line fluttering around the front of the main cabin. I also looked hard for sign of dogs—I think I was a lot more afraid of the Creigh dog pack than any lurking cops.

We still had the same problems with respect to approaching the cabin down that open hillside, so my plan involved getting back into that escape tunnel, whose entrance was beneath the lone tree fifty feet away. I pointed it out to Greenberg, who was duly impressed with the Creighs' tunneling ability. I'd brought a shotgun instead of my rifle, and we each had a handgun. I had mine in my utility vest, along with a flashlight, extra ammo, a knife, and some water. Baby had his Glock in a hip holster and a flashlight. I wanted to get back into the house via the escape passage, make sure Grinny and her prisoners weren't actually just sitting there in the kitchen, and then explore some of those other passages we'd seen on our way out.

With all that blubber onboard, I couldn't feature Grinny Creigh making it through that narrow passage up to the main escape route, so I was pretty sure that she'd never left the Creigh compound. The house, maybe, but not the clutch of buildings. Nathan's henchman had obliquely confirmed that when he told us Grinny had deliberately pointed us away from the cabin and out to the glass hole. Even a sheriff's office forensic team hadn't been able to find the escape tunnel, so I figured there had to be other hidey-holes buried back there behind that cabin. They'd had decades to dig and hide, and this couldn't be the first time they'd had to go to the matresses in all that long history of smuggling and worse. Wherever she was holed up, it probably did not involve a lot of physical exertion to get there. On the other hand, I had to admit that she could just as easily have gotten into a vehicle right there at her front door and been driven off to Arkansas. But my instinct was that she was lurking in a hole somewhere, like the spider she was.

I'd asked Baby on the way over how in the world a bunch of drug-running hillbillies had managed to get into the horrible trade in pediatric organs. He surmised that they'd started by peddling kids to the truck-stop pimps throughout the South, then graduated into selling them into organized kiddy-porn and pedophile sex rings, the bulk of which operated in or around New Orleans.

"All those semis," he said. "You know, with the big living quarters behind the cab? Perfect way to transport thirteen-year-old girls and boys across the country. There's a known market for blue-eyed blonds in Washington, no questions asked and big money. Probably only been a matter of time before someone with connections in the courier systems approached them about upping the ante."

"But harvesting organs? Hayes said he knew about them going to the hospital lab, but he thought it was for abortions. Carrie and I thought it was for sterilization."

"That'd be bad enough," Baby said, "but you're saying they took them over to that lab, put them to sleep, and then harvested. You gotta wonder who thought that one up."

"Three guesses."

"Yeah, well, you have to remember, they've been doing shit like this for generations up here. Probably didn't seem like a big step to them."

"Which mystifies me even more," I said. "If they've been doing evil shit for decades, how come they've never been taken down?"

He thought about his answer. "I think it's because nobody cared, as long as they were doing it to themselves. We only got into it because the meth coming down out of the hills was reaching flood stage. But it's not like we've been putting serious assets against them—those are reserved for the urban cocaine and heroin traffickers. You know, the guys bringing it in by container-load through Miami or over the Mexican border on NAFTA semis. Basically, DEA is just too damned busy to fool with what has been up to now a pretty low-viz and very remote problem."

I'd thought then that if this was considered a low-visibility problem, then the rest of the nation's drug problem must be positively galactic in scale, but I kept my silence. If anyone appreciated that, it would be a street agent like Greenberg. Some day I'd ask him if his thoughts on the "war on drugs" were similar to mine. Right now it was time to get moving.

"Pet the doggies?" I asked in a quiet voice, and both shepherds crowded around, circling my legs and rubbing hard in return for ear rubs and patting, even as I told them in my kindest voice that they were a pair of worthless, blockheaded, deer-chasing, flea-shedding hair-bags who couldn't catch a sleeping cat if they tripped over one. They positively beamed.

Getting them down into the escape tunnel was harder than I'd anticipated, and if surprise had been the objective, we probably blew it right there. The dogs slid and scrambled their way down that slanting plank and then barked at us when we didn't join them fast enough. We found the lanterns Carrie and I had left, lit them, and put away the flashlights. Then we regrouped at the junction of the tunnel coming up from the cabin basement and the bricked-up wall. I described where the one tunnel came from, and Baby asked if we could defend ourselves if someone was down there in that hidden room with a twelve-gauge as we climbed down out of the ceiling. I had to admit that we'd probably get our asses shot off, literally.

"How about this walled-up tunnel, then?" he asked, running his hands over the roughly mortared stones. He had to squeeze in between two of the three big ceiling support posts planted right in front of it. I had to hunch over, as the roof of the tunnel was only six feet, if that. The floor was hard-packed earth with a thin layer of dust. Everything was a dull yellow-orange in the kerosene lamplight. The air quickly began to stink of kerosene smoke.

"It may have caved in or just simply be too dangerous to use," I said. I slapped the stone with my hand and mostly hurt my hand—it was solidly embedded. The shepherds watched us in the lantern light with a bemused expression.

Baby got out a pocketknife and began to test the edges of the stone wall. He could get the blade in about two inches all around except on the bottom. He leaned back against the center post and then grunted.

"What?" I asked.

"This post just moved," he said, standing up and going around to the side away from the stone wall. Then he reached up and grabbed the top of the post and pulled, and damned if the post didn't come down like a big lever arm while the stone wall lifted slowly out of the ground maybe two inches. We heard a dull snap under the door as if a ratchet had fallen into place. The post was now at a forty-five-degree angle, and it wouldn't move anymore.

"Okay, so it lifts and separates," I said. "But does it open?"

Baby pushed on the wall right in the middle, and nothing happened. I then stepped forward and pushed on the right-hand side, and the thing began to pivot, like a big stone flapper valve. There was obviously a pin of some kind dead center, so the wall ended up at about an eighty-degree angle to its original position. A warm flow of air came through the opening, smelling faintly of straw or hay.

I pointed a flashlight down the passage beyond, which revealed a tunnel identical to the one we occupied. There were three posts on the other side just like the ones we had on this side. The difference was that there were many footprints in the dust on the floor, and this one went down at the same angle as the one coming from the cabin.

"If anyone's down there," I said quietly, "that pressure release will let them know this door just opened."

"What's that smell?" Baby asked, sniffing the air. "Barn? Hay? Straw?"

"Yeah," I said. "Maybe this connects to that barn where they chained me up that night."

"So—we go?"

"These guys go," I said, and sent the shepherds down the passageway. If there was going to be an ambush, they'd sense it. They might not survive it, but we would. We picked up our lanterns and went after the dogs, Baby first and me in trail and still hunched over to keep from banging my head. I kept looking back, half-expecting that stone door to swing quietly shut like it always did in the movies, but it just sat there. Baby saw me looking and suggested we wedge it open. We went back through and wrestled with that post lever until we broke it off at the ground, which should keep anyone from closing it behind us.

The tunnel went straight for maybe two hundred feet and then hooked hard right, where it ended in a wooden door. The dogs were milling around in front of the door, but they weren't excited. We could hear air whistling past the cracks around the door, and the barnyard smell was stronger here. There was a normal latch on the door, and black iron hinges on the other side. This thing had been here for a while.

"The lady or the tiger?" Baby said, drawing his Glock.

I pulled the shepherds back to me and took a position that would let me cover the opening as the door swung back. Baby put a lantern down just out of the arc the door would take when opening, lifted the latch as quietly as he could, flattened himself against the wall, and pulled the door open quickly.

Over the barrels of the shotgun I saw ten anxious eyes staring at us from a dark room. We'd found the kids.

Now: Where was the spider?

24

The door had opened into one of the shed barns, but not the one in which I'd been penned up. There was a double door at one end, hay piled up to the roof on one side, and a wall of farm implements on the other. There was fresh straw on the floor and a malodorous bucket in one corner. A second bucket with fresh water and a tin cup hung on one wall by the doors.

Baby stepped into the room first, and the children recoiled when they saw the gun in his hand. I followed him into the room and told them it was okay, we weren't going to hurt them. The lantern revealed a ragtag collection of blankets on the floor. The children were all little girls, maybe eight to ten years old, dressed in plain, floor-length frocks, which were universally too large for them. They were pale, thin, and frightened. Two were sucking thumbs, a third had badly crossed eyes, and the other two had skin infections on their jaundiced faces. They all looked scared of the shepherds.

Baby put away his Glock and knelt down on one knee to talk to the kids, while I went to the doors and tried to open them. There was a good-sized crack between the doors, and I could see a heavy keeper bar across them. I got out my boot knife, slid it through the crack, and lifted. It came up and then fell off the blade when I got it past the brackets. I pushed the doors ajar a few inches and looked out. In the time we'd been walking the tunnels, the night had turned misty and colder. I could see the main cabin way off to my right; the barn where the dogs had been kept was right next door. The moon was barely visible, but it provided a diffused light in the mist.

"What've we got?" Baby asked.

"Fog's coming in," I said. "Nothing moving out there for the moment. Better move that lantern, though." I didn't want to be silhouetted. And we still hadn't found Grinny Creigh.

"These kids are starving," Baby said. "And scared."

"Wards of Grinny Creigh," I said. "They ought to be scared."

He shook his head in dismay. "Barely human, some of them," he mused.

"Problem is, how do we get them out of here?"

"Yeah," he said, looking sideways out the partially opened barn doors. "We try to make a run for it, and she's out there in the weeds with some of those dogs?"

"What if we could go back through the tunnels," I said. "That would reduce our exposure to a fifty-foot run across open ground. Once we got into the rock passage, we could defend ourselves, and then get to the vehicle."

As if in answer to my what-if, we both heard something, a noise in the tunnel from which we'd just come. One of the kids was staring at the open door, and then she started to cry. I sprinted for the door as I recognized the sound of running feet—far too many running feet. The shepherds recognized it, too, and leaped for the doorway at about the same time I got the thing slammed shut. Ten seconds later there were multiple thuds against the door and dark growls of frustration. So much for getting out through the tunnels, I thought. And Grinny had joined us on the web. Her web.

Baby had brought the keeper bar into the barn and then secured the barn doors using the brackets on our side. There was a lot of snuffling and growling going on in the tunnel and just that simple door latch keeping the door closed. I jammed a pitchfork up against the panels of the door.

"What time is it?" Baby asked.

I looked at my watch. It was twelve thirty in the morning.

"They'll find that note when they go looking for you," he said. "Then they'll come here. All we have to do now is wait."

"She's here," I said.

"Oh, yes," he replied. "She's here."

I peered through the crack between the barn doors. There was a cold draft coming into the barn, and the mist had deepened outside. I could see out into the building complex, but not very far out into the yards beyond.

"Well, we sure as hell can't go out there," I said. "There'll be dogs and probably some black hats with rifles waiting. Don't suppose your cell works, does it?"

He shook his head. I'd checked mine; same deal—no signal. Some of the dogs on the other side of the tunnel door must have heard us talking, because they began to jump against the door. The pitchfork held, but just barely. The kids were watching the door with terrified expressions. They apparently were all too familiar with Grinny's dog pack.

"Hay bales," Baby said, and we started stacking bales against the door. We got twenty of them set up, which had the effect of reducing the scary noises and also putting a thousand pounds of weight in front of that door. I went back to the front door to keep watch.

"What would you do if you were Grinny's crew right now?" Baby asked.

"I'd surround this barn with dogs and black hats and then set it on fire," I said. "Solve all my problems at once."

He nodded. Apparently the same thought had occurred to him.

"Still glad you came?" I asked.

"Wouldn't have missed it," he said. "How far is it to the main cabin?"

"Maybe three hundred feet," I said, opening the door a crack to make sure.

"If we could get over there before she organizes her troops, we'd have that hidey-hole underground and a shot at that one escape tunnel. Here we have what's called a barbecue pit."

He had a point, but it was getting really foggy out there. We'd never see a brace of dogs coming, and they'd probably hit the kids before they hit us. We both looked out the front door. A substantial mountain fog looked back. Then, somewhere along the hill, a dog began to howl. Before I could shut them up, my shepherds howled back, and we were treated to a two-minute wolf-pack duet echoing across the ridges, strangely muted by the fog but eerie all the same. I let them go to it; I wanted whoever was out there in the trees to know there were four of us in here, not just two.

The dogs in the back tunnel went quiet when the howling started. The kids watched my shepherds with total fascination. Somehow the howling inside had comforted them a little bit. Baby was right: They were a motley-looking crew, all of whom would have been the subject of taunts at school for their defective appearance. But they were little girls, and the witch had been sending them to a butcher.

"Cover me," Baby said. "I'm going to see if I can find some water and buckets nearby."

I put the lantern over in one corner near the girls, told them it was going to be okay, and then took up position just outside the door with the shotgun. Baby slipped out, gun in hand, and went left, in between our shed and the next one. The fog lay over the grounds like a wet white veil, quiet as a coiled snake. The dogs on the hill had stopped their racket, and mine were plastered to my legs. I stood out there for five minutes, listening. I should have sent them with Baby, I thought, although they might have taken off after sounds in the fog.

Sounds in the fog. There was something out there.

I slipped back into the barn and closed the doors down to gunport width. Then I realized Baby might return in a hurry and opened one about a foot. Frack bristled at the foggy darkness, and I told him to stay. I went down on one knee to lower my profile. Tendrils of fog probed the doorway and chilled my ankles. Where the hell was Baby? I heard more snuffling behind the tunnel door, and one of the girls began to whimper again.

Suddenly, out front, an orange glow flared in the fog. Then a second one, then two more. Two were close together, the rest spread out. They were far enough away that all I could see was the flickering light, but it was obvious I was looking at torches. Lots of torches. Then a disembodied voice spoke out of the fog.

"Lawman!" the voice called. "*You* in there." It was Grinny's voice.

I said nothing, but got down flat on the ground with the shotgun pointed out front.

"*You* in there, speak up, damn yer eyes," she said. Even her voice was hateful. There were some old shingles on the floor by the door. I picked one up, slanted it across my mouth so that my voice would be pitched to the right, and answered her.

"I don't talk to women who murder children," I called back.

"Shet yer mouth with that talk," she called back. "You's the one gonna die tonight."

I wondered if perhaps Baby was out there, doing some kind of a flanking movement. If he could surprise them from the side, I could release the dogs and attack them in the face. Had to keep her talking so I'd be able to locate them. The torches made it harder, not easier, to pinpoint where they were.

"We've got Nathan hanging by a hook at the glass hole," I called back. "Talking to some federal friends right now. Then they're coming here."

"Maybe not, sport," Baby said. "Look behind you. In the corner, by the kids. I think your little love note came with you."

I blinked. *What?* His voice had come from the same direction as Grinny's. A cold, sinking feeling filled my stomach as I realized where he'd gone.

I looked. My note to Carrie was on the floor. They might yet come, but not because they knew I was here.

"That you, Special Agent?" I said, trying to keep my voice neutral. "You're in this kid-killing thing with that monster?"

"Consider it culling, not killing," he said from somewhere out there in the fog. "You saw them: Most of 'em aren't going to make it past puberty anyway."

"Especially if you and mother-of-the-year out there are selling their innards."

"Hey?" he said, almost pleasantly. "We need to stop wasting time here. You and the demon spawn in there are history anyway. Or here's a deal—you get to walk away, take your chances with the black hats in the fog. You do that and I'll make sure those kids go to the county."

"Under their own power or in plastic bags?"

"They don't know anything, sport," he said. "We don't need them dead— just out of here."

"Oh, right, Special Agent," I said. "I have your word as a murderer on that, do I?"

He didn't answer that. Now I knew why the DEA team had never succeeded in getting at the Creigh operation, and how Grinny had known what we were up to with such precision. Son of a *bitch!*

I tried to see through the fog to locate them, but they were still just voices in the mist, framed by flickering torchlight. She must have her whole damned crew out there, I thought. Minus the two trolls up at the glass hole.

"So how come you didn't pop me when you had the chance, Special Agent?" I called. "Up there on the mountain tonight?"

"'Cause yer *mine*, you son of a bitch," Grinny shouted back. "I ain't afeared'a no law. We buy and sell law up here. I want your hide for Rowena. Fair's fair."

"So that's the deal, Baby?" I called. "You were just taking orders?"

Greenberg didn't answer, and I noticed that the nebulous points of light out there in the fog seemed to be separating. I slid back into the barn, pulled the lantern over, and cranked the wick down to its lowest position.

"Well, shit, what's it goin' to be, lawman?" Grinny called. "Feelin' a mite skeered, are ye? Ain't like it was out on the road, is it, when you kilt my sweet baby Rue."

"Your sweet baby Rue shot at me and lost," I said, desperately trying to think of what to do.

"Cut her down, clear'n simple," she replied. "Blowed her head clean off. You gonna burn for that. You'n 'em gully rats in 'ere."

As if to confirm that observation, a bolus of orange light rose into the fog and then came down in my direction as someone threw a torch at the shed. It landed on the tin roof with a clatter, then rolled off and landed in some grass. The fog had dampened the grass, but it wouldn't stay damp for long. I had to do something.

"C'mon, sport," Greenberg called. "That trash in there isn't worth all this. C'mon out here and palaver—the money in this thing is positively amazing."

Fucking unbelievable, I thought. Children as sausage. I wanted to scream.

I threw back my head and howled like a frustrated wolf. Nothing happened. I did it again, and then both of my shepherds joined in. I went out the door in a crouch, moved to the right a few feet, and howled again. The shepherds came to the door and got into it in earnest. Some of the black-hat dogs howled back, thrilling the mountain fog. While the animals were doing their thing I sprinted straight out toward the torchlight, shotgun cocked and pointed forward, until I could make out some figures spread out in an arc, holding torches. One of them was much wider than all the others, and I didn't hesitate: I stopped, knelt, raised the shotgun, and fired right at her, then let go the second barrel at the shortish figure standing next to Grinny. Then I jinked sideways while all hell broke loose back there in the fog, with guns going, dogs barking, and several torches hitting the ground as the black hats scattered.

I blasted back through the barn doors, jacking new shells into the shotgun. The shepherds dove in behind me, and then rounds started to smack against the walls and bang off the tin roof. I leaned around the doorjamb and fired two more shells into the darkness out front and then pulled the doors closed. Then I frantically began piling the hay bales into two rows, extending from the tunnel door to the front door, creating a channel between the two. A rifle bullet went by my head close enough to make me wince, and I could dimly hear shouting out front in between gunshots. The kids were flat on the ground, their eyes squeezed shut, grimy little hands over their ears. A bullet blew up their water bucket.

I piled the bales up three high, then partially opened the front doors and fired two more rounds in the direction of the torches. I knew I wasn't hitting anything, but I fired low, hoping the sounds of buckshot slashing through the weeds would encourage the black hats to at least back away. Then I went to the tunnel door, reached over the row of bales, knocked the pitchfork away, and tripped the latch.

Four seriously ugly dogs charged into the makeshift run between the bales and bolted right out the front door, which I slammed shut behind them. Then I yelled at the girls and the shepherds to come with me. I swept them all into the tunnel and shut the door before the dogs outside figured out what had happened. I hadn't had time to the grab the lantern, so we were in utter darkness. I switched on my flashlight, reloaded the shotgun with my last two shells, and then herded my little crew of terrified children up the passageway, the shepherds running ahead. Behind us I could hear bullets hitting that door. I should have barred it somehow, I realized.

My plan was to get out to the crack in the ridge while the bad guys dealt with whatever damage I'd done with the shotgun. I was pretty sure I'd hit Grinny, and hopefully also Greenberg, if that had been him next to her. I'd done the last thing they would have expected: gone right at them while my shepherds distracted them and their cur dogs, two-legged and four-legged.

We reached the stone-wall door and slipped through it. I made the girls hold hands to keep them together. Every one of them was crying, but they moved obediently. The lever post was broken, so I couldn't close the door, but I didn't think anyone would come through for a few minutes, anyway. What I didn't know was whether or not there was a sentinel or two at the hillside entrance to this tunnel. As we trotted along through the dust in the silent tunnel, I wondered how badly I'd injured the fat lady. With all that blubber, she might not have been really hurt at all. On the other hand, it just took one pellet between the eyes to have the same effect as a .38-caliber bullet. One could always hope.

We reached the crude stairway up to the hillside tree. I gathered my desperate little band and told everyone to be quiet. I went up the stairs and listened. Then I turned out my light and pushed the trapdoor open a little. I couldn't see anything but gray darkness, then realized that that was because the fog was up here on the hillside, too. I would not be able to see any guards, but then they should not be able to see me, either. I beckoned Frick and hoisted her through the trapdoor.

"Find it," I told her quietly, and she disappeared into the fog. It would take her about a minute to figure out that she didn't know what she was looking for, but if there were other dogs out there, we'd both know it before then. She came back a minute later, panting but not alarmed.

I got my little crew out of the tunnel and to the base of the lone pine tree without incident. The kids were holding hands in a chain of grimy death grips and staring out into the fog as if they expected Grinny to materialize like some kind of giant succubus. As did I. Then the gunfire resumed down at the Creigh cabin.

I listened, but my brain wasn't comprehending. What were they shooting at? Were the black hats getting ready to charge the shed? And if so, why? It'd be much better to simply burn it and all the evidence. Then I heard the unmistakable sound of a street-sweeper and I knew what had happened: The cavalry had arrived.

"C'mon, kids," I said.

We followed the tiny brook that flowed down the hill from the crack in the ridge to get to the entrance and then went single file, dogs ahead, until we came out the other side onto Laurie May's property. We were halfway down the hill when we heard vehicles climbing the lower field. I was ready to move back into the crack when I saw the blue strobe lights pulsing through the fog. Frack came alongside and nuzzled my knee.

"You know what, buddy?" I said. "The paperwork on this one is going to be positively phenomenal."

25

Phenomenal didn't do it justice. Three days later I was sitting at the riverside bar of Rocky Falls's main hotel when Carrie Harper Santángelo joined me. She'd been spending a lot of daylight hours at the courthouse and the Robbins County Sheriff's Office, and evenings with Big Chief, who was recovering in the local hospital.

I'd been drinking more and enjoying it more these past few nights, although there had been the occasional bright moments with Carrie.

"Is it soup yet?" I asked, and she smiled. She was doing that a lot lately, especially since she'd introduced me to the oldest hangover preventative known to men and women.

"One more hearing tomorrow and you're free to go back to beautiful downtown Triboro," she said. "This one will be on Nathan's shooting Mose Walsh."

"I feel really bad about that," I said. "He tried everything but leaving town to not get involved. I should have just taken no for an answer."

"As I remember, he showed up on his own out there," she reminded me gently.

"Yeah, but only after I told him about the kids. He was enough of a cop to get to hurting over that. When they gonna let him out?"

"Tomorrow," she said. "They think they have it under control now."

Mose had been whacked pretty good by the rifle bullet, which had also creased his chest and cut him from one side to the other. The more serious problem had been a *Staph. aureus* infection, which raised its ugly head the night they got him back there. He'd been bitten by several insects while lying on the ground, and one of the little dears had given him something far more dangerous than a bullet wound.

"They catch that damned doctor?"

"It's better than that," she said.

"Meaning?"

"Meaning he was a doctor but he wasn't. He was the senior lab tech at the county hospital, but, unbeknown to them, he had been a doctor once upon a time in wild and wonderful West Virginia. General surgeon. American, not foreign. Lost his medical license because of a prescription drug habit."

"How'd he get a license here in North Carolina?"

"Apparently, through the good offices of M. C. Mingo."

"Also hooked up with Grinny Creigh. Fancy that."

"Un-hunh. Anyway, he went off the grid, ended up here under false everything. He wasn't claiming to be a doctor, just a tech."

"But he knew how to harvest pediatric organs."

"He knew enough to keep it sterile and where the parts were," she said. "And it wasn't like he had to keep his victims alive during the surgery."

"Is he talking?"

She shook her head. "They're calling him Mr. Miranda. But of course Greenberg *is* talking, so eventually they'll wrap him, along with Nathan."

"Greenberg," I said, signaling for another drink. "That son of a bitch." The bar was filling up and the noise level was rising, which was probably a good thing.

"He wouldn't be the first DEA guy to get too close to his work," she said. "Feature being blind *and* going through withdrawal."

"Works for me," I said. My two shotgun blasts into the fog had had satisfying results. Baby Greenberg had taken a pellet in each eye and both hands; he was now sightless. Grinny Creigh had been hit eight times, but all in the blubber belt. It had probably hurt like hell, but I hadn't done any real damage, other than that she'd bled like a stuck pig. The EMTs, all six of them, had struggled to get her slippery carcass onto a backboard and then into a gurney out there in the field. They had her six feet from the ambulance when the one strap long enough to fit around her broke and dumped her on her neck, which, happily, snapped like a twig under the impact of three-hundred-plus pounds of fun, love, and joy. She was now taking up space in a prison quad unit, quite out of her mind with rage.

Nathan was in jail with two hands that didn't work very well anymore, and he wasn't talking, either. His lawyer was threatening to sue for police brutality; all that was missing, unfortunately, was the guilty policeperson. I certainly didn't count, and since Carrie wasn't with the SBI anymore, neither did she. Greenberg had been wrong about the state's ability to retrieve bones from the glass hole; its icy depths and the absence of any living creatures in the alkaline crater preserved everything. Nathan was still young enough to do a meaningful life sentence or six.

The North Carolina Attorney General's Office had sent a team of prosecutors into Robbins County to handle the various high crimes and misdemeanors. We had reps from all the federal alphabets poking around, including some I didn't know about. My official report to the FBI had ended up in mailroom limbo, because, of course, Baby Greenberg had never called anyone down there to go find it. Carrie's hate mail, on the other hand, had provoked an impressive media shitstorm in Raleigh. Said storm finally galvanized the big Bureau into acknowledging that there was this wee problem up in Robbins County, something which, of course, ahem, they had known about for some time, you realize.

The kids were in county social services protective custody over in Carrigan County, because, as it turned out, there'd been some collusion between the Robbins County Social Services, M. C. Mingo, and Grinny Creigh. Apparently an imbecile's liver was just as useful as a normal kid's liver, and the social services reps knew where both kinds were living, courtesy of all those welfare checks. Monsters, all of them. They were claiming coercion, but the bank records would tell the tale.

We kicked around the specifics of tomorrow's hearing and then went into the dining room to have dinner. And maybe just a spot of wine—I looked forward to some more hangover prevention. Carrie, naturally, never suspected a thing. She'd become adept at reserving some doggie-bag tidbits from restaurants, and I was rapidly becoming second fiddle in the shepherds' household. She'd been spending more time than I thought was necessary with Big Chief, and I wondered if that professional cocksman was trying to snake me. I'd waxed eloquent a couple of times on how infectious staph could be.

"You going back into the state womb?" I asked her when we'd finished dinner and were waiting for coffee. I'd been curious for some time now, but had been reluctant to ask until it looked like we were winding the thing down.

"I had a sit-down with Sam King just this morning," she said.

"Lemme guess: The offer's still technically on the table, but they don't really mean it?"

"Something like that," she said. "They mean it, because there are some harpies up in the employment standards division who are more than ready to pounce with a discrimination ruling. But it probably would be 'awkward,' as he put it. This case has achieved some real notoriety."

"And you were the one who went to the media with it, which people in the SBI don't do if they expect their career to prosper. Especially people in professional standards."

She laughed. "That's always a sin in a bureaucracy, isn't it?"

"Mortal," I said. "Some pundit inevitably asks why you thought you had to do that if your organization was worth a shit in the first place. Hurts the bosses' feelings. The Bigs gonna be okay?"

"Them? Who'd screw around with those guys? They'll be fine."

I recounted how I'd felt, leaving law enforcement. How I thought my identity had been stolen, or at least lost. How I'd always felt just a bit superior to the average civilian in the street, but now had to watch my speed on the highway just like everybody else. She said she was still feeling that way and wondering if she ought to go back but in some other department.

"I was a senior *female* civil servant," she said. "I can force the issue if I want to."

"You don't want to do that," I said. "You'd always wonder about everything that worked for you after that—was it merit or the harpy effect."

"I suppose," she said. "But then there are these little niggling details of a mortgage, health care, a car payment, and retirement."

"You could always do what Mose did—become a wilderness guide. It's not like you don't know some interesting places to go see in them thar hills."

For a moment she got this dreamy expression in her eyes, as if that thought had crossed her mind. Aided and abetted by that conniving fake Injun over at County, no doubt. The one with the big nose, or something. But then she sighed and shook her head. I tried another tack.

"You're vested in your state retirement," I pointed out. "And my company can take care of those other matters—we need more lady agents at Hide & Seek Investigations. By the way, where do I send *my* bill?"

She cocked her head to one side. "Your *bill?*"

"As an SBI operational consultant? I believe we had a contract. I have some really spiffy timesheets made up."

She started to laugh. "They never canceled that?"

"Not to my knowledge," I said. "King told me to go home, but he never said, 'You're fired.' I don't believe you ever canceled it. Far as I'm concerned, I've been on the clock the whole time."

"They're going to shit little green apples," she said, still laughing.

"They'll pay it, too," I said. "Or I can always try your trick with one of those operational reports going in the mail, now that I know where to send it. Inquiring minds have a right to know. Think of the recruiting impact."

"*Big* green apples," she said. "I'll think about your offer. That might be fun."

Eat your heart out, Big Chief. I ordered more wine.